THE QUICK AND THE DEAD

D. B. SIEDERS

CITY OWL
PRESS

THE QUICK AND THE DEAD
Soul Broker, Book 3

CITY OWL PRESS
www.cityowlpress.com

Cover Design by Mibl Art. All stock photos licensed appropriately.

Edited by Tee Tate.

For information on subsidiary rights, please contact the publisher at info@cityowlpress.com.

Print Edition ISBN: 978-1-949090-54-3

Digital Edition ISBN: 978-1-949090-53-6

Printed in the United States of America

To my readers,
Thank you

"Thank you...for gracing my life with your lovely presence,
for adding the sweet measure of
your soul to my existence."

–Richard Matheson, "What Dreams May Come"

PRAISE FOR D. B. SIEDERS

"A unique cast of characters drives this beautifully crafted tale that demands you keep a box of tissue on hand. WAKING THE DEAD is a soul-wrenching look into the decisions one must make about life and death, not only for one's self, but for a loved one. Ms. Sieders knows how to put words on paper that touch the heart, and invigorate the mind." - *4.5 Stars from InD'Tale Magazine*

"Revolution brews in the spirit world. Vivian and Lazarus encounter a vibrant cast of allies—among them mambo woman Bijoux Briggs and Vivian's sister Mae, who was disabled in life but is powerful in the afterlife—and develop a love connection despite their complicated past." - *Publisher's Weekly*

"D.B. Sieders is a unique storyteller. CROSSCURRENTS is a mix of science fiction and fantasy that is woven together perfectly. Ms. Sieders's characters are distinctive and the story is imaginative and fun." - *4.5 Stars from InD'Tale Magazine*

"For paranormal romance readers who are looking for something a little different, Lorelei's Lyric could be your first step into a whole new world." - *Romantic Reads and Such*

"Sieders delivers a well-written and intriguing supernatural world with a plot that pulls you in and characters that keep you turning pages until the very end in FIRESTORM." - *ARC Reviewer*

"In WAKING THE DEAD, there is an emotional, raw honesty in Vivian and her struggles to care for her sister, Mae. It's so rare to find a heroine, one we root for, who is not a saint but is desperately trying to do the right thing and is not always perfect." - *ARC Reviewer*

"D.B. Sieders has a charming way with language, bordering on zany, sarcastic, and gritty. Waking the Dead is realistic, unique, honest, humorous, bittersweet, a little flirty, and a dark journey of hope. It is an addictive must-read!" - *5 Stars from Liz Konkel, Readers' Favorite*

THE SOUL BROKER SERIES

BY D. B. SIEDERS

Waking the Dead

Raising the Dead

The Quick and the Dead

Chasing the Dead (Short Story)

PROLOGUE

She floated in the place between here and there...what was it called again?

"Between life and the afterlife."

Her body materialized. Her body, but not her body—she'd never had this kind of body before she moved to the afterlife. Not that she remembered very much from that time, the time before she came to the place between here and there and...someplace else. That place had been dark, filled with many sad and hurting things, many angry things and they hurt one another. It was a place of great suffering for the things there.

"Souls. You freed thousands upon thousands of souls." The voice was one she knew. He was from the time before the afterlife, just before she moved on to the afterlife. Before she died.

"I..." The word formed and sounded strange to her. Her voice before the afterlife hadn't been in her control. She'd learned some words from Mother and Father and Sister, and others from television, but speech had been impossible for her then.

The bearer of the voice, the man—and not man, wearing a body not his own from before the afterlife—touched her hand, holding it in his larger, warm hand.

She gasped.

"Hello, Mae. It's good to see you here."

His hand was so warm, and it filled her with comforting warmth that seemed to come from the inside out. "You were there...*before*. You brought...something to me and to Sister. It was...nice, but more than nice. I'm sorry. Words are hard."

He smiled, his eyes a lovely shade of green, his hair dark, his face... beautiful, but that wasn't what people said about men. Her thoughts clarified, and she breathed deeply, without pain or the crunching rattle in her chest like before, when she'd been alive.

"It's all right," the man said. "It'll come to you. I had a hard time, too, but maybe not so hard as you. I was able to, *ah*, I was, um..."

Her lips curled into a smile. She loved smiling. And laughing, but it seemed a little wrong to laugh at the man as he struggled to find words. His cheeks were red, and he looked away. Strange. She didn't like it. Her mouth turned down in response to her anger. It reminded her of the before time when people didn't want to look at her. People pretended she was not there, talked around her, and she could never talk to them because her body didn't work like their bodies.

"Look at me and say words to me. I am not invisible."

"No, you aren't," he said, meeting her gaze with a lopsided grin. "You're a lot like her. I didn't realize it when we first met. You were different. I was afraid to say that, to say something stupid like I was normal and you weren't when we were alive. It seemed rude."

She shook her head, confused. "I *was* different. There is nothing rude about what is true."

He sighed, pulling his hand from hers. She missed the heat and the feeling that was more than nice. Running a hand through his hair, he walked around the place between here and there. Most of the others who crossed through this space were eager to move on. Grey, silent, without scent or taste or texture, it was the place that the others used to travel from the afterlife to the world of the living. For her, it was a place of calm and respite, the place that reminded her of the time before, when she'd been alive.

She was not alive now, but she had not yet gone to the place that awaited all departed souls who chose forever. It wasn't time. This place between here and there was home enough for now. She took a tentative step, marveling at how her legs supported her body and allowed her to move when she wanted. And she was high, standing, looking at the man without stretching her neck—she could control her neck sometimes when she'd been in her own body before the afterlife, but it was hard. People were always above her when she was in bed or in a chair.

Now she was tall, and she could walk. She wanted to run. When she tried, her feet became tangled and she fell forward. The man caught her.

"Easy. You have to learn to walk before you can run. As far as the truth not being rude, well, I'll take your word for it. And in the spirit of being honest, my normal was nothing to be proud of. I wasn't a nice man when I was alive, especially near the end."

She let him ease her back up to stand. When he tried to pull away from her, she held on to his hands with hers, refusing to let go. "You were nice when you came to me and to Sister. You helped me, and you helped her. She was sad and angry. You helped. What is the word for that?"

He made a strangled sound somewhere between a laugh and a sob. "Comfort. I wanted to give you both comfort and peace. It was my job, but I would have done it anyway."

She smiled. "You said I was like her. You mean Sister?"

He nodded, then he met her gaze again, his filled with anger and worry. She knew anger and worry. Mother, Father, and Sister had been angry in the time before, and worried—about her.

"Why are you worried?" she asked. Something deep inside the core of her being awakened. She'd unleashed it when she'd moved to the place between here and there and then beyond. Power. Power to do something to help.

His face relaxed. Had she given him comfort and the thing called peace?

"I'm worried about your sister, Vivian. She's in trouble. I...let her down and now she's in trouble. I need you to help her."

"Of course I will help Sister. I love her."

He tightened his grip on her hand and whispered, "I do, too."

"What is your name?" she asked. She'd forgotten. When she'd known him before she moved to the afterlife, he'd talked more to Sister. To Vivian. That was Sister's name, but to Mae, she would always be Sister."

"I'm Zeke. I was your guardian, and Vivian's guardian, for a while. But she saved me. You saved a host of souls. And if we can save Vivian now, we might just save every soul alive now and yet to be."

CHAPTER ONE

"In point three miles, take ramp, on right, to Natchez Trace Parkway."

Ignoring the robotic voice of her GPS, Vivian Bedford pulled her car onto the shoulder of Highway 100 just shy of the ramp, put it in park, and leaned forward to place her forehead on the steering wheel. She heaved a deep sigh. Postponing the inevitable could prove unwise, but she needed a moment.

She had not yet taken the time to say goodbye to her life.

She closed her eyes and let the cadence of gentle rain falling on her windshield wash over her. Tennessee didn't often experience the soft kind of rain. The weather normally wavered between bone dry and downpours. But today light rain blended with an autumn chill to create a low, crawling fog that permeated the landscape. Even in the midst of her latest crisis, auburn and amber oak leaves, mixed with the brilliant golden yellow and orange maple foliage, soothed her aching soul. This had always been her favorite time of year. She wondered if her own maple looked as lovely.

She wondered if she'd ever see it again. She wondered if she'd ever see Zeke again, and the thought opened a gaping hole in her soul. No, there was no time for this...grief? Confusion? She'd deal with it later. Right now, she needed to deal with the present, with her exile.

She needed to deal with the reaper.

"So, what happened to my house?" she asked.

Her passenger sighed. She didn't know what he found more exasperating—her questions or yet another delay. He would answer her, though. He always did. He probably felt he had to.

The reaper depended upon her for his survival now.

"It's being rented. Your friend Kay Clemmens is managing the details. I'm certain you'll find it in good order when you return."

If I return. "So Kay still knows I exist?"

"Yes, though she is the only living soul granted that privilege. You understand it's for the best?"

"Understanding doesn't make it any easier."

She was being unfair. If she found her situation unfair, she could only imagine how Lazarus Darkmore felt. In saving her life and soul, the reaper had become mortal and lost much of his considerable spirit powers. He was also now vulnerable to illness, injury, death, and that final end would put him at the lowest level of the reaper hierarchy.

Not a good position for someone with as many enemies as Darkmore.

Vivian never meant for that to happen, but it didn't ease her guilt. Of course, resentment and guilt walked hand-in-hand along the winding road in her heart. She resented the burden of caring for Darkmore and hated herself for resenting it.

She hated owing him.

Plus, she'd gotten herself entangled in the politics of afterlife management. The price of that entanglement? Not only had she inadvertently rendered a high-ranking reaper mortal, she'd been forced off the grid of the realm of the living. She and Darkmore traded life, at least her life, in Nashville for a life on the run from the guardian spirits she'd crossed one time too many. Vivian Bedford: soul broker, spiritual intercessor and liaison between the living and dead, keeper of the ancient and high-ranking reaper Lazarus Darkmore, enemy of the Archangel Guardian Council and, on account of that last part, accidental revolutionary.

I'll never be able to fit all that on a business card...

The sound of the passenger side door opening jolted her out of her latest self-pity break and back to reality. Darkmore stood a few feet away from the car. He raised his arms over his head and stretched. She was still getting used to seeing him in normal clothing. He'd traded his standard white suit for Levis and a polo shirt. At least they'd saved his Stetson. He filled out the jeans nicely, though, especially from the rear. If he had to be trapped in human form for a while, at least he'd look good doing it.

Darkmore started walking away, which raised Vivian's internal alarm. They needed to get going. Every guardian spirit in Nashville, Tennessee, and probably the world at large would be looking for them. Mississippi meant safety. Probably. She clung to that belief now.

The alternative held little appeal.

She opened her door and called out after him, "Where're you going?"

"I'm off to answer the call of nature," he yelled back.

That's a first. Bet he hasn't peed in a few centuries.

Powerful spirits assumed the illusion of a living, human, corporeal form by channeling their spirit energy and building a body out of the elements around them. Those illusions were convincing and...functional in many capacities. She'd seen many of them eat. Most did so with relish, no doubt missing that which was denied them and their senses most of the time. But she'd never known any corporeal spirit who'd needed to tend to other human bodily functions.

Certainly not Darkmore, the scariest, most powerful reaper this side of eternity. He'd frightened her when they'd first met, when he'd been hell-bent on claiming her soul by any means necessary.

He still scared her, but that didn't make her any less responsible for his well-being now that he wore a true mortal form

"Need any help?" she asked, hoping he'd say no.

"I *have* done this before, my dear. I'll be back in a moment."

Shaking her head, she closed her door and engaged the automatic door locks. It wouldn't keep spirits out, of course, but the living posed a threat, too. Hyper-vigilance in all of its pathologic glory, but in her position it had become a survival skill.

She closed her eyes for a moment and focused on channeling spirit energy, something the living weren't supposed to be able to do. Part blessing, more curse, and a whole lot of responsibility, the power was something she'd need to learn how to fully control if she had any hope of fending off the guardian spirits. Woefully outmatched, she had to protect herself and

Darkmore. Sparks flickered beneath her fingertips as power coursed through her body. Friends and allies had allowed her to absorb their spiritual burdens before leaving her life behind, fortifying her for the journey ahead to what she hoped would be safety.

And more living soul brokers. Strength in numbers was all she could count on now.

She gazed up at the concrete overpass emblazoned with "Natchez Trace Parkway." It dwarfed the green metal truss bridge they'd crossed a few miles back, the one that spanned part of the Harpeth River. It felt like her beloved city had closed the door on her. Facing the beginning of the long road to Jackson struck her like the slamming of a very large door.

She put her head back on the steering wheel and waited for the reaper.

———

A knock at her window jolted Vivian awake.

A stranger stood outside of her car. She cracked her window just enough for conversation, trying to stop the surge of panic rushing through her. They didn't need this kind of attention, especially when there were so many threats lurking around every bend in the road. Plainclothes or undercover cop? Spirit in disguise? Garden-variety pervert or serial killer?

Shit!

"You doin' all right in there, little lady?"

"I'm fine," she replied, trying to smile and catch her breath simultaneously. She didn't do a very good job. "I must have dozed off for a minute."

"Maybe you ought to get a hotel or something."

"I'm just waiting for my...traveling companion to come back. He had to make a pit stop."

"Oh," he chuckled. "That him?"

She spied the reaper walking back to the car. He tipped his hat to the stranger. *Nice of you to show up!* "Yes, that's him."

"Good afternoon," Darkmore said, extending his hand. God, no good could come of this. He may be mortal, but she had no doubt that Darkmore could still kill this human and absorb his soul. Or he could simply toy with him, forcing the man to see and experience his personal worst nightmare in vivid and terrifying detail by way of a reaper-powered head fuck.

"Howdy," the stranger replied, offering his own hand. "The little lady here fell asleep. I was just checking to make sure she was all right."

"I thank you kindly. Looks like it's my turn to drive." Darkmore accepted his hand and Vivian held her breath. If the stranger was a guardian or reaper in disguise, Darkmore could blow their cover. If he was simply a Good Samaritan, then the reaper could unleash the man's darkest fears and deepest agony.

And feed from it.

"Lazarus, please," she said, keeping her voice steady. "Let's go."

Darkmore held on to the man's hand a little longer than necessary, and the man's gaze went dark. Then Darkmore winked at her, the bastard, but thankfully he let go of the man's hand.

She shot him a nasty look as he helped her out of the car, as much to disguise her terror as to express exasperation. She shuffled over to the passenger side, trying to ignore the testosterone-fueled exchange between the stranger and the reaper. Plopping herself down, she tried her best not to slam the door. She shut her eyes and counted to one hundred and twenty-two, stopping only after Darkmore closed the driver's side door and pulled back onto the road.

"Take ramp, on right, to Natchez Trace Parkway."

CHAPTER TWO

Vivian didn't know how long she'd slept. Her intention had been to stay alert and awake, of course. Spirit willing, flesh weak. She remembered, vividly, the moment they'd entered the quaint wooden gateway onto the Trace proper after a short stint on the overpass. It was like taking a step back through time. They'd left metropolitan life well before, trading the civilization of West End Avenue and Belle Meade glamour for the rolling hills of west Nashville. From there, city life morphed seamlessly into pockets of suburban charm mingled with farmsteads and even a bit of redneck splendor.

But upon entering the Trace, no homes, shopping centers, office high rises, or other cars interrupted the tree-bordered meadows that flanked the windy stretch of two-lane highway. Their only company, aside from a couple of Lance Armstrong wannabes, had been a flock of wild turkeys loping close to the highway's shoulder.

Her heart sank further when she spied a field of gold and green nestled to the right of the trace. Not the black-eyed Susans from her glimpse of the paradise she'd lost, but the goldenrod flowers were close enough to open old wounds. The reaper could ease her pain, feeding from her misery, but that was a temptation neither of them could afford to test. They moved on, and she had the sense that her return to paradise would be long and difficult.

Assuming she ever made it back.

So she'd closed her eyes in a moment of reflection, or perhaps deflection, and then drifted off to sleep.

She might not have known exactly how long she slept, but it had been long enough to give her a king-sized crick in the neck from dozing too long with her head rammed against the door. She also heard a voice that didn't belong to Darkmore, and she cursed herself for letting down her guard.

Someone else was in the car, someone she hadn't invited along on their escape to join the rebellion.

The voice, low, feminine, and decidedly seductive, belonged to Uphir. Vivian had met the demoness only once while working with Darkmore, but once had been enough. Sly and attractive if you could overlook the cloven hooves, she sometimes worked with the reaper as he tormented souls not long for this world and destined for the dark side of the afterlife. The wicked souls they targeted had it coming, though the brutality with which they doled out karmic justice sickened Vivian's human sensibilities, as did their obvious enjoyment of their work. Judging from their last encounter, Vivian suspected Uphir had a thing for Darkmore and enjoyed playtime with him as well.

She didn't like Uphir. More to the point, she didn't trust the demoness. It was more than jealousy, which Vivian could admit was part of the issue. In spite of her fear of the reaper, Vivian was...fond of him, and now had become protective. Uphir's sudden appearance brought out those protective instincts. She didn't like being caught unaware with Darkmore in such a vulnerable state. Uphir was a fickle ally with the instincts of a predator. In his weakened, mortal condition, Darkmore might become prey.

Instead of attacking, Vivian pretended to sleep so she could eavesdrop and find out what the demon wanted and if she posed a threat.

"How did you find us?" Darkmore asked with his trademark calm.

"Worried, my darling? After all we've been through?" The demon's voice had become a low purr.

Excuse me while I lose my lunch.

"Oh it's nothing personal. Given our current predicament, you'll understand my concerns about being tracked by my associates, not to mention the competition." Darkmore's reply was cool and distant. It made Vivian happier than it should have.

Uphir huffed. "Well, if you must know, Earl has proven to be rather more useful than I anticipated. He can sniff out even the smallest trace of spirit energy and track it to the source."

Well surprise, surprise. Vivian wouldn't have figured the guy had it in him.

Earl was one of Uphir's human servants. Vivian met him recently while working on a particularly nasty reaping with Darkmore and Uphir. A small man with a penchant for outrageous demon cosplay, pathologic devotion to his mistress, and a hunger for power, Vivian hadn't been fond of the man—assuming he was still mostly man. He'd probably been one of those "nice guy" types who spent a little too much time in his mom's basement harassing women online. No wonder Uphir was able to nab him. She may have treated him like dirt beneath her feet, but she'd given him the power he'd never possessed in normal life.

And he appeared to like being treated like dirt beneath her feet. Whatever. That was their business, not hers.

"Earl? Really? I never would have guessed it."

"Tell me about it," Uphir said, voice dripping with disdain. "How's yours, by the way?"

"Vivian? She's not mine."

"So you keep saying. She has a useful talent, though. Does she often improvise?"

Vivian assumed Uphir was referring to the unexpected blast of spirit energy she'd dealt to a child rapist while working with Darkmore. He'd had it coming, and she wasn't sorry that she'd broken protocol. Still, she'd brought more unwanted attention to Darkmore, which couldn't be good for either of them.

Had she known then what she knew now, she would have just killed the bastard.

"She's a bit of a wildcard, indeed, but intriguing," Darkmore answered, without really answering.

"Is that why you've abandoned your post to travel on this fool's errand?"

"Uphir, you surprise me. I would have thought you'd be amused, tormenting Uriel and his associates on the Council. It could be good for business. Care to join us?"

Vivian fought to keep her breathing steady as her heart rate skyrocketed. What the hell was he playing at? Inviting a demon to join them? It wouldn't take her long to figure out that Darkmore's mortal coil was now permanent. She could claim his soul, his service, and make his newfound life a living hell.

And she'd enjoy every minute of it.

This was such a mess. A mess of Vivian's making.

But she'd had no choice. Darkmore had put himself in the line of fire for her, absorbing a burst of powerful guardian spirit energy meant to kill her. No doubt the rogue guardian spirit would have claimed her soul and brought her back to the Archangel Guardian Council in chains. In the face of a spirit energy crisis, Uriel and his fellows were running the afterlife version of a pyramid scheme, siphoning more spirit energy than the guardian spirits who mediated crossings could handle. Former mortals recruited to afterlife management by the Council upon death, guardian spirits were charged with using the life force released by a soul as they crossed to another plane of existence to help the soul cross, saving what was left to protect themselves and souls in peril from competing reapers. Only the high-level guardians and the Archangel CEOs had become greedy, demanding more and more energy from guardians in the field.

What they were doing with all of the energy they amassed was a mystery, but it couldn't be good.

As a living soul broker, Vivian had the unique ability to collect spirit energy from the living, something no guardian or reaper could do. It wasn't pretty. The living didn't suffer—quite the opposite, actually. Vivian could take in their burdens, the heavy weight of sorrow they carried, and convert it into a version of spirit energy. She suffered in the process, but it gave her some nifty powers, including the power to heal. After Darkmore saved her from the rogue guardian's blast, he'd been badly injured. She'd had no idea if the damage was permanent to the reaper, so she'd channeled all of her energy into healing the reaper.

It had worked a little too well, rendering him fully mortal and subject to all manner of parties interested in soul harvesting.

Darkmore had made a lot of enemies over his long existence. He was in as much danger as she was. So why on earth would he invite Uphir, a hungry demoness, to join them?

Uphir's voice brought her attention back to eavesdropping. "Tempting...are you sure Vivian won't mind?"

"Ask her yourself," Darkmore said. "She's awake."

Opening her eyes and fighting hard to not to glare at Darkmore, Vivian sat up and turned around in her seat. "Hello, Uphir. Nice to see you again."

"Charmed, my dear," she purred. Vivian resisted the urge to roll her eyes. Making the demoness angry wouldn't help anyone.

"So, what brings you out here to our, um, car?"

"I'm checking in with Darkmore, and I come bearing news. Earl has been tracking guardian movement in the area. I suggest you stop at the first campsite near Hohenwald and lie low for the night. Perhaps even until tomorrow afternoon. There are unaffiliated spirits lingering in a nearby cemetery who are sympathetic to your little revolutionary cause. You'll be safe under their watch. I can advise you when it is safe to resume your travels."

"Gee, thanks. Why go out of your way to help us?" Vivian asked. It probably wasn't a good idea to antagonize her, but she didn't appreciate the demon's attitude.

"I have a vested interest in Darkmore's well-being. Besides, Earl is rather fond of you."

"Really?" The last time she'd encountered Uphir's slimy little minion, she'd made it clear what she thought of his pathologic devotion to his mistress and her...activities.

"Of course. We very much enjoyed our last meal. Take good care of my associate." With that, Uphir disappeared before Vivian's eyes.

———

They pulled into the Meriwether Lewis site a short time later, much to Vivian's irritation. They'd made precious little progress on the journey to

Jackson, Mississippi, home to the so-called rebel guardian spirits and other living soul brokers. She didn't relish the prospect of spending time at a campground in the boonies, virtually defenseless against the guardians pursing them.

Plus, Darkmore was starting to get on her nerves. It wasn't his fault, but that didn't make the irritation any easier to bear.

He'd been calm and quiet during most of the drive, speaking only when she'd asked a specific question of him or chatting with the demon. He had to be angry with her. It was her fault that he was mortal. She hadn't meant to do it, but her rash actions had left him in a nearly defenseless state and tied him to her. Sure, they'd worked together before her screwup, and they had established a rapport of sorts, but she was under no illusions about Darkmore's interests. He was a reaper. When they'd first met, he'd wanted her soul. Later, when he found out what she was and what she could do, he wanted her service. After that, they'd become sometimes partners, and Darkmore served as insurance against her guardian spirit boss' exploitation. She'd fed him her excess spirit energy and he'd protected her from guardian spirit control. It was a relationship of convenience, beneficial to both parties. But he'd gotten more than he'd bargained for when he saved her ass and became stuck in a fragile mortal body. If she were in his position, she'd be furious.

That probably explained the silent treatment. She could hardly blame him.

But, given her druthers, she'd have preferred to hear him shout, swear, or even punch her rather than deal with his silence and indifference. It unnerved her. And now he walked the grounds seemingly without a care in the world, circling the monument marking the grave of the famous explorer. She might as well join him, since they'd be staying in the area for a while. Not that there was much to see, as far as she could tell. The memorial itself looked like a miniature pyramid with a metal stovepipe stuck on top.

Not very impressive.

Milling around a bit, she walked over to a plaque labeled "Grinder House." She glanced at it, read the dates, and the blood drained from her face. Deciding not to shout his name, she jogged over to Darkmore and asked, "What day is it?"

Darkmore chuckled. "I wondered when you might inquire about the date and time. It is October 11. October 11 of the year we left when we traveled to Uriel's realm."

She hadn't even thought to worry after the potential shift in time they might have experienced. *Nice to know a problem I hadn't even considered is a non-issue.* "I was afraid of that. You don't suppose he'll put in an appearance, do you?"

"Who?"

Oh, the reaper was so exasperating. "Meriwether Lewis. He died on this day like, I don't know, about two hundred years ago." The ghost of a famous explorer who might attract unwanted attention from the spirit world by putting in an appearance. Just what they needed.

Darkmore shrugged. "Just because he was murdered doesn't necessarily mean he wants to visit the scene and relive it year after year after year."

She didn't know whether to be relieved or disappointed. She'd only met the spirit of one famous person. Though Eddie was pretty cool, she'd often thought it might be fun to hobnob with more...influential folks. A man who'd made it into textbooks certainly qualified. But now was not the time to chase dead celebrities. They needed to keep a low profile.

"Don't be so glum, my dear. We won't lack for company. Why not take the opportunity to learn about life during the early days of your nation?" He spread his arms and gestured to the remnants of the dead, the ones she'd been pointedly ignoring.

He was right. The site was teaming with spirits dressed in pioneer getup along with a few Native Americans. Like most non-reaper and non-guardian spirits, they lacked the energy to assume a corporeal form. Lost and lonely spirits, or perhaps those who chose to remain tethered to the realm of the living rather than cross over, these wispy and often transparent manifestations maintained a safe distance from Vivian and Darkmore. In spite of his mortal body, he apparently still carried the aura and presence of the grim reaper he had been not so very long ago.

She looked him up and down. "They don't seem too friendly. You seem to have that effect wherever we go."

Darkmore looked around with his normal nonchalance. Then he turned back to her, cocked his head, and replied, "True. Perhaps we should introduce ourselves before the rumors start flying."

Before she could stop him, Darkmore sauntered over to a group of male settler types, one of whom stepped forward and gave him a wary eye. She marveled at the clarity of the spirit's manifestation, not to mention his stature, or rather, lack thereof. People really were shorter back then. His features were clear and visible down to the gritty black stubble on his chin and the dirt under his nails. People of that era apparently didn't bathe much either. He puffed out his chest, straightened his hat, one of those black colonial numbers that reminded her of Captain Jack Sparrow, and faced down Darkmore.

"State yer business, fiend," he said. Some of the other male apparitions in his company located their courage and flanked him.

Ballsy move for dead guys who couldn't even manifest their lower halves.

She stifled a giggle that would have been wholly inappropriate for the moment. God, what was wrong with her? Likely stress. She'd have to find a better way of coping.

Darkmore stood his ground but maintained a respectful distance. He even removed his hat. "Good afternoon, my brethren. I am called Lazarus Darkmore," he offered, making a low bow and gesturing to Vivian as he spoke. "My companion and I are merely passing through your territory. We mean you no harm, I assure you."

"I doubt that, sirrah. I've never known a spirit of your kind to come seeking room and board, nor to be traveling with a quick wench at that."

"Hey, who you calling a wench—"

Before she could finish, Darkmore had invaded the spirit's space. He actually held onto the spirit's arm, which shocked Vivian. Apparently being mortal hadn't rendered the reaper entirely helpless. He still had some of his powers.

"Mr. McClung, I would ask that you show my traveling companion, Mistress Bedford, the respect befitting a lady. Surely you remember how. Even after the passing centuries you remember your lady, don't you?"

The spirit of Mr. McClung trembled, and his eyes grew wide. "Do not speak of her, ye devil!"

"Beloved Rachel, treasured wife and mother, lost to the fever as so many were in those days. You were both so young and she bewitched you with her innocence." Darkmore spoke low, almost purring to the man, bringing him back to his darkest hour and savoring his pain. Reapers thrived on suffering.

Vivian looked away, all too familiar with the Reaper's methods and the havoc he wreaked on his victims.

"Of course you remarried, but you were cold and remote to Rebecca, weren't you? She could never replace your Rachel, and you made her suffer for it."

"Stop!" McClung pleaded.

"Oh, you sought solace in all manner of vices, but no drink, gambling boon, or harlot's body could fill the void, could it? Had you been a better husband in the first place, had you protected her and kept her away from the bearers of the foul contagion, she might have lived. You often wonder, don't you?"

Vivian mustered her courage and prepared to intervene, but Darkmore released the spirit. Naturally, the reaper took a moment to draw out his pain in the form of light energy before he backed off fully.

He wasn't the sort to miss a good meal.

"Now then, shall we try this again?"

"P-pleased to make yer acquaintance, Ms. Bedford, Mr. Darkmore," McClung muttered. The other spirits, all of whom had stepped back, made small bows and nods.

Unsure what proper etiquette had been back in McClung's day, Vivian settled on a friendly nod. "Nice to meet y'all, too. Have you had any trouble with guardians or reapers lately?"

McClung's gaze shifted to another male settler spirit. He stepped forward and removed his hat, speaking softly and with his gaze on the ground. "Yes, ma'am. They've been coming through our lands for a fortnight, recruiting."

"I see," Vivian said. No wonder these spirits were on edge. "Let me assure you that Darkmore and I aren't with them. In fact, we're headed to

Jackson to join some other folks who'd like to keep things the way they are in this realm and the spirit world."

The spirit nodded and stepped back. McClung looked at her with an unreadable expression but didn't speak. Vivian sighed. She was weary, on edge, and not at all in the mood for a standoff.

"We do not intend to overstay our welcome, nor do we plan to interfere with your personal affairs," Darkmore said, courtesy personified. "All we ask is that you extend us the same courtesy. And, of course, alert us if you detect any guardians or reapers in the area for the duration of our visit."

McClung stood his ground and stared at the reaper. Vivian was duly impressed. She'd fainted after her first encounter with Darkmore. After a moment, McClung turned back to the same spirit who'd informed them of guardian and reaper invasions and said, "Angus, fetch the woman."

Angus disappeared, leaving Vivian and Darkmore standing in silence with the male spirits. Vivian stifled a yawn and resisted the urge to stretch. That would probably set McClung on another tirade about unseemly wenches, which would do no one any good.

Angus reappeared, along with the spirit of striking woman with flame red hair and pale skin straight out of a Celtic fairy tale. The other ghosts moved away from her, averting their spectral gazes. This spirit manifested in vivid detail, a startling contrast to the faded, almost colorless appearance of her fellow ghosts. Vivian stared into her sparkling green eyes, and she sensed more power in this particular spirit than a garden variety lost and lonely manifestation.

"Miss Bedford, Mr. Darkmore, this is Maeve. She has agreed to protect you."

Uh huh, more like keep an eye on us. But a spirit like her would also be a good lookout.

Darkmore bowed low and said in his smoothest voice, "It is an honor, Mistress Maeve."

It struck her as odd, but then again, so did most things about the reaper. For all they'd worked together, Darkmore remained an enigma. Remembering her manners, Vivian added, "Thank you so much for your guidance, ma'am."

Maeve nodded to them both and then disappeared.

"I guess she'll be keeping a low profile," Vivian said.

Darkmore shot Vivian a warning look and then turned back to McClung. "I thank you, Mr. McClung, for your hospitality and accommodation. We will endeavor to be worthy guests and trouble you no longer than is necessary. Good day, sir." He tipped his hat, took Vivian gently yet insistently by the arm, and guided her away from the spirits. Once out of earshot, Darkmore took the opportunity to scold Vivian. "Do try to restrict your commentary on the manner in which the spirits we encounter choose to aid us. They can be of help or a hindrance. I'd rather they help."

"Well, she just up and left. Besides, why are they so hostile? Jeanne told me we'd be welcomed." Jeanne was one of the good guardians. It had been Jeanne who'd put her in touch with another living soul broker—the man whose rebellion they were traveling to join. Before then, Vivian hadn't realized there were others like her, living soul brokers helping—or being exploited by—guardian spirits. Her own guardian spirit had exploited her, but he'd also protected her from the Archangels on the guardian council as long as he could.

Wherever Ezra was, or more likely wherever the guardian council had imprisoned him, she hoped he was okay.

"Your friend Jeanne is a young guardian, green and full of optimism. She most likely underestimated the extent to which the guardian council has infiltrated and antagonized free spirit communities. They are right to be mistrustful."

"Jeanne was supposed to give them a heads up. Besides, Uphir said these spirits would be sympathetic to us."

"Perhaps Jeanne was unable. And, from Uphir's perspective, this was a king's welcome. At any rate, for the sake of our continued safety, let's assume we're more or less on our own in hostile country."

"Fine. I'm sure your little buddies have been extending their influence, too, judging from the reaction you got," she snapped, regretting it immediately. She shouldn't kick the reaper while he was down.

"Naturally. We reapers have to keep pace with the competition."

Vivian wondered if he intended to do a little recruiting for his kind along the way but decided not to ask.

She doubted she'd like the answer.

CHAPTER THREE

After struggling for nearly forty-five minutes to gather kindling and wood, not to mention racking her brain on fire safety protocol from memories of her days as a girl scout, Vivian managed to get the campfire going. Busy was good, though. So was silence. Darkmore possessed the ability to sit, stand, or work for hours in silence. Too bad most humans couldn't do that. He'd made himself useful by unpacking and assembling their tent, unfurling their sleeping bags, and dragging their clothing and supplies out of the car and to the campsite. She settled on spearing a couple of hotdogs with skewers and securing them neatly in the vee of a tree branch she'd rigged for support. She fiddled with how to arrange them so they'd sit close enough to the fire to cook, but not so far into the flames as to char. Satisfied with her work, she settled herself into a lawn chair that Darkmore had unfolded for her and tossed him a cheese stick.

"Thank you," he said.

"No problem."

Vivian settled back in her chair and closed her eyes. *Not too long, otherwise you'll fall asleep.* She breathed in the cool night air and made a mental note to grab some extra blankets. Autumn's debut meant the possibility of frost. She could cure cuts, bruises, sprains, and some pretty severe internal injuries, she wasn't sure if her spirit healing powers could ward off pneumonia.

Then again, she'd brought back a dead reaper, so the odds were pretty good, right?

She opened her eyes and took a moment to savor the stars. On a clear night, thousands were visible, especially out in the country without the glare of streetlights getting in the way. She spied the three stars making up Orion's belt, one of the few constellations she could recognize.

"So, was he real?" she asked. The silence had become uncomfortable again, so she risked engaging the reaper in conversation, one that didn't involve their current perilous circumstances.

One that didn't involve what she'd done to him.

"Excuse me?"

"Orion," she said, pointing up at the night sky. "The hunter? I was just wondering if he was real, and if you...knew him?" Darkmore had once professed to being familiar with the goddess Athena, so why not?

Darkmore smiled. "Some myths are simply myths, Vivian."

"Oh," she said, shaking her head. Needing a distraction, cheeks flaming embarrassment at her stupid question, Vivian got up, dusting off her jeans. "I'll throw something together for dinner."

She grabbed the skewers, using her shirtsleeve to protect her fingers from the hot metal, and set about dressing the hot dogs. She pulled some fixings out of the cooler and wished for the first time that she'd remembered to grab onions and chili. At least they had ketchup, mustard, and relish. Vivian slathered a heaping helping on top of each dog-filled bun and added some chips and apple slices to the plates. She then handed one plate to Darkmore along with a beer.

"Thank you," he said.

"It's no trouble."

"But it is."

That floored her. The reaper had a way of doing that. It used to be his favorite pastime.

Apparently, it still was.

He heaved a sigh when she didn't answer. "This is trouble for you, not to mention troubling."

"Well excuse me for trying to be polite," she snapped. It wasn't fair. But the tension of the past weeks needed a place to go. Darkmore made a convenient target.

"Be honest, Vivian, if not with me then at least be honest with yourself."

"What do you want me to say? Wait," she said, holding up a hand. "Don't answer that. Let's just eat, okay? I'm tired and I don't feel like a fight."

"It is only natural to feel angry based on your experience. Being saddled with me in this state wasn't something you bargained for, was it?"

"No, you're right. It wasn't. Satisfied now?"

I so do not want to have this conversation.

He held her gaze and spoke with a clear, steady voice. "No. Admit it. You resent having to care for me, or at least feeling like you must care for me because guilt and your sense of honor demand it."

She closed her eyes and counted to ten, then said, "Why are you hell-bent on dragging all of this out now? McClung's suffering didn't satisfy you?"

She put her plate down on her chair none-too-gently and started fussing over the campsite. Ducking into their tent, she fluffed the pillows and smoothed their sleeping bags. That task complete, she emerged from the tent, grabbed a stick, and stoked the fire. She looked around for something else, anything else, to do. It was the only way she could keep avoiding the issue the reaper had so eloquently described. Even in mortal form, he possessed power to see into her heart and soul, unearthing dark resentments and buried feelings she'd rather ignore.

Darkmore sat in silence, watching her.

"I'm going to check the car and make sure we got everything," she muttered. "May I please have the car keys?" she said, heaving a deep sigh and avoiding his gaze.

He handed them over without a word and she scurried back to the car, tail between her legs like a scolded dog. She felt his eyes on her back until she rounded the bend in the gravel road that led back to the parking lot. Vivian jogged the rest of the way, longing for the warmth of the car almost as much as she longed to get away from her charge.

Almost.

She climbed into the car and turned the ignition, shivering as the blast of cold hit her at full force. Cursing herself for leaving her beer behind, she rubbed her hands together and waited for the heat to kick in. Fuck Lazarus Darkmore and his fucking perception. Why couldn't he leave well enough alone? He knew her history, of course, and had used it against her when they first met. At that time, she'd been in the midst of caring for her sister Mae. Total care. Mae's many disabilities and illnesses left her completely helpless. The role of caregiver had taken its toll and Darkmore had relished her pain. Now, it seemed, he was determined to force her to confront the uncomfortable parallels that her responsibility for him presented. Should he die in his current mortal form, he'd be fodder for reapers, demons, or worse. Guardians.

Maybe he wanted to feed from her suffering, assuming he could still do so in human form. Wasn't that a cheerful thought? Then again, a meal was the least she owed him, and it wasn't so different than what she'd been doing before, allowing him to take in the burdens she carried and use the spirit energy. When the burdens had belonged to others, giving them to the reaper had been a relief. Not so when he took in burdens that were all her own.

When the reaper fed from the darkness in her own soul, she had to relive the pain of the burdens she carried.

She fought the hot tears threatening to spill down her cheeks and wished for her cell phone. *Who would I call?* Aside from her friend Kay, none of those who'd known and loved her remembered that she existed. No one alive, anyway. It was for their own safety as well as hers. Running and rebelling meant severing all ties. She had no way of reaching out to the Padre, better known as Lloyd Montgomery. In life, he'd been a Catholic priest and unlikely ally turned friend to Vivian. A dear friend. His death had hit her hard. Now, in his new role as a guardian, he was working on the inside to subvert the system while she was off to join the rebels. She wished she could talk to him.

God, she wished she could talk to Zeke. They'd parted on...not bad terms, but uncertain terms. He said he still loved her, and she believed him, but so much had passed between them. And she had to leave him—again—before they could reconcile.

The tears fell then, as they often did when Zeke was on her mind. Guardian spirit, friend, lover, protector, he'd been many things to her. And she'd let him go, trading her soul and service to the guardians so he could claim a spot in paradise,

That hadn't worked out.

She wiped her tears and put Zeke out of her mind. Too bad they couldn't stay in a hotel. TV would give her a welcome break, though knowing her crap luck she'd get stuck watching a marathon of some horrible reality show. She spotted something out of the corner of her eye, bright and moving fast. What the hell?

Shaking her head, her gaze darted in the direction she thought whatever she'd seen had moved.

The glowing orb hovering outside the front window stopped her thoughts.

It almost stopped her heart.

Reflex mixed with shock enabled her to place her head in her hands and lean over the steering wheel, but not so fast as to let the hovering spirit know she'd spotted it.

She hoped.

She didn't have to fake the sobbing and near-hyperventilation.

Breathe in, breathe out. Just breathe, stay focused, and don't look up. Don't look up. She sensed the presence just outside the car, which was good. It hadn't come inside. It didn't cast any shadows inside the vehicle, making it impossible for her to track by sight. She fought the urge to bolt from the vehicle.

The temperature rose inside the car.

Vivian trembled, wondering how long she would have to sit in the car before it would be safe to open the door and walk away. She couldn't run. It would know that she knew and saw. The blazing hot thing outside her car was a guardian, or something the guardian spirits were using to track her. Had to be. The guardians ran hot. It was their tell, the only warning she'd have that they were near. They would find her. They would find Darkmore.

She couldn't breathe. She had to get out. She had to make sure they didn't find the reaper.

The light hovered beside her and she had to squint, but she covered by leaning her head back and rubbing her hands over her tear-filled eyes. If she squinted or blinked or flinched, it would know. Most normal humans couldn't perceive entities or energies from the spirit realm. If she kept calm and didn't acknowledge its presence, the light might mistake her for an ordinary human and leave her be.

Checking her reflection in the rearview mirror, she wiped her eyes and tried to make her expression reflect sadness rather than terror. She'd had a year to practice acting like she couldn't see spirits in the presence of the living. Time to put those skills to the test.

Heaving a deep breath, she turned off the ignition, opened the driver's side door, and used every ounce of restraint she possessed to exit the vehicle slowly. She shut the driver's side door and locked the car. Then she took one step and a breath.

The light followed.

Vivian took another step, stumbling a bit out of fear. A whimper almost escaped her throat as panic seized her muscles. She stooped down and rubbed her ankle.

Breathe. Focus. Get up!

She registered a chill in the air again, in spite of the light's proximity.

Vivian got up and started walking again. With any luck, the guardian would get bored soon and move on.

Of course, guardians had plenty of time to grow patience.

The temperature dropped enough to make her shiver. That and the fading light gave her enough impetus to keep going. Slow and steady steps carried her about halfway back to camp. She hoped. When she rounded the bend, the glowing light of the fire confirmed it.

The other light had gone.

The chill crept closer.

She caught a movement, something lurking just outside the light cast by their campfire. Her pulse, which had barely slowed from her encounter with the guardian sentinel, started racing again. She needed to keep walking, but her feet refused to cooperate. Cold sweat broke out on her body when she noticed the orb of light again. It hovered at a more comfortable distance but refused to leave.

Walk, walk, you can do this, you just have to walk.

She remained frozen to the spot and the orb inched closer. The shape lurking in the shadows moved closer, too. It moved with a familiar, sleek grace. She could no longer convince herself that she'd imagined it. They were closing in, the light and the shadow.

She bolted.

Vivian felt rather than saw the orb closing in on her, though whatever moved in the shadows remained out of her sight. Strong arms gripped her, and she screamed and thrashed. If she was under attack, she was at least determined to fight back. Just before she was able to muster the first sparks of spirit energy, his voice stopped her.

"It's all right," Darkmore whispered, his voice low and gentle. "Calm down. It's just me. I didn't mean to scare you, honey."

Honey?

He loosened his grip and held her at arm's length. He appeared to be examining her. *What the hell?* Surely he'd seen the guardian, or at least felt its presence. Confusion filled her along with adrenaline, robbing her of the ability to speak or think.

"You gave me quite a fright, running off like that, especially after an argument. Here," Darkmore said as he wrapped a blanket around her shoulders. "Let's get you back to the fire and get you fed. You'll catch your death out here."

The reaper wrapped his arm around her shoulders and pushed her head against his chest. Then he started to walk back toward the fire, dragging her along with him. After they'd walked a few paces, he whispered into her ear.

"Don't speak, just follow my lead." She doubted she could speak even if she wanted to. Her panic began to subside into numb weariness as the heat from the guardian sentinel faded. That had been a close call. Too close. Darkmore had kept his wits, thank goodness.

She certainly hadn't.

He sat her down in front of the fire and then grabbed her plate, offering it to her. She could only stare. Moving closer, he broke off a bit of hotdog, and held it to her lips.

"The guardian is moving on, but he isn't gone yet. Be a good girl and eat your dinner so he won't become suspicious again."

She accepted the hotdog, chewing slowly and trying hard to swallow. Her raw, dry throat made it difficult, as did the cold night air. Darkmore held a bottle of water to her lips and encouraged her to drink.

"You only have to hold yourself together for a little while longer. He's almost out of sight," Darkmore reassured.

"What about the other spirit?" Vivian whispered with a rasp.

"There is nothing else out there for you to fear. Are you ready to sleep?"

"I'm not sure I can."

He offered her a small smile, stood, and helped her to her feet. After leading her to their tent, he helped her settle into one of the sleeping bags. He'd even placed the cushioning pad beneath it. After fussing over her pillow, he held the sleeping bag open for her to crawl inside before tucking her in.

When he started to leave, she grabbed his hand, taking more comfort in the contact than she had a right to savor. She hated displaying fear or weakness, but she really didn't want him to go.

He squeezed her hand lightly but didn't let go. "I'm going to add a few more logs to the fire and clean up a bit. It won't take long. I'll come back."

Feeling foolish, she nodded, releasing his hand. After he left, she focused on finding her inner calm and listened to the sounds of night all around and of Darkmore settling their campsite for the night. She suspected he was making extra noises for her benefit.

He stepped back into the tent after about thirty minutes, zipping the flap after he entered. After a few moments, he climbed into his own sleeping bag. He'd probably sleep like the dead. She wished she had that skill.

She rolled over and prepared herself for the long night ahead. Too tired to cry anymore, but too wound up for sleep to claim her, she couldn't even muster a proper sigh of exasperation. It threw her off balance when she Darkmore's sleeping bag covered body curled up against her back.

A fresh wave of panic seized her. How far did he want to take this charade? She could admit to herself that she found him attractive, and there was at least one occasion when she'd come close to succumbing to that attraction. Shortly thereafter, she'd received a brutal and terrifying reminder of what he was. She might be able to look past his darkness, his hunger for suffering, his lust for pain, while in mortal form—someday. After the events of the night and with the prospect of a potential audience, however, she was decidedly not in the mood.

"Relax, my dear," he said, rumbling near her ear. "Though I suspect you'd enjoy a rut in the great outdoors, my intentions are entirely honorable."

"So says the grim reaper," she replied with a snort. The sarcasm did little to hide the tremor in her voice, but her fear had to be obvious. Heart racing, body stiff, nails digging into her palms as she clenched her fists—everything about her current state screamed fear.

He laughed, but he didn't move.

"Well, if you aren't in the market for a good 'rut,' what is it that you want?" she asked.

"For you to relax and get a good night's sleep. We both need to be rested and strong for the journey ahead." He moved closer and turned her body to face his. She was about to protest when he brought his mouth close to hers. His index finger on her lips stilled him.

"Let me," he whispered. "I'll be full, and you'll be calm."

Realization dawned and she relaxed a bit. He wasn't seeking affection or something more carnal, then. Not exactly. He was offering to take her fears, sorrows, and burdens. This was how he collected spirit energy from her. It wasn't quite a kiss, but it didn't make the exchange less intimate.

Or less dangerous. Spirit energy was powerful and left a signature for those who knew how to detect it. Even garden-variety ghosts, lost and lonely spirits, could detect the energy that fueled the more powerful of their kind. If the sentinel guardian was still close, it would be able to detect their energy exchange, too.

"We can't risk using our spirit energy, Darkmore," she pleaded. "They can track us."

"And I," he said, closing the gap between their mouths. "Am *very* good at covering my tracks."

He placed his mouth on hers and drew out her terror in wisps of red light. He'd done so before, as part of their original bargain of trading the burdens she collected from the living in exchange for his protection. The trade worked well for both of them, since she didn't like carrying around all of that human suffering, whereas he found it delicious.

Of course, most of those exchanges occurred in the light of day rather than in a shared sleeping space with their bodies curled close together.

Apparently Darkmore felt it too, since she detected his arousal pressed against her. It was mostly likely involuntary. He hadn't been a truly mortal man for a long time and, if she was being honest, the sensations she experienced were far from unpleasant. Maybe she didn't mind that so much either, and the thought disturbed her more than her earlier encounter with the sentinel guardian.

Before she could panic, Darkmore released her. He turned her back around so that her back now faced him and he snuggled close.

"Thank you, Vivian. That was…satisfying."

"What are you doing?" Her voice was sharper than she'd intended. She wasn't as angry with him as she was with herself. Her response to him had frightened her.

"Shh, I'm spooning you. Sleep. No harm will come to you. I'm here."

In spite of her lingering fears and disturbing thoughts, she succumbed to the peace he'd given her and, eventually, to sleep.

CHAPTER FOUR

She slept remarkably well considering her close encounter of the deceased and dangerous kind, not to mention her encounter with the softer, protective side of the reaper. Even more remarkable, she woke before Darkmore. She took a moment to watch him sleep, awed by the novelty of the experience. She'd wondered more than once if guardians, reapers, or other dwellers of the spirit world ever slept. She'd only seen Zeke, her former spirit lover, asleep once. He'd been in corporeal form and more at peace than she'd ever known him to be.

That had been the day she'd let him go.

Or so she'd thought at the time. God, she missed him.

She pushed the stray thought aside lest the memories and her unresolved feelings about him overwhelm her.

Those feelings may never be resolved, since she was unlikely to see him again anytime soon—if ever.

Darkmore didn't snore, didn't toss or turn, and she barely detected the rise and fall of his chest. *Figures.* Only he could manage to sleep like a babe even in the middle of their flight from the spirit establishment. If the reaper feared anything, he hid it well.

She stepped out of the tent and into the chill of the morning. It took some time and a few false starts, but she worked out how to operate the portable propane stove so she could set about the most important task of the morning: making coffee. She thanked her lucky stars that she'd had the foresight to pack plenty of instant coffee packets, settling on mocha for her first cup.

It didn't take long for the water to boil, and as soon as she'd mixed the packet of tasty goodness into her thermos, she decided to take a little stroll. If the guardian sentinels were still around, she needed to do a better job playing ordinary human. Even if they weren't, she needed to clear her head and stretch her legs. With any luck, they'd be able to make it to Mississippi today without further delays, which meant at least five hours in the car. Her legs and back ached just thinking about it. Thinking about her next awkward conversation with Darkmore made her head ache.

One look at the brilliant blue sky, with clarity only a crisp autumn day could muster, and she stopped questioning the wisdom of her decision and started walking.

A small flock of Monarch butterflies fluttered nearby, and she took slow and silent steps toward them. They busied themselves gorging on the nectar of fall flowers, some of which still glimmered with the early morning dew. She watched as one uncurled its tongue and slid it gently into the center of an awaiting flower. Naturally, her first thought came straight out of the gutter, but she also found a measure of peace while watching the slow beat of their amber and black wings. *They hatch, they feed, and they grow. They transform, they emerge, and they feed some more. They mate, they lay their eggs, and they die.*

Would that human life was so simple, not to mention the afterlife.

"Sleep well?"

At least Darkmore had the decency to make some noise this time so she'd know he was coming. "I did. You?"

"Very well. I must confess, there is a certain satisfaction in a well-earned night's rest. I'd forgotten that for a time, so I suppose I should thank you for enabling me to experience it again."

"Right," Vivian muttered. She'd managed to avoid the uncomfortable conversation they needed to have, but they sly reaper had turned small talk into a trap.

"Come, sit with me for a while," he said.

"I still don't want to talk about this."

He offered her a small, patient smile. "You'll feel better once we do. I'll make you another cup of coffee."

She stood and stared at the ground.

"I'll make breakfast, too."

"You really aren't going to let this go, are you?"

"Bacon or sausage?"

She sighed. No help for it. "Sausage. Throw in some eggs and I'm there."

Vivian walked back to their campsite with Darkmore, glad for his company in spite of lingering fear and guilt. Conventional wisdom held that she shouldn't like him, shouldn't trust him, and most certainly shouldn't feel responsible for keeping him safe. By all rights she should be terrified, and she knew all too well the terror of which he was capable of making her feel.

He curled up with you and helped you sleep, and now he's making you breakfast. Just go with it.

While cursing her inner voice, something else occurred to her. "Do you know how to cook?"

"Yes."

"I mean, do you how to cook with modern camping gear?"

It was a valid question. The reaper had, after all, lived his first life well before Christ, or the common era, as was often substituted for the Biblical time scale reference. He gave her a bemused look as he managed to turn on the propane stove. On his first try.

Vivian decided to multitask, figuring it would make the conversation easier. She set about packing up their blankets and sleeping bags while she spoke. "So you were right last night. I admit it. I didn't bargain on taking care of both of us and it bothers me, but not for the reason you probably think."

She waited for his response. When he didn't answer, she continued. "Don't get me wrong, I do have an aversion to caring for the helpless on account of Mae and I'll own that. You know it as well as I do."

And he did. When they'd first met, when the reaper had first targeted her, he'd used his powers to see into the darkest parts of her soul, using what he found there to try and claim her. He'd wanted Mae. Vivian's disabled sister was a powerful reservoir of untapped spirit energy. It made her a prize coveted by both guardian and reaper spirits.

Only most of them were incapable of tapping into the living as an energy source. Vivian could, a side effect of her status as a living soul broker. To get to Mae, the reaper needed Vivian.

Exploiting all of the unspeakable resentments she harbored at being her sister's sole caregiver, Darkmore had nearly claimed her. Then again, Vivian's guardian spirit, one of the few souls she thought she could trust, had wanted Mae, too. The fate of Vivian's soul had been secondary to his goal.

Darkmore had wanted Vivian.

First for her power as a living soul broker, but later, he'd wanted her for...her. It didn't change what he was or what he'd done. He was a predator, a reaper of souls subjected to torment and terror in his dark realm.

"You're right," Darkmore said, his gaze darkening with the memory and the pleasure he'd taken in her pain. "I know."

He claimed and tortured souls. It was his purpose, his nature, and he relished his work. But the souls he claimed were wicked. If the reaper darkened your door, you'd done something in life to bring him there. And guardian spirits were anything but angelic, their lust for power and spirit energy at odds with their duty to ferry righteous souls to a better plane of existence. Her guardian spirit Ezra had traded her soul's safe passage for a chance to settle an old grudge with the reaper. It was how she'd become a living soul broker, trapped between the world of the living and the world of the dead.

There was plenty of moral ambiguity to go around on both sides.

"But you aren't helpless," Vivian continued, averting her gaze. "Mortal or not, you still have some of your powers, your wits, and a gigantic set of brass balls."

She heard him snort, so she knew he was still listening. "What bugs me is that I did this to you. You went out of your way to keep me safe and I returned the favor by trapping you in your mortal body. I hate that."

"I see," he said. After a moment, he added, "Why do you hate it so much? You didn't intend to trap me. Plus, as you reminded me in your rather colorful way, I possessed you against your will, which ultimately led to my injury at the hands of your guardian attacker."

Vivian rolled her eyes. Having a debate with the reaper was exasperating at best, infuriating at worst. He could never agree with her, and even when he did, he found a way to twist things around until he left her angry, confused, and, loathe as she was to admit it, hurt.

"Do control your temper. I have an obligation to play Devil's advocate, you know."

"Bad puns aside, you're right. You did help get yourself in this situation, but I asked for your protection. Wallace shot that blast through you that was meant for me, so you saved me. Again. And what did I do? I royally screwed up the healing and left you stuck in your mortal form."

"And what does that mean to you?"

"Damn it, it means I still can't control my stupid fucking powers that I never wanted in the first place. And it means I owe you. I hate owing anyone."

She huffed, and then set about disassembling their tent with her excess aggression. Good thing the tent fabric was tough. After she finished wrestling with the tangle of poles and polyester, she gathered up their trash from the previous night. She was about to tackle the cooler when Darkmore persuaded her to sit and eat.

After a few bites, a few deep breaths, and another half cup of coffee, she felt a bit better. "These are good, by the way. How did you learn how to cook in modern times?"

"The Food Network."

The Grim Reaper watched the cooking channel? Who'd have thought?

Her shock must have registered, since the reaper offered her a wry smile. "Truly, cable television is one of many things I enjoy in this realm. During my off time."

"So you like more than just Westerns?" She'd found out early in their acquaintance that Darkmore had a thing for old western flicks. That's where he'd picked up his fondness for Stetson hats, and possibly where he'd found inspiration for his mortal form. He could've been a young Robert Redford with icy blond hair, chiseled features, and deceptively winning smile.

Not that she thought of him that way. Much. There was the time not so long ago when she'd asked him to be her date for a friend's wedding, but that had been desperation. Her ex-lover had been the best man and had brought the woman he'd dumped her for—the one he'd cheated on her with —to the wedding. Pride and anger, two of the seven deadly sins, had driven her to ask Darkmore to accompany her.

More than that, several small and not so small acts of kindness, unexpected and more powerful because of it, had built trust between them. Only a few threads, but it had been enough.

Until she'd seen him work, helped him torture a damned soul, seen how much he enjoyed it.

"I like many things," Darkmore said, gaze knowing, as if he'd read her confusion and dismay. "Now then, as to your debt to me, are you more disturbed at the prospect of causing me harm, the idea that you must 'fix me,' or how I might calculate the terms of payment once I am restored?"

Just when she was getting comfortable, he just had to go and say something so cold, so calculating, and so reaperish that she had to start from scratch.

"All great questions, but I think the second is foremost on my mind. Have you thought about asking Uphir? I thought she was the expert for your kind."

"Though she suspects something is amiss, I'd rather not. Her rates are far too high. Any other ideas?"

She'd been afraid of that. Uphir might help him, but he'd spend eternity in her service. Someone as powerful as the reaper would rather face all of the legions of hell than serve another. "I was hoping the folks in Mississippi might be able to help. Barring that, at least I'll be free to use my powers again when we get there and can work under their protection. I'm surprised you haven't come up with something, given your vast experience."

He appeared to consider. "I've seen many things in my time, and I've chosen to return to the mortal world in human form through the conventional route, though never truly human of course. I've witnessed reanimation of a corpse. Not very pretty, but quite an impressive feat. This, however, is an entirely new and different experience."

She knew Darkmore was difficult to surprise and even more difficult to impress. That she'd had enough power to do something that he hadn't expected or seen gave her a brief surge of pride. Not good. She shouldn't get smug, since the whole thing had been an accident. Plus, she still felt guilty for putting him in this predicament. He didn't seem particularly distraught, though, which made her more than a little suspicious.

"So, about yesterday...that little number you did on McClung, was that a gargantuan bluff?" she asked.

"Hmm," was all the response he offered.

"And last night, when I was in trouble, you came running awful fast." She paused, deep in thought. "Plus, you managed to suck the terror right out of me."

Why hadn't it dawned on her before?

She stared at him for a moment before asking, "So, exactly how much of your former powers do you still have?"

He grinned. "I believe most remain intact. You've been worried about that for a while, haven't you?"

"Yes," she said, voice sharper than she'd intended. "And you were more than happy to sit back and watch me worry over it, weren't you?"

"You are at your best when you are hell-bent on protecting those for whom you care. More often than not, you're at your worst then, too. At any rate, regardless of the outcome, I'm guaranteed to get my fair share of wonderful meals while traveling with you. Shall we?"

Too stupefied to do anything else, Vivian helped pack up and followed the reaper.

CHAPTER FIVE

They made good time on the Trace from Hohenwald to Tupelo, Mississippi, birthplace of Elvis and a convenient place to break for lunch. Vivian volunteered to drive the first leg if for no other reason than to claim sole rights to their music selection. After his little morning confession, she felt the overwhelming urge to discover what type of music the reaper found most offensive so she could play it often over the course of their trip.

They stopped at the Visitor's Center and parted ways for a pee break and to stretch. She longed for a shower, especially after a glance in the mirror reminded her of the ill effects that too many days without shampoo and excess humidity had on her curls. Plus, her grays were peeking through again. She did a quick sniff test and figured she could go at least another day before she became overripe, but she really wanted some soap, lotion, and a good shave for her neglected legs.

Being on the run wasn't as romantic in real life as it seemed in books or the movies.

She joined Darkmore at an outdoor picnic table and opened her not-so-appetizing cheese stick. Chancing a glance at him, she smiled while he swallowed a grimace along with his processed food product. At least she had some company in her misery.

"You have a visitor."

"Huh?" Vivian asked after she swallowed a cracker.

Darkmore motioned to some nearby trees. When she looked, she saw Jeanne and an unfamiliar spirit waiting. They were both in corporeal form.

Jeanne looked much as she had the first time Vivian met the young guardian, who was, in fact, truly young. She'd died young, robbed by cancer of a chance to complete her pre-law studies, to experience the richness of adult life. Recently departed, Jeanne was also a young guardian spirit, though she possessed the power and skill of a much more seasoned soul broker. Being a dedicated student likely hadn't hurt, and she'd carried that trait with her into the afterlife along with her youthful appearance. With shoulder length honey-colored hair, gorgeous round face, a trim figure, and a bright, bubbly personality, she was a brainiac in sorority girl's clothing.

Jeanne's companion, on the other hand, was anything but bubbly.

Vivian turned to back to Darkmore, eyebrows raised. As far as she knew, Jeanne was one of the "good" guardians, if a little too eager and irritatingly perky. She'd assisted Vivian in her flight from the guardian council and put her in contact with Waylon Briggs, leader of a rag-tag band of mortals who, like Vivian, were living soul brokers who could commune with the dead. She wanted to trust Jeanne, but she'd been double-crossed by enough guardian spirits to be wary.

And something about the other spirit had the hairs on the back of her neck standing at attention.

"Go," the reaper said. "See your friend. I'll finish this abysmal excuse for a lunch and then find some more ice."

She hesitated, scanning the area for any signs of ambush.

"You needn't worry. They are alone. Go on. I'll be nearby in case you get into trouble."

On impulse, she gave Darkmore a quick peck on the cheek, surprising them both, and then jogged over to the tree line. Jeanne beamed and grabbed her hand, pulling her deeper into the patch of forest for privacy. She embraced Vivian and filled her with a healthy dose of warm guardian spirit energy. Though taken aback by the unexpected display of affection, she had to admit that she'd missed the peace that guardians could deliver. She also reminded herself that Jeanne, the spirit world's version of Cheerleader Barbie, was a hugger.

"It's so wonderful to see you," Jeanne whispered.

"You, too," Vivian said, and meant it.

After a long moment, Jeanne released Vivian and held her at arm's length. Vivian became more than a little self-conscious. Jeanne manifested as she'd appeared in life: young, blonde, and extraordinarily put-together. The other spirit was equally striking, though in a markedly different way. With her dark hair cut into a severe bob, black jeans and a black T-shirt, and fathomless toffee-colored eyes, this guardian's aura screamed power and danger.

Not unlike Darkmore. Vivian liked being under this spirit's scrutiny even less than the reaper's. The unnamed spirit stared a hole through Vivian, like a big cat judging the quality of a potential kill.

Great. Another fan.

Since running wouldn't do her any good, she'd have to trust that any friend of Jeanne's would do her no harm. Rather than lower her gaze or betray any signs of the fear coursing through her, Vivian ignored the spirit and focused her attention on Jeanne. "I know I look like shit. Real camping will do that to you. What's the latest on the home front?"

Jeanne smiled. "You don't look *that* bad, but you'll be pleased to know that it's safe to grab a hotel. We've been working hard to throw Uriel's forces off your trail."

Vivian bristled at the mention of the Archangel's name, anger temporarily displacing fear as the dominant emotion. "Really? That's surprising, because last night I had a run-in with a spirit-energy seeking missile."

Jeanne's face fell and Vivian immediately regretted her snippiness. It wasn't the young guardian's fault that she had a target on her back.

Jeanne apologized before Vivian could offer an apology of her own. "I know and I'm so, so sorry we couldn't get him off your tail in time! But you must have put on a good show. My intel has it that they think you're heading to the New York base."

"Just how many bases are there?" Vivian asked. It would be a good idea to learn as much about the rebellion as she could, given that she'd be joining it soon.

"At least ten and more factions are forming every day. But not all are on the same page," Jeanne added, her normally perky features growing somber.

"Sounds like they need a leader." Vivian had been joking, but something in Jeanne's expression made her suspicious.

"They do," Jeanne said a little too eagerly.

"Wait a minute." Vivian held up her hands in protest as realization dawned. "I signed on to keep my friends safe and change Darkmore back, not so I could become the General Custer of your rag-tag band of ghost bandits."

The comment earned her another dark look from Jeanne's buddy.

Jeanne, who'd grown accustomed to her frequent outbursts, hardly missed a beat. "No, no, you don't have to worry. Waylon's the man for the job. But he needs all the help he can get right now. You've got firepower, healing power, and talent. Just work with him, help him, and try to encourage him, okay?"

"Fine," she said. How hard could that be? "Any ideas how I can put the reaper back to rights?"

Jeanne beamed. "I've been in contact with some spirits involved in Voudon. They have more experience with this sort of thing. They'll be in touch once you get to Jackson."

Voodoo? Seriously?

"Oh no, not Voodoo. Don't call it that or you'll offend them," Jeanne admonished. Freaking guardian spirits. They could read the thoughts of humans, though they usually only pried when necessary. Jeanne, being Jeanne, opted to listen in more often than the rest of her kind.

"It's not like what they show in the movies—the spirits and practitioners are benevolent. They're on *our* side. The Archangel Council has blackened their reputation for years so they could control all crossings and collect the spirit energy associated with crossings."

"All right. I get it," Vivian said, taking a step back and holding up her hands in surrender. It sounded like something the Archangels would do. "I'll try to keep an open mind."

The Archangel Guardian Council, who sat at the top of what had to be the largest pyramid scheme in the universe, had tried to control her, just as they controlled her mentor. "Mentor" probably wasn't quite the right word for Ezra, the guardian who'd roped her into the soul broker business. He was a tricky bastard, prone to giving her just enough information to get her in trouble without cluing her in on the endgame of afterlife management politics or the risks inherent in her work.

Steeling herself and tamping down on her anger, Vivian asked, "Any word from Ezra?"

"Nothing much yet. But don't worry. He's insinuated himself back into the Council's good graces, and I'm sure he'll be in touch once he has some information we can use."

Yeah, he's really good at insinuating himself into the confidence of others.

Ezra, the first spirit Vivian ever met, had come to her in the guise of friend and mentor. Only after he'd earned her trust did she learn his true purpose—he'd come to claim Vivian's soul on behalf of the guardians. Darkmore, the only entity in this game who'd been completely—if brutally —honest, told her that Ezra liked to play both sides. Jeanne seemed to think that Ezra was still firmly on their side, the side that wanted to stop ripping off spirit energy and use it for the intended purpose of helping souls cross. Vivian believed his loyalty rested with himself and no one else.

Jeanne must have guessed where her thoughts had led her. Or perhaps the young guardian had read her thoughts. Some guardian spirits could do that. "Oh, Vivian, I know you're mad at him, but you have to understand the situation. We've been trying to avoid open rebellion with the Council for so long. You know, trying to change things from within?"

She nodded reluctantly. It made sense and fit with Ezra's natural style of playing politics. And she knew a thing or two about playing both sides for protection and survival.

Jeanne's features relaxed a bit as she continued. "Ezra's been walking a fine line, working with the rebellion in secret while staying in the council's good graces. He just couldn't tell you everything."

Vivian snorted and rolled her eyes as a fresh wave of anger washed over her. "Oh, I don't doubt his skills at lying and double-crossing. I've experienced that first hand." Ezra was also inclined to keep secrets—the kind that had cost her and those she loved dearly.

"Any word from Zeke?" Her voice only shook a little and she held Jeanne's gaze.

Jeanne's gaze darted to the left before returning to hers. The young guardian was about to lie to her, and her chest went tight as dread warred with anger. More secrets. With Zeke, it was always secrets.

"He's working for the cause...and for you. That's all I can say."

"Fine. I won't ask again. Just promise me you'll..." *What? Tell him I miss him? Tell him I still love him? Tell him to come and take me away from all of this? No.* "Promise you'll look out for him."

Jeanne dropped her gaze and nodded, remaining oddly quiet. The other spirit just kept glaring. Before her patience reached the breaking point, Vivian said, "Okay, what gives?"

Jeanne kept her eyes on the ground. Vivian mustered enough manufactured courage to turn to the other spirit and say, "I'm Vivian, by the way. I'd say nice to meet you, but we haven't been introduced, and you don't seem particularly happy to be here, if you don't mind my saying so."

That earned Vivian a smile. Not exactly friendly, but not unfriendly, either. It would do. She understood. Hard to know whom to trust in afterlife management these days.

"I was called Marguerite in life," the spirit said in a softly accented voice, extending her hand. Vivian accepted. It was warm and her handshake firm. Marguerite's eyes reminded her of Darkmore's, ancient and fathomless. She had to be a very old guardian spirit. Her accent had likely softened over centuries—or more—making it impossible to identify, at least for Vivian. Likely not as old as Darkmore then, whose crisp, flawless Midwestern American accent was too flawless to be genuine and perfected with untold eons of practice in blending with mortals. Then again, perhaps Marguerite used her accent as a disguise. Ezra's good old boy Southern charm was disarming, hiding his power and the threat he posed, making those he met underestimate him.

A change in the atmosphere brought Vivian's attention back to her companions. The temperature rose, but she didn't think it signaled anger from the guardian spirits. Other strong emotions could bring out their power and the heat that came with it, though.

Marguerite had turned back to Jeanne, and Vivian noted the softening of her gaze. *Looks like Jeanne got herself an upgraded mentor.* Jeanne's former mentor, Wallace, hadn't been very nice. In fact, he was the rogue guardian responsible for Darkmore's condition and the rest of their current mess. Uriel and the guardian council had given him the green light to stop Vivian at all costs, and the rogue had taken his work very seriously. Instead, Vivian had sent him to spirit realms unknown. Good riddance.

"Well," Marguerite said, stern look back in place. "Perhaps I should give you and Jeanne a minute." She nodded to Vivian before placing a comforting hand on Jeanne's shoulder.

After Marguerite disappeared, Vivian shook her head and grabbed ahold of Jeanne "Whatever it is, just say it. I've had more suspense the past twenty-four hours than I can handle." Though curious about Marguerite, safety and survival were her top priorities.

Jeanne looked up at her with big blue eyes and for a moment appeared even younger. Those eyes held pleading. "Vivian, Marguerite is more than my mentor. She's my lover."

She stared at Jeanne for a full thirty seconds before laughing. She couldn't help it. At least half was due to relief. No bad news, no new threats, and no imminent danger—the adrenaline that had been spiking in her veins for the past several weeks needed an outlet.

When she regained her composure—mostly—she said, "*That's* what this is all about? Seriously?"

"Stop making fun," Jeanne said, looking sullen. "Do you have any idea how hard that was for me?"

She tried, but she just couldn't stop herself. Every time she caught her breath, she'd take one look at the young guardian and lose it again. Jeanne made like she was preparing to vanish, so Vivian grabbed her and gave her a good-natured pat on the back.

"Don't be like that. I'm not making fun. I'm just relieved."

"Why?" Jeanne asked, suspiciously.

"What do you mean why? I thought you were going to lay some more seriously messed up spirit crap on me, or tell me someone else I love died, or give me more bad news." Some of the tension drained from her body along with the laugher. God, that was the first real laugh she'd had since leaving Nashville.

Jeanne offered a shy smile, apparently pleased with Vivian's answer, or her reaction. "Well, I guess I didn't think about it like that."

"Why was it so hard to tell me? Did you think I'd be mad or something?" As far as she was aware, she'd never said or done anything that could have been construed as homophobia. Maybe this was baggage from Jeanne's mortal life. The world was changing, but plenty of folks clung to deeply held prejudices that were hard to let go, especially when challenged in the form of a friend or family member.

Jeanne shrugged, casting her gaze to the ground. It wasn't like her. The Jeanne she knew was a fighter. "I'd hoped not. I mean, I never had the chance to, you know, come out, while I was alive. Maggie's been after me to tell someone I know in the mortal realm so I'd, you know, have closure."

Yup. Mortal life baggage it was.

Vivian was touched that Jeanne had chosen to tell her, even though she'd hardly had any other choice. Vivian was the only mortal Jeanne communed with, as far as Vivian was aware of at least. Still, Vivian accepted it for the gift of trust and friendship it was.

Since Jeanne probably expected a measure of irascibility from her anyway, Vivian decided she might as well play her part while offering reassurance. "Let me 'splain something to you, Lucy. I went from having a guardian hit man chasing me to having the entire freakin' guardian council on my ass. My whole life has been erased, I'm on the run, and I've got to take care of and put up with yon reaper. Your gayness is the very least of my concerns."

Jeanne gave her a sheepish grin. At least Vivian had got her laughing.

"Look, I don't care who you sleep with, or 'commune with' or whatever you call it. You love who you love, right?"

"Right," Jeanne answered. She was crying. Vivian had never seen her cry.

"Hey," Vivian said, chest squeezing tight with concern. At least it wasn't fear for safety this time. After a moment's hesitation, she pulled the guardian spirit into her arms. Awkward, but she figured she should at least try to offer some comfort. It was what she did for the living, after all.

What she'd done, she corrected. She was a rebel, now. Presumably that meant fighting, but perhaps her empathetic connection with humans, the ability to absorb their burdens, would help the rebellion leader. Was that what Jeanne had meant when she suggested Vivian offer him support?

Now wasn't the time for more questions, though. She turned her focus back on Jeanne. "It's fine. Who am I to judge? I mean, it's not like I haven't participated in a little human-on-guardian action. That's about as unnatural as you can get, aside from cross-species."

Not that she thought of her time with Zeke as unnatural. He'd been her protector, friend, lover, and shelter from the storm that had become her life. Their time together had been brief, but she'd loved him fiercely. And she'd let him go, doing what she thought was best.

Then he'd come back, but things between them weren't right. They hadn't had time to make them right before she left—yet another regret. He said he'd fight for her. Would he wait for her?

And then there was Darkmore.

Driven by some strange compulsion at the thought, she added "And… I'm seriously considering giving it a go with a reaper."

She could've played if off as a joke, at least before she clapped a hand over her mouth. Holy shit. Why had she said that?

Because it's true.

Jeanne laughed and let go of Vivian so she could dry her eyes. "I'm surprised you haven't already. You are quite a rebel."

Vivian had expected an admonition, not a joke. "Thanks for not judging me, either."

Zeke would judge, but then again, he'd "reconnected" with his living wife while hiding from Vivian. He was hardly in a position to judge.

"I'm not like the council," Jeanne replied. There was something in her voice that gave Vivian pause. The council would definitely have a problem with a guardian or soul broker they considered one of "theirs" fraternizing with a reaper. She'd learned the hard way that they also had a problem with guardians fraternizing with the living. But guardians with guardians? Seriously?

Unless…

"What? They have a problem with folks like you? They have a problem with your relationship with Marguerite?" Vivian couldn't quite bring herself to call Jeanne's partner "Maggie."

"They have a problem with a lot of things." Changing the subject, Jeanne said, "Go on and get back on the road. You should be able to find a nice hotel along the way. One with room service. And a shower."

"Thanks," Vivian said with mock indignation. "I'll do that."

Jeanne hesitated for a moment, and then planted a kiss on Vivian's cheek. "Thank you."

Then she disappeared.

Vivian leaned against the tree and let Jeanne's words sink in. She could breathe easier, at least for the moment, it seemed. With the guardians off their trail, they no longer had to hurry. Truth be told, she didn't really want to hurry into the unknown now that their safety no longer depended upon it. She reflected on all she'd lost and fought the bitterness she'd kept at bay since they began their journey.

"No, I won't think about all that right now," she said aloud. Instead, she decided to focus on their more immediate needs. She rose, dusted off her grimy jeans, and marched off to find Darkmore.

CHAPTER SIX

"May I ask where we are going in such a hurry?"

Darkmore had played along when Vivian ran back to fetch him and their belongings. She'd packed up the car at lightning speed, cursed her fingers for failing to type faster while programming the GPS, and sped out of the Welcome Center's parking lot with enough speed to leave skid marks. All the while, the reaper maintained his calm and followed along.

"Jeanne says the guardians are off our trail."

The reaper didn't seem surprised. He had probably known before Jeanne clued her in. "That is welcome news. If that's the case, why the rush?"

Taking a deep breath and deliberately relaxing her white-knuckled grip on the steering wheel, she said, "I want a shower. A long one. And I want a really good meal, a soft bed, and..."

She didn't have to look at Darkmore to know he was smiling. *Smug bastard.* At least he didn't push her to finish her thought.

They'd kept to the Natchez Trace Parkway as long as possible, and its sweeping vistas of red, gold, and orange fall foliage. The sharp contrast between the dull grays and bland landscape flanked by the interstate was jarring by contrast. They'd make better time but leaving the shelter of forest and pasture for the openness of civilization left her uneasy. She didn't like being so exposed and couldn't help checking her rearview mirror.

After twenty miles of uncomfortable silence, Darkmore spoke. "So we are seeking more comfortable accommodations?"

"Yup."

"What about that one?"

Darkmore's finger pointed to the boxy hotel looming in the distance, presumably located just off the next exit. Bland and boring, it looked like every other cheap chain accommodation they'd passed during the last several hours. Bone deep weariness tempted her to stop, but after weeks on the run and the greater part of two years living in fear of the spirit world, she craved respite. A bit of rest and a moment of peace before they faced the looming battle that awaited them—if she could have that, she could face what was to come.

Though he would never admit it, she suspected the reaper needed a respite as well. It had to be terrifying for a creature as ancient and powerful as Darkmore to be trapped in a mortal body, his essence contained within such a fragile vessel, subject to all of the discomforts that came with a body that was slowly dying. He hid it well, but she hadn't missed the way his joints had popped and cracked at their last stop, the way he'd limped a bit while human limbs adjusted to motion after a few hours of sitting in cramped quarters, how he shivered in the cold. That had hit her like an arrow through the heart. Cold was his nature. His presence had soothed her during Southern summer heat waves during his frequent visits, like a welcome breeze or a crisp mountain stream.

It pained her to know that she'd taken that from him.

He needed warmth, sustenance, and rest as much as she did, and not in the sterile, impersonal space.

"Nope," she said, shaking her head. "If we're going to stop for a few days, we're going to do it in style. At least, as much style as you can get in Boonieville Mississippi."

"A few days." It wasn't a question, and he didn't sound surprised, exactly. Just thoughtful.

Maybe this was a bad idea. She hadn't budgeted for it, as her original plan had been to get to Mississippi and find the afterlife management rebels as soon as possible. But God, she really needed a break. "Um, maybe. I'll have to check the finances, but I think we can afford it."

"You needn't worry about payment, Vivian."

She chanced a glance at the reaper. She couldn't read his face, so she turned her gaze back to the road ahead. "No, I'm not completely unprepared, you know. I *do* work in finance—scratch that, I *did* work in finance."

Something else she'd given up because she'd crossed the guardians.

"At any rate," she continued, "I like to be prepared. I figured I might have to disappear someday, or go on some sort of secret guardian mission-type trip, or get away. I planned ahead."

"And you think I did not?"

She jerked in surprise, though she shouldn't have. A creature as old and as clever as the reaper hadn't survived this long without planning. Of course he'd have resources. She'd be willing to bet he had caches of wealth hidden all over the world, and possibly in a few other realms.

She checked her rearview mirror. Aside from a couple of sedans and a slow-moving pickup, they had this stretch of interstate to themselves. She changed lanes and pulled onto the shoulder. After she put the car in park, she took a deep breath, turned, and looked at Darkmore.

"How much we talking about?"

He smiled then, flashing that shit-eating, smug grin that infuriated and inflamed her all at once.

"More than enough."

"I already told you I don't like owing you—"

"It's only money. In my case, quite inconsequential—at least before my transformation. Now, it is essential for our survival. And our comfort."

Vivian thought for a moment, her accountant's brain crunching numbers almost of its own accord. She'd planned for six months at most. It had been all she could manage during her stint as a part-time soul broker. Who knew how long they'd be on the run? Perhaps she could have squirreled away a bit more, but there had been so little time.

"Do not trouble yourself. I've simply been around longer."

She turned back, put the car in drive, and pulled back onto the Interstate after a quick glance over her shoulder. She checked the GPS. They weren't far.

"I'll think about it. In the meantime, though, dinner is *definitely* on you."

———

"Did you have to screw around with the concierge?" Vivian asked between bites of

steak. She hadn't spoken much since their food arrived via room service. Between a long, hot shower, a change of clothing, and her first decent meal in days, she'd been too wrapped up in the blessed act of unwinding.

He smiled, apparently lost in savoring his own meal. "I may be mortal in form, but I am still a reaper. I require sustenance beyond this fine meal."

She swallowed hard. Misery and torment were the reaper's bread and butter. Often enough, he "sweetened" his victims before feeding from them, touching raw nerves and dredging up their deepest, darkest fears, secrets, and horrors. Not quite the same as harvesting soul energy—he gathered that when he took a departed soul to his dark realm of torment, or when he relieved Vivian of the burdens she collected from the living—it still filled him with a form of existential nourishment and satisfaction. It was his nature, but having once been on the receiving end of his sadistic brand of play, watching him work made her uncomfortable.

That was probably for the best. She couldn't afford to get too comfortable with Darkmore. They may be allies, if not quite friends, but it wouldn't do to forget what he was.

"Fine, but did you have to include the bellboy, the folks in the elevator, the guy who delivered our food?"

"Speaking of which, why are we eating in our bedchamber? I would have been more than happy to escort you to a fine dining establishment nearby."

She shrugged. "I like room service. I get it whenever I can."

Darkmore stopped eating and gave her one of his inquisitive looks.

"It's not a very interesting story," Vivian said. She took another bite. No need to waste a warm, medium rare rib eye on anyone's account.

"Tell me anyway."

She took a long moment to savor the tender bite of steak, chased by a sip of wine, before answering. "Fine. We always took el cheapo vacations when I was a kid, on those rare occasions when we went anywhere. Dad worked hard. So did mom, but she didn't get paid to be a caregiver. Money was tight for a long time, especially with Mae. Hell, the conversion for the van alone was over ten grand." *Not to mention Mae's wheelchair, Mae's specialized bed and occupational therapy-designed equipment, Mae's doctor visits, Mae's meds...*

Vivian stopped her train of thought soon after she stopped speaking. Her sister wasn't a subject she enjoyed revisiting in the presence of the reaper. Both reaper and guardians had been drawn to Vivian largely because of Mae and her disabilities, since mortal souls trapped in incapacitated states provided vast spirit energy reserves. She still associated her first encounter with the reaper with the terrible night on which she felt the full force of her own anger and resentment at caring for Mae. He'd fed from her deeply that night.

Oddly enough, she didn't sense his influence, the pull of his hunger, or any sign that he was savoring her emotional burdens now. Maybe he was being...polite. She'd never known him to miss a meal, though. Then again, he'd just fed from the misery of hotel staff.

His expression hadn't changed. He simply nodded, encouraging her to go on. She blew out a breath and then spoke.

"So once I was out on my own and stayed in my first upscale hotel, I ordered room service because I could. I was at a work conference in Atlanta, my first, so I was excited. I felt like I'd finally made it. I remember the man wheeling in this cart with beautiful, silver-covered dishes. He was dressed just like a maître d' out of a five-star restaurant, and he uncovered the trays full of steaming food, poured my glass of wine, and unfurled my napkin..."

"You needn't be embarrassed, Vivian."

"What makes you think I am?" she snapped.

"You don't seem to be comfortable with this particular topic. Is it because you suppose I find your fondness for this bit of luxury quaint and foolish, or is it because you were thinking of your sister?"

She sighed. Why couldn't he just let stuff go? "I don't really care if you think I'm quaint. I like room service, and I make a point of getting room service at least once whenever I go on a trip. It's my thing."

"Fair enough. And Mae?"

"I don't want to talk about Mae with you."

"Why not?"

Vivian waited to answer, finishing her last bite of steak and savoring another sip of wine. She'd be damned if he cheated her out of the meal. When she finished, she steeled herself and looked Darkmore straight in his ice blue eyes. "I don't want to talk about Mae right now because I'm just getting comfortable with you again. If we talk about her, I'll have to think about what you are and what you did to me when we first met. And then..."

She trailed off, wishing she'd kept her mouth shut. He couldn't make her talk, and she didn't owe him an explanation for why she did anything. She shouldn't have made it personal. Sure, they were allies, and if she'd kept him safe since she turned him mortal, he'd returned the favor a thousand times over. He'd protected her from guardian spirits long before he'd needed her for anything—anything other than the burdens she collected and converted into spirit energy.

That's all he needed her for. All he wanted. Those small moments of intimacy they'd shared, that one memorable kiss that had been about more than sharing spirit light, those surely hadn't meant more to him than staking his claim on a meal ticket.

He didn't want her.

But the reaper was a persistent hunter, and patient. He wouldn't let it go.

"And then...what? What is it that you want?" Darkmore asked, his cool, smooth voice barely above a whisper. His gaze was intense, filled with hunger of a different sort.

She froze, despising herself for the admission of weakness. She knew what she wanted from him, but warred with herself over wanting such a creature as the reaper. Unsure, frightened, and angry, she got up from the table, slipped on her shoes, and grabbed her jacket and car keys. The reaper rose from his seat as well and moved as if to stop her.

"I've got to go out and get a few things, and some air. Why don't you grab a shower and I'll see you when I get back?"

"Vivian—"

"Please," she said, refusing to meet his gaze. She hated begging.

"You still fear me," Darkmore said. He stood right beside her. She could feel his cool presence and his power. It beckoned her. He placed his hands on her shoulders. She flinched.

"Let me go," she murmured. The tears she'd fought threatened and she despised herself. She wouldn't break before him. Never. Not before this creature who fed on human tears.

He released her and she ran.

————

She stood in front of the side entrance to the hotel, key card in one hand, door handle in the other, and her mind no clearer than when she'd left the man on the other side.

Odd that she thought of him as a man now, not as a reaper, ally, occasional guard, or source of vexation. Friend, perhaps, or friendly. Theirs had always been a mutually beneficial relationship, but she'd grown to see him as more than she had when he'd first darkened her doorway.

Now, above all else, he was a man, flesh, bone, and as mortal as she. And waiting upstairs, behind another door.

She'd returned after an hour of soul-searching coupled with a few errands. When multi-tasking failed to keep her from wallowing in angst, she'd wandered back. Now, she struggled to make herself open the door. Her time away had done little to settle her anxiety or help her find the answers she'd sought within herself. She regretted running from him. Again. It smacked of cowardice.

She had the right to fear him, of course. He was a reaper of human souls, his prey and sustenance. Vivian had looked deep enough within herself to realize that the same darkness that frightened her also held her fascination. He'd once told her that he was neither good nor evil. She'd seen him use his powers to drag living souls to his dark realm, deserving souls to be sure, but he *liked* it. He reveled in it. More to the point, she'd tasted his power and liked it, too.

What does wanting someone like Darkmore make me?

On the other hand, the same reaper had also shown her kindness and helped her. Her spirit powers enabled her to alleviate the deep burdens of souls in pain, which she absorbed within her being through spirit light. Darkmore relieved her of those burdens. He'd protected her from the rogue guardian who sought her destruction and the powerful guardian spirit council who'd unleashed him. They sought to control her. The reaper granted her free will.

His arms had enfolded her the night before, chasing her fears away.

And he'd never lied to her. That was more than she could say for the guardian spirits she'd encountered, the so-called "good guys." Ezra came to her in the guise of a Good Samaritan, comforted her during her darkest days and protected her from the reaper. But he failed to mention that his true purpose was to claim her soul. Instead, he allowed her to live, a decision that left her burdened with the unwanted spirit powers she now possessed, not to mention the ability to see and commune with the unseen dead all around. Ezra's lies led to this heartache and more.

Her protector and guardian spirit Zeke had loved and comforted her. He became her lover, and she'd lost him because of Ezra's lies. His soul had been meant for Darkmore, but Ezra took him. Zeke had done terrible things during his life, atrocities that condemned him to a sentence in the frightening and cold realm of purgatory and damnation in which the reapers dwelled. Instead, Ezra sentenced him to serve as his right-hand helper. Vivian had found a way to free him, tried to send him to a place of peace.

But Zeke hadn't gone.

He returned to her for a time, but his lies ultimately broke her heart. He'd promised to fight for her before she fled her life and home, just as he'd promised to protect those she loved and left behind. But he had others to protect, others to love. A living wife and two children with whom he'd maintained...contact. She couldn't compete with that, and she shouldn't be angry with Zeke for turning to them when he thought she'd sent him away, but she was angry, and hurt.

Stop. She couldn't allow herself to think on Zeke right now. It felt too much like betrayal.

It reminded her too much of his betrayal. And what he thought was hers.

"I will not run from this," she whispered aloud, almost like a prayer.

She registered a chill in the air, one she suspected had nothing to do with the crisp autumn evening. Risking a glance over her shoulder, she thought she caught sight of a shadow flashing around the corner of the building. Perhaps she should investigate, but she wasn't foolish enough to do so without backup. She'd have to find Darkmore.

Vivian slid the key card into the slot, opened the door, and walked inside. Taking the stairs two at a time, she arrived at the door to their room and repeated these actions. She scanned the room, but he wasn't there.

"Lazarus?" Whispering his name in the darkness of their room proved a little too intimate for her comfort. The reaper had always unnerved her. That he unnerved her for different reasons now sent a shiver down her spine, and not from cold or fear.

"In here," he called.

The sound of his voice eased her fear. Surely he would register any other spirits in the area if she could. Shaking off her jitters, Vivian removed her coat and slipped off her shoes and socks. She walked barefoot through the dark hotel room toward the bathroom door, its frame glowing from the light on the other side. Inhaling deeply, she noted the fresh scent of lemon soap. Beneath it, she smelled the reaper. He smelled of a crisp autumn day, of snow-covered pine and evergreen, and of man.

Throwing caution to the wind, she opened the door and went to him.

He stood before the mirror, wearing a damp towel slung low across his hips and nothing else. His broad chest glistened with droplets of water, and Vivian stared as they trickled through the golden hair covering it. She'd never seen him in such a state of undress and could not help staring. His mortal form, sculpted and chiseled with well-defined muscles, captivated her. Of course, he'd chosen it for that very reason. The beauty disguised the danger. His gaze met hers by way of the mirror. Those eyes hadn't changed, and in them she could see the endless ages through which he'd traveled. Under any other circumstances, she might have been mortified to be caught in the act of such blatant gawking, but his gaze encouraged her exploration.

The look he gave her answered her hunger and beckoned her forward.

"What are you doing?" she asked, her voice quavering.

He rubbed the patch of whiskers that ran along his jaw and down his neck. The hair was darker than the blond locks on his head, darker than his chest hair that had captured her attention moments earlier. His beard matched the color of the hair that extended from his naval down below the line of the towel he wore.

Heat pooled low in her belly as she moved closer to him.

"I was thinking about shaving," Darkmore said quietly, his eyes never leaving hers.

She wondered how long it had been since he'd shaved his beard. Mortal men took such a mundane act for granted, yet the reaper seemed to regard the prospect with a strange mixture of innocent amusement and reverence. Something dawned on her then, like the last piece of a puzzle sliding neatly into place.

He feeds on human experience, too. The whole of it, not just the darkness.

He picked up the can of shaving cream from the vanity and sprayed a generous dollop into his left hand. Long fingers then massaged the white foam into his skin. He rinsed the excess from his hands and then reached for the razor, its sturdy metal handle and sharp, gleaming blades a good fit for the reaper in the form of man.

Vivian grabbed it first.

"Let me," she said. Insinuating herself between the reaper and the vanity, she hoisted herself up until she sat on top of the counter in front of him. With her free hand, she reached out for his body and pulled him closer until he rested between her thighs.

Her hands steady, she slowly ran the razor across his face, taking care not to nick the skin that covered his angular jaw. Gentle strokes of her hand followed the path of the blade. He stood still and watched with his unfathomable gaze. His mortal body, however, could not hide his arousal. His breathing became labored. She could feel his excitement through the towel and the fabric of her jeans.

After she removed the hair above his lip, she grabbed a washcloth and soaked it with warm water. She ran the cloth over his face and traced his smooth skin with trembling fingertips, daring to run her fingers through his hair when he offered no protest. The dampness that clung to his white-blond locks softened the coarse texture. Darkmore closed his eyes and a soft groan escaped his lips.

That groan broke her.

She put her arms around his neck and pulled his mouth to hers. The softness of his lips surprised her, as did their warmth. She'd expected cold. Reapers always came with a chill, sometimes as refreshing as a soothing spring breeze, sometimes as icy as despair, but always cold.

Now, her reaper burned.

She moaned and covered his hands with hers, needing the feel of those warm, strong hands on her flesh. She brought them up to cup her breasts in a silent plea. He pressed himself closer to her and deepened their kiss in response, teasing her nipples through the fabric of her shirt. She slid closer and moved her hands to his hips, pressing her body against his and gasping. Need chased away any lingering doubts, as did his utter beauty and the skill his kiss and his clever fingers promised.

She yanked at her shirt and pulled it unceremoniously over her head. Her bare flesh met his, and she clawed at his back and slid her hands down in an attempt to remove his towel. His hands found hers and stilled them.

She growled in response.

Whispering words in a language she did not comprehend, he trailed kisses along her jaw and down her neck. She fought to free her hands so she could grab him and pull his hot mouth to her aching breasts, but he held her firm.

"Please," she whispered.

"Patience," he whispered. "Patience."

"I want you," she pleaded, her doubts replaced by blind need for a respite from her life's turmoil, the comfort of a lover's touch, and the need to care for him, too. "I need you."

"Then come with me," whispered, wrapping her legs around him and lifting her from the counter. She kissed him hard as he carried her to the bed, protesting when he removed her from his body. He placed her on the bed and gently pushed her down, trailing kisses along her neck and teasing her breasts before moving lower and removing her jeans and panties. Her lips parted in anticipation as she watched him unwrap the towel from his waist.

He was beautiful and still carried that otherworldly presence, all raw energy and wisdom, an untamed creature with the power of ages. But in his mortal form, they could, at last, meet on equal terms. Fear had long deserted her. She burned for him.

"Roll over for me, Vivian," he said. She squeezed her thighs together in anticipation and did as he asked. Her belly rested on the bed, tangled in the sheets as she waited for him. Darkmore rewarded her by covering her body with his, and she spread her legs in invitation.

His hands moved with slow softness that frustrated and inflamed her. She bit the pillow and then tried to roll back over. He held her still and said, "No."

"No?" She panted.

"You might be satisfied with a frantic coupling for our first time," he said in a dark, husky voice. "Yes, I think you would be more than satisfied. Soft and gentle isn't your style. It wouldn't be, of course. You are intensity. You crave the battle for control, for dominance, and you never submit easily, do you, Vivian?"

She bucked and tried to wriggle away from him. Frantic seemed like a good idea to her, but the reaper seemed intent on talking first. He talked too much sometimes. She growled.

"You'd like that, but I would not. Not for our first time," he said with finality. He placed his body over hers and she reveled in its heat, in spite of her irritation. He'd read her right, of course. But that didn't mean she'd give him the satisfaction of showing it. She would accommodate him. For now. Until the moment he dropped his guard and she could strike.

Then he'd give her what she wanted, and he'd savor every moment.

CHAPTER SEVEN

"Shh," he whispered, caressing her cheek with his as he moved atop her. She relaxed until he raised both of her arms above her head and held them firm in his grasp. His weight pressed down on her, and with her arms immobilized, she lay completely at his mercy.

It wasn't necessarily unpleasant—which was alarming in and of itself—but being at the reaper's mercy was dangerous.

"Be still. I will not harm you, Vivian, nor will I force myself upon you."

"Then what's with the bondage game?"

He laughed, cool and smooth and she marveled at the effect his voice had on her even in his mortal state. She cursed him silently, as well as herself, for wanting to play along. This was, or had been, her game. She set the terms.

"My dear, if this were a game of bondage, do you not think I would be more creative? I've had eons in which to explore all manner of deviations."

OK, that was creepy. Oddly enough, her earlier misgivings and doubts didn't return in spite of his mock threat. Doubtless it was true. She'd seen him "play" with his food often enough. But the game would be different with her, in this time and space, and in his mortal form.

"I'll file that under things-I-really-don't-want-to-know."

He laughed again and she felt it rumble through his body and hers. "Don't knock it 'til you've tried it."

Sexual frustration warred with rising anger. Was he toying with her? He wanted her, too, or at least his mortal body did. But that didn't mean as much as mind and soul. For all she knew, he could be goading her into frustration and misery so he could feed from it.

Had she mistaken his earlier tenderness, those small kindnesses?

"I don't want to try it, and at this point I'm starting to think I don't really want to try *you*, so could you kindly remove yourself from my body?"

He didn't remove himself. Instead, he insinuated himself closer to her. *How is that even possible?* Then he just lay still. She heard his slow, even breaths, and could even hear his heartbeat over the pounding of her own. While she didn't feel physical discomfort, she began to register a spike in her mental unease. He didn't move. She couldn't.

"Lazarus?"

"Yes?"

"What are you doing?"

"I'm savoring you," he said, placing a whisper of a kiss on her cheek and another at the base of her ear. She shivered. He placed more light kisses along her left shoulder and moved her hair so he could reach the nape of her neck.

Ignoring her gasps and writhing he continued to plant soft kisses along her neck, over her right shoulder, and along her right arm, whispering low at each pause along his mouth's journey.

"Did you think I would rush this? The ages have tempered my being with patience, Vivian. I do not seek quick couplings. I've experienced far too much that this realm and infinite others have to offer to be satisfied with taking you fast."

She wasn't certain of her capacity for coherent thought or speech, nor did she care. Not that she'd admit that to Darkmore. Evidently, he did want her, and on more than a physical level. She should have known, and she cursed her earlier doubts and misgivings.

He stopped. Why—Oh, he'd asked her a question.

"Well, given your vast experiences and appetites—"

He bit her lightly, and all she managed after was a husky groan. He'd made his way back to the nape of her neck, apparently enamored of the reaction his attention there earned him on his last visit.

Maybe that last question was rhetorical. He probably wanted to shut her up.

Too bad. She could play his game, too. Making him wait could be fun, but it could also serve to soothe those lingering doubts she still harbored, allowing her to relax and savor what was to come.

"As I was saying," she said, squirming to get away from his mouth. "Given your experience and appetites, what makes me so special to you?"

He didn't stop his kisses, nor did he miss a beat with his answer, "You are a novelty. You must understand, even with all of my experiences, as a mortal I have never coupled with a being capable of channeling spirit energy."

"What? You can't be serious!"

She was disappointed when he stopped his kisses, but she had no one but herself to blame this time.

"You do not believe me."

"Well, no...I suppose I don't. You told me before that you've lived many mortal lives, for your morbid research purposes."

"Your point?"

"Well, I just assumed that your colleagues kept tabs on you and dropped in from time to time. Other reapers? Uphir?" The demoness had been awfully chummy with him. He hadn't minded. Surely they'd been lovers. Maybe they still were.

He chuckled. "You always utter Uphir's name with a particularly nasty brand of venom. Are you jealous?"

"You didn't answer my question."

He laughed again and she felt the loss of his body. She rolled over and found him stretched out beside her, gloriously naked and quite aroused. She had another moment to regret opening her big mouth before he spoke.

"Ah, now that we have eye contact once more, we can resume the age-old ritual of pre-coital chit-chat, if you insist."

No matter the situation, the reaper maintained his calm demeanor and air of nonchalance. Granted, she realized he would always have her beat in years, not to mention snappy comebacks, but a tiny part of her hoped that he'd show some reaction to his current situation. If being trapped in a mortal body and facing a major demotion upon death of said body didn't do it, nothing would.

The reaper always managed to throw her for a loop.

Naturally she'd indulged in a few fantasies starring Darkmore. More than a few, if she was being honest. None of those imagined encounters took place in a generic hotel room in the middle of rural Mississippi. Perhaps she should have gotten them a room at Union Station when she'd had the chance. He'd been a big hit at her best friend Sue's wedding, not to mention a rather stimulating date and the perfect package to flaunt in front of her lying, cheating ex-boyfriend and his new piece of tail. Of course, Darkmore had been the one to put the brakes on sex when they'd returned from the wedding reception, otherwise they could have had some fun back at her place.

She'd had some unfinished business at the time. Zeke had come back to her, and the reaper had stepped aside rather than fight the guardian spirit. He'd allowed Vivian space to choose. He had a thing about free will.

She forced herself to stop reminiscing, lest memories of her former life, the one she'd lost—possibly forever—spoil the moment.

"To answer your question, Vivian, I did not indulge in sexual congress with corporeal spirit dwellers during any of my mortal lives. It would have defeated the purpose."

"The purpose?"

"You said it yourself. I was there for research. To acquire a human perspective required me to be fully human. The only stipulation I insisted upon during those journeys was that I assume my rightful place in the reaper hierarchy upon my return. Often enough I received a promotion in exchange, but no spirits interfered with my mortal experiences."

"Makes sense, I suppose," she conceded. "So you still want to gather new experiences?"

"What else could possibly be of interest for me? Now your turn. Why do you despise Uphir?"

"I don't *despise* her. But I'll admit that I don't like the thought of you and her together."

"Ah, jealousy. Don't make that face, Vivian. It does not become you."

He stood and stretched, giving her a lovely view of his physique. She enjoyed the rear view as much as she had the front.

He turned back and offered her a small smile. "I did not mean it as an insult. Your reaction is natural and very human. Given a few centuries, you'd probably lose most of it. Your temper, however, could take millennia to cool."

"Gee, thanks."

"What else would you like to know before we commence with my, ah, new experiences?"

"I'm not sure. I'm still surprised you never...communed with any guardians or reapers while human. What about your first life? Didn't the reaper who claimed you show any interest?"

"I died rather young the first time around, so no."

His expression didn't change, but something about Darkmore's tone left her desolate. What could possibly induce a reaper to collect a child? She couldn't ask him, not then. It seemed too personal, and she wasn't sure she wanted or needed to know the answer. Going down the rabbit hole had never made her feel better about anything where the spirit world was concerned. Instead, she sat up and patted the spot on the bed next to her.

He sat, maintaining a deliberate distance between them, and waited. She wasn't sure what to say, so she settled on a slight deviation from her initial line of questioning. "So tell me, Lazarus, how did you lose it?"

"Lose it?"

"Yeah, you know, your virginity. I'm assuming that if you died young, you didn't get around to popping your cherry until you became a reaper. Or was it during your next life?"

"Ah, I understand," he replied. "It was actually during my apprenticeship period, perhaps seventy-five years after my death, give or take."

"Why so long?" Vivian asked. Given her own endless fascination with sex, she found it difficult to believe that anyone would be willing to wait so long.

"I had other priorities," he said. "As pleasurable as I've found the activity in subsequent years, my visits to the mortal realm, particularly in corporeal form, were occupied with more...fundamental pleasures. Now, your turn. Tell me about your first time."

He'd piqued her interest and then shifted topics. Typical. "Well, I was a late bloomer myself."

His eyes widened and his brows shot up.

"Don't look so surprised!" Vivian chided, giving him a good-natured punch on the arm. "I was in my twenties, college actually, and I've more than made up for it since."

"I see. Tell me about the lucky gentleman responsible for your deflowering, my dear."

"He was a bit older, more experienced," she offered, and he smiled in appreciation. Of course he'd find her notions of "older" and "more experienced" quaint by comparison. It was odd, sharing stories as she might with a normal, human lover. Odd, but pleasant, and she relaxed for the first time in months.

"Naturally I was as curious as I was nervous, but he took great care to make my first experience special, and the many I shared with him after. You?"

"Hmm," he said, thinking. Maybe it was hard to remember after so long, or maybe he thought she'd be disturbed by the details. "It happened rather by accident."

"Were you male or female?" The reaper once told her he'd lived many human lives, some as man and some as woman. He preferred male, he claimed, as he'd been born that way originally, but having both experiences had made him more well-rounded, with a better understanding of the full human experience that made him an effective reaper.

"I was male, and a rather charming female entertainer from the royal Babylonian court caught me alone in the palace one evening and enjoyed corrupting me—I believe she enjoyed it more once I'd gotten the hang of things, but all in all she was rather a patient instructor."

"Oh! A harem woman, huh? Sounds like something straight out of Arabian nights."

"We were Persian, not Arab, but yes, Scheherazade might have found room for us in one of her thousand and one tales."

"So," Vivian murmured as she scooted closer to him. "She was patient, huh?"

"Yes."

"Is that how you became so patient?"

"Perhaps." He'd moved closer while they talked. Enfolding her in his arms. "Would you care for a demonstration?"

"I think I could stand that. But..."

"Yes?"

"Maybe I need a safe word."

Darkmore laughed. He laughed so hard, in fact, that he released Vivian from his iron grip and fell back on the bed. She'd become enamored of the reaper's laughter on those rare occasions she'd heard it. It warmed her heart and soul to a degree that matched the heat of her body.

Once he'd recovered, he said, "We really need to work on your trust issues." With a look of pure devilry, he added, "I have just the thing for it."

She arched a brow at him but remained seated. She enjoyed watching his nude form move about the room while he searched. The sight made her giggle.

She stopped giggling when he used one of her scarves as a blindfold. A mixture of fear and arousal filled her. Arousal won out as the timbre of his voice caressed her ears.

"I'll leave your hands unfettered, I think," he whispered, letting his own fingers trail lightly over her flesh. "I can always persuade you to still them later."

His lips and tongue followed his fingers, giving her a little thrill each time as she tried to anticipate when and where his touch would fall next.

Vivian endured his slow, meticulous exploration until desire and frustration compelled her to reach for him with trembling fingers. True to his word, he stilled her hands with his. Her lungs ached from panting and trembling morphed into quaking. When he'd pushed her body to its limit, he claimed her mouth as he pulled her up and cradled her body to his.

"Please," she pleaded. "Now."

"As you wish," he whispered back. He lifted her with strong arms and positioned her astride him. She braced herself on his shoulders as he entered her.

Their union complete, he removed her blindfold and met her eyes.

"Vivian," he whispered.

"Again," she replied.

He lifted her once more and slowly, slowly brought her back down upon him. He maintained the same slow, deliberate pace, pushing the limits of his mortal body. She matched his rhythm and held his gaze the entire time.

The reaper's eyes fascinated her, alive and filled with all he'd seen, all he knew, all he was and had been. The heat of passion did nothing to mask the cold depths of his nature. He was still the reaper, but he was also human. Beautiful, fragile, fierce, and vulnerable by turns, that was part of his essence, too. He gifted her with his entirety, his honesty, and his need.

She tensed and cried out. So very close. So was he. His eyes widened, his breathing accelerated as he gripped her. "Now, Vivian," he said. "Let go!"

She exploded in a burst of blinding light as she came. Golden rays flowed from her body as Darkmore watched in awe. He met her lips, taking in her light as he found his own completion. She poured all of herself into that light and he accepted all that she was, and then they closed their eyes in shared rapture.

———

Vivian awoke some time during the night, still entangled with the reaper. She'd apparently fallen asleep on top of him, and she took a moment to savor the warmth of his body beneath hers. She rolled off him and gently stroked the skin of his chest and arms, enjoying the feel of his muscles beneath her fingertips. Though she certainly appreciated the form he'd chosen, smiling wide as she remembered their union, the first of many she hoped, she remained curious about his many lives.

"That tickles," he murmured, grasping her wrist and rolling over to pin her beneath him.

"Sorry," she said, chuckling softly. "You didn't give me the chance to do much exploring earlier. Not that I'm complaining."

He smiled, then rolled to his side and pulled her close. "What's on your mind, Vivian?"

"Lots of things," she said truthfully. After a moment's hesitation, she added, "But for starters, will you promise me something?"

"It depends."

Of course it would. The reaper lived by his own code of honor, and his word was part of that. He wouldn't make promises he couldn't keep.

"When we set you to rights and you are able to choose your form again...I would like to see you. I mean, I'd like to see what you looked like before. In your first life."

He remained silent, and Vivian felt his sigh. She worried that she'd offended him somehow. Perhaps he felt her request crossed some boundary, or maybe he no longer cared to share emotional intimacy with her now that he'd experienced her flesh and tasted her spirit. Of course, he'd offered to take her with him not so very long ago, to serve by his side, presumably as his eternal companion. Then again, he hadn't specified the duration.

"I'm sorry," she whispered, rolling to the side of the bed and sitting up. She cursed herself for asking too much too soon. He'd been right in his earlier assessment. She wasn't demure or shy in her desires or drive. Perhaps he was the old-fashioned sort. The thought made her feel uncomfortable in her state of undress and decided she'd grab her nightgown.

She shivered, rose, and prepared herself for a long, cold night.

"Come back to bed." The reaper's voice startled her.

She hesitated, but then reclined again lest she offend him further. She closed her eyes and focused on keeping her stupid tears at bay and her breathing even. God, she'd become such an emotional mess. *Why can't I just keep my mouth shut?*

"You can stop warring with yourself. I assure you, my darker appetites are sated. For the moment."

She refused to give him the satisfaction of an answer. He'd consumed her spirit light, her essence, which included a healthy dose of the fear, anger, and sorrow she carried for her exile, for all she'd lost and all she might still lose, and for what she'd done to him.

When he spoke again, his voice held a trace of amusement. "My other appetites, however, are another matter entirely." He reached for her hand and pulled it below the sheet to show her.

Familiar warmth spread through her body and she grasped him harder, earning a deep groan for her trouble. She moved closer, seeking his lips as she happily prepared herself for a decidedly warmer night ahead. He obliged, whispering in her ear, "Yes, Vivian. I promise."

Before her brain filled completely with the fog of lust, she remembered the sense of being watched that she'd experienced earlier in the evening, when she'd run away from him, and her desire. "Are we still safe here?"

"What makes you think we are not?"

"I thought I saw something following me on the way back here. Something cold. Have you sensed any other reapers in the area?"

She felt his soft laughter rumble through his chest. "You worry too much."

"Well someone has to—"

He stilled her mouth with a deep kiss and followed with, "Relax. You needn't fear anything in the immediate vicinity for now. Why not enjoy the respite while it lasts?"

"But—"

"Leave it for now. If something comes tomorrow, or if tomorrow doesn't come, then what we have right now is everything," he whispered. "Best savor it."

For once, she listened.

CHAPTER EIGHT

Silence was golden, but Lazarus Darkmore apparently preferred conversation on road trips. "You are a tapestry of fascinating contradictions, Vivian Bedford."

"What's that supposed to mean?" She glanced away from the road long enough to glare at Darkmore.

They'd been on the road for a couple of hours, leaving the respite and comfort of the last few days far behind. Back on the Natchez Trace, their progress was slower than it would have been on the Interstate, but steady. She could hold onto the illusion of security and seclusion by sticking to the scenic, winding roads sheltered by trees, meadows, and farmland. The autumn splendor soothed some of her discomfort, but apparently not enough to go unnoticed by the reaper.

And naturally he'd poke and prod her until he discovered the source of that discomfort, whether she wanted to share or not.

"You expressed your displeasure at the tedious pace of our journey a few days ago. As I recall, you used a plethora of charming phrases with which to convey your frustration."

"Yeah. So?"

"The day after that, you expressed your desire to remain at our charming hotel indefinitely."

"Hey, you weren't complaining." Her tone was laced with indignation, but she flashed him a wicked grin, the smile of a very satisfied woman.

"No, I found our detour to be quite pleasant."

She arched her brow and said, "Pleasant? That the best you can do?"

Darkmore chuckled. "I believe I made my thoughts on the subject abundantly clear." As he spoke, he moved his fingers over Vivian's thigh, lightly stroking and tracing patterns as he moved up. "Besides, I prefer to show rather than tell."

"Keep that up and I'll have to stop the car for a more detailed demonstration," she said, taking his hand in hers. The gesture comforted her more than it should have. "Or we might end up in a tangled mass of metal at the side of the road. Now then, you were saying?"

"Ah, yes. After expressing your desire to lock me away in our hotel for an eternity not two days ago, this morning you proceeded to rouse me at a most ungodly hour and insisted that we needed 'get our asses in gear.' A rather charming turn of phrase, by the way."

She'd never admit it out loud, but he had a point. There was no need to rush. Still, as tempting as it might have been to stay another day and night, she'd grown restless and wary. They should get to Jackson as quickly as possible, and part of her was anxious to do so. Since she had nowhere else to go and no way to avoid the coming fight, she'd resolved to do whatever she could to bring whatever conflict was coming to an end as quickly as possible.

So she—so they—could return to the way things had been before. So she could go back home.

Still, her determination warred with the conflicting desire to avoid the danger and darkness to come. She'd had more than enough to last a thousand lifetimes, but given what she was, what Ezra had made her with Darkmore's help, she could never escape—live as a soul broker or die and still serve, but without the ties that anchored her to normalcy and life. She could, however, practice avoidance and spend some more time basking in the calm before the storm. After browsing through some brochures she'd found in the hotel lobby, she'd found the perfect pretext for avoidance. They were going to do a little sightseeing on the way. Nature always had a calming, healing effect on her, and her soul could stand a little more soothing.

Maybe the reaper could do with a little soothing as well.

"I changed my mind. It's a woman's prerogative." She spoke with what she hoped was casual indifference, but the reaper could probably see right through it.

"Indeed."

"I thought it might be nice to visit the Cypress Swamp while we're still on the Trace. I've never seen a swamp before." That was true enough.

He didn't say anything. That bugged her more than his incessant teasing, and he probably knew it. Either that, or he found her idea of a mini-vacation quaint. Or maybe he thought she was nervous in the wake of their new...intimacy? Relationship?

Since he refused to fill the silence, she kept talking. "Look, I know you've probably seen a thousand swamps, and deserts, and mountains and —well, pick a landscape. I haven't." She didn't risk a glance his way.

"My dear, you have such a knack for taking an innocuous statement and turning into a source of conflict."

She'd fallen into his trap again. Or was it her trap? Damn the reaper. "Are you trying to piss me off?"

The corners of his lips curled into a sly smile, one that made his blue eyes twinkle with amusement. "I needn't try very hard, but no. It was actually a compliment."

"Calling me a walking contradiction is complimentary?"

He gripped the handle above his door as he answered. "Mind your speed, please, and your steering."

She took a deep breath and focused on the road. Lowering her blood pressure would take longer, as it always did with the reaper, but he was right. Oh, the irony. A nearly fatal car crash had put her in the crosshairs of the spirit world. It wouldn't do to kill herself and the newly mortal reaper in one now.

Slowly, Darkmore released the handle and straightened in his seat. Had she really scared him? That was more jarring than their earlier intimacy. "In answer to your question, yes. As exasperating and mercurial as your moods can be, they are as refreshing as they are unpredictable."

She cleared her throat, hoping to hide her reaction to his earlier fear. Then she said, "That still doesn't sound particularly complimentary."

"Consider the source. Recent circumstances notwithstanding, my greatest enemy is and has always been boredom. It is the enemy for all ancient beings. You are many wonderful and terrible things, but you'll never be dull. Ah, I believe this is our stop."

With monumental effort, she shifted her focus from the reaper and managed to park. The crisp autumn air infused her lungs when she stepped out of the car, and a survey of the landscape filled her with giddy anticipation, renewed by yet another startling revelation—he found her intriguing.

No, that wasn't quite right. She'd intrigued him from the beginning. When the reaper first came calling, he'd toyed with her rather than claim her soul. Not because he'd been unable to claim her—she was under no illusions about his power and capacity for cruelty, his appetite for darkness. Her soul's darkness had called to him. No, he'd been both fascinated and infuriated with what she was. The guardian spirit who'd been meant to claim her soul had left her alive, trapped between the world of the living and the dead, and it had granted her the power to channel spirit energy while still alive, a living soul broker. He'd also coveted her power to channel spirit energy from the living, something not even the most powerful spirit, guardian, or reaper could do.

He couldn't take from the living, but he could take it from her, if and when she chose to give it. She'd held out on the guardians, but freely gave her excess energy to the reaper. He took the heavy burdens she collected from the living, giving her sweet relief as she fed his darkness. Convenient, symbiotic even, but she'd never realized she was particularly interesting to him on more than a superficial level.

That she could interest an entity such as the reaper in something other than a predatory sense was extraordinary.

She tossed Darkmore the keys and jogged to the trailhead, pausing briefly to read the requisite description etched on the wooden placard. A realm of trees, water, and reflections to soothe a tired soul? She could stand a little of that.

"Are you coming?" Vivian yelled back to her companion.

"Go on. I'll catch up."

Perhaps he sensed her need for solitude, or maybe he wished for some of his own. Either way, she was pleased with the opportunity to explore on her own. As far as she could tell, they had the entire area to themselves. It was probably too cold for alligators, but she could always spot birds. And the patch of colorful deciduous trees along the water's edge deserved a look. Their leaf litter framed the wide, moss-covered bases of the bald cypress clusters that jutted out of the inky water. The odd patch of algae added an extra touch of green. Smaller cypress knees peeked out intermittently, adorning the scene with angles and a sense of texture. The morning mist that hadn't quite dissipated still clung low to the earth.

In short, it was a hidden paradise, and she was eager to discover its secrets.

She continued along the trail, utterly delighted to discover the network of overwater wooden bridges. Walking slowly, the better to savor the peace and beauty of her surroundings, was her intention. But each step, turn of her head, or sidelong glance filled her hungry gaze with a new scene more gorgeous than the last.

Movement on the opposite shore captured her attention and she quickened her pace. Once there, she wondered if she'd let her imagination get the better of her. Something was off. She stopped to focus on what her senses might reveal, on the sights and sounds around her. Only, there were no sounds. They'd all stopped.

That couldn't be good.

She shivered from a mixture of fear and a familiar drop in temperature.

"Darkmore, this isn't funny," she yelled. "Quit messing around and come on out!"

She waited a few moments. Vivian considered calling out for him again, but out of spite decided against it. He'd enjoy that too much. Instead, she turned with a huff and prepared to walk back the way she came.

If she hadn't looked up at the last minute, she would have run right into a hundred and fifty pounds of menacing canine blocking her path back to the bridge.

The lone wolf sat on its haunches as it stared at Vivian with dusky eyes, ears perked and pointed forward as it regarded her. She stood frozen in place, not wanting to make any sudden movements. Running would only entice the predator to give chase. The wolf didn't move, but Vivian knew enough to be very afraid. She'd never seen one this close, at least without the safety of a moat and chain link separating her from danger. Park rangers always dismissed sightings east of the Mississippi, except for the grudging acknowledgment that some still stalked the forests of Maine.

Apparently, those park rangers were wrong.

She took a slow, cautious step back, keeping eye contact and raising her hands to appear bigger. If she could convince the wolf she was a threat, perhaps it would slink back into the swamp and leave her unmauled.

"Go on, get out of here," she growled, taking another step back.

The wolf rose and began to stalk toward Vivian, snarling and with ears back. Vivian kicked up some dirt and leaf litter. She glanced around for a large stone or a stick, anything she could use as a weapon as the beast continued bearing down on her. Grabbing a medium sized branch, she swung it in the wolf's direction and let out a primal scream.

Instead of slinking back and fleeing, the beast swatted and answered with a raspy, high-pitched howl that echoed through the swamp.

She fought the urge to run, trading fear for anger. Unlike most mortals, she had powerful weapons of the supernatural variety with which to defend herself.

"I didn't come this far to be dinner!"

She crouched low and threw a blast of red light at the wolf, aiming for the beast's head. No point in messing around with death on the horizon, endangered species act be damned.

The wolf vanished before Vivian's energy struck her.

Vivian yelped first in surprise and again when she heard the bulky cypress crash into the water. The smoke rising from the sunken hardwood showed her blast would have been lethal if it had hit its mark. She spun around, mind and body on high alert as she tried to predict where her assailant would materialize next.

"Come on out and fight," she screamed.

Within the span of a heartbeat, the impact from behind knocked her to the ground, immobilized by the wolf's powerful, muscled body. It left her winded and unable to see, though she made an attempt to frighten the creature by firing bursts of light blind. She curled her fingers and fired again, hoping like hell she could get the beast off of her long enough to get her bearings, get up, and fight or flee.

The scent of burning flesh and an angry canine wail let her know she'd hit some part of the wolf, which she could only assume was some sort of demonic beast. Ordinary wolves didn't vanish and rematerialize. The wolf shifted its weight, and Vivian managed to roll out from under it and onto her back. She knew the risks, but reckoned she'd be in a better position to do some damage to her otherworldly attacker.

The wolf pounced on her and placed its face close to Vivian. The animal's hot breath seared her face in spite of the chill it carried. Any closer and massive fangs could graze her nose. A tilt of the animal's head could put Vivian's tender neck into the perilous grip of bone-crushing jaws. Whatever this creature's true identity, it held Vivian's life, and quite possibly her soul, in its grasp.

"What do you want with me?" she asked, gasping for air. The beast had knocked the wind out of her when she pounced. Fear-induced hyperventilation didn't help.

The she wolf—Vivian had gotten a close enough look to identify the beast as female—cocked her grey head to one side, regarding Vivian. Then the wolf snarled and leaned in closer. Vivian closed her eyes and wait for the attack. Hopefully it would be quick and relatively painless. The weight on her chest grew heavier and she felt the air being pulled from her lungs.

Panic struck and she thrashed her head from side to side, struggling to close her mouth. She remembered the old fairy tales of werewolves. They'd come and steal your life, and your soul along with it, condemning you to transform into a ravening beast at every full moon. She'd always dismissed the belief as silly superstition. But as she'd learned over the past year, some of those superstitions proved to be all too true.

Using the last of her strength, she raised her legs and torso in an attempt to fling the wolf from her body. The beast growled a warning and Vivian swore she heard the animal inhale even deeper. She waited for suffocation overtake her.

Instead, she felt a rather familiar pull.

Her eyes flew open in time to watch the wisps of red light escape from her mouth and enter the open mouth of the wolf, rays carrying her terror and rage with them. The wolf's pink tongue flicked out along its mouth like a pet dog who'd just indulged in a treat.

Its sandpaper tongue grazed her cheek. Then she felt as well as heard the low rumble of a friendly, yipping bark

What the hell?

The wolf continued to alternate between grooming herself and laving Vivian with her tongue. She rubbed her face against Vivian's cheek, the texture of her rough whiskers a stark contrast to supple fur. Vivian's breathing had returned to normal. She felt the freshness of cleansing relief that always came with transfer of the burdens she carried. Still, she remained uneasy. This reaper in feline form was nonetheless a reaper.

And this reaper wasn't Darkmore.

"All right, already. You're full, we're both clean—sort of—so can you let me up now? My back's getting sore."

The wolf stared at her and then whined softly, at least as softly as was possible for a canine of her size. She raised a large paw to Vivian's face and delivered a playful swat. One claw nicked her left cheek.

"Ouch! Seriously, you've had your fun, now get off already!"

The wolf blew a puff of light into Vivian's face and then leapt off of her.

Vivian breathed in the light and felt a cool rush of raw power fill her being. She rose as the musky scent of earth, decaying leaves, the pungent aromas of long-gone wildlife filled her senses. Her ears perked forward at the sound of scampering along the periphery of the clearing.

Vivian pounced.

I pounced? Why am I still so low to the ground?

Rational thought abandoned her as her keen eyes spotted a flash of black taking flight. The harsh caw triggered the urge to pursue, the mad desire to capture and kill. The flash of black whirred past. Vivian followed.

She barely had time to register the blur of amber, gold, and gray in the landscape around as her focus narrowed to the target ahead until tunnel vision overcame her, leaving her aware only of her prey. It flew low to the ground as it taunted her. She matched every turn and followed at inhuman speed. Strength and power surged through an unfamiliar body, and she felt as well as heard her primal howl.

Her howl grew louder when the black bird swooped down and clawed her hindquarters. She whirled out to capture it in strong, bone-crushing jaws. It managed to elude her the full impact of her bite, but not before she gave it a good scrape. Vivian stopped long enough to savor the blood on her tongue. She wasn't certain what she found more shocking—her jaws, the irresistible drive to taste the blood of her enemy, or how much she relished the coppery tang of the blood.

They continued the chase until the raven led her to another clearing. Vivian stopped just inside the tree line as awareness of another presence filled her keen senses. She crouched low and inhaled through her nostrils and mouth as she tasted and smelled the creature. The scent was male and musky, though not unpleasant. Her sensitive paw pads picked up vibrations in the earth as the creature moved.

He'd scented her as well.

Ears back, teeth exposed in a snarl, Vivian slinked out of the brush and spotted a massive black bear. Though her perspective was arguably skewed, he looked more massive than the ones she'd seen before in normal life. He darted from side to side and growled in frustration. She rose, figuring that it would be best to display confidence and ferocity so as to avoid an actual fight. Head high, ears forward, and still sporting her snarl, Vivian loped up to the bear and stood less than three feet in front of him.

Instead of answering her challenge and invasion of his territory, the bear kept turning and shaking his head. He sniffed at the air all around paced the ground in front of her. She quirked her head, perplexed at his lack of response. Then it dawned on her.

He doesn't see me!

She was about to belt out another howl when the bird appeared and settled on the bear's shoulder. The raven's black eyes burned with malice, deceit, and a smug invitation to catch him if she could. Rage snuffed out all thoughts of danger and she lunged. The bear caught her scent and movement. He swung a massive paw and knocked her aside.

She felt the blow throughout her lupine body but recovered quickly. She managed to catch the bear's flank with her own fierce jaws as he swatted again and rolled away before he had the chance to land on top of her when he lunged. She circled in an attempt to get behind him, but his sense of smell appeared to compensate for his apparent lack of vision as he matched her movements.

She became aware of other creatures surrounding them in the clearing, like spectators at a boxing match. The bear seemed to relax as they made their presence known. They gazed at him with reverence, even the smallest and most helpless. He roared, and they moved until he stood between them and Vivian.

She couldn't speak, but she conveyed her desire by looking skyward and growling. The raven cawed and then landed behind the bear. He hopped along the ground, pausing to peck one of the smaller creatures with his sharp beak. A bit of light escaped from the wound and the bird took it in, leaving the small beast shuddering.

She leapt over the bear and grasped the bird in her mouth. The other animals set upon her with claws, fangs, and hooves digging into her flesh. Vivian tried to throw them off, but they were too many. If she released the raven, she might be able to escape. But then none would be safe from its wickedness. One snap of her powerful jaws would end it, but they might end her.

The raven cried out and the others called the bear. Then, the great black beast bore down upon her.

She'd have to choose quickly.

"Vivian."

She heard the familiar voice even as she braced for the blow.

"Vivian!"

————

She bolted upright and brought her hands to her face to shield it from her attacker.

I have hands again.

"Vivian, calm yourself."

She dropped her hands and saw the reaper's face in front of hers. He looked concerned, which was pretty unusual for him. She couldn't recall any of her previous forays into the realm of spirits producing that kind of reaction, save one.

The one in which she'd traveled to his own dark realm.

"How long have I been gone?"

He quirked a brow and answered. "By my estimate, you were ahead of me by around five minutes. I came upon you lying prone on the cold ground but a moment ago. If you traveled to another realm, it cost you no time in this one."

She accepted his proffered hand and he pulled her up. Fussing over her, he ran his long fingers over her body in search of injuries and scanned her with his icy eyes. It left her with odd mixture of embarrassment and excitement.

Under his scrutiny, she processed the odd mixture of sensations coursing through every fiber of her being—embarrassment, arousal, and exhilaration. Power and hunger lingered after her strange trip to what she figured was the spirit realm's version of Wild Kingdom.

"Whoa," she said, batting the reapers hands away so she could pace up and down with excitement. "That was incredible!"

"Be still and let me examine you."

"I'm fine. Better than fine, actually," she said, giving Darkmore's hand a little pat of reassurance before the details of her bizarre encounter came spilling out. "I was walking along, and I came across this wolf, which is weird since they're supposed to be long gone east of the Mississippi and this far south, right? Anyway, I saw the wolf, only it wasn't a wolf...it was one of you guys, you know? A spirit. One with a lot of power. I think she was a reaper since she came with a chill. She knocked me down and sucked out my light. Then she gave me some of hers and I just, I, well, I *became* her. I mean, I think I did. Maybe she knocked me out and I just had some crazy, screwed up dream or something."

The reaper just stared at her. His normal calm and intractable expression had replaced concern and he coolly regarded her. She huffed and rolled her eyes. This might be everyday, run-of-the-mill stuff for him, but even in her ever-expanding universe, it qualified as spectacular.

"Look, I know you've seen and done it all, or pretty near to it, but this is seriously blowing my mind—"

"There's no need to become defensive, Vivian," he replied as he turned and surveyed the area. He seemed almost distracted. She was about to go off on him again when he spun around, brought her close, placed his mouth on hers and drew out her light energy with more force than she'd ever felt.

Once she got her bearings back, she shoved him off and hit him with a small burst of spirit light for good measure. A brief moment of remorse led her to say, "Look, sorry about the zap, but you need to grow some manners. I don't mind feeding you. Truth be told, I enjoy our exchanges. But I'm not going to stand back while you manhandle me to get it, understand?"

He didn't answer, apparently still lost in thought. Then a small smile graced his features. Vivian's body responded to his roguish display and she silently cursed herself for it.

"Okay, when you're done sitting there and looking like the cat that ate the canary, how about filling me in?"

The reaper turned his attention back to her, though he was obviously still distracted. "I beg your pardon?"

"You've figured something out. Care to share?"

He stood up and dusted himself off. Then he looked at her and said, "You've been granted a rare and wonderful gift, my dear, one not often granted to mortals by this particular spirit guide. She was a powerful seer in life."

"Huh?"

"Our protector from the Hohenwald community, Maeve, has taken it upon herself to follow us. And she's apparently granted you a vision of the future."

Her eyes went wide, and she looked around for a place to sit, settling on the edge of the wooden bridge. She opened her mouth and closed it, struggling to settle on which of about a thousand questions to ask first. After three or four tries, Darkmore chuckled and sat down beside her.

"At a loss for words? That is rare indeed." He teased, as always. She gave him a good-natured slug on the arm, followed with a grudging smile.

"Why don't you start by telling me what happened, what you experienced in the vision?"

She recounted the tale, earning a few more chuckles from the reaper as she described the thrill of encountering a wolf in Mississippi and the thrill of the hunt. He became more sober, though, when she told him about her attack at the hands of the bear and his followers.

"If Maeve offered you a vision, then she was most likely trying to accomplish one of three things, possibly all of them."

Tendrils of dread wrapped around her gut, but no good ever came from blind fear. Forewarned was forearmed. "Am I going to like any of them?"

"Probably not right away, but you may find the message valuable in due time. She may have been testing you. In fact, I would wager your initial battle with her in her wolf form was a test of your power, fighting skills, and your courage. She only offers guidance to those she deems worthy."

Her expression must have screamed disbelief, as he added, "Guardians and reapers, as you call us, are capable of assuming many forms. The possibilities are boundless and not restricted to human, of course. All of the earliest cultures revered the natural world on which they depended for their survival. They both feared and venerated many of the mighty beasts they hunted and with whom they competed for prey. That was true of Maeve's people, and she came from a long line of female holy women who kept the old traditions alive after St. Patrick brought Christianity to the Emerald Isle. She brought them to the New World and was ultimately burned as a witch for her trouble."

That made sense. Then again, she'd never seen the reaper or any other spirits take on animal forms—at least not that she realized. She'd mistaken this Maeve spirit for an actual wolf at first. She tried picturing Darkmore in animal form, but it didn't seem right. He was a beast, of course, a cunning and seasoned predator, but she couldn't think of him as anything less than...civilized.

As if reading her thoughts, he said, "Naturally my kind and my esteemed colleagues on the other side of the spectrum have always been more than willing to mold ourselves to fit the beliefs of our mortal charges."

"And to exploit those beliefs in order to screw around with us."

"Tsk, tsk. Always so negative. The ancient Celts were clever enough to recognize the connection between the púka, fae, and other shape-shifters and the realm of spirits."

"So all of those myths about shape-shifters and werewolves aren't just legend?"

He laughed. "No, but it is to our advantage to maintain skepticism among you mortals."

"Or just scare the hell out of us," Vivian said, grumbling.

"Oh not at all. They bring messages from the spirit world through visions and come to carry souls to the Land of the Dead. Of course, tricksters may also use their talents as teaching tools for brash or foolish mortals." He added a wink at the end.

Vivian replied with an eye roll and her middle finger.

Ignoring the obscene gesture, he continued, "As I was saying, once she deemed you worthy, she offered you a vision in order to warn you, threaten you, or guide you in your quest."

"So, in this vision, I became a wolf, wound up chasing a raven, and then came across a giant, blind bear and a whole herd of other forest creatures who wanted to stop me. How on earth am I supposed to figure out what that means?"

"Perhaps her meaning will become clear once we reach your contact in Jackson. I can tell you that the raven is often known as a trickster."

Cryptic messages, secrets wrapped in mysteries and, more often than not, half-truths and lies, were part and parcel of the spirits. She'd yet to meet one who gave her a straight answer, even the reaper. Asking him for more information about the vision would be useless.

So, she settled on asking another burning question. "Hey, what about Bigfoot?"

He hesitated, wincing. "I don't know if I should go into that."

Did he not know her at all? "Oh come on. Tell me, tell me, tell me!"

Sighing, he shook his head and acquiesced. "The guardians came up with the Meh-Teh form first." He must have registered her blank stare, since he tried to clarify. "Meh-Teh? Migoi? Yeti?"

"Yeti? The Abominable Snowman is a guardian?"

He winced again. It was funny. "Well, yes..."

"You're not giving me the whole story, are you? Don't hold out on me, reaper."

Darkmore sighed, but she knew she'd won when he spoke again. "It's a bit of an embarrassment, since a rather competitive reaper assumed the form of Sasquatch in a fit of one-upmanship. Since then, newly minted reapers and guardians sometimes break the rules and appear as such creatures as a sort of practical joke." He shook his head again in distaste. "Very immature. Wreaks all sorts of havoc with mortals and distracts from our work."

Vivian burst out laughing. She laughed so hard, in fact, that she slipped off the edge of the bridge and back onto the cold ground. Darkmore kept shaking his head, which made her laugh even harder.

Once she recovered, she asked, "So can any of your kind or the guardians appear as an animal? I'd just like to know if I need to add that little trick to my ever-growing list of pesky perils."

He shrugged. "Some can, some can't."

"Can you?"

"I indulged in cross-species projection a time or two, but it isn't as much fun as one might think."

In response to her questioning look, Darkmore said, "Fleas are most unpleasant."

"Wuss." She teased. Then she sighed in regret. Given the vision she'd suddenly been gifted, it was likely prudent to get to get to Jackson without further delay. Seemed as though their mini-vacation had come to an end just as it was beginning. "Well then, I suppose we'd better get back on track."

Vivian stood up and took a moment to soak up the beauty of their surroundings. She squeaked when Darkmore grabbed her from behind.

"I thought I told you to grow some manners and ask me nicely before just helping yourself," she began. His trail of hot kisses along her neck stopped her protests.

"I thought you might enjoy a rut in the great outdoors before we continue our journey."

She couldn't argue with that.

CHAPTER NINE

They arrived in Jackson later than they'd anticipated, mostly because Vivian did, in fact, enjoy rutting in the great outdoors. Darkmore had remarkable stamina and enthusiasm to match, even in fully mortal form. Night skulked along the streets by the time they reached the outskirts of the city. A mixture of anticipation and raw nervous energy crept up her spine as they pulled into the gravel parking lot of the agreed upon rendezvous point. The tires squeaked as she parked, and Vivian's body jerked as the car went dead. She stared up at the ramshackle structure.

The place was a total dump.

"I think we just landed at the Dew Drop Inn."

"I beg your pardon?" the reaper asked, apparently oblivious to the fact that the joint in front of them reeked of redneck. "If I read the sign correctly, I believe we've landed at the Burnin' Bush."

"I take it you're not a Charlie Daniels fan," she muttered. Neither was she, but having grown up with "classic" country, she was familiar with the bearded, bad Santa-looking singer. With a sigh, she double-checked the address that Jeanne had given her.

As she feared, this was, indeed, the right place.

Putting the car back in drive, she found a space between a beat-up old Ford truck and a dingy Dodge van and parked. The latter lacked back and side windows. *Can you say 'serial killer'?* She glanced at the dashboard clock. It was only 8:43 and the parking lot was already packed. Not good. She figured they must be far enough away from town for this place to rank as high nightlife among the locals. Judging from the men milling around outside for a smoke, she also figured those locals for backwoods hicks. They weren't the type to welcome outsiders.

She and Darkmore wouldn't exactly blend.

Especially Darkmore.

"I don't have a phone number or anything else to go on, so we'll have to go inside and look for Waylon Briggs and his buddies," she said.

"And that troubles you?"

"It does." Vivian tried to ignore a couple of wolf whistles from the peanut gallery on the front porch. "I'll admit to having a bit of redneck in my roots, but this is a whole other level."

"These mere mortals still inspire so much fear, my dear? I'm surprised."

"Habit," she replied, and immediately regretted saying it out loud.

"Do tell."

"I'd rather not."

"You know I'll find out anyway." It wasn't a threat, but a promise. Darkmore enjoyed delving into her psyche far too much to let anything go, especially something that obviously bothered her.

"Probably, but right now I'd just like to get in, get this done, and get out without anyone getting hurt." Of course she was afraid of these men. The womenfolk didn't look too friendly, either. All the supernatural mojo in the world wouldn't help in a fight with the natives if it blew their cover.

She'd have to keep calm, keep the reaper calm, and keep his fragile mortal body out of danger.

Darkmore's eyes widened and he stared at Vivian with a frightening intensity, and not a little incredulity. "Do you actually doubt my ability, your ability, *our* ability to protect one another from *them?*"

Ugh, of course the reaper wasn't going to make this easy. No matter how ancient or experienced, testosterone and pride were an inconvenient and dangerous combination. "No, dumbass, it's *them* I'm worried about, not to mention our cover!" That was also true. Hopefully the spin she'd put on her anxiety would soothe his ego enough to avoid trouble. "Now get out of the car, follow me, and for fuck's sake let me do the talking."

Without waiting for a reply, Vivian grabbed her keys and exited the vehicle. She slammed the door a little harder than necessary. Muttering a few choice words, she finger combed and fluffed her hair. After a moment's hesitation, she unbuttoned her blouse and pushed the girls up until they nearly spilled out of the thin fabric, glad her mother wasn't there to see. Tattoos would have helped, as would a bit more muscle and grit, but this was the best she could do on short notice.

"Are you coming?" she asked with a huff. He'd taken his time exiting the vehicle. Had she been willing to look at him, she was certain Darkmore's smug grin would have pissed her off and turned her on all at the same time.

"You admonished me to follow you and to keep my mouth shut, so I think I'll content myself by bringing up the rear."

And enjoying the show.

With a deep breath, she plastered on her best slightly drunk Southern Belle wannabe smile and sashayed toward the entrance. By some miracle she managed to avoid stumbling on the uneven ground, and she even earned a few more wolf whistles from some of the rowdy good old boys loitering out front. She felt her smile tighten and her fingers dig into her thighs hard enough to bruise them through the layer of denim, yet she forced herself to toss her hair and swish her hips a little more as she sauntered past them and into the bar.

Her impression of the place didn't improve once inside. Though the statewide smoking ban appeared to be enforced, judging by the crowd outdoors, the stench of decades-old tobacco and wasted lives permeated the interior. Bare bulbs hovered over worn pool tables, casting a harsh light over inked biceps and grimy beards. Beer bottles littered the booths flanking the pool tables. A few old timers lurked within their shadowed depths while nursing a bottle or glass of liquid comfort. There weren't many women present, aside from a few sassy barmaids and worn out truck stop whores. Figured, since the Burnin' Bush didn't appear to be the sort of establishment suited for wives or girlfriends.

Vivian spied a few jarheads scattered throughout the crowd and graced each with a genuine smile and an extra shimmy. Redneck or not, those fellas had probably served at least two tours in some stinking desert or another halfway around the world, so she figured she'd give them an ogle pass in the way of gratitude.

After a quick glance behind her to make sure the reaper remained as inconspicuous as possible, Vivian sauntered up to the bar, grinned wide and said, "How do, friend? How about a Bud for me and my feller, here?"

"Why sure, purty legs," he replied, grinning back. Bless his heart, he only had about three teeth in his head.

She grabbed Darkmore's hand and yanked him down on the barstool next to her. The barkeep plopped down two bottles in front of them. She took a long draw, downing about a third of the bottle before casting a nervous glance at the reaper, who followed suit. He grimaced, and she hoped she was the only one who noticed.

"Y'all ain't from around here," the barkeep said. It wasn't a question.

"No sir, we've been on the road a spell. Came in from Nashville as a matter of fact." She thickened her accent and leaned over the bar a bit, hoping to distract the man with a peek at the girls. It had been a while since she'd gone out honky tonkin' in a slaughterhouse. The fewer questions, the better.

"Hew-whee, city folk, huh?"

"Naw, we work in the city, but we're country folk at heart."

He eyed her and Darkmore, and after a moment his eyes went wide. "Y'all ain't in the business, are you?"

Vivian thought fast. It wouldn't be a bad cover, and it could explain the reaper's rather unconventional appearance. Blue jeans and flannel shirt aside, he stood out. If they'd landed in *Deliverance* country, he just might find himself in more danger than she would.

Better to let the barkeep think they were minor Music City celebrities. As long as she didn't have to actually sing, they could pull it off.

She leaned in and gave the barkeep a conspiratorial wink, along with a better view of her cleavage, "Keep it down, friend. It's hard to get out and about without drawing a crowd."

He winked and nodded, "Lookin' for some new material, huh? Well, don't you worry none. Your secret's safe with me."

His statement didn't inspire much confidence, but it was too late to backtrack. Besides, she needed to focus on finding Waylon Briggs. Her knowledge of the man consisted of a few chats online and Jeanne's vague description. They hadn't gotten around to trading photos, since Vivian needed to skip town shortly after contacting him online. Her online searches didn't turn up anything either, but given his status as a living soul broker, he probably kept a very low profile. Being an Afghanistan war vet and a fireman, she figured he'd be big and burly. She'd visualized him a few times under cover of darkness, picturing a tall Irishman with a tight ass and some real skill with the spirit light. This had been before her relationship with Darkmore had moved to the next level, of course, but heat crept up her cheeks as she remembered. Darkmore, who had remained silent as promised, gave her a small smirk that made them burn even hotter.

She wondered if the bastard could still read minds while trapped in mortal form.

Familiar notes emanating from the old jukebox in the corner jolted her back to reality.

The old song traveled from her ears to her brain, where it set every raw nerve ending on fire and inspired a host of flashbacks involving fluffy mullets and bad karaoke. Winos and home décor were an arguably odd combination, but it fit the overused theme of hard drinking men and long-suffering women in the musical genre like rhinestones and rodeos.

Vivian spun around on her barstool and shot daggers at the reaper with her eyes. "What the hell do you think you're doing?"

"Setting the mood."

"First off, did it occur to you that someone might wonder how the jukebox turned itself on? Second, stay out of my head, especially the child-hood soundtrack section. Third, if you put "She Thinks My Tractor's Sexy" into the queue, I will blow your head off and send you back to the bottom of the reaper barrel myself."

He smiled a predatory smile that managed to inspire hunger rather than fear. "You really are fetching when you're angry."

"Fuck you," she said through gritted teeth.

"Perhaps not tonight, given your vexation with me, but maybe later."

Vivian closed her eyes and counted to ten. Then she flagged down the toothless bartender of the Burnin' Bush. "Excuse me, but we're lookin' for an old friend tonight and was hopin' you could help. You know a fella name of Briggs?"

His formerly smiling face turned hard and he said, "Briggs don't come here much."

"Oh," she replied as she tried to suppress a surge of panic. "Is there another bar nearby? Maybe he just gave us the wrong address." Damn it, she'd let the accent slip. She needed to get a handle on the situation and decide if retreat was in order.

"The Bush is the only place in town." He gave them the once over and said, "I didn't figure someone like you'd be associatin' with that type."

She wasn't sure what "type" the man referred to, but the feral gleam in his eyes had her settling on retreat. *Time to backtrack and get out.*

"Well he's more of an acquaintance. Friend of a friend." Vivian batted her eyelashes and smiled even brighter. When in doubt and in a den of rednecks, she thought it best to play dumb.

Before he could answer, Vivian felt a bump at the back of her stool. She turned around and found herself way too close to a greasy-haired man in jeans and a ratty old T-shirt. He was also covered with the acrid scents of beer and lust. He leaned in and said, "Evenin', miss. Buy a purty gal a beer?"

"That's sooooo sweet," she answered, pitching her voice an octave or two higher. "But we need to be on our way. Still got a long drive ahead of us."

He leaned in closer and whispered, "Why don't you leave the little queer and try on a real man for size?" His eyes looked glazed, and Vivian wondered if he was drunk, stoned, or maybe both.

"I'm gonna have to ask you to back off now."

Anger warred with fear, but she held her ground and refused to back away. She also refused to look to the reaper for help. Feminine pride wouldn't allow it and she felt more than capable of fighting her own battles. His hand crept up her thigh and she stifled the urge to strike him.

Apparently, estrogen and pride could be a lethal combo, too.

"I believe the lady wishes to be left alone."

Shit! Darkmore somehow managed to wedge himself between Vivian and her would-be attacker. She put a hand on his shoulder and squeezed hard, hoping a bit of pain would remind him of his promise to keep a low profile. He shook her hand off and spoke to the man in an icy, calm voice.

"Do sit down, Mr. Milford."

To her surprise, Milford took a seat on the stool formerly occupied by the reaper. He kept his gaze locked on Darkmore's the entire time, apparently under the reaper's influence. Having experienced it herself a time or two, a jolt of fear surged through her psyche.

"Now then, Mr. Milford, why do you insist on soliciting the attention of women who are clearly out of your league? Even if you did manage to enchant my companion through alcohol or the drugs in your back pocket, the all-to-brief encounter wouldn't erase the shame. No matter how many whores you bed, you'll always see her face and remember, won't you? Your long-suffering wife whom you abandoned while she battled cancer, when she could no longer service your carnal desires."

"H-how do you know about Janelle?"

"Oh, you've had a brush with my kind before. Remember your near overdose from last year? No one else came to your bedside—not your brother, or your mother, not even the children you sired. They despise you."

"No," he whispered, his eyes shining with unshed tears. The predatory impulses had fled at the reaper's first words. He'd looked confused at first. Now he looked like prey.

"Lazarus, stop. We need to get out of here." A group of burly men from a corner pool table had taken notice of them. They probably weren't Milford's friends, exactly. Milford didn't look the type to have many friends. But he belonged here, and small communities like this took care of their own, especially when confronted with outsiders asking too many questions about the wrong people.

The reaper hungered. Being trapped in a mortal body had left him vulnerable in the physical sense, but he seemed to retain most of his powers. And his appetites. She could hardly blame him. The pathetic creature in his claws deserved to be there if half of what Darkmore had said was true. Being a rapist was reason enough to draw the reaper's hunger. Add in neglect of a terminally ill spouse and probably a laundry list of other deadly sins, and he was a meal fit for a reaper.

But not with an audience. The reaper didn't appear to notice as the men shuffled closer. He kept on talking, tormenting the evil little man in his clutches as wisps of the man's life force left Milford and fed Darkmore.

"Oh yes, Thomas, they do. In a few years they'll forget the toys, trips to the beach, Little League. All they'll remember is dear old drunken daddy slamming the front door to the home they lost shortly after when no one could pay the bills."

"Stop," he said, placing his head in his hands and shuddering.

"What the hell's goin' on here?"

Vivian felt the hair on the back of her neck rise at the sound of the barkeep's raised voice. Every eye in the joint focused on her and the reaper. Unless they were willing to burn the place down and destroy every human in this hellhole, they'd be lucky to make it out alive.

They could, but it would be breaking the rules. More than their lives would be forfeit if they called that much attention to their presence.

"Tommy, you ain't crying, are you?"

After a few moments of uncomfortable silence, the bartender burst out laughing. A few others joined in before the catcalls started.

"What's a matter, Tommy?" a rough voice shouted. "Your boyfriend there break up with you?"

"Shit, someone stick a quarter in the juke. Tommy's got a tear in his beer!"

"Shut the fuck up!" Milford roared. He'd managed to shake off the reaper's spell and looked like he was ready to take a swing at Darkmore. Milford might be soft in the middle, but his fists were meaty enough, and whatever he did for a living gave him plenty of muscle in his upper body.

Time to split.

"I don't think our friend is gonna show, so we'll just be on our way," Vivian said, slapping two twenties on the table and grabbing the reaper by the hand. He didn't move, so she tugged harder. Vivian turned to give him a verbal lashing, but one look at his posture and focus on Thomas Milford set off more alarm bells.

Mr. Milford was filled to the brim with delicious rage, shame, and anguish. And the reaper was still hungry. The man's earlier pain hadn't satisfied him. Darkmore had only a taste of the ugliness in Milford's soul instead of a full meal.

Vivian slapped him as hard across the face as she could manage.

Then she yelled at him. "Get your no good, drunk ass up and walk it to the car! I swear I can't take you nowhere."

The look he gave her in return would have chilled her to the bone even if she hadn't known he was a reaper. He might have found her intriguing, entertaining, and a worthy companion, but she was under no illusion that she was more important to him in this moment than his need to feast on human suffering. She stood between the reaper and his prey. It wasn't a good place to be.

But she had to protect him.

In spite of her fear, she leaned in close and put a shaking arm around him as though to help him out of his chair.

"Not another word," she whispered with a hiss. "Let's just get the hell out of here before something bad happens."

They made it as far as the parking lot before something bad did happen.

CHAPTER TEN

Vivian figured Tommy boy might be dumb enough to follow them, but she hoped they could hop back in her car and hightail it out of there before he caught up with them. What she didn't count on was the reaper slowing them down. On purpose.

"Git on back here, you fuckin' freak!"

A few more crude comments and laughter let her know they had a small audience trailing them. *Just keep walking. Don't engage them. Just keep on walking.*

"I'm tellin' y'all, he's some kind of mind-readin' freak!" Milford shouted.

"Aw Tommy, quit talkin' shit!"

"He sure is purty, though. Put him in a dress and gimme enough beer and I'd probably fuck him."

"I said git on back here, freak," Milford yelled. "Don't be hidin' behind some fancy little city cunt. Be a man!"

The reaper pulled free from Vivian and spun around to face Milford.

"Lazarus, don't! It's not worth it—"

He punched Milford in the gut. The man doubled over in pain but didn't fall down.

"Hey faggot! Get your goddamn hands off my brother!"

Against her better judgment, Vivian tried to get between the men so she could drag Darkmore out of there. Instead, strong arms gripped her shoulders and a dirty palm covered her mouth. They pulled her away even as she screamed in protest. She bit the filthy hand over her mouth, earning a curse and a cuff to the ear. Four other men jumped Darkmore.

She watched in horror as their fists collided with the reaper's face. To his credit, he gave as good as he got from them even without using his spirit power. Once he'd recovered from the initial shock of the attack, he dodged many of the other blows. Darkmore delivered fewer punches with greater effect, driving up through his legs and body to transfer as much impact to his opponents as possible. He even managed to knock one man to the ground and break his nose judging from the blood and the man's cries of pain.

One small and vicious-looking pit-bull of a man broke a beer bottle and came at Darkmore. The reaper ducked to miss the sharp glass, but lost his balance and landed on the ground. When the man charged him again, Darkmore threw gravel at his face and used the resulting blindness to knock the bottle out of his hand and push him hard against a nearby car. The lapse in attention to his other attackers, however, earned him a kick to the back of the knee. He collapsed and another man came up from behind and whacked him with a tire iron.

Vivian flailed and kicked her attacker as she tried to free herself. Judging from the grunt of pain and muffled curses, one of her kicks landed between his legs. When she felt his grip relax, she elbowed him in the ribs, and he let her go. She ran to the reaper.

The two men left standing took turns kicking Darkmore. Vivian recognized the steel-toed work boots, imagining the damage they likely inflicted on the reaper's mortal body. She leapt on the back of the bigger man and wrapped her arms around his neck. He smelled of cheap aftershave and stale sweat. The man managed to grab her arms and dug into her flesh with his fingers and ragged nails. It hurt like a mother, but the adrenaline coursing through her veins allowed her to ignore it and focus on getting free.

She had to stop them before they killed the reaper. If he died, his soul would be fair game for others of his kind, creatures with appetites as dark as his, if not darker. He'd be at the bottom of the ladder, the newest and lowest reaper. Given his long existence, he'd made more than a few enemies. If he fell into the hands of those enemies, they would torture him and feast on his suffering until his essence shattered.

She couldn't lose him. She wouldn't.

Vivian bit her opponent hard on the shoulder. He backed up and slammed her into the side of the white serial-killer van, knocking the wind out of her. She didn't know if she'd be able to hold onto him much longer, but at least they'd stopped kicking Darkmore.

A loud shot rang out in the night, then another. The sounds echoed through the dark lot before a booming voice shouted, "Break it up!"

The crowd of drunken brawlers and spectators hit the ground or scattered. Vivian's attacker dropped her and ran. She crawled along the ground toward Darkmore, trying to ignore the sharp jabs of gravel. Her knees fared better, being covered by jeans, but her hands and elbows stung. Pushing aside her own discomfort, she touched the reaper gently on the shoulder.

"Lazarus, can you hear me?"

He didn't respond. More alarming, his breath was shallow, and she could hear crackling and wheezing when she put her ear to his chest. He probably had a whole host of internal injuries, but her primary concern was for his lungs. Vivian's experience caring for her disabled sister left her all too familiar with signs and symptoms of respiratory distress. She worried his lung had been punctured by a fractured or broken rib. A hospital wasn't an option. Too many questions. They'd call the police, which would draw too much unwanted attention.

Ignoring the chaos around her and the danger still posed by the unseen gunman, she focused on the reaper. Memories of Mae pierced her heart, and the familiar wave of protectiveness and resentment welled up in her chest. Damn him for putting her through this again—the terror, the guilt, the knowledge that she and she alone was responsible for keeping him alive and knowing she didn't have the power or force of will to do it. She'd lost her sister. If she didn't act, she'd lose Darkmore, too.

She lifted him by the shoulders and cradled him in her arms, focusing all of her mind and energy on the reaper's broken body.

She felt the familiar pull as light emanated from her open mouth, her nose, and her eyes. Channeling all of her pain, doubt, anger, and sorrow, she pressed her lips to Darkmore's and willed him to take in the spirit light that would both feed and heal him. He jerked and she had to release him for a moment while he coughed and caught his breath.

"What happened?" he whispered.

"You got your ass handed to you by a bunch of rednecks," she said, blinking back useless tears. "Now hold still and let me heal you."

He took a small breath and swallowed her light, then took a deeper one. Those deeper breaths meant his lungs were healing, thank God. Some of the bruises on his face began to fade. She hoped the same healing mojo was working its magic on the injuries she couldn't see.

To her surprise, he covered her mouth with his hand to stop the flow of light.

"I wasn't finished. You need more—"

"It's enough," he said, grimacing. He was clearly still in pain. Vivian opened her mouth again, but he cut her off.

"We have more pressing matters to attend to right now."

The reaper nodded at something behind her. She turned and squeaked with surprise as she came face to knee with a strange man. He was dressed in camo and had a gun in his right hand.

"Congratulations," he said, his voice deep and silky, like smooth single malt Scotch. "You passed the test and then some."

"What?"

He barked a laugh, put the gun back in its holster, and offered her a hand. The reaper managed to sit up on his own and had scooted away from her. She hesitated for a moment and then took it. Standing almost eye-to-eye, she recognized the man as one of the soldiers she'd smiled at in the bar. The man looked to be in his late thirties to early forties, splashes of grey mixed in with his dark, buzz cut hair and beard stubble. The easy smile and relaxed posture didn't diminish his aura of danger, and she didn't miss the few sparks of green light that escaped the fingertips of his free hand.

"Sergeant Briggs is gonna love this," he said, still chuckling. "Come on, let's get your friend in the van."

CHAPTER ELEVEN

Vivian followed Chester Newman, gun-toting second-in-command to the Briggs rebel force, as he drove the reaper. They'd tucked Darkmore into the back of the white serial killer van, which Chester owned. She wasn't happy with the situation, wasn't happy leaving her injured and vulnerable reaper in the hands of a stranger, but the van would be a more comfortable ride. They traveled around five miles to what looked to be an aging apartment complex located not too far from the Burnin' Bush and still in the boonies on the outskirts of Jackson. Classic 1970s construction, the bland brick rectangle buildings held six units each, three across and two up. Not exactly quite ready to be condemned, but probably not too far from it, the building appeared deserted save for a few vehicles parked near the back and lights visible from inside a few of the units.

Chester referred to it as 'headquarters.'

He led Vivian to one of the unoccupied units and left her to unload their belongings while he fetched Darkmore. The small apartment had little in the way of creature comforts, but it was warm, clean, and safe. After she'd hauled in the final load of their belongings, she plopped down on the couch. Exhaustion, not to mention the aches and pains associated with brawling, took over. Exhaustion won.

A sharp sting in her arm jolted her awake.

"Ouch! What was that?"

She opened her eyes and saw a very large man leaning over her. His hair was also cut short, military style, and he wore desert camo, too. Like Chester Newman, he filled out his camo pants, not to mention the tight, sandy T-shirt that covered broad shoulders and ripped biceps. Definitely military, or ex-military, he had light brown skin and brown eyes, and a face that was probably warm and inviting when not scowling.

Remembering the events from earlier in the evening, she panicked and jumped to her feet. Adopting a defensive stance, she asked, "Who are you? And where is Darkmore?"

"Your friend is resting in the other room. He's still a little banged up, but should be fine in a few weeks. I hear that's thanks to you. You didn't tell me you had so many useful skills, Miss Tennessee Woman."

"*You're* Briggs?"

He smiled, revealing bright white teeth and dimples, "That's right. Expecting someone a little different? Maybe someone a little whiter?"

She tried to hide her shock, embarrassed that he'd recognized it. Then she decided to hell with it. With everything else that had happened over the past few weeks, this little faux pas seemed pretty trivial.

"Yeah, I guess I did. With a name like Waylon I was expecting a bubba."

"My Mama liked Waylon Jennings. Don't ask me why. I can't stand that shit." He grinned at her. "She was white, so maybe it was an ethnic thing."

Vivian rubbed her arm sore arm and remembered the rude awakening. "Hey, what in the hell did you stick me with anyway?" she asked, eyeing the medical bag resting beside the couch.

"Tetanus booster. Didn't know how long it'd been since you had one. Before that, Hep B." When she gave him a look of confusion, he continued, "Chet said you bit some guy in the parking lot."

"*That's* your biggest concern? Tetanus and Hepatitis?"

He shrugged, "It's the best I can do. If you got HIV from him, you're shit outta luck."

It hadn't occurred to Vivian that she might have to worry about such ordinary issues as blood borne diseases.

Briggs just stood and watched her with a smug grin on his face. His eyes were sharp, though, and they seemed busy sizing her up. She returned the favor and let her eyes roam over him. Returning her gaze to his face, his dimples caught her attention once more. They would have seemed out of place on such an imposing man, but he'd dropped the scowl and wore a look of wry amusement.

She forced herself to quit staring. White women and black men did often mix in the new South, but prejudice still ran deep, and she knew her daddy would be rolling over in his grave at the thought of her ogling Briggs. As quickly as that thought popped into her addled brain, she set it aside. Her first thought was a product of her upbringing. The second thought, which was a reflection of her character, told her this wasn't a man to be crossed, but he was also a man of his word and one to be trusted. Hours of online communication combined with instincts she now trusted served her well.

She pushed the spark of interest aside out of loyalty. She supposed she was officially with the reaper, which brought her focus back to more immediate concerns.

And a few questions.

"Why didn't you show up tonight? And what did Chester mean when he told me I'd 'passed the test and then some?'"

"He meant just what he said. You passed the audition." His face remained as bland as his tone, as if they were discussing the weather instead of a near-brush with death.

Anger brewing, she spat out her reply. "*Audition?*"

"You didn't think we'd just let you waltz right in without knowing what you could do, would do, and more importantly, would not do with your spirit powers, did you? I've worked too hard to recruit and protect my people to trust just anyone."

White-hot rage filled her, so intense that it was almost cold. The reaper's influence? Possibly, since half of her anger was on his behalf. Briggs had put them in danger, deliberately sent them into enemy territory to be ambushed. That was as twisted as any trap ever set for her by guardian or reaper spirits, the common enemy they were supposed to be fighting. Allies didn't do that. Allies fought beside you, had your back, and kept you safe—Briggs was supposed to be her ally.

When she spoke, her soft, low voice made up for lack of volume with a rumbling growl. "You invited me here, under your protection, and I agreed to serve as an ally. But instead of meeting us and offering safe passage to your base, you sent us into that redneck hellhole filled with humans who had no idea what kind of danger they'd face if our cover was blown. Granted, it would be no great loss to humanity, but we could have been killed. Lazarus almost *was* killed."

She emphasized the last by allowing the spirit light to spark from her finger tips and glow beneath her skin. "Lazarus is under my protection. You don't want to test him, or me."

He met her threat with a neutral, almost bored expression. "I had to make sure you wouldn't go and do something monumentally stupid like cast spirit light in front of civilians."

"And if we had?"

"Y'all would've been on your own."

Vivian fought the overwhelming urge to shoot a blast through Briggs' head. Instead she slapped him hard across the face. To her surprise, he didn't make any move to defend himself or to strike her back. He just stood his ground and stared at her. The second blow, however, he blocked by grabbing her wrist.

"I understand you're pissed off, and I'll give you one pass. One. The people here are under my protection. I don't bring strangers in lightly. You don't want to test me, either."

She wriggled free and tried to clamp down on her temper. Judging from his grip, the man had allowed her to free herself. He didn't have to let her go. Rage still boiled the blood in her veins, but she held onto it and let his words sink in. She and Darkmore had been running from the spirit world for a while. Briggs had been on the run longer, and he likely had a lot of living soul brokers with him. Good leaders took care of their people, they protected as well as ruled. She didn't agree with his methods, but she understood.

If Briggs accepted them, he'd protect her and Darkmore from any threat with the same ruthlessness.

"Fine. I get it. We're in now? We're good?"

He nodded. She spun on her heel and went to check on Darkmore, finding him in bed very much as she and Chester had left him around an hour before. Chester had left the small lamp on the nightstand lit. Bruises had bloomed on the reaper's swollen face, and she silently cursed herself for not attending to him sooner. Pulling back the covers, she unbuttoned his shirt and exposed his chest, hissing at the evidence of his beating. More worrisome was the damage she couldn't see. Not sure if she'd fully healed his internal injuries back at the bar, she took a deep breath, focused her energy, and bent over him so she could deliver the healing rays.

"No," Darkmore rasped, turning away from her and groaning.

"Stop squirming and let me finish healing you," she chided, her tone gentle.

"I don't want you to finish healing me."

That stumped her, and her next words came in a not-so-gentle tone. "What? Why not?"

"Because the greatest wisdom comes from suffering."

Unbelievable bastard. Heaving a deep sigh, she said, "That's cute. You can stitch that on a pillow for me after I fix your hands."

With great effort, the reaper pushed himself up to sit, groaning as he turned to face her. Her last comment had failed to amuse him. His icy eyes bored into her and she reminded herself that, injured or not, he was still a reaper and could inflict any number of torments upon her body, mind, or soul.

Then again, reaper or not, he was being a stubborn jackass.

"Seriously, what gives?"

He heaved a sigh and groaned again. When he spoke, his voice sounded harsh and strained. Vivian wondered if he was fighting pain or anger. "Are you at all familiar with Eastern philosophy?"

"Not really."

"One ancient branch, which happens to still be quite popular in the modern era, holds that humans derive wisdom from three sources: personal study, personal experience, and personal suffering. The last is the greatest form of enlightenment. I ought to know, as I have inflicted immeasurable suffering throughout the ages in an effort to educate my charges."

She wanted to yell, to scream and rage and hit him with the lamp. Yeah, that would teach him to interfere with her "healing" touch. Instead, she cocked her head to the side and said, "That's an interesting way to look at it. Your point?"

"My point, Vivian, is that I've been a fool."

She stared at him, jaw hanging. First off, the volume of his declaration surprised her, as did his tone. The reaper rarely raised his voice or lost his cool. Second, he had always carried with him an air of supreme confidence and omniscience that she found extremely irritating most of the time.

At this moment, she found the loss of said confidence quite alarming.

"I thought I had experienced enough suffering in my many mortal lives to understand all facets of the darkness you humans carry in your souls. I have endured *everything*, Vivian," he said, his gaze open and raw, filled with things no soul should know, let alone share. "Every manner of disease, injury, loss, violation, and cruelty humanity can inflict on its own has been mine to live. And yet, I've never once feared for the fate of my spirit."

Perhaps prompted by her look of confusion, he continued, "I knew what awaited me on the other side, you see. No matter the pain or terror, it could be easily endured with the understanding that it was, in fact, temporary. I would carry my lessons with me upon the end of each incarnation and apply them in my own realm. But now..."

"You've never faced death?" she whispered as realization dawned. Her chest went tight, and she had to look away and blink back unshed tears. "*Really* faced it? Not even in your first mortal life?"

He closed his eyes and turned away. "That experience was another matter entirely."

His tone and the anguish in his voice prompted her to drop the subject, at least for the moment. Instead, she let his admission sink in. She hadn't often contemplated her own mortality, at least before becoming involved with the spirit realms. It was something she took for granted. *We're born, we live, and we die. We can die anytime.* People of faith took comfort in their firm belief in eternal paradise, but no one really knew for certain what awaited in the great beyond. Trying to imagine going from a position of invincibility to one of utter uncertainty made her head spin. Even Jesus had known he'd get to go back home to Papa while he was hanging on the cross, according to the Biblical accounts. What if he hadn't?

She'd entered the reaper's room with every intention of healing him. She had half a mind to pack up and leave after Briggs' little stunt. But now she questioned the wisdom of that decision. Here, they would be protected, or at least among those like them. Extra eyes, ears, and spirit power couldn't hurt. Out there, he'd be as vulnerable as any human, perhaps more so.

"Lazarus, I—"

"I do not want your pity, Vivian, nor do I wish to burden you. Tonight's fiasco was my doing. I broke my own rule when I turned and struck Milford. I made it personal. And now I must face the consequences."

"So you can punish yourself?"

"So, I will remember next time," he answered, laughing bitterly. "As I believe I once told you, life is often painful, but it does teach us a thing or two. It would appear to be my time to practice what I preach."

Her first reaction would have been to scoff, or possibly rant and rail at the reaper, who had never seemed more human. A stubborn, human man hell-bent on proving how tough he was by wallowing in the misery of his own making was both exasperating and infuriating. But...he was hers, at least for now. Ranting at him wouldn't do any good. Human he may seem, but he was a reaper, an ancient creature of myth, legend, and more than the occasional nightmare. Mortal men didn't often heed advice offered by their women, and being much older, arguably wiser, and more experienced than she, Darkmore was unlikely to listen to her if she wasn't very careful and thoughtful in her approach.

She intrigued him, and part of that appeal came from her unexpected nature. Very little surprised Darkmore, one of the consequences of a long, long existence. But she had, she did, and if she was clever, she could do it again.

He intrigued her as well, and challenged her always. If she wanted to help him, she'd have to meet the challenge on his terms and bend them to suit her own.

"Would you excuse me for a moment?" she asked, after taking a few moments to make some tough decisions.

"I did not intend to cause you discomfort, Vivian. You don't have to leave."

That was interesting. An almost apology, and invitation to stay, a subtle request that she stay, as if she would abandon him?

"I have no intention of leaving," she said, which was true. "I just need to have a little chat with Briggs."

He nodded and then slowly lowered himself back to rest on the bed. Vivian left the room and closed the door behind her. When she returned to the small living room, Briggs stood up from the couch. He looked at her with something akin to awe, which was not what she'd expected from the tough-as-nails leader of the mortal soul broker rebellion.

"Been eavesdropping?"

"It's my house," he said with a small shrug. "Your friend in there, he's a reaper?"

It was a question. Darkmore had always been an enigma. In his current state, he'd be even more mysterious to those in their world. She didn't want to reveal his weaknesses to Briggs. Not yet. But she owed him honesty.

"Yeah."

"But he's mortal. How'd that happen?"

She sighed, suddenly very, very tired. "I healed him after my little spat with the rogue guardian, the one I told you about during our chats. The reaper saved me, and I thought I was saving him. I guess it worked a little too well."

"Will it work on any spirit? Can you do it again?"

It wasn't what she'd expected. He wasn't angry with her for bringing a reaper into their midst, nor did he seem particularly interested in using Darkmore's powers. True, reapers weren't known for being cooperative, but they were powerful, much more powerful than she was, and much more useful in a battle with guardian spirits.

Or so she believed.

Vivian could almost hear the gears turning inside his head, and it got her thinking, too. With spirit firepower, healing powers, and the ability to trap potential enemies in a mortal form, she was a valuable asset in her own right. From what she'd learned, not all living soul brokers had her gift of healing, and she suspected no others had the ability to render mortal powerful spirits capable of forming temporary corporeal forms. Captured spirits could be questioned in the same manner as any vulnerable mortal, and she suspected Briggs would have no qualms about using extreme and creative interrogation methods.

Vivian could be used as a formidable weapon, which made her suddenly more interesting. Apparently, Waylon Briggs took a rather Machiavellian approach to leadership.

Well, she could play princess to his Medici prince.

Adopting a neutral tone, she answered his question. "I probably could do it again if circumstances dictated, and if properly motivated."

He gave her a bland stare. "Room, board, and safety aren't enough for you?"

She laughed, letting bitterness and resentment seep through. "I think I have more than enough reasons to question my safety after your little stunt at the bar tonight. I can pay my own way, and if I contribute to your little rebellion then I believe I should expect something in return."

He laughed then. "Seems I've gotten myself a little mercenary. What exactly do you propose?"

Time to bargain, then. There were many things she wanted. Most of those things were things Briggs couldn't give her. But she had a mistake to correct and a debt to repay. If she had to sacrifice freedom and allegiances and put her life and soul on the line, she needed to at least make sure her debt was settled.

"I'll lend my spirit powers, including those that heal and can render spirits mortal, to your cause. In return, I want you to help me find a way to return the reaper to his former state."

His gaze widened a fraction of an inch, the only visible sign of his surprise. "What makes you think I have that kind of information?"

Good question, but her instincts told her he was the key to helping restore Darkmore to his original state. She thought back to what Jeanne had told her earlier. Jeanne mentioned contacting spirits involved in Voodoo. Wait, she'd called it something else. Maybe Briggs would be familiar with spirits in the same circle.

"Know anyone who does Voudon?"

"I do," he said, without hesitation. "You think a Houngan can help you?"

What the hell was a Houngan? No matter, she'd bluff now and look it up later. "I'm told someone like that might."

He grinned, which gave her pause. She hoped she hadn't fallen into a trap, since he seemed to be more pleased with negotiations than she'd expected. "Tell you what, Miss Tennessee. Let's see what you can do in training tomorrow and I'll arrange an introduction. You'll have to get in good with my contact yourself if you want help."

"Training?"

"Yeah, training. You arrived at a good time. Got a new batch of recruits set for testing tomorrow morning. We start early. Chet can give you a wakeup call. We'll talk more after. Wear something warm." Briggs picked up his medical bag and made to leave.

"Leave that here, if you don't mind. I've got some doctoring to do."

Briggs gave her funny look, but then nodded and walked to the front door. Vivian walked with him. In spite of her misgivings, he had offered them shelter and a safe haven. She vowed to at least be civil to the man until she decided whether or not she liked him.

"There's food in the fridge. You want anything else, Chet can direct you toward town. Get some rest. You're gonna need it."

"Good night to you, too," she quipped.

Instead of taking offense to her attitude, Briggs offered her a wry smile. "I don't coddle, and I don't have time for Southern charm these days, but I'll treat you fair and keep you safe if you do your part."

She nodded, waiting until he'd made it across the parking lot before shutting and locking the door. Though tempted to go straight back to the reaper, she had enough caregiver experience to take the flight attendant approach: put the oxygen mask on yourself first before assisting others. Brigg's hadn't lied. The refrigerator and pantry were stocked with essentials. She made herself a ham and cheese sandwich and poured a tall glass of milk to wash it down. While she ate, she warmed up some soup for Darkmore.

While the soup cooled, she grabbed the medical bag and then made a trip to the bathroom, from which she retrieved a washcloth and soap, and filled a shallow bowl with tepid water. Vivian carried these items back to the bedroom, where she found the reaper dozing. Nudging him gently on the shoulder, she roused him and helped him to a sitting position, propping his back with a couple of pillows.

"Take off your shirt."

"I beg your pardon?"

"You heard me." It remained unbuttoned from her earlier examination. He arched his brow at her, but did as she asked. She wet the washcloth, dabbed it lightly with soap, and then sat next to Darkmore on the bed. When she tried to bring it to his face, the reaper turned away.

"Hold still," she chided. "You want this to get infected?"

"I already told you to not to interfere. Do you ever listen?"

"Boy, you really are a fool."

Judging by the look on his face, he clearly hadn't expected that response. Under normal circumstances she might have found it amusing. Instead, it filled her with a heavy sadness.

She didn't make eye contact or raise her voice. It wasn't that kind of battle. Instead, she spoke quietly while she wrung out the wet cloth. "For someone who claims to be an expert on the human experience, you're pretty lousy at recognizing the fundamentals."

After a long moment, he said, "Explain."

"Aside from pain and suffering, there's a lot more to the human experience. This," she said as she gently caressed the cuts and bruises on his cheek, first with the cloth and then with her fingers, "is caring."

Vivian traced the cloth along each wound on his face, his neck, and his chest. After she'd cleansed and rinsed his skin, she patted him dry with a clean towel as she whispered, "This is concern."

Vivian followed with a salve, and then trailed kisses along his injuries. "This is compassion, Lazarus." The reaper slowly relaxed his rigid posture under her ministrations. His taut muscles loosened, his breathing calmed, and the bitter chill she'd experienced when she began to care for him faded. The sensation emanating from the reaper felt like a refreshing breeze.

When she finished, she brought him a bowl of soup and a glass of milk. They sat in companionable silence while he ate. After she cleared the dishes and helped him brush his teeth, Vivian turned off the lamp on the nightstand and climbed into bed with him. Mindful of his injuries, she curled up next to him and placed her hand over his.

"This is comfort."

Darkmore didn't speak, but she heard his sigh and felt his fingers grip hers before he relaxed into slumber.

CHAPTER TWELVE

Vivian left Darkmore safe in bed while she showered and got ready for training. Luckily, Chet's soft knock at zero-dark-hundred didn't rouse the reaper. Before she left, she kissed him lightly on the forehead and fed him more of her spirit light, smiling as she watched the cuts and bruises fade from his skin. He'd probably be a little pissed off at her for disregarding his request that she allow him to take his lumps like a man, but he needed his strength in order to face whatever battle might be coming, not to mention potential run-ins with their new allies. She shut the door and locked it with the key Chet had given her, and then followed Briggs' second as he headed for the big field behind the apartment complex to meet the other recruits.

Mississippi didn't experience autumn's chill to the same degree as Tennessee, but she found herself wishing for a sweater. Best not whine, though. Drill Sergeant Briggs didn't strike her as the type to take kindly to whining, especially since he'd *told* her to dress warm. Briggs stood before the group of new recruits, not at attention or with the air of authority she'd expected.

He looked bored.

Maybe it was part of his tough guy act. The recruits looked anxious, though she didn't understand why. It wasn't like channeling spirit energy and zapping enemies was all that hard to muster or control once you got the

THE QUICK AND THE DEAD   111

hang of it, or got over the initial shock. She'd had plenty of practice during her time working for the guardians. Oh, and there was that brief but memorable trip to Darkmore's realm where she fought off a gang of nasty monsters and helped liberate a host of trapped souls. She'd been thrown into battle, and while she hadn't come out of it unscathed, she had emerged as a tested warrior. She'd survived.

Maybe the others hadn't endured the ordeals she had.

"Listen up, people," Briggs began, his voice booming. "Welcome to boot camp. I've met with each of you individually, so we'll skip the whole going 'round in a circle playing get to know your new best friends. Do that on your own time. We're here to train and train hard."

He had everyone's attention, which was a good thing for a leader. Vivian was surprised he hadn't brought any of his seasoned veterans along to help, though. Maybe he just believed in using a personal touch.

"Before we get started, I need to know what sorts of bad habits and lousy skills y'all have picked up, fucked up, or God forbid, come up with on your own. Then we're going break them and train you right. The establishment has some well-trained field agents, so we've got to train harder. It ain't the fat cat higher-ups that scare me, it's the newly dead on a mission. That's how they roll."

Briggs was right about the newly dead, but in her experience, the fat cat higher-ups were plenty scary. Members of the Archangel Council who ran the guardian spirit operation had power. The tithes they collected from field agent spirits who mediated crossings kept them stocked with spirit energy. Their little pyramid scheme had actually created an energy crisis in the guardian spirit realm that helped inspire the rebellion. Uriel and his buddies were the bigger threat as far as she was concerned, but she was no master strategist, nor was this her rebellion. If taking out enemies from the bottom up had been working for Briggs and his mercenaries, she'd go along.

"This, ladies and gentlemen, is how we roll," he said. Then he shot a focused burst of red light out of his index finger. The tight stream hit the middle of the bull's eye mounted to the bale of hay at least a football field length away. The shot was clean, leaving a hole roughly the diameter of a nickel all the way through.

And it didn't even ignite the hay.

Impressive.

Vivian's blasts normally inflicted substantial collateral damage. She'd have to work on that.

"Aim between the eyes of a guardian, or reaper and you'll disable him, or her, long enough to grab the target and go. We're saving souls here, people. You're up first, Lewis!"

A tall man, presumably Lewis, shuffled over to Briggs. Lewis carried himself with a hunched posture and could have easily been mistaken for a much older man were it not for his mop of honey blond hair and the smooth, unmarred skin of his hands. His eyes darted about and his hands shook a little.

Briggs clapped him hard on the shoulder and said, "Don't think about it too hard, brother, just do it."

Lewis adjusted his heavy-framed glasses, pushing them back up to their proper position on his narrow nose, and shot the equivalent of a lightning bolt from at least four fingers, which meandered toward the general direction of the target and splintered into at least three side branches. It hit the outer rim of the bull's eye and set the adjacent hay ablaze. Some of Briggs' minions appeared then and put it out with a fire extinguisher.

"Power? Check. Aim? You've got to work your ass off on it," Briggs said. Lewis nodded and walked back toward the crowd of recruits.

"Gutierrez, you're up!"

A petite woman pulled her dark hair into a ponytail while walking over to Briggs. He'd moved to another target, though now that they'd put out the fire on the first one it seemed perfectly serviceable to Vivian. Gutierrez squinted, held up her right hand, and produced some impressive, multi-colored sparks. Apparently angered by the lack of *oomph*, she stood a little straighter and tried again. More sparks flew laterally, but she wasn't able to muster any specific bursts toward the target.

"¿La pasión? Sí. ¿El poder? No del todo," Briggs said.

"You have a terrible accent," she spat, in perfectly unaccented English, before spinning around and stomping back to the group.

The next few displays ranged from comic to downright frightening in terms of both raw power and utter lack of control. Briggs didn't take notes, and kept his commentary to a minimum, which made Vivian question the point of the exercise. *Maybe we're just playing the spirit light version of "mine's bigger than yours" or some other macho crap.* She heard her name and walked quickly toward their leader.

"Bedford," he drawled. "Miss Nashville Tenn-e-ssee herself. Let's see what you got."

Vivian stood straight, tensed her jaw, and focused her mind on tossing the light. She had a moment to admit to herself that she'd been pretty lax about practicing. True, she'd hit a rascal of a spirit called Junior not long ago, but he was a lost and lonely spirit at the time and pretty easy pickings. The child rapist she'd blasted had been incapacitated, and she'd fired from close range. She'd done a good job dispatching her rogue guardian stalker though, even if Darkmore had suffered collateral damage.

No point in dwelling on it now. She fired.

Her blast lacked the crisp, laser-beam quality of Briggs', but it flowed clean and found its mark. The hay didn't ignite right away. Not bad, overall.

And then, she felt Briggs' blast.

It didn't hit her outright, but her right cheek burned, and she smelled the acrid scent of singed hairs. Adrenaline prompted action first. She crouched low and fired again. This shot lacked finesse but surged with power. Briggs ducked. He wasn't able to deflect the blow with his own light, she noted with grim satisfaction. Using his delayed reaction to her advantage, she fired again.

He rolled out of the way and fired an invisible burst of energy that hit her in the chest and knocked her over.

Briggs sauntered over to her as she recovered, placing his foot over her midriff. "That all you got?"

He then crouched beside her and whispered in her ear, "You think I'll go easy on you because you're a woman?"

That pissed her off.

Vivian grabbed him by the throat. The element of surprise allowed her to wrestle him to the ground and straddle him. She had the good sense not to fire on him at such a close range, but she could deliver another kind of low blow. Focusing her mind, she inhaled deeply, taking in thin wisps of red light from Briggs as a barrage of strange, disjointed images flooded her.

.   .   .

Everything is grey. The earth, the distant mountains in the horizon, the worn asphalt upon which they travel, and the buildings they sweep past. All is grey except a few patches of scruffy green along the road, and the brilliant yellow and red flames they're heading for.

The flames are almost obscured by billowing smoke.

They're surrounded by chaos. Men and women running or racing past in vehicles of desert camo that blends in with the surroundings, as do the camo-clad soldiers. A loud explosion behind them causes the road to tremble as their driver struggles for control.

They swerve.

Another impact and the vehicle is lifted from the ground and lands hard on its side. Screams of pain echo all around. Red floods the grey, as does charred, blackened flesh.

Crawling from the remains of the vehicle, eyes fix on the spot of deep purple that interrupts the grey landscape. The spot moves closer. It's a woman, judging from the curves beneath layers of billowing purple fabric. The form extends her hand. An electric jolt of raw power fills the broken, battered body as they grasp hands, flesh to flesh.

"Hey, Tennessee! You all right?"

Vivian opened her eyes and found, to her surprise, someone other than Briggs hovering over her. This man was younger, had a full head of hair that fell past his shoulders in dreadlocks, and looked more than a little alarmed. No wonder, given the show she and Briggs had put on. She recognized him as one of the new recruits but hadn't caught his name. Thankfully, he helped her sit up.

"I think so," Vivian answered, shaking her head. After getting her bearings and swallowing back bile, she asked, "What happened? The last thing I remember is tussling with Sergeant Sneak Attack."

Vivian heard nervous titters and looked around. A crowd of other newbies surrounded her. She didn't see Briggs.

"Well, you had him in a choke hold and started putting on some kind of badass light show. You hit each other good. He did the same to you, and then y'all both passed out."

"So where is Briggs?"

"He woke up first and took off in a rush. Told us to wait for Chet. What'd you do, anyway?"

"Well, I got pissed off for starters. Being blindsided tends to do that." She rubbed her sore neck and rolled her shoulders. The real soreness would hit later. For now, she'd let the adrenaline in her system keep it at bay.

"I didn't know you could shoot it out of your mouth."

"That wasn't shooting, that was..." She struggled with the explanation. Channeling conscious spirit energy from a living person gave her visions of that person's life, usually their worst memories, in vivid detail. The empathetic connection gave her a glimpse into the person's soul while relieving them of their burdens.

He'd taken some of her conscious energy as well, but damned if she felt lighter. Then again, Briggs didn't strike her as empathetic. Maybe he got something different from the energy he collected. There was so much she still didn't know about her own power, let alone the gifts—or curses— carried by other living soul brokers.

She hated to admit it, but Briggs had reminded her how much she still needed to learn after putting her in her place.

Best keep her answer simple.

"I drew out his spirit energy," she said with a shrug. "I guess he took some of mine too, so we'd be even."

The young man looked confused, but Vivian caught nods of recognition in some of the others. She felt a little jolt of giddiness at the prospect of comparing notes with them. If she hadn't gotten herself into too much trouble with Briggs, that is. He might kick her off his team before she got the chance to learn anything.

The man shook his head, chuckling, and then offered Vivian his hand and hoisted her up from the ground. "That was something else. You got some nerve, Tennessee!"

"Thanks, I think. What's your name?"

"Barry, but y'all can call me B."

"So, now what do we do?" Gutierrez asked.

"Start making yourselves useful."

Chet walked toward them, carrying a stack of clipboards. As he passed them out, he said, "When we're not training, we all pitch in for operations. Once we sign you off, you can go on assignments."

"What kind of assignments?" Lewis asked.

"Briggs normally handles the briefing, but most of our missions involve facilitating crossings for those souls the guardians leave hanging. We've recently started liberating targets from the establishment."

"Liberating? You mean kidnapping?" B asked, suspicious.

Chet shook his head. "We prefer to think of it as apprising the clients of more cost-efficient alternatives for afterlife transition. The establishment steals their life force when they cross and barely leaves them enough to make it to the next life."

"What a minute," Vivian began. "Your group can actually lead souls to other realms?" She thought they were here to fight the guardians, as in an outright battle. This sounded more like a rescue operation.

"That's right, Bedford. And we don't suck all of their energy out in the process." Of course, Briggs' team could take a percentage of a deceased soul's spirit energy while mediating a crossing. Even a much smaller portion than the guardians usually demanded would be powerful, especially if they didn't have to give a portion to the guardian council hierarchy. With enough time and patience, Briggs and his mercenaries could accumulate enough spirit energy to fight and win a battle with some of the key players on earth.

Not that it would do much good. The Archangel Guardian Council could easily replace field agents. If the goal was to take out the guardians, it wasn't a smart strategy. Not that she could think of a better one, but she expected Briggs to have a better plan. Maybe he did. She hoped so.

"But without the energy, how can you complete the journey? How do you navigate to the correct realm, and without detection?" An older gentleman asked. She'd been wondering about that as well.

"Those are great questions, Long. We've identified several routes that the enemy uses infrequently, and we always send scouts ahead. As for energy, the journey requires far less than the amount guardians and reapers claim from the client."

That made sense. Good public relations move, too. While she'd like to think that giving souls a better option for crossing to the next realm was reason enough for the operation, Chet seemed as shrewd and calculating as Briggs. It was a great way to recruit living soul brokers. Worn down and weary from the suffering they witnessed, not to mention exploitation at the hands of the guardians for whom they were forced to work, giving the new recruits something good to do would build morale.

They'd be useful and in control, choosing their own cases and healing the departed. She couldn't think of a better way for Briggs and Chet to build trust and loyalty.

They certainly weren't building good relationships with their sparkling personalities.

Beyond that, it would be an excellent way to recruit bona fide guardians. Some of the souls they helped would likely be tapped for duty as guardian spirits, and they were much stronger and less vulnerable than living soul brokers with fragile, mortal bodies. That made more sense. Clever strategy, building an army by stealing new recruits from the evil empire.

After being barraged by twenty different questions at once, Chet held up a hand and yelled for quiet. Once he had their attention, he continued. "All of your questions will be answered during the course of training. In the meantime, I need volunteers for daily operations. If you will kindly refer to your clipboards, you'll see your assigned duties as well as those you may choose based on the skills you've brought with you."

Vivian wasn't terribly surprised to see she'd been assigned to medical. She'd just started scanning the rest of the list when she overheard a couple of guys in the back sniggering. They pointed to Gutierrez, and one said, "I guess we know who's on maid patrol, huh *mamacita*."

Gutierrez narrowed her eyes into angry slits and snapped back. "Actually, I have an MBA from Harvard. What do you two idiots do with your time that's worth anyone's while?"

"Well, we don't go stealing jobs from real Americans for starters," one shot back.

"I was born here, you idiot!"

Vivian had enough scuffles over the past twenty-four hours. "I only have a bachelor's degree, but I've worked in loans for over ten years," she told Gutierrez. "Think they need help with the bookkeeping?"

Exhaling, the flush in the woman's face softened and she moved the hard glower from her mouth as she looked at Vivian. "Yeah, we can tackle finances together. Chet showed me the office earlier," Gutierrez said.

"Sounds good. I'll have time until I'm called to tend to the injured."

Gutierrez shot one final glare at the two smartasses, before she nodded to Vivian. "Come on. I'll teach you all about allocations and overhead. Let's go."

They'd almost made it out of earshot when the bigot's buddy had to go and shoot off his mouth. "What in the Sam Hill are we supposed to do then while these chicks are messing up the money?"

"They can always use more help in the kitchen," Gutierrez offered smiling sweetly. Then she turned and started marching back across the field.

Vivian had the feeling she and Gutierrez were going to get along just fine and dandy.

CHAPTER THIRTEEN

The books weren't in terrible shape, and Vivian was relieved to find that the Briggs rebellion had some pretty substantial financial backing. Maria Gutierrez explained that most of the recruits turned over part of their personal savings and assets when they joined. When Vivian commented that most cults had the same requirement, Gutierrez assured her that it wasn't mandatory and that each recruit decided if and how much to contribute. The only thing Briggs demanded besides hard training and discipline was pitching in with operations.

Gutierrez had learned all of this during her week of orientation. Since Vivian had been thrown straight into training, she'd missed the intro course. Maria gave her the condensed version while they sorted through computer files, online accounts, and printed spreadsheets.

Briggs, it turned out, owned the building that housed headquarters, which he'd originally purchased with the intent to fix it up and keep regular tenants. In addition to providing shelter and training facilities, Vivian discovered that he'd invested all of his personal assets into the rebellion coffers. *At least he puts his money where his mouth is. Literally.*

"So what's your story?" Vivian asked. She'd finished going over the last of her spreadsheets. The rest of the work would have to wait until she and Gutierrez compared notes and brainstormed ways to improve the operations investment portfolio for the long term while making sure they still had enough to cover the rebellion's costs in the "real" world.

It would be very interesting to know how the rebellion stored spirit energy, assuming they were collecting. The guardian spirits could hold quite a bit in their realms, as could reapers. As a living soul broker, Vivian could only hold so much power before her mortal body suffered. The mental and emotional side effects of those burdens were no picnic either. She'd have to ask Briggs if there was an easier way to offload it.

Wouldn't Darkmore love that?

Gutierrez didn't look up from the computer screen, but she did answer Vivian's question. "I was on my way home from work, home being New York by the way, and I had a heart attack."

"So you were supposed to die," Vivian said. That's what had happened to her. The car crash that opened her connection to the spirit realms should have been fatal. Her reprieve from death came with the price of service in afterlife management. Death might have been better, but she suspected she'd have been tapped to serve a term under Ezra's mentorship anyway, ferrying souls to the other side and collecting energy for the grand afterlife pyramid scheme.

Gutierrez's lips curled into a sly smile as she continued to type. "That's what Armando told me."

Ah, Armando. Reaper or guardian? Either would do, she supposed. After all, she'd been caught between spirits from both sides—Ezra from the guardian side and Darkmore from the reaper side and, of course, Zeke. He'd been caught in the middle, too.

And, in spite of her best efforts, he'd remained trapped between worlds. *I'm so sorry, Zeke.*

She shook off that unpleasant thought. Not the time to open old wounds.

"How'd you get away?" Vivian asked.

Gutierrez winked and smiled. "I charmed him. What about you?"

So much for putting unpleasant thoughts aside... Keeping it short and sweet, she said, "One of my guardians took me out in trade with a reaper."

"Interesting. Did you charm him?"

Not until much later... She stood and stretched, taking a moment to decide how best to answer. "It's complicated, but I made a bargain to release my other guardian, the *charming* one, and my sister. After I took a trip to the dark side with the reaper, I let loose a whampload of spirit energy and got upgraded to indentured servitude."

Gutierrez nodded. Interesting. Vivian expected surprise, but maybe her story wasn't all that unusual. Or perhaps Gutierrez had been through worse.

"It happens a lot. If they get the living to do some of their dirty work, they don't have to spend as much of their energy."

That made sense.

"Greed's universal. I should know. I worked on Wall Street."

Vivian didn't really want to know which was worse.

————

After more skills assessments and a crap ton of written evaluations, Chet informed Vivian and the others that a shorter version of orientation would take place over dinner. Bone weary and hungry, she hoped if the two rednecks from earlier were on kitchen patrol that they actually knew how to cook. Joining Barry "B" Johnson and Gutierrez at one of the newbie tables, Vivian enjoyed surprisingly good pork BBQ and southern-style green beans. She'd promised to bring Darkmore a plate, so it surprised her when the reaper came strolling in, looking good in tight jeans and a thermal pullover.

The residual scrapes on his face just made him look more dangerous.

He sat down beside her and surveyed the others at the table.

A mortal reaper in a den full of angry mercenaries bent on shaking up the afterlife establishment, and he still strutted around like he hadn't a care in the world. Like he ran the place. She didn't know whether to be angry or impressed.

Gutierrez eyed him with a mixture of suspicion and carnal interest, which made Vivian's temperature rise. B looked at him like he was the devil, and Lewis, the shy man from the field, swerved to avoid their table. Of course, Lewis had looked pretty fragile earlier, which could account for why Briggs treated him with an uncharacteristic gentleness.

Vivian surveyed the scene, heaved a sigh, and said, "Everyone, this is Lazarus Darkmore, a reaper. Darkmore, this is everyone. I'd introduce them, but you've probably scanned them all anyway."

"And Southern women are supposed to have such impeccable manners," he drawled. "You are, however, correct. I am familiar with Ms. Gutierrez through mutual associates, though Mr. Johnson's story is...unexpected."

"Say what?" B actually made the sign of the cross and looked as though he wanted to stake the reaper through the heart.

"Don't take it personal, B. He's like this with everyone," Vivian replied. The comment about mutual associates confirmed her suspicion that Gutierrez's Armando was also a reaper.

"Given his ethnicity and address, one might expect he dodged a bullet, quite literally."

"That's racial profiling!" B said.

Vivian put her head in her hands and murmured, "This is not happening, this is not happening..."

"Were I to take the form of my native ethnicity in this era, I suspect I'd endure more than you, but that is irrelevant. No, Mr. Johnson indeed dodged a bullet, just from the other side of the law." Darkmore thanked the wary young man who served him a plate and began eating. Leave it to the reaper to stir the pot and then leave it boiling over.

"You were a cop?" Vivian asked.

"In training. Some meth heads tried to pop a cap in my ass. Almost worked, too," B answered, pulling down his shirt collar and showing them the scar on his neck."

"Anatomy 101—that's not your ass," Gutierrez quipped.

"It's an expression. Anyway, my designated guardian zapped me to a waiting room or something and left me there forever. I didn't have time for that shit, so I left."

The room went silent as folks from other tables put down their clinking silverware and shushed one another so they could eavesdrop. Not that Vivian blamed them. She leaned on the edge of her seat and waited to hear B's story. It reminded her of the last soul crossing she'd mediated before going rogue. She'd met the spirit later, still on this side of eternity, having been abandoned by the guardian spirits responsible for her crossing.

They'd drained the poor woman and left her to languish in some in-between realm, the bastards. Seemed like they'd done the same thing to B.

"What do you mean you left? How do you just leave limbo?" Gutierrez asked. Vivian had to admit she was curious as well. Both she and Gutierrez had gone directly from life to living soul broker work without any red tape.

"I just got up and walked out. I remember wishing I was back home and boom, there I was." B leaned back and nodded his head, posturing like a proud peacock.

B just went up a notch or two in Vivian's estimation. Not only had he escaped limbo, he'd come back with his mortal body and the powers of a living soul broker. He had guts, brass balls, or was just foolhardy.

Nah, he just did what he had to do.

"Of course, your guardian came back," Darkmore said between bites, pausing to wink at B.

Vivian braced for a fight, getting her feet beneath her and pushing away from the table. She wouldn't hesitate to zap the reaper if he got out of line. Better her than Briggs.

"Fear not, Vivian. I do not intend to feed on Mr. Johnson's suffering. I simply want him, and the rest of you, to be aware of what you'll soon face."

Judging from the brief flash of fear that crossed B's face, Darkmore managed to hit a raw nerve. The reaper was right, though. She suspected they all had some idea of the dangers inherent in going against the ancient guardian regime. Vivian wondered, looking at Darkmore, if they'd also be going against the reapers at some point. She'd be curious to hear Briggs' thoughts on the subject, whenever he decided to speak with her again.

Would the old adage about the 'enemy of my enemy is my friend' hold true? Would the dark side remain neutral? Perhaps they'd seize upon the weakness of the other side and take over. Vivian shuddered at the thought.

B stared at Darkmore for a long moment and then gave him a single nod. "Yeah, my guardian came back, mad as hell and scared, too. I wouldn't give him more energy, so he roped me into taking energy from the living. I drew the line when he went after special needs kids."

"And you have the scars to prove it," Darkmore said, smiling.

B didn't offer to show those scars, assuming they were physical.

"Okay, kids." Chet's voice boomed from the kitchen door. "We've got a few hours of training before we split up into teams. I'll text you your assignments. Briggs wants new recruits paired with our veterans for soul crossings. The rest of our seasoned members will be with me."

B yelled, "What'll you folks be doing?"

Vivian didn't expect an answer, but Chet flashed an evil grin and said, "Raid on the enemy. Train hard and we'll let you in on the action."

B grinned back. "That's what I'm talking about!"

Darkmore studied Chet, though Vivian couldn't tell if he liked the man or wanted to consume him. It made Vivian glad they'd be assigned to a different unit. She didn't see into the hearts and souls of mortals like Darkmore did, but she knew his hunger. Briggs' second might not be safe with them.

Honestly, none of the souls in the rebellion were safe with them, but the same was true for the reaper. She'd be walking a fine line, balancing his need for protection with theirs. Her phone pinged. Digging into her back pocket, she pulled it out and read the text that sent a shiver of dread down her spine.

It was from Briggs.

You're with me. Bring the reaper.

CHAPTER FOURTEEN

They drove in silence, the dull and dreary landscape a blur of brown and grey. It made her unutterably homesick for the crimson, gold, and cinnabar decorating her home state. There was no joy in Jackson's autumn. Not just the urban decay in the city streets, but the landscape beyond lacked the color and variety of Tennessee. And it was still hot and humid. Briggs had told her not to expect seasons when he'd invited her to his hometown. He hadn't been lying.

Maybe living here had shaped her host as much as the far away desert in which he'd fought more than enemy soldiers.

"Who is she?" Vivian asked.

Briggs ran a hand over his face, clearly not in the mood to talk about the vision he'd given her. She probably should've waited for a more private moment to ask. Darkmore sat in the back, his expression a mask of polite interest. Briggs wouldn't want to give the reaper any ammunition to use against him. But she sensed there was something Briggs wanted or needed from her, even if he wouldn't admit it outright.

"Someone you weren't supposed to see."

She let out a humorless laugh and glanced to the backseat. "I showed you mine."

He gave her the side eye and said, "This ain't a democracy. I'm doing you a favor right now. Don't make me regret it."

She bit back a smartass remark and went back to staring out the window. They'd traveled a few miles outside of the downtown area and into an older neighborhood. Small houses that screamed post World War II boomer lined the narrow streets. Most had been kept up, she was pleased to see, with neat, if bland, lawns bordered by chain link fences. Some had carport add-ons with newer cars resting beneath. Most were painted, the colors a jarring contrast to the dismal sky and uniformly dead landscape.

What sort of favor did he think he was doing? He certainly wasn't favoring her with his company. That was for damned sure. At least he hadn't attacked her. She'd have to wait, it seemed, to find out where they were going and what he planned to do when they got there.

Not for the first time, she was glad to have the reaper at her back.

They pulled into the driveway of a house with new powder-blue siding and a charming lawn. To her surprise, the grass was green. Every other house on the street, along the drive, and as far as she could tell, the entire state, was brown with only a hint of green in patches. Hanging baskets of blooming flowers cascaded from hooks along the carport's roof. She marveled at the reds, yellows, and purples, not to mention the fragrance that caressed her senses when they exited the vehicle. It was like stepping into a patch of spring.

An older woman wearing an apron stepped out on the front porch, looking like she'd stepped out of a 1950s sitcom. White curls blossomed out of her scalp and around a face distinguished by a strong jaw, high cheekbones, and striking blue eyes. The woman wore plenty of makeup, but wore it as well as she wore her age. She crossed her arms and scowled at Briggs, cocking her head to one side, her gaze as intense as a bird of prey's.

"Her stories are on. She won't talk to you right now. Come back in an hour."

Briggs grinned. "Come on, Auntie. That's no way to greet your favorite sister's son."

The woman kept the scowl, but her gaze lit with wry amusement. "You're my sister's only son, thank the good lord. Why aren't you working?"

"Station'll call if they need me. I got some folks here who need to contact the loa."

Briggs' aunt made a sour face. "I don't like it. You know I don't like it. Coming here to my house and asking for that ungodly—"

"It's my house, Auntie," Briggs said, not unkindly, but firm. "You don't have to like it, but you'll respect Gran and her ways."

She sighed and looked away. "I take care of her, don't I?"

Briggs walked across the lawn, up the steps, and enfolded the woman in a warm embrace. "You do."

Briggs turned his head and nodded to Vivian and the reaper. "This is Vivian Bedford from Tennessee, and her friend, Lazarus Darkmore. Auntie Olive takes care of Gran better than Gran's good for nothing son ever did."

Olive, who'd pulled out of her nephew's arms to get a better look at them, laughed and patted Briggs on the back. "Just like you took care of me when my Otis passed. Your daddy was no good, but you? You're your mama's boy through and through."

Vivian made her way to the front porch and extended her hand. "Pleased to meet you, Miss Olive."

Auntie Olive eyed Vivian with interest as she shook her hand. "You don't look the type to go running around looking for mumbo jumbo."

Darkmore coughed, which Vivian suspected was meant to cover a scoff. Plastering on what she hoped was a winning smile, Vivian said, "You'd be surprised."

To her surprise, Darkmore bent low and kissed Olive's hand, a move that made Briggs all but growl. Olive didn't mind the attention at all, gushing over his manners while ushering them into the house.

The interior was dark, a combination of small windows covered with thick curtains and dark wood paneling. Heavy furniture in faded wood made the room seem smaller. No, that was memories of her late sister's room. To any other person, the space would feel homey and welcoming. All it inspired in Vivian was claustrophobia and a muted sense of unease. A couple of prints hung above a floral sofa. A matador and an elegant Spanish lady surveyed the scene with eyes that seemed to track their movements. Surrounding these were a variety of family photos spanning generations. She recognized a younger Briggs standing between a woman who resembled Auntie Olive, presumably Briggs' mother, and a tall, imposing man in military uniform. Unlike his son, Briggs senior's head was covered with tight, cropped curls, his dark eyes filled with wariness. She recognized the look. A veteran who'd seen too much, done too much to return to normal life.

Waylon Briggs had that look, too. He'd seen too much in a faraway desert.

Faded rugs covered much older carpet, clean but worn, and a collection of knickknacks that only an older woman could assemble littered the surfaces of end tables, an old sideboard, and an ancient stereo system that probably hadn't played a tune in several decades. More family photos were scattered between the detritus of porcelain figurines, souvenir ashtrays from places like Destin, Myrtle Beach, and one from Las Vegas.

Those photos showed a long tradition of interracial marriage in the family, a testament to the family's legacy of defiance and fortitude. Some of those pictures were taken prior to the 1960s when anti-miscegenation laws were still on the books and brutally enforced—officially and otherwise. Vivian considered how that mixture of family pride and constant vigilance would shape its members.

Olive had disappeared through a heavy door after inviting them in. She reemerged with a tray full of drinks and cookies. Sweet tea, most likely, and she'd bet those cookies were homemade. She accepted a glass and a cookie with thanks, as did Darkmore. Briggs took a glass and sat on one of the mismatched love seats.

Taking his cue, Vivian and Darkmore sat opposite him on a small sofa, leaving Olive to take what was clearly the seat of power in the room. Most recliners didn't normally double as a throne, but most recliners didn't host Auntie Olive. For all of her deference to her nephew, it was clear that Olive was in charge in the household space.

Olive took a sip of tea before speaking, her attention focused on Briggs. "She's been better this week. She'll be glad to see you."

"You mean she'll know me this time," he said, almost snorting. "Even when she doesn't recognize me, *they* do."

A moue of distaste crossed her fine features, but she didn't comment. Presumably "they" were something of the supernatural realm. His Gran must have a connection, then, like her grandson. Either Olive refused to believe, which seemed unlikely given her straightforward manner, or she was uncomfortable with it.

"They might not like your friends," Olive said, studying her cookie. "They give her enough trouble. She deserves her peace."

Darkmore spoke, his voice pleasant and neutral. "We'll preserve her peace. I give you my word."

Briggs gave the reaper a sharp look. Olive, apparently still in the grip of Darkmore's charms, flashed a shy smile. "Did Waylon tell you about her?"

Vivian tensed. She had no idea what Darkmore intended, but it likely wasn't good. Not necessarily evil, but the reaper was rarely neutral. It was in his nature to inspire and inflict pain, cause chaos, stir trouble. Olive had done nothing to deserve the reaper's...interest.

Not as far as Vivian knew. She shuddered. The reaper could see into the deepest darkest corners of mortal hearts, minds, and souls. Vivian had experienced that firsthand.

As if sensing her discomfort, Darkmore relaxed his posture and smiled. "She carries far too many burdens. Most of the elders do. Vivian has a...calming effect on troubled souls. Whatever the loa share with us will not harm or frighten one such as mambo asogwe Bijoux Briggs."

Briggs barked out a laugh filled with more bitterness than mirth. "She hasn't been *that* for a long time. Stopped practicing when she left Haiti, around about the time her mind started going soft."

Olive scowled at him. "Fine way to talk about your elders. Suppose you'll badmouth me when I get dementia."

"No badmouthing. It's the truth." Briggs turned to Vivian, pointedly ignoring the reaper. She didn't blame him. Darkmore knew more than he should. Being trapped in corporeal form hadn't robbed him of his dark gifts. "We brought her here in 2010, after the earthquake. She was already old then. Probably would've died if we'd left her. Never was the same after the move."

"Alzheimer's," Olive said.

"Trauma," Briggs countered. "She doesn't want to remember what happened, so she sits and watches soap operas all day and lets the loa come and go as they please."

Vivian frowned. "What are the loa?"

Briggs kept his eyes on the reaper while answering her question. "Spirits. Not Bondye, but those a step or two lower, like the saints in Catholicism. They're intercessors."

Like us, she thought, or more accurately, like guardian and reaper spirits, perhaps. Intercessors, but for what? Did they intercede between the world of spirits and living? Did they grant favors to the righteous or faithful? Were they evil or benign, or both, or neither?

"What do they do, and what do they want in return?" she asked.

Briggs turned his unreadable gaze to her. "The spirits can offer advice, if they feel like it. Some look out for their descendants, or take care of unfinished business if they can find someone to act as their instrument. Some carry messages or prophecy. Some are probably just bored if they haven't moved on."

That was interesting. Then, all of a sudden, it dawned on her. Voudon. Jeanne told her she'd been in touch with some of the spirits familiar with the practice, and Briggs had mentioned he knew someone. That had to be it. No wonder the reaper was so interested. The key to severing the ties that bound him to his mortal form might be found in these spirits.

But at what cost?

Briggs clearly wasn't keen on dragging his Gran into it. She didn't blame him. Guardian spirits and especially reapers craved the life forces of humans who were infirm, vulnerable, and unable to live the sorts of "normal," functional lives that most people took for granted. That he'd allowed Vivian to bring Darkmore astounded her. Darkmore, who'd coveted Mae's powerful soul trapped in a helpless shell of a body and, she hoped to all the fates, a blissfully unaware mind.

"Will you excuse me for a moment," Vivian said in a voice that only shook a little. "I need some air."

Darkmore blocked her escape route through the door they'd used to enter, so she spun on her heel and stumbled from the living room through a hallway that led to a mudroom, one with a door leading outside.

What she found in the backyard took her breath away.

CHAPTER FIFTEEN

The green lawn and hanging flower baskets she'd seen in front of the house had nothing on the backyard.

Bordered by the same chain link fence, most of the metal was concealed by winding vines, shrubs, and trees, enclosing the small patch of paradise from the outside world. Like the front, green accentuated by brilliant bursts of color filled the small space. Flowers grew in haphazard patches. The patches were bordered by stones or pieces of wood and were free of weeds, but without rhyme or reason behind the design. Old, rotting barrels sprung from the ground like relics of the trees they'd once been and filled to bursting with petunias, marigolds, dusty millers, and other familiar plants.

Strange. They were past the season for these flowers. It was time for mums and winter pansies, not heat-loving varieties that had already withered and died in the Tennessee chill. Mississippi was warmer, but not that much, and the surrounding landscape was so dry and barren.

A vision of Zeke's grave flashed through her mind, yellow blooms and green in the midst of winter, and her heart lurched with the ache of loss and desolation.

"Olive? Is that you?"

The voice was strong and clear in contrast to its bearer. Sitting in the corner of the yard under the shadow of wisteria was a woman dressed in dainty button-down shirt and slacks pressed to perfection, her gnarled hands on her lap. She held something resembling a well-worn handkerchief, twisting it as if nervous.

"No, ma'am," Vivian said, taking slow, careful steps toward the woman so she wouldn't spook her. "My name is Vivian. I'm a...friend of Waylon's. He thought you could help me with a, um, a spiritual problem."

Dark, vacant eyes turned to gaze at Vivian. The woman was beautiful. Vivian was pleased to see her clean hair shining in the bright autumn sunlight, shimmering almost as brightly as her painted nails. Olive clearly took good care of her, as did Briggs, apparently. For all of his bitterness and military stoicism, the man cared for his family. Vivian stopped a few feet short of the woman's bench.

Something else glowed around her, brighter than her shiny hair and fancy nails, brighter than the sun in the sky above her.

Waylon Briggs' Gran carried more spirit light energy than any living soul Vivian had ever encountered, except for Mae. Power, raw and enticing, emanated from every pore. How did they safeguard her from greedy guardian and reaper spirits, especially with a living soul broker at the ready for harvest?

Mrs. Briggs shook her head and finally seemed to see Vivian. She furrowed her brows and clutched her handkerchief tighter. "Were you talking to me, honey? I am sorry. My mind is not what it once was. I get confused..."

Vivian's heart broke for her. Before time and age ravaged her mind, she must have been a force to be reckoned with. Her voice ran over Vivian like a warm summer breeze, lovely with a hint of French, but it held a trace of power and authority. Darkmore had called her mambo asogwe, her title spoken with great reverence. Lazarus Darkmore said many things about humanity, but reverence was not something he bestowed upon most mortals.

Bijoux Briggs must be powerful.

Vivian knelt beside her. "It's okay. I didn't mean to disturb you. Your flowers are beautiful."

A smile graced Mrs. Briggs' face, one filled with childlike delight. "They do grow well here, don't they? And in all seasons, even when it gets hot enough to fry an egg on the sidewalk. Weather is no match for the loa."

The hairs on the nape of Vivian's neck rose as the temperature around the woman rose. She blinked as the energy and light flitted to and fro, taking shape and then disappearing before she could make out the faces of the spirits. The light came closer. Vivian fought the urge to flinch, to back away, and to run in terror.

"It's all right," Mrs. Briggs said. "They are curious about you. They want to taste your light and know you."

"Bad idea," Vivian said, standing and backing away. "The last time one of the powerful dead tasted my light, it didn't end well. That's why I'm here."

Mrs. Briggs' face changed. A new, different intelligence shone through her gaze, this one darker, cunning. It smiled, twisting the old woman's face into a rictus of malevolence.

"Yes. You are a raiser of the dead. Rare. Coveted. These fools would have you raise them, too." The entity flicked Mrs. Briggs' wrist, indicating the spirits floating around them. "Fools. They would be trapped in a mortal body, a sack of meat decaying all around them. There's no freedom in such a form."

"Who are you?" Vivian asked. "One of the loa?"

"I am the one you seek, soul broker. You want to free your reaper. What would you offer me in exchange for the means to free him?"

Bargaining with the spirits was tricky, particularly unknown spirits. The temperature suggested guardian spirit, who tended to run hot. But that didn't necessarily mean "good." And she had sense enough to realize that there was a lot more out there than she'd seen. Darkmore might know this one, but she wasn't ready to bring him into the negotiations quite yet.

Nor was she ready to bring Darkmore near Mrs. Briggs, the fragile mortal vessel for a vast and tempting well of spirit energy.

"I don't know who or what you are, so I cannot imagine what I have that would be of value to you."

The laugh that came from Mrs. Briggs' throat was deep, rich, and malevolent. It was also familiar. Vivian knew very little about Voudon, but Darkmore had briefed her on the basics. Rather than being all about dark magic and blood rites, it seemed to be steeped in the African tradition of honoring one's ancestors.

"You're Waylon's father?" She tried not to make it sound like a question. Her intuition was good, but not infallible. If she'd played her hunch wrong, she might offend the spirit.

"No, child, but you're on the right path. The body I've borrowed is one of my line, as is Waylon. As for what you might have to offer me, you've managed something necromancers through the ages could only dream of—you raised the dead."

She shivered, hoping it didn't show. "Not exactly. Darkmore wasn't dead." Not as far as she knew. "At least, he was more than a departed spirit."

"You caught him," the voice said, dark and full of avarice. "He's bound to this plane and bound to you. You own him."

"No," she said, horrified at the prospect. Did this evil spirit want to own Darkmore? She didn't intend to return him to his former state to turn him over as a slave. That was the very fate they were trying to avoid. Should Darkmore die while trapped in this mortal form, his soul would emerge as that of a newly departed, powerless, low on the afterlife management totem pole, and fair game for any more powerful spirits to claim.

Darkmore had made a lot of enemies over his long, long existence. Plenty of spirits would be pleased to own him. Their vengeance would be slow, painful, and quite possibly eternal.

But the spirit would know that. Apparently, he knew she wanted to set the reaper free. So, it stood to reason that he would want her to raise another spirit from the dead, possibly to own and control. Though she knew little of the loa, possession of those who venerated these spirits was part of the ritual, just as the powerful spirit currently occupying the body of Waylon's Gran had possessed her. It was a temporary arrangement as far as she knew.

If the loa depended upon possession to work their magic and enforce their will upon the world, having a living minion would come in handy.

"You want me to make a zombie for you?" she said, incredulous. "That's a little cliché."

"Your reaper isn't a zombie. He has free will...for the most part. But if you command him, he will do your bidding. You might not even have to use your authority, smitten as he is."

She'd have to think on that little revelation later. The idea of commanding the reaper, or any living or formerly living entity, was uncomfortable. Such power could be seductive and, she feared, addictive.

"But you want me to resurrect someone, or encase some spirit in a mortal form. To be honest, I'm not sure how I managed the first time. I only wanted to save Darkmore, to heal him so he wouldn't die in his corporeal form."

The spirit smiled at her. It was all wrong on the old woman's face. The regal, wizened face wasn't made for that kind of malevolence. "You'll call upon those powers again when the time is right, and you'll save two lives and many souls."

That didn't sound too bad.

"There will be a price."

Vivian sighed. "Isn't there always?"

"Don't be flippant, child. You've only glimpsed at what awaits beyond the veil, but enough, I think, to respect it, revere it, and fear it."

Vivian bit back a smart-assed comment. She may not like whatever had taken over the old woman, but it was right. There was much to fear in the afterlife. She'd seen suffering on a scale barely fathomable during her trip to the reaper's dark realm. His was but one of many, and the dark things that lived in those places, that ruled them, knew what scared the souls trapped within. The dark things brought terror, pain, and ultimate suffering to life in vivid, agonizing detail.

Speaking of dark things and torment, it was time to end this conversation. "What do you want from me?" she asked.

"Maeve's vision revealed most of what I want. There's a traitor in your midst, one my descendant cannot—or will not—see. A trickster. You must root out the trickster and put Waylon back on the path he wishes to follow, futile though it may be."

The trickster, the raven...that must mean Briggs was the bear and she the wolf symbolized in her vision. Yeah, finding someone in Briggs' blind spot would be problematic on so many levels, not the least of would be convincing Briggs when she found the traitor. She had access to finances, which could prove useful. A traitor in their midst might be siphoning cash, if the traitor's motive was sabotage. The other currency in which the rebels dealt, soul energy, could prove more problematic. First, she'd have to discover where the rebels stored their excess spirit energy.

Darkmore could help.

Then again, there could be an easier explanation, one in plain sight. "Are you the repository of soul energy?"

The entity possessing Mrs. Briggs said, "No." Her expression was neutral, almost deliberately so.

"Let me rephrase," Vivian said. "Is mambo asogwe Bijoux Briggs the repository?"

Mrs. Briggs' face split into a malevolent grin. "She receives what Waylon collects. My descendant isn't completely stupid. Neither are you, it seems. No one in the rebellion knows about the mambo. Should the traitor discover her, it would be disastrous."

The fact that Briggs trusted Vivian, not to mention the reaper, with such a secret, spoke volumes of the trust he apparently had in her. Or was it simply part of the bargain? She'd offered her services in exchange for his help in freeing the reaper. Was it honor, or did he suspect something was off with his rebellion?

"Why does he trust me? Why do you?" she asked.

"This isn't the first time you've gotten your reaper friend out of a jam, and at great personal cost. You've freed many souls, used your gifts to assist the living, and you defied the Archangel Guardian Council. Your sense of honor and your abilities make you a valuable asset to my descendant. And to me."

"Why don't you just tell Briggs all of this yourself?"

"Where would the fun be in that? I don't get out much. There are so few vessels, and I have what you might call a timeshare arrangement with the mambo. I'm an observer, as is the nature of the loa...mostly. And before you ask, no, he won't believe you if you simply tell him. Blind spot. My descendant does everything the hard way, much like you. Do we have a bargain?"

"Not yet," she said, thinking fast. "You want me to look out for Waylon and raise someone from the dead for you in exchange for restoring the reaper to his former state. You've asked me for two things that will apparently cost me. What else will you grant me?"

The entity laughed. "You certainly live up to your reputation for recklessness and audacity. I cannot grant your greatest wish. You shall always be a soul broker in this life."

"And the next?"

"That is not for me to say. But the mambo and I can give you something else you crave. Half your payment in advance, the full payment upon completion of your end of the bargain."

Before Vivian could ask what the entity meant, Mrs. Briggs' face changed. The malevolent smile faded, replaced by an expression of awe, wonder, and...love. Vivian took a step back as the old woman rose from her chair, handkerchief falling away. Whatever had taken over the mambo's body didn't seem to harbor ill intent, but she'd seen too many spirits to believe that this one wasn't dangerous.

Whatever it was, it was powerful. The energy pouring from Mrs. Briggs nearly brought Vivian to her knees.

"Don't be afraid." The voice was female, oddly accented, as if English wasn't its native language, but Vivian couldn't place the accent. The spirit paused, running the mambo's tongue over teeth and working her jaw as if testing the host's capacity for speech.

But Mrs. Briggs could speak on her own. Whatever had afflicted the old woman had ravaged her mind, not her body. Perhaps the spirit had suffered some speech impairment in life? The body of Mrs. Briggs took a tentative step forward and then reached out and grasped Vivian's arms to steady herself.

Power coursed through Vivian's body, rolling in waves that threatened to pull her under. Images flashed through her mind—blurred faces, amorphous shapes, some moving, some still.

She desperately wanted to track the shapes. Her heart ached when they moved out of her narrow field of view. Sometimes she could will her head to turn, but mostly it did what it wanted. At least she could track them by sound. When they didn't turn on the noisy machines and when they weren't all so loud, she enjoyed hearing their voices.

They sometimes spoke to her. She tried to speak to them, but the noises she made didn't sound like their words. Though she'd stopped trying to mimic how their mouths worked long ago, she grunted and could often manage to touch one of them. She liked it when they stroked her cheeks and hair, when they gave her food and drink, when they gave her something she could grasp in her hands. Her hands didn't work like theirs either, but she liked the way the strips of fabric wound around and through her fingers.

She liked the girl with the red hair. The one they called Sister.

Vivian reached out with a shaking hand and stroked the old woman's cheek. The entity inhabiting the mambo's body sighed and leaned into her touch, and then placed a hand over hers. Between the lump in her throat and tears streaming down her face, it was hard to speak. But there was so much to say, so much she wanted to tell the spirit inhabiting Mrs. Briggs, so many questions she needed to ask.

But she sensed the time for their visit was short.

"Mae," she whispered, voice hoarse with emotion. "I thought I'd never...see you again. How? I thought you'd moved on to the next place. A better place."

The look of horror must have registered on her face, since Mae laughed through the mambo. Strange. The face and form belonged to Mrs. Briggs, but some subtle shift in expression or gesture made it clear when someone other than the old mambo was speaking. More than that, it was her eyes. The gaze that shone when Mrs. Briggs had been alone in her person had shown confusion, the bleary-eyed vacancy that came with dementia or, in the few moments when she was herself, wisdom and cunning. The first spirit who'd possessed her, the ancestor, had held cunning and cruelty as well as wry amusement.

The spirit of Vivian's sister shone through the mambo's gaze with love, childlike wonder, and power. So much power. It moved through the body Mae inhabited and then surged through Vivian like a jolt of lightning, making it hard to breathe. The energy Vivian normally absorbed from the living and those ready to cross was potent, but nothing compared to this.

Did Mae still carry the spirit energy that had been trapped within her while she lived?

A horrifying thought made Vivian grab the mambo by the shoulders. It was like latching on to a live wire. "You aren't still trapped, are you?"

"No," she said. Then, noticing Vivian's discomfort, she pulled the spirit energy back within the mambo's body. "I am free to come and go, but it is... difficult to speak with the living without a conduit. I would have come sooner, but you've been hidden."

"Yeah," Vivian said, wiping tears from her eyes. "I got into trouble with the guardian spirits and had to go on the run."

She cocked Mrs. Briggs' head to the side as if thinking. Then she nodded. "You are here to fight them. Good. They are greedy. They take too much and leave souls in limbo. I would feed them all if I could but I, too, am on the...run?"

"From who? Did the guardians get to you, too? Mae, you can—"

Mae held up the mambo's hands. "Slower, please. I have to use the mind of this woman to...understand your words and reply. Speech is strange."

Oh, God. Of course it would be.

In life, Mae's disabilities left her completely helpless, incapable of speech, most voluntary movement and, Vivian had thought, comprehension. Based on the memories she'd shown Vivian, Mae had some limited perception of the people and things around her, as well as a deep longing to interact with those people. Profound frustration had flowed through Vivian's mind, Mae's frustration with the inability to express her wants, needs, and feelings.

"I will see you again," Mae said. "Soon. The other spirit promised. I am safe and fighting with you. He is with me. Our guardian. I will carry the light this woman's body holds to spirits in need, as I have each time her kin have brought it to her. Bring more. As much as you can. We almost have enough."

"Enough for what? And who is with you?" Vivian now understood part of the mystery of Briggs' operation. He and his rebels mediated spirit crossings at a discount and took the energy they collected to Mrs. Briggs, a woman who still held the power to commune with spirits in spite of her mental decline. Spirits like Mae could take that energy and distribute it to other spirits in need, mediating more crossings.

But that last part, the part about almost having enough, gave her pause. What else was Briggs up to?

"I have to go," Mae said through Mrs. Briggs, with obvious reluctance. "Find the one who is working against Waylon and bring the light he has hidden. We need all we can before we strike."

"Strike? Wait, Mae, are you telling me we're going to war with the Archangel Guardian Council?"

This time the smile that graced the mambo's face was full of battle lust and the zeal of a new soldier. "Yes, and we will bring them down. Every. Last. One."

CHAPTER SIXTEEN

To his credit, Briggs didn't ask too many questions about Vivian's chat with his Gran. When she'd stumbled back into the living room, he'd simply arched a brow and asked if she had what she'd come for. She'd said yes and then told him she had some things to do before she came back for another visit to sort things out with the reaper.

If he was curious, confused, or troubled, he didn't let it show. He'd simply nodded, thanked his aunt for her hospitality, and after giving Vivian and Darkmore a chance to do the same, he drove them back to base.

When they got to the apartment Vivian shared with the reaper, Darkmore excused himself out of courtesy, giving her a chance to speak with Briggs.

"Work on your aim," he said. "We're going on a raid in two days. Got a lot of trapped souls holed up at the old asylum. I need you and Chet at my back."

That was surprising. "Thought you weren't impressed with my demo."

"Never said that, Miss Tennessee. I pushed you to see what you could do. Next to me and Chet, you're the best we've got, especially out of these new trainees. You saw that for yourself."

True, but something else bothered her about the situation. "Who else do you have on board besides the other trainees? You've been at this for a while. Where's the rest of your team?"

Briggs grinned. "Most of those who pass our boot camp go on to other cells. The other rebel cells aren't organized enough to know their elbows from their asses. Dangerous. We send out our fighters to keep their people alive. Most of them end up running the show once the regulars figure out their leaders are shit."

"I get it," she said, sardonically. "Plant enough of your guys in the other factions and you can get them all on your side."

Briggs' grin widened. "I plant my gals, too, Miss Tennessee. Spirit light fighting requires skill, not brute strength. And I'm keeping more of us alive. Not many living soul brokers out there. We need as many fighters as we can get. And, yeah, I want them on my side. We need strategy, unity, and discipline if we're going to win this war."

"And spirit energy?" she said.

His smile faded and he started to pace. "What else did Gran tell you?"

She leaned against the door and forced her body to relax. It would do her no good to rile her new boss up. She needed him to trust her if she was going to save his operation from the traitor in their midst. Briggs may be arrogant and ruthless, but he was right. Even in the short time she'd spent in his camp, she could tell it was a well-organized operation that protected its members while giving them the skills they needed to protect themselves and others. It wasn't just ruthlessness and fear that inspired loyalty to him. The soldiers he'd planted in other rebel groups could just as easily decide to split and work for their own interests and agendas once they rose through the ranks to become leaders.

But they hadn't.

The records she and Gutierrez reviewed showed that most, if not all, of the rebel groups scattered throughout the Americas trusted Briggs to manage their finances, and Gutierrez had heard that Briggs spent hours on the phone and Internet discussing strategy and coordinated attacks.

His former trainees appeared to trust him implicitly.

"Okay," she said. "Tell me more about this mission, and the war that's coming."

"The mission is just what I said. A raid on the Mississippi Asylum for the Insane."

A cold chill crept up her spine, one that had nothing to do with the reapers. "Insane Asylums are still a thing? That seems so...barbaric."

Briggs shrugged. "Not really. It shut down in the 1930s, but it was open long enough to accumulate a bunch ghosts who can't pass on—and some the guardians won't let pass on."

"Won't let? I don't understand—"

The blood froze in her veins as realization dawned. Those bastards. Guardian and reapers spirits coveted people with mental challenges and illness as much as those with physically incapacitating disabilities. They accumulated an abundance of unspent spirit energy as a side effect of their conditions. Rather than offering a peaceful crossing to the afterlife, one that would free them from the suffering they'd endured while living, it seemed the guardian spirits in charge of this part of Mississippi had exploited the souls of the inmates and kept them as an energy source.

"They're using them as batteries. That's sick!"

"It is," Briggs agreed. "We're going to set them free and take what energy we can from them, hopefully enough to make a move on the Archangel Guardian Council."

It seemed like a good strategy, and yet... "How does that make us any better than the guardians?"

Briggs scowled. "You want all of that energy to go to the enemy? Or get wasted?"

"No," Vivian said. "I want the spirits we liberate to use it. I've seen what they can do. My sister," she paused, fighting the lump in her throat and unshed tears. "When she died, she set millions of souls free from the reaper's realm, and she used only a fraction of her power. We should get these spirits on our side."

She braced for a fight. Briggs wasn't the type to take unsolicited advice, especially from someone he considered a subordinate. He had no reason to trust or believe her. There was only one way to convince him, but the prospect filled her with more dread than her visit with the mambo had.

But she'd seen into the depths of his soul. Whatever happened on that far away war zone had nearly cost Briggs his life. He'd only survived by becoming a living soul broker. Like her, and the others in his camp and in scattered cells throughout the US, his near brush with death had left him between worlds. As if that wasn't traumatic enough, he'd become an unwilling agent of the guardian spirit who'd claimed him, forced to serve and deliver spirit light until he managed to break free.

The least she could do was share her story, which would also show Briggs the truth of her words.

Before he could pull away, she channeled a low burst of light from her fingertips and grasped him by the arm, focusing on her memories.

Car crash, blood, a dying man.

Zeke.

She took his hand and he filled her with the cold of the reaper and the heat of the guardian, two powerful forces vying for his soul. Breath and life were leaving his body, and she couldn't stop it. She wanted, needed to save him.

She failed.

The vision of a friendly looking old redneck flashed through her mind. Ezra, the guardian who was supposed to collect her soul, his warmth and comfort soothing the ache of the man's loss—of Zeke's loss—and the well of sorrow she bore by caring for her disabled, dying sister.

Memories of Darkmore, the reaper Ezra had cheated by taking Zeke instead of her, flooded their connection. The reaper's icy rage found a target in her soul. He reached into the darkest corners of her heart and soul and unleashed unspeakable horrors.

At the center of it all, the heart of the matter, was Mae.

Filtering through the worst parts of that horrible night when the reaper almost inspired Vivian to harm her helpless sister, she showed Briggs her story. She and Zeke working to protect Mae from the reaper, only to find out that Ezra had his sights set on Mae, too, eager to harvest the spirit light that coursed through her broken body.

Finding out the truth—she'd been meant to die, but Ezra let her live and took Zeke instead, robbing the reaper of his soul and making a play for the prize that was Mae's soul. Losing Zeke. She'd lost them both, and there was still a gaping hole in her soul that hadn't healed from the loss, might never heal.

She willed the memories forward, unwilling to relive the pain of betrayal, loss, and longing.

Bracing herself against him, she fed Briggs the memory of her sister's soul crossing through Darkmore's dark realm, unleashing her spirit light to set free the souls trapped there in hell, purgatory, or whatever other name encompassed the despair embodied in that horrible place.

Light flashed, Mae's light, and then Vivian's mind went dark.

"Damn." Briggs' voice sounded hoarse and ragged.

They were on the ground. Shit, had she passed out? Double shit, she'd fallen on top of Briggs, her limbs tangled with his and her body pressed tight against him. Vivian fought the urge to scramble, which would likely result in more friction than either of them needed or wanted in this awkward situation.

Oddly enough, the physical awkwardness went a long way to alleviating the emotional aftermath of the encounter.

With great care and near painful slowness, Vivian rolled her body off Briggs and scooted away. He sat up and scrubbed his face with both hands. She didn't know if he was hiding tears or exasperation, but she took the opportunity to wipe away her own tears and regain her composure.

"How long was your sister..."

She smiled in spite of herself. Seemed she wasn't the only one suffering from an acute case of awkward shyness. Briggs didn't usually have trouble being blunt. "You mean how long was she severely disabled? All her life."

"Huh," he said. "At least Gran had a good run when her mind was there. I'm sorry."

"Me, too." Vivian wasn't sure he'd heard her whisper until a large, warm hand landed on her shoulder. She patted his hand and met his gaze. "So will you think about recruiting some of those hostage souls? If they can do a tenth of what Mae managed, they'd make powerful allies."

"You think you can get through to them?" He stood and stretched.

"They weren't all there in life. Can't imagine decades in the tender care of their guardian captors has helped."

That was true enough. In her experience, lost and lonely souls were too scared or too far gone for conversation, let alone reasoning with—though she'd had some success with an old lost and lonely ghost who'd latched on to a friend's young son and became his protector. Maybe Junior could help?

She'd have to figure out how to summon him, but that would be the least of her worries. Briggs was planning a raid. The damaged, vulnerable, tortured souls would be even more traumatized by a battle. Some of them might even get injured in the crossfire. It would be better, smarter, to find a way to get a message to them, let them know to stay out of the way or be ready to rise up against the guardians holding them captive.

That thought was on the tip of her tongue, but something held her back. If the vision she'd received from Maeve, "kindly" interpreted by the loa she'd encountered earlier, was to be believed, Briggs had a traitor in his midst. That traitor might be after spirit energy, sabotage, or a coup to oust Briggs as leader. No matter his—or her—motivation, the souls at the asylum were at risk. She couldn't stop Briggs from sharing her advice with his inner circle, though she could ask. But she could protect those poor souls by warning them ahead of time that they couldn't trust anyone but Briggs.

And she'd have to do that in secret.

"All I can do is try," she answered. "If we can take out the guardians keeping them captive and do it quickly, I'll give it my best shot. If they'd rather just cross over, we can go with your plan and harvest a bit of their energy as they go. But if even a few want to join, it might give us an edge when we go against the council. What have we got to lose?"

Briggs appeared to consider, which gave her time to think. She'd need an excuse to sneak off base and find a way to speak to the spirits at the asylum without being detected by the guardian sentinels. And she'd have to make sure no one from based tailed her. Everyone in camp was a suspect at this point.

It was a toss-up which of those tasks would prove most challenging. Darkmore could likely help, but his mortal body left him with limited access to some of the powers he held as a sometimes-corporeal reaper. But they could still conceal themselves from the living, at least temporarily, with enough spirit energy.

At last, Briggs nodded. "I'll give you one shot. You'd best work fast and make it count."

"Fair enough. Let's keep this plan between the two of us for now," she said, relieved. Then, as inspiration struck, she added, "I'll need a little time off to check in with the guardian who sent me to you. She's great with lost, lonely, and tortured spirits. She can help me figure out the best way to earn their trust without making them run."

Briggs' expression hardened and she mentally kicked herself. It had been the wrong thing to ask, she realized too late. He wasn't a trusting man, couldn't afford to be, and she'd raised his suspicions. To his credit, he quickly schooled his features to neutrality and said, "No can do, Tennessee. I need you and everyone else here training hard. You'll have to make do with what you've got in the way of persuasion."

Shit.

On his way out the door, he said, "I'll see you at dinner. You and Gutierrez are on KP tonight and for breakfast tomorrow. After that, you'll hit the training courses with Chet. Rest while you can. The next couple of days will keep you busy enough."

She let her head fall back against the floor as soon as Briggs shut the door, and closed her eyes. *I'm not cut out for political games or intrigue,* she thought. No poker face, no subtlety, and no filter. It was a wonder she'd kept her association with the reaper secret from the guardian spirits for so long.

A sudden cold chill danced across her skin, part caress, and part sting.

The sting intensified, almost as cold as the reaper's voice. "You shared your light with him."

CHAPTER SEVENTEEN

She froze. Darkmore's cold voice, deceptively soft, was as predatory as seductive. It took her back to the time when she'd first encountered the reaper. He'd been purely predatory then, hungry for her pain, her suffering, for vengeance against the guardian who'd claimed the soul meant for him instead of taking her. Before she intrigued him, before he wanted her for more than her power and as the instrument of his revenge, he'd come in the guise of temptation. Beautiful, mesmerizing, and dangerous, he'd promised to grant her what her dark heart most desired.

Freedom from the burden that was Mae.

She shuddered at the memory, fresh in her mind after sharing it with Briggs. Sharing had apparently upset the reaper, which was puzzling. He'd never had a problem with the spirit light she shared with Ezra, her guardian mentor, or Zeke, her guardian spirit lover. In fact, when Zeke reappeared in her life not long ago, the reaper, though clearly interested, gave her space to take care of her "unfinished business." No signs of jealousy or male territoriality. The reaper was a patient hunter. After all, he had eternity on his side.

Until now.

She took a deep breath. He was closer now. She felt his icy presence surround her. Every instinct screamed fight. Her fingers flexed, the energy coursing through her seeking an outlet, desperate to defend against the threat. Anger rose from the reaper and found its answer in her. She didn't have time for this nonsense, and neither did he.

Suddenly, his presence was gone.

Her eyes flew open and she jumped to her feet, fear and anxiety replacing rage. Had he left? God, this day was turning into a clusterfuck of confusion, impossible tasks, and missteps.

"I'm here."

She spun around and spotted the reaper in a dark corner of the apartment, his face shadowed. She couldn't read him. He'd locked his energy and essence down tight, hiding. But she'd felt the intensity of his emotions.

"I'm sorry," she said, not quite sure what she was apologizing for.

For betrayal? No, she hadn't done anything wrong with Briggs. She'd needed the man to understand what the trapped souls they were set to liberate could do, and telling him would not have been enough.

She was still guilty over his mortal state and suffering, of course. That was part of it. But the feeling that left her aching, longing, and profoundly sad came from something else.

She'd changed the reaper.

He sighed heavily and stepped out of the shadows. "It is I who should apologize. Jealousy is delectable in others, but I find the emotion... distasteful in myself."

Taking a cautious step forward, she said, "And I'm sorry for that, too. I brought you to this, I—"

He reached out and grabbed her shoulders, enfolding her in his arms in a fierce, almost painful embrace. Oddly, the bone crushing pressure eased her deep, aching soul. A cool balm in the heat of helpless anger and regret, a calm in the midst of the storm, she held on to the reaper with all of her might.

"I didn't like you sharing with him," he whispered into her hair.

"It didn't mean anything. I had to show him what the souls he's after can do if we can bring them to our side instead of stealing from them. If I help Briggs, the loa will help you."

He stilled. Though his emotions were still clamped tight, she caught a hint of something odd. Sorrow? Regret? Longing?

"I know," he said. "I still didn't like it."

She pulled back and he allowed it, meeting her gaze with his fathomless, too-knowing eyes. With a breath for courage, she reached out and cupped his cheek, sliding her hand up to the nape of his neck and pulling him down for a kiss. Dropping her guard, she unleashed her spirit light, giving him all she was and all she had, holding nothing back. The darkness and light of a lifetime poured out of her into the reaper. He devoured what she offered and demanded more, deepening the kiss and holding her steady as she fed him all that she'd seen and done, all of her hopes, dreams, nightmares, and deepest desires.

All that she was.

That was it, she thought. The reaper didn't simply crave darkness. He enjoyed feasting on suffering and delving in to the darkest corners of human hearts, but there was...more. He craved experience, knowledge of the human condition.

What was it he'd said the night they arrive in Jackson? *I thought I had experienced enough suffering in my many mortal lives to understand all facets of the darkness you humans carry in your souls. I have endured everything.*

But had he really? She didn't think so.

Looking back over all she'd been through with Lazarus Darkmore, she found him to be as much a student of the human condition and its darkness as he was teacher in the dark purgatory of his realm. He wanted to know people, what made them think, act, tick, break, and triumph.

He wanted to know her.

And now, he did.

She pulled away, trembling, feeling as though she'd been psychologically and spiritually flayed. Exposed, vulnerable, completely open to the reaper in mortal man's clothing. What would he do with what she'd given him? Her base, primitive instincts told her to run. He was a predator, a stealer of souls. Darker instincts coiled within her and screamed that she become predator. Spirit light coursed through her body and soul. He hadn't taken all of her light, not even a fraction. Her greatest weapon coiled in her fingertips, just beneath the surface and ready to strike.

She forced it back deep within her. Darkmore was not her enemy. He'd saved her from the greed of the guardian spirit who played as mentor but used her for his own gain. He'd protected her from the guardian council at great personal cost. She would not destroy him. He was hers to protect.

Darkmore's eyes were shut tight, breath ragged and rasping, his body in the grip of small tremors.

Summoning her courage, Vivian cleared her throat and said, "So, are we good?"

"No," he said, his voice low and husky. "But we will be."

He kissed her, hard and bruising, pulling her against his body and then pinning her to the wall. She should have been terrified. Even in his mortal form, the reaper possessed an unnatural strength of body, mind, and will. He could destroy her, had nearly done so once, not long ago.

Now, his coolness soothed the fire raging within her soul and gave her shelter from all of life's storms. He met his match in her as she savaged his mouth and raked her nails hard down his back, rough enough to bruise, to wound, and he welcomed it, growling his approval.

He bit her lip and she screamed, pushing him back, wrapping her legs around his waist, and holding onto him, an anchor in a roiling sea. Instead of fighting her, he brought them to the ground and surrendered to her, at least for a moment. Once she straddled him, he ripped off her shirt and bra, savaging her flesh. Breathless, wanting, she tore at his clothing until he rolled them and somehow managed to disrobe them both.

The soothing balm of his chill contrasted with their rough joining. In spite of his power, he again yielded to her, allowing her to engulf him with all that she was, pouring her light and her heat and everything she had into him. He craved human experience. She gave it to him until they were both breathless and spent.

————

Drifting off to sleep, she caught a glimpse of a faraway land, one of sand and stone, hot and dry, a village built from sandy stone, windows covered with rich fabrics. The decadent scents of roasting meat and grain filled her senses, as did the unexpected rush of water. An oasis? No, a river, they were close to a river. Men and women dressed in robes, some drab, some brilliant in color and luxurious in texture, heads covered or dark, braided locks swaying with the movement of the people in sandaled feet upon dusty streets.

There, yet not, in the logic of what had to be a dream, she wandered the streets with no sense of time or place, though it was surely some ancient time. No cars or any other machines, no lights, but plenty of animals and manpower in the streets and the fields beyond. There were sheep and goats, but no chickens. Horses and ox-like beasts transported people in chariots and—

She stopped, or perhaps whatever lens allowed her to visit this strange place came under her control when she spotted a man busy etching symbols upon a stone tablet. No, not stone, it was clay. The symbols weren't from any language she recognized. She moved on, drawn to a small dwelling at the end of one of the side streets, shadowed from the heat of the day and secluded. A sound, raspy and gurgling, came from within the dwelling. It called to her, but also filled her with dread and a strange revulsion she couldn't explain. The pitiful cries almost masked soft sobs. A harsh female voice spoke, and all sounds stopped.

She didn't want to see what was inside those walls, but she could not look away.

Past the linen curtain that covered the entrance, inside the dark space, a woman sat on a stool, her eyes red and swollen, tears still falling freely. Another woman, this one dressed differently, richly, adorned with jewelry and tattooed, head shaved. She exuded authority and power. Priestess? Shaman? Healer?

The woman on the stool sought a healer, but not for herself. The bundle on the ground in front of her feet writhed and wiggled. It was the source of those strange sounds, the sounds that were wrong, inhuman. Something came loose from the bundle, its shadow large and looming in the light of the fire. A limb? But it was...wrong. The skin was blotched, almost... rotting. Sores covered it, and there were misshapen stumps where fingers should be.

Tiny fingers, the fingers of a baby.

Oh, God, she wanted to run away. She wanted to snatch the thing that should have been a child and...what? Heal it? It looked beyond healing, beyond hope. The gurgling sounds were achingly familiar, the sounds that came from Mae's ailing lungs. The baby could barely breathe, the inside of its body likely as ravaged by disease and decay as the outside. The woman, this poor creature's mother, begged the priestess for help.

Vivian begged, too, knowing that her plea was in vain. There were no herbs that could cure, no salves to sooth, no teas, potions, or incantations that could right the terrible affliction. She doubted modern medicine would help, or would have helped, since what she was witnessing had occurred in the past. The priestess muttered under her breath, then paused. Something caught her attention, something lurking in the corner of the room. The mother didn't appear to notice, but Vivian saw it.

Saw *her*.

Felt the chill on her skin and bone deep terror. This was a reaper.

First reaper. Names whispered through Vivian's mind—Ereshkigal, Nyx, Nephthys, Persephone. She would have many names, but here, she was only death. She had come for the child. The priestess approved.

Vivian screamed.

———

Strong arms enveloped her as she came to her senses. She was in bed. He must have carried her there after she'd fallen asleep. Cool waves of calm filled her as Darkmore stroked her back and whispered soothing words in a language she didn't understand, yet was familiar.

She pulled herself together and met his gaze. "That was no dream, was it? It was a vision. Was it yours?"

His face turned to stone, gaze remote and older than any she'd ever seen. Oh, yeah, it had been a vision, something from the past, from *his* past. He hadn't meant for her to see, or perhaps he regretted showing her after the fact, but this was deeply personal for the reaper.

"I trusted you," she said quietly. "I showed you all of me, Lazarus. Everything."

"And you wish the same of me," he said. It wasn't a question. He knew.

She blinked back tears and fought to keep her voice steady. Perhaps she'd read him wrong. True, they'd shared much, and he cared for her. He wanted her for his own, but she'd thought...

Hope was a dangerous thing. Stupid. He was only with her because she'd rendered him mortal, trapped him in this body and, accidentally, bound him to her.

"Never mind. Forget I mentioned it. I can leave if you like and sleep on the sofa."

She tugged at the sheet. Stupid, considering he'd seen her bare soul as well as her naked body, but she'd had enough exposure for one night. If he didn't want to share his secrets, she didn't want to know them.

He put an arm around her and sighed. "Must you always run away?"

She bit back an ugly reply. He was right, of course. What the hell, she'd already given him the deepest, darkest corners of her soul, and the brightest. Another confession hardly mattered. "I forgot...until now."

"Forgot what?"

"What you are. What I am in comparison. Insignificant by comparison, hardly a blip on your radar after thousands of lifetimes and millions of souls. It's not your fault. You're stuck with me and in your mortal form, and this is just another one of many experiences you'll add to your collection."

He took a breath, and she rushed to finish before he could speak. "It's fine. Forget it. Let's go back to the way things were and make the most of our time together before I restore you to your original form."

"My original form," he said, the bitterness in his voice giving her pause. "Trust. Insignificance. You aren't the only one who forgot until now. Sometimes I forget how human you are."

"I haven't been human since the night we met."

He laughed, the bastard. "You're confusing me with your guardian mentor, but let's put that aside for a moment. You have such capacity for understanding, empathy, and for antipathy and cruelty, the struggle to balance them making you very, very human. But your human nature, your youth, and your stubbornness blind you from the truth."

Her tears fell freely now, and she didn't bother to hide them. Mustering the last of her strength, she met his gaze and, to her surprise, found him smiling, his eyes red and blazing with emotion she hadn't thought he had the capacity to experience.

"I don't understand."

He smiled. "I gave you exactly what you asked of me. And I found it... uncomfortable. It's been a long, long time since I've had such a human reaction. I must apologize, faulting you for yours."

A fresh spark of hope ignited within her. He wasn't sending her away, he wasn't hiding. He'd given her...she still wasn't sure, but it had been something. Something that she'd asked for, but she couldn't quite piece it together.

He pulled her down and spread the covers over their bodies, spooning her, her back to his belly. Then, just as sleep claimed her, he whispered, "You said you'd like to see what I looked like before, in my first life."

"Mmm," she sighed, his words barely registering.

"I showed you."

CHAPTER EIGHTEEN

True to his word, Briggs trained Vivian and the other newer recruits hard. B was a crack shot, mastering spirit firepower on the first full day. Cop skills must've helped. Even better, B was generous with his time and shared his skills. Not that Gutierrez needed it. She marched onto the training ground, pushed her way to the front of the line, bumping the rednecks who'd hassled her when we first met, and proceeded to hit every single target in a rapid succession of light bursts.

Then she hit them all in reverse. With her other hand.

"You little hustler," Vivian said, impressed and more than a little scared.

Gutierrez smirked. "You don't give all your secrets away the first week. Always have something in your back pocket. Now, Bedford, what you got?"

Vivian grinned. What she lacked in fancy finger work and showmanship, she made up for in power and range. She suspected the reaper had fed her some of his power, but much of it was her own. She'd spent time with the new recruits and the old guard, serving as an ear to bend while collecting emotional burdens that she converted into spirit light.

Unfortunately, none of those folks were the traitor based on the flavor of their burdens or their memories. And all of them worried about having enough spirit light for the battle to come, which wouldn't be an issue for a traitor with a secret stash of spirit light. Darkmore hadn't had any luck in his surreptitious readings, either.

Good news? It gave her plenty of ammo, but she'd have to ration it. The upcoming raid would require plenty of firepower and strategic use.

God, she still hadn't figured out how to get a message to the souls at the asylum.

A blast of light rushed past, grazing her cheek with a wicked burn.

"Sorry," Lewis shouted.

"Don't be," she yelled back, clutching her cheek. "My fault. I wasn't paying attention."

A second blast came from behind, but she ducked, anticipating it, and took aim at the direction of the blast. The light burst before making contact with the building, creating the spirit energy equivalent of shrapnel. Not enough to damage, but enough to show her attacker she meant business.

"Good save, Bedford."

Chet emerged from around the corner of one of the outbuildings. His specialty appeared to be ambush. He'd spent the greater part of the morning putting mixed teams of veterans and new recruits through their paces, simulating attacks from above—trees and rooftops outside and rafters and windows inside—as well as below, from trenches, underneath bushes, and beneath tables. She figured something would be coming around a nearby corner. Chet's training and her instincts had worked in harmony.

"Yeah, well, a real hardass drilled those moves into me."

He grinned, rubbing the skin beneath his singed T-shirt. "You're welcome. Remember them and you might just live long enough to save some souls. And you," he yelled, pointing at Lewis, "nice job going for that shot."

Lewis had grown in skill and confidence. He still wasn't the best shot, but he was outstanding when it came to covering his teammates and spotting hidden enemies. He'd managed to find Darkmore seventy-five percent of the time—no small feat. Apparently, he'd been gifted with a guardian spirit's intuition when he'd become a living soul broker.

She'd been surprised when the reaper had joined them for training.

When she woke up, realization hit her like a slap in the face. The dream... vision...whatever it had been, and the pitiful, broken infant tucked away in a dark corner of an ancient shaman's chamber.

It had been the reaper's first form from his mortal life, long, long ago.

And the reaper who'd claimed his soul, and the fathomless well of spirit light he carried, had been the first reaper?

She had no idea what to think or how to feel, other than profoundly sorry for the suffering Darkmore had endured in his brief mortal life. The thought had ripped open the scar on her heart she carried from Mae. No wonder the reaper had been drawn to her sister. If anyone in the universe understood her, it was the reaper. Vivian had often wondered if Mae had been aware of the horror that was her existence, an intact mind trapped within a damaged and diseased body. In the brief moments she'd communed with her sister's soul, she hadn't had the courage to ask.

She didn't have the courage to ask Darkmore, either. And she suspected he might not be inclined to answer if she did. Or worse. He might relish her reaction, feeding from it.

Careful what you wish for.

And yet, what he'd revealed to her was a gift. She doubted few if any entities in this life or the next knew what he'd once been, or how he came to be. She'd bared her soul to him, and he'd done the same, hadn't he?

"Bedford? You with us?"

She shook her head, cursing. Her wandering mind would be the death of her, literally. As tempting as it was to muse on the deeper meaning of what Darkmore had shown her, she needed to focus on preparation for the raid, and she needed to come up with a plan to speak with the lost souls at the asylum.

Oh, and rooting out the traitor in their midst. Nothing like impossible tasks.

"Yeah, sorry."

"Break time," Chet said, surprising her. "Bedford's not the only one who's tapping out. We need you at your best for the mission. Can't wear you out now. Go rest. We'll reconvene at thirteen hundred hours. That's 1:00 for you pansy ass civilians."

Well, the break would give her time to work on her third task. She hadn't had much time to get to know the other rebels, aside from Gutierrez. Being the only women, they might have bonded by default, but Vivian admired her spirit, her skill, and her no-nonsense approach to the situation. Gutierrez was outgoing, too, and had spent more time with the rest of the rebels. Vivian, being holed up with the reaper, hadn't had much time to play the get-to-know-you game.

Since there was no time for that now, picking Gutierrez's brain was her best bet. And she had the perfect way to do it.

"Maria?"

Gutierrez, who'd been gathering her belongings, paused. "What's up?"

Vivian ran her fingers through her hair, no doubt showing the mixture of dark and grey roots peeking through her signature red. She'd noticed Gutierrez's highlights had faded since their arrival, too, and she'd also noticed the color kit her gal pal had brought home from their latest shopping excursion.

Vivian had bought one for herself, too.

"Wanna hang out at my place? We can do our hair and talk about boys."

She grinned. "You're on!"

———

Vivian closed her eyes and savored the sensations of warm water and strong fingers massaging her scalp, groaning in pleasure.

"That good, huh?"

She opened her eyes to a smiling Gutierrez, her foil-wrapped locks twinkling in the light from the bathroom. Gutierrez had transformed the bathroom in her unit into a makeshift salon, stacking pillows and arranging towels into a comfortable seating area on the floor and using the detachable shower head to rinse away hair color with suds. Whatever shampoo and conditioner she used smelled heavenly, like honey and citrus. High-end stuff, like the coloring kit she'd bought.

She'd turned her nose up at Vivian's cheap kit but said she could probably "work with it."

"How come you're so good at hair?" She practically purred with delight. Gutierrez was a whiz with finances, skills honed by her days spent as a raging bull on Wall Street. Finding her to be not only competent but skilled to the level of a professional in hair color was a pleasant surprise.

"My mom. She owned her own salon in Brooklyn. Worked her ass off to put food on the table and put me through college and business school. And before you ask, she wasn't a single mom. My dad worked his ass off, too."

"I didn't assume anything."

Gutierrez snorted. "Keep telling yourself that, *gringa*." She said it with a smile.

It was Vivian's turn to snort. "You keep telling yourself that, *mi amiga*. Now hurry up with the rinse job so I can get the goop out of your hair."

They made more small talk while Gutierrez put more goop, or product as she called it, in Vivian's hair and pre-styled it for a later blowout. Trying to give her the same experience that she'd received, Vivian carefully removed the foil and rinsed out the highlights. Then she lathered the woman's thick locks with the same fancy shampoo, giving her what she hoped was a relaxing scalp massage.

"So, what's your take on the team?"

Gutierrez sighed deeply, a small smile playing at the corners of her lips. "They're coming along. I'm okay with you and B, and maybe Lewis, but not Long, and definitely not your reaper."

A spark of outrage on Darkmore's behalf shot through her before she shut it down. She could hardly blame Gutierrez. The reaper was scary, even in mortal form. And the enemy of one's enemy didn't necessarily make for a good friend.

Then again...

"What do you have against reapers? Wasn't your Armando one?"

Gutierrez's smile widened. "Yeah. He was a reaper. Still is, as far as I know."

That gave her pause. "You aren't in touch anymore?" Of course she had a million questions, but she didn't want to give away her motivation for this line of questioning. Gutierrez was smart. She could smell bullshit and was capable of recognizing an interrogation when she heard one.

Gutierrez went very still, her posture stiff beneath Vivian's fingertips. She fought the tremor running through her body, maintaining pressure and soothing roll of fingers along Gutierrez's scalp.

When Gutierrez spoke again, her words took Vivian by surprise.

"No. You looking for a way out?"

CHAPTER NINETEEN

Vivian scrambled for a response. How did she want to play this? Would Gutierrez speak freely if she thought Vivian was looking to break free of the reaper, or was it a trap, or a test?

"Oh, so we are going to talk about boys?" Gutierrez said slyly.

"Maybe," Vivian replied, reaching for the handheld showerhead to rinse the shampoo out of Gutierrez's hair. After rinsing, using the opportunity to gather her thoughts. "Of course, Lazarus Darkmore is hardly a boy."

"He's no man, either."

"True, he's not human, no more than any guardian spirit. We aren't fully human, either."

Gutierrez barked a laugh. "You're smarter than you look."

"Gee, thanks." Vivian applied a bit more pressure than necessary while applying conditioner, and a bit more nail action. "I was smart enough to get the reaper on my side against the guardians."

Gutierrez shrugged. "Good on you. You're nothing special here, though. Neither am I."

Seeing an opening, she took it. "Neither are Long or Lewis. Jury's out on B. I suppose Briggs and Chet are the special ones."

"No, they've just been at it longer. We're all small time, for now. When we get enough energy, we'll be big time, if we can keep it."

Gutierrez surprised her again. She rinsed the conditioner out of Gutierrez's hair, marveling at the shine and how even the fluorescent bathroom lights played with the highlights. Wrapping the mass of locks in a towel turban, she helped Gutierrez to her feet. "So Briggs really means to take on the Archangel Guardian Council?"

"And bring it to its knees. Too soon, if you ask me, which he didn't, but we've got a decent shot."

"Why too soon?"

Gutierrez gave her the side eye. "How many rebel bases you think he's got?"

Vivian shrugged. She'd seen the books and gone over the finances with Gutierrez. The finances were solid, as far as she could tell. After all, they didn't need conventional weapons, political backing in the human world, or much in the way of materiel. It wasn't clear from the books, since they didn't provide details on regular soldiers—only commanders. Still, how many living soul brokers could there be in the world?

"I figure a couple hundred. From what Briggs tells me, strategy can compensate for numbers."

"And energy," Gutierrez says. "Briggs has a stash, or so I hear. No one knows where he keeps it, but I overheard he and Chet talking. This big raid should give him enough to make his move on the council."

Vivian knew where Briggs kept his energy, or rather, with whom, and she understood why he kept that information secret. Question was, who else knew?

"Does Chet know where it is?" Vivian asked, wondering how much Briggs trusted his second in command.

"Don't think so, and Chet wants to keep it that way for now." Vivian must have looked puzzled, since Gutierrez added, "Less risk if Chet gets captured. It's happened before, seconds getting taken while defending their lead and teammates. A couple of bases out west lost their reserves before Briggs instituted new rules."

"What happens if Briggs gets taken out?"

Gutierrez toweled off her hair, examining the results in the mirror. She seemed pleased, which made Vivian happy. She wasn't certain she could trust Maria Gutierrez, but she liked the woman. Under different circumstances, they might have been friends. At least they were on friendly terms.

It made using her for information much less palatable.

"Isn't that the question?" she said. "Briggs probably has a plan, like someone on the outside who's supposed to deliver a message to Chet if he gets taken out or captured."

That was interesting and made sense. Who could it be? It wasn't her. The only reason she knew about Briggs' grandma was on account of the reaper. Aunt Olive didn't seem the type of woman to get mixed up in after-life management business or rebellions—she'd been uncomfortable enough with the family connection to Voudon and the loa. Still, Olive was devoted to her nephew, so it was possible.

More questions than answers. Figured.

"So you looking for a way out with your reaper?" She spoke as she applied mousse to her hair and began finger styling it.

"No, I'm looking for a way to right a wrong. I owe him. He had my back when it came to guardian politics and energy tithes. And, well, I..." *Like him?* That sounded ridiculous even in her own head.

"Let me guess. It's complicated."

It sounded like a social media status cliché, but that didn't make it less true. Vivian nodded.

"Armando came in handy, too. I didn't go under when the subprime mortgage bubble burst because he had a sense about things. He made us filthy, stinking rich, mostly because he liked human luxuries. He liked me, too. The feeling was mutual, for a while."

Vivian smiled wryly. "Wow, all I got was a stipend and a house full of corporeal spirits. They almost ate me out of house and home." She had to yell, since Gutierrez had started using the hair dryer.

"Oh, yeah, *los diablos* eat your food, drink your booze, and wreck your life, and all you get in return is a lousy job you never wanted. Guardian spirits are the ultimate scam."

Vivian twirled her newly red locks around her fingers, creating what she hoped would be gorgeous ringlets when they dried. "So you're team reaper?"

"I was, until Armando decided to feed from *mi abuelo*."

That hit a little too close to home for Vivian. She dropped her hairbrush with a clatter and cursed under her breath. Gutierrez didn't miss a beat with the dry and style routine. Whatever emotions she was experiencing, Gutierrez had them clamped down tight. Vivian had no desire to pry, though it would be necessary if she wanted to relieve her fellow soul broker of her burdens. As far as she'd seen, only Briggs shared that ability, though her healing powers appeared to be unique among her fellow living soul brokers. Lewis had guardian spirit intuition, Gutierrez was a pro at wielding spirit light, much like Chet, and it made her wonder what else her allies could do.

What the traitor in their midst might be able to do.

"Y'all got room for one more?"

Vivian didn't know whose scream was loudest, but Gutierrez's shot was better. The only reason she didn't hit B was because he was freakishly fast. One minute he was behind them, his evil grin reflected in the bathroom mirror, and the next he appeared on the sink, sitting and whistling at the damage Vivian and Gutierrez unleashed on the wall.

"Damn it, B, you need to stop sneaking up on people. It'll get you killed!" Vivian yelled.

"And you're wasting energy, *pendejo*. You should save it for the raid."

"Just practicing," he said. Then, he turned his suddenly serious gaze on Vivian. "Speaking of getting killed, you're asking an awful lot of questions about reapers and such, especially for someone who brought her reaper with her. What gives?"

Shit. Darkmore's secrets weren't hers to tell, and revealing his weaknesses might get him killed before she could restore him. And B had been spying on them? For who? She doubted the man was simply curious.

B laughed. "Red, you have a terrible poker face. I could read you even if I hadn't been a cop."

"She has trust issues," Gutierrez said, glaring at B. "You aren't helping.

Vivian shifted her gaze back and forth between the two. A groan she couldn't control escaped her throat as she slid down the wall. Oh, God. She'd been played.

Gutierrez crouched down in front of her, a wry smile tugging at the corner of her lips. "Don't beat yourself up. We've been feeling you out, too. Congratulations. You passed."

Crap on a cracker, how did she end up in this ridiculous game of spy versus spy?

"Great. Do I get the password to the club house and the secret handshake?"

B snorted and Gutierrez's smile widened. It was weird. These two weren't traitors. She'd bet her life on it. But they were acting shady. Of course, they'd called Vivian out on the fact that she was acting shady.

"How about you tell us what you're looking for. I bet it's the same thing we want." B frowned then and said, "Don't misunderstand. We're not out to get Briggs or interfere with his operation. We just have our own...interests."

Gutierrez rolled her eyes. "Way to go, Sherlock. Why don't you just tell her everything?"

"She's all right, Maria. A conduit like her wouldn't be here if she wasn't. She'd be off stockpiling spirit light and going kamikaze on the guardians and Archangels and getting blasted to oblivion."

"Not that stupid," Vivian said. "I'm here to save souls and get some of the more powerful ones on our side. Something's brewing." She paused, not wanting to tell them too much—not about where Briggs kept his stash, about the souls in the asylum, or about Mae.

Mae needed the stash Briggs' traitor was apparently keeping...

"So who would stockpile and go rogue?" Vivian asked. "Someone like that could get us all killed, and we all know that in this business, death is only the beginning."

Gutierrez and B went tight lipped and quiet. So much for trust. Damn it, she didn't have time for this. None of them did. She pulled herself up off the ground, dusted off her butt, and heaved a deep sigh before speaking.

"There's a traitor among us. Intel is from at least two sources, one reliable." Mae was reliable. Jury was out on Maeve, even though Darkmore seemed to trust her. "Whoever it is, they've got a stockpile of spirit energy and they're waiting to make a move. Given how big this raid is and the souls in play, I figure it'll happen then."

"What are you going to do about it?" B asked.

"I have absolutely no idea," she said, the weight of helplessness and frustration bearing down on her like a landslide. "If I can find them, I'll do what I can to stop them. Briggs is apparently blind to whoever it is, so convincing him to take it seriously is out. If I can't, I'm going to do everything I can to protect the trapped souls when it goes down."

"Why are you telling us?" Gutierrez asked.

"I don't know. Maybe I needed to get it off my chest? I like you both, and that's the God's honest truth. I'd hate to see y'all get caught in the crossfire."

"That may be true, but I'm guessing there's another reason." B grinned at Gutierrez.

Gutierrez grinned back and said, "You can't do this on your own. You need allies. You need us."

"We're in," B said. "We'll do our own investigating and we'll have your back. You got ours?"

Vivian smiled. A spark of hope ignited within her for the first time since she and Darkmore arrived in Jackson. "You know it. And I'll tell you what I find. Where are you two planning to start?"

"With Chet," they said in unison.

"Good. I'll be working on a way to sneak out and get a message to the souls at the asylum. Darkmore can help with that. If we can keep them safe, we might be able to get a few on our side."

They all shook on it and decided to split up and mingle before accelerated boot camp training recommenced. On her way out the door, Gutierrez turned to Vivian and said, "If you do decide to part ways with your reaper, I'll help you."

CHAPTER TWENTY

Vivian collapsed onto the sofa and closed her eyes, barely acknowledging the reaper when she walked past him. That had been standard operating procedure for her since his revelation—and hers. Those exchanges had been far more intimate than their physical relationship, and it had left Vivian confused, anxious, and exposed in a way that made her want to hide. Given Darkmore's self-imposed distance and manner, she suspected he felt the same way.

He was becoming more and more human with each passing day. Powerful and deadly with many of his supernatural powers intact, but still human. More human than he'd ever been in any of his past lives, and it was changing him. What he was becoming and the possibilities his transformation opened frightened her more than his darkness ever had.

He sat down next to her and took her hand, a very human gesture. God, she hoped he didn't want to talk. The mental and emotional energy it would take for *that* conversation was more than she could muster.

"Take a moment to catch your breath, but you need to prepare for a quick jaunt."

She opened one eye and looked at his handsome face. He'd shaved again, as he seemed fond of doing. Memories of his first shave since becoming mortal warmed her more than she liked, which was stupid. Wait, a jaunt? What did he mean?

"We can't leave. Briggs and his guards are watching us, or have you forgotten?"

The reaper shook his head. "No, I haven't forgotten. The guards are simply irrelevant."

"I don't understand. Unless you've been holding out on me and can still do that spirit materialization transport thing, there's no way we're getting out of this house undetected."

Darkmore grinned. "Trust me. You won't like it, but it will get us in and out with our captors none the wiser."

Briggs and his band weren't exactly captors, but they did have her and the reaper under heavy guard. Between that and exhaustion from two days of hard training, she could barely keep her eyes open. The reaper's warning about not liking whatever he had planned sent a jolt of adrenaline through her body.

Some wake-up call.

Darkmore walked to the kitchen and came back with two steaming mugs of fresh coffee.

"Liquid courage?" she asked.

He looked at the ceiling, the corners of his mouth twitching. "No. Just something to keep your hands occupied."

Before she could protest, a dark vortex appeared above them, dropping Uphir into their living room.

"Son of a bitch!" she yelled, nearly dropping the coffee mug. "A little warning next time?"

Uphir smoothed her form-fitting pencil skirt and gave Vivian a teen-worthy eye-roll. Shifting her gaze to the reaper, she flashed a wicked grin and said, "You'll owe me for this."

He bowed low over her hand, brushing his lips over her skin. "Lovely to see you, my dear. I believe you'll find that this matter concerns you as well."

"Fine. We should go before one of these uppity mortals catches a whiff of my power."

"Go?" Vivian stared at the pair. "How?"

Darkmore pointed up at the swirling vortex of darkness. Knowing the demoness, it was a gateway to one of her torture chambers. Uphir was supposedly the underworld's leading medical authority, but she seemed interested in healing only as a means to extend the lives of her victims, torturing them to the brink of death, only to bring them back from the edge so she could repeat the process and feast on their agony. Not that her victims didn't deserve it. The child rapist she'd brought Vivian to heal deserved what Uphir and the reaper did to him. That didn't bother Vivian.

What bothered her was how much Uphir and the reaper *enjoyed* feasting on the wretched soul's suffering.

And now Vivian was supposed to just hop into this demon's portal and trust that she'd see them safely to their destination?

And what about the tortured souls?

Vivian carefully set her coffee mug down and braced for a fight. Meeting Uphir's gaze, she said, "You don't touch them."

Uphir went very still, from the roots of her raven hair to the tips of cloven hooves, the only visible sign of her demonhood. No, scratch that. Her eyes shifted from a rich chocolate brown to deep crimson, and Vivian swore scales rippled beneath the smooth flesh of her neck. Darkmore heaved a sigh, swore under his breath, and grabbed Vivian's arm, yanking her up through the portal before she had the chance to scream.

———

Vivian had traveled through vortices created by spirits before. Not her favorite mode of travel, but the waves of nausea didn't last as long as her first trip.

The demon portal was an entirely different experience. Pitch black, reeking of ozone, and painfully loud, only the reaper's grip on her arms kept her from being torn asunder. Screams echoed from somewhere in the void. Uphir probably kept some of her victims trapped in this...place? Limbo? Or, fearing the demon and her tender mercies, some of the souls she claimed may have taken their chances and escaped into the portal's ether.

From their shrieks, some likely regretted that choice.

A biting chill pierced her flesh as they flew at breakneck speed through the void. Too fast. She couldn't breathe, could barely hold on to the reaper. Risking a glance at his face, she was shocked to find it contorted with the same agony. His diminished powers and mortal body rendered him as vulnerable to the demon portal as she, and yet he'd still come with her, knowing the risks.

He must have sensed her thoughts, since he twisted his lips into some semblance of a grin. "Hold on tight. The landing will be worse."

"What—"

In the next instance, they crashed to the ground with bone breaking impact. Darkmore had positioned his body beneath hers to break her fall, damaging himself in the process. This time, he didn't object when she used her light to mend his body, ignoring her own aches and pains until he was fully restored. She rolled off the reaper and sat up.

Big mistake. Her head spun and her ears were ringing with remembered echoes of screams.

"Do we," she began, struggling for breath, "have to go back the same way?"

The reaper grimaced, which was answer enough. He rose and offered her a hand, pulling her off the cold, grass-covered ground. At least it had given them a softer place to land than the nearby asphalt. That was about as far as her night vision went—no streetlights, no nearby homes or businesses, no passing cars. They appeared to be out in the boonies.

"Where are we?" she asked, wondering if they were even still in Mississippi. Her heart lurched in her chest as a sudden longing for home hit, stealing her breath.

Darkmore touched her shoulder and then ran his hand down her arm to clasp her trembling hand. Uphir dropped in front of them, landing gracefully on her cloven hooves and glaring at Vivian.

"What?" Vivian growled. It was stupid, but she figured the demon had gotten back a bit of her own during the spirit travel roller coaster ride from hell.

Instead of lashing out, Uphir flashed a wicked grin and transformed from an attractive human-sort-of woman—aside from the goat feet—into a seven-foot-tall, horned beast with a bifurcated tail and pitchfork.

"Do pick your jaw up off the ground, my dear," Darkmore said, dryly.

Turning his attention behind Vivian, he said, "Earl. How nice to see you again."

"It's Lothar."

The deep growl of a voice made Vivian spin around. She barely stifled a scream when confronted with a reptilian creature that appeared to be half man, half dinosaur. The dinosaur half included a head full of teeth fit for a T Rex and clawed talons.

Vivian gulped, and then regained enough composure to say, "Nice upgrade."

He grinned, baring more sharp teeth. "My mistress is generous when I please her."

Uphir sneered at her minion. Vivian figured Earl—he'd always be Earl to her—was a masochist who enjoyed being belittled and humiliated by the demon. Not really wanting to know what other special treatment he might enjoy receiving, she turned her attention back to the reaper.

"Let me ask again. Where are we and why are we wherever we are?"

Her night vision had adjusted enough to see that they were at some sort of rural crossroads. In Mississippi. Oh, God, she didn't know whether to laugh, cry, or scream.

She settled on a bark of laughter as a tall man in a dark suit and hat materialized, cigarette dangling from his lips and a guitar slung across his shoulder. She stopped laughing when he leveled her with his gaze, fathomless and cold to the core. The shade of the Blues Legend turned his icy gaze on the demon and her minion, disdain dripping from his aura, before turning his attention to Darkmore.

"You the only one dressed decent," he said, his Southern drawl as smooth as aged whisky on the rocks. He flicked his cigarette, the spectral ash disappearing into the night. "What's your story, Red?"

It took Vivian a moment to realize he was speaking to her. Star struck, and more than a little wary, she said, "I'm with him. Didn't pick him up at a crossroads, and I still have my soul."

He grinned wide. It made him look more human, but the otherworldly quality he carried still had the hairs on the back of her neck standing at attention as a chill gripped her to the marrow of her bones. "That so? I bet there's a story in there. You can maybe tell me after. Right now I expect you want those touched souls. Found a couple wandering the grounds. They followed me here."

"Hey, I tracked those souls," Earl said, sounding entirely too whiny for a man in his current form.

Cutting off the petty spat that was brewing, Darkmore inclined his head. "We are obliged to you, Kalunga-ngombe."

The shade barked a laugh. "I ain't the lord of the underworld—not yet. I just work for him in these parts. I'll bring the souls out with one song. You got ten minutes, then I'm gone, and they gone with me."

A jolt of excitement went through Vivian. She could warn them, let them know that help was on the way and that, if they chose, they could stay and use their power against their captors, the guardians, and maybe the whole damned council.

If she could get through to them—in ten minutes. No use worrying about time limits. She looked at the man from myth and legend and nodded. "Bring them, please."

He winked, settled his guitar, and began to play. Chords rang out in the still of the night, haunting, sultry, and like nothing she'd ever heard before. When he sang, it wasn't the high-pitched, on the edge voice she'd expected, like a man on the run from the rougher side of life. The voice was that of a man whose demons on his trail had caught up to him already, raw, deep, and it grabbed Vivian by the soul and clung to her.

One by one, lost and lonely spirits emerged from the darkness, drawn to the music and its power. She doubted any soul, living or departed, could resist such a call. God, for all the pain and suffering her connection to the world of spirits had caused, it had allowed her to witness sights and sounds beyond belief and so beautiful as to seem unreal. If the man's music held even a sliver of the magic it held on the other side of the grave, it still would have been the closest thing to magic she'd ever heard.

It ended too soon, and it took a moment for her to recover. Clock was ticking. "I have a message for you to take back to the others," she said, disturbed by the vacant stares of the spirits. "I'm with a group of living soul brokers. We want to set you free and help you cross over, if you want to move on. If you don't, we want you to join us and help us set other souls free. You have the power to break their chains and bring the guardian spirits to their knees."

The souls didn't stir, didn't move, didn't even flinch with the drop in temperature as the reaper and demon moved closer. Damn it, it wasn't their fault. They were lost souls, lost in life due to mental illness and God knew what other horrors, and now they were being held prisoner by the very entities who were supposed to send them on to peace. By the spectral remains of their clothing, some of them had lingered for more than a century. Dirty, ragged skirts and petticoats hovered above the bare feet of one young woman. A boy with scars carved into his wrists still carried the chains that made them, and a man with a shaved head, emaciated to a degree that made Vivian think he'd actually died of starvation, stood naked.

"Please," she whispered. "Please, you have to tell the others. When the rebels come, they'll be shooting spirit light to destroy, not to disable. We don't want you or the other prisoners to be caught in the crossfire!"

"They can't hear you, my dear," Darkmore said. "And I cannot read them. Perhaps if I were...as I was before, I could see into their darkness, but not now."

Uphir's sharp gaze landed on the reaper. Shit. He'd given too much away. The sadistic bitch would know his weakness and make it her mission to exploit it. She tightened her grip on the reaper's hand and stared at the demon in her frightening form, refusing to drop her gaze.

"He's mine," Vivian said. "Come after him, and you'll deal with me."

Uphir grinned. "Why would I want him when I could have you? If the reaper no longer has the power to guard his get, then you're fair game."

Without thinking, Vivian channeled spirit light, not from the misery she carried, but from a long-ago memory. She was a young girl holding a tiny, fragile infant in her hand, cooing and babbling things only children understand. The baby smiled, drooling and wiggling small limbs as Vivian's younger self squealed in delight. Smelling of powder, sour milk, and innocence, it was the first time she experienced the fierce kind of love that bonded protector and protected. Mae was hers to love, to teach, to nurture, and to cherish. Together, they would discover the world and all of its wonders.

She hadn't realized there was a time before Mae's disability, a time when their family had been filled with the promise of two full lives, filled with hope, filled with possibility.

Uphir shrieked as the light hit, transforming her back into her woman form. Even her feet looked like an ordinary human's. No cloven hooves or fur. She huddled on the ground and glared up at Vivian, hissing.

Vivian might have gloated, had she not been shocked. Going after the demon was stupid. Sure, she could channel spirit light and had helped take out a few rogue guardians and spirits, but testing her unpredictable powers on a creature like Uphir? Monumentally stupid.

Still, Uphir didn't know that. Probably. Best keep up the pretense of I-meant-to-do-that for Darkmore's sake, as well as her own.

Earl roared, baring fangs and slashing out with claws. She was tempted to blast him, too, but Uphir's pet masochist would probably enjoy it. Best to just ignore him. Or perhaps she could salvage the situation.

"Stop that! Go grovel at the feet of your mistress, you useless sub!"

Earl obeyed, shrinking back to his normal size and crawling on hands and knees to Uphir. The demon had gathered herself enough to rise—on cloven hooves—and savage her dignity. She kicked her minion, who then proceeded to give Vivian a sly smile.

Good. She'd allowed Uphir to save face, done Earl a favor by allowing him to defend his mistress, who'd rewarded him with the punishment he craved, and hopefully secured their return trip back to the apartment.

"Five minutes, Red." The Blues Legend stood bathed in moonlight, strumming the odd chord here and there. He seemed amused. Whether it was her outburst, the demon's reaction, or the fact that she'd wasted precious time in a pissing contest when she should have been trying to get through to the lost souls, she wasn't sure.

"What do I do?" The question was rhetorical, but Darkmore answered. "Nothing."

She whirled around and stared at the reaper in stunned silence. "What?"

He offered her a sad smile, equal parts understanding and pity. The reaper had once seemed so otherworldly, so ancient, so remote, and so utterly inhuman. In this moment, the reaper had never seemed more human.

As was she.

That was it, then. She'd done her best, used her power and influence to get here, call the spirits she needed to protect to this place, and deliver her warning. And yet, in the end, she couldn't make them listen, couldn't get through to them. For the first time since becoming a living soul broker, she'd failed.

"Time's up."

The Blues Man grinned and nodded at Vivian. With a last look at the moon, he made magic with his voice and guitar, disappearing into the night with the lost souls. The last thing she heard as she entered the portal was a song about a red-haired woman trying to save the world.

Zeke's words came back to her then. *We have at least two weapons against our baser natures, though—faith and free will.* She'd have to have faith that somehow her message had been received. What the spirits did with it was up to them.

And what she did next was up to her.

CHAPTER TWENTY-ONE

They were on the move at sunset.

The white van rolled down the highway, the first in a series of mixed vehicles loaded with Briggs' teams. It was the same white serial killer van Chet had used to pick Vivian and the reaper up from the Burnin' Bush. The bloodstains on the tattered upholstery were probably from the reaper's bloodied and battered body. She wondered what a forensic examiner would make of a sample. If her healing energy had truly rendered Darkmore fully mortal, did he carry the DNA signature of a normal human? Would it be a match to any other living humans?

She doubted it, since the form he wore was that of an entirely different man, different race, different physical condition, perhaps different enough from what was as close to arcane *Homo sapiens* DNA as one could get. But the blood in his veins was real enough, as were the fading bruises, the hairs of the beard he shaved, his fingertips—she'd been close enough to see the whorls that made up his fingerprints and the lines running along his palms.

Her cheeks heated at memories of what those hands and fingertips could do.

No, she couldn't afford to think about that right now. They were on the eve of battle and too much was at stake. And her plan to protect and defend the lost souls involved other...complications. She'd have to shove a whole host of emotions aside to deal with the next few hours.

Of course, it was difficult to push those emotions aside when the reaper was sitting next to her in the van. They'd chosen seats on the back bench, away from the others. Darkmore had probably done it out of courtesy, since he still made most of the team uncomfortable. It was his nature.

When the silence proved as uncomfortable as the weight of his gaze, she said, "Let me guess. I'm still a fascinating tapestry of contradictions."

He smiled. "I suspect you always will be, but that's not what I'm thinking."

She should not ask...she definitely should not ask...

"Okay, so what are you thinking?"

He leaned forward in the seat, closer to her, close enough for her to get lost in his coolness, his wintergreen and fresh snow scent. It reminded her that even in this human form, he was still reaper.

"I'm thinking you're up to something. I do hope it's devious. I could use a little fun."

The way he said "fun" was so creepy and reaperish. He was trying to get under her skin, and damn it, it was working.

She flexed her fingers, feeling the spirit light roiling beneath her skin, pulsing and eager to escape. They'd all received a fresh infusion of energy from Briggs before leaving HQ, and Vivian had fed the reaper the sorrows she'd converted into useful energy. Unfortunately, taking in those burdens hadn't given her any new information or clues as to the identity of the traitor. Not that she'd expected much. The team members who came to her for relief were volunteers. Unless the traitor was arrogant and stupid enough to try his or her luck fooling Vivian, it wasn't much of a trap.

The actual trap she'd designed was better, but much riskier and more dangerous. She didn't doubt he'd come through, but facing him again? No, she couldn't think about that. She needed to focus on the trapped souls, her fellow soul brokers, and keeping Briggs safe. That was her mission right now.

She'd focus on the fallout after.

Darkmore leaned closer, rubbing his cheek against her, catlike and intimate. She resisted the urge to pull back—or lean in closer. "None of that right now. We need to focus."

He ran his nose along the shell of her ear, sending shivers down her spine and along all of her sensitive nerve endings. "I'll keep you safe, Vivian. I always do."

And I'll keep you safe, too, even if you don't like my methods.

Before she had the chance to open her mouth and say that out loud, he pulled back and surveyed the van's other occupants. Gutierrez and B were on her team, which was great in that she trusted them, but also dicey since they might have had more luck finding the traitor if they'd been split among the other teams.

Fortunately, she'd recruited a few unofficial teammates to keep an eye on the others.

"Do you want to know?" she asked. Why had she said that? Was she trying to pick a fight with the reaper?

Of course she was. Fighting and anger were much easier than dealing with other emotions—like guilt, dread, and the oddest sense of anticipation.

His smile fell and he went still. "It's still so strange, no knowing what you're thinking."

She twisted in her chair, eyes wide and jaw gaping, an unbecoming sight, no doubt. "What do you mean you don't know? I showed you *every-thing* not too long ago."

"And I showed you." The words were muttered, almost to himself. "Nevertheless, since my...transformation, I've become less adept at gleaning the thoughts of mortals, unless, like you, they open themselves to me."

That was new, and more than a bit alarming. She'd noticed the physical changes, of course, and some of the psychological changes, but had not fully appreciated the extent of his mental and preternatural transformation.

"I'm becoming more human with each passing hour," he said, no trace of anger or judgment in his tone. He seemed...thoughtful, bemused and, to her surprise, pleased. "I never thought I would experience the fullness and richness of humanity. It is beautiful, frightening, wondrous, and heart-breaking. The form encasing me is so dynamic. Every cell and fiber moves, breathes, regenerates, and degenerates. I feel it living and slowly dying all around me."

She blinked back tears. God, she'd done more damage than she realized. Were they running out of time? If this mission failed, if she was unable to root out the traitor and keep Briggs safe, would the spirits channeled through mambo asogwe condemn the reaper to irreversible mortality?

"I'm sorry," she whispered. "I'll make it right." Somehow. She hoped it was a promise she could keep.

"I'm not."

She stared at him, wide-eyed and shocked, so shocked that she didn't bother blinking back her tears. He wasn't sorry? He was losing powers he'd possessed for millennia. He would suffer illness, injury, and he would die, his soul like any other, ripe for the claiming.

And there were many dark forces that would gladly claim him for an eternity of torment and degradation.

The corners of his mouth curled into a small smile. "I've existed a long time, Vivian, but I've never lived—until now. I told you once that experience is a great teacher, the only thing truly worth pursuing. This experience is a gift. To live a life filled with limitless uncertainties and limitless possibilities."

"But you'll suffer, and die, and your soul will be sucked into eternal darkness."

"That, too, qualifies as an experience," he replied with a dismissive wave of a hand.

"How can you be so flippant about it?"

Heads turned, and the van swerved a bit. God, she'd practically yelled the last part.

Gutierrez's gaze bore into hers, clearly giving off a "you okay girl?" vibe. The driver, one of Briggs' senior team leaders, cursed and told them to keep it down.

B smirked. "She dodged one multi-vehicle car crash. It's what got her here in the first place."

Darkmore turned his gaze to the other occupants and all commentary ceased. They turned away, giving Vivian and the reaper the illusion of privacy. She didn't see the look on the reaper's face, but she'd witnessed his scary-as-hell looks in the past. Seemed he wasn't fully human yet after all.

When he turned back to Vivian, his gaze was once again serious, but not scary. "I'm aware of the risks and what awaits me in the afterlife should I die in this form. I also have several contingency plans and hiding places in this world and the next. Places that can accommodate you as well."

A warm feeling in her chest warred with the coolness of the reaper. His chill had lost some of its potency, another sign of his growing humanity. He'd asked her to come away with him once before. She'd been too frightened and too angry at the world of spirits, and he'd terrified her—with good reason. He'd offered her a place at his side as a reaper, as his equal and, eventually, as his better. A goddess, a queen of the darkest realms of the afterlife, a Persephone to his Hades, only she wouldn't ascend from the underworld to bring renewed life.

She hadn't considered his offer then, had no compunction to go with him willingly, but she'd traveled to his dark realm in order to save her sister, a willing sacrifice. Instead, she helped free a host of the souls trapped in the dark realm from the evil entity who dwelled within it. On her way out, she asked Darkmore to ascend with her.

He'd said he was already home.

Here, now, in this moment, he was her equal. Part of him remained tied to the darkness of the underworld and his time as a reaper of souls, but those ties were closer to her own with the afterlife as a living soul broker. He was more human than he'd ever been—partner, lover, man. To join him as a human being, mortal, vital, living?

"You don't have to decide right this minute, Vivian, but soon. Think it over, will you?"

Those were the same words he'd used when he'd first asked her to be his. His smile told her it was deliberate. Free will. He hadn't forced her then, and he wouldn't force her now, even though she'd forced mortality upon him.

Swallowing hard, she reached up with a trembling hand to touch his face. "I will think it over."

The van made a sharp right turn. "Heads up, people. We're almost at the rendezvous point. We go in on foot. Stick close and remember your training. These guardians will be shooting to kill, and they'll drag your souls into their service after they drain you dry, so don't get hit. Y'all ready?"

They all shouted out various forms of "yes" and "hell yeah" and "affirmative" with a couple of whoops thrown in for good measure and bravado. He was right. Death was the least of their worries.

She hoped the reinforcements she'd called in would be enough.

———

The largely defunct Mississippi State Hospital consisted of a sprawling campus with neoclassical-style buildings that appeared more like a college campus than a lunatic asylum, at least by day. As they approached under cover of night, red brick darkened to the color of dry blood in the moonlight as white columns glowed a ghostly white.

It wasn't the only glow.

Energy, spirit light, pulsed in the air around them, through the ground, on the wind rustling through tall grass and tree leaves, and from all around. No wonder the guardians made this place one of their strongholds. It would no doubt be guarded like Fort Knox.

When she'd said as much, Briggs laughed. "Not their style. Too many of them hanging around would draw unwanted attention. Ask your friend the reaper."

Darkmore agreed. The others of his kind would covet this repository of soul energy and the lost souls within, though claiming them could prove problematic. If a reaper took the damaged souls, it would represent a policy violation. The mentally ill, even those who committed violent acts, were not in their right minds and therefore weren't fair game for reapers harvesting the souls of the wicked.

By the same token, guardians were breaking the rules by keeping the souls of former patients trapped here, siphoning their vast energy stores. They should have ferried the souls into the afterlife long ago. No moral high ground for the so-called good side. These guardians were definitely no angels.

The teams split and scoped out the buildings and grounds, scouting for the position of sentinels securing the perimeter and the prison housing the souls, and seeking the highest concentrations of spirit light. They were banking on the theory that their own soul broker energy would blend in enough to be undetectable above the high background levels, but that was a gamble. They needed to locate their targets, strike, and extract the souls as quickly as possible while minimizing collateral damage.

She fell back, the reaper at her side, and then split off from the group. It wasn't strictly disobeying orders, since the small copse of trees was within their assigned scouting territory, but she failed to inform Briggs or Chet.

A fact that did not go unnoticed by the reaper, though he waited until they disappeared into the shadows before speaking.

"Is this a part of your devious little plan?" he whispered, voice laced with amusement. Ugh, the bastard was having fun.

Of course he was.

He may not be able to read mortals as well in his current form, but he had no trouble tasting spirit light from souls. She'd seen him harvest a few souls brought to him by Uphir. Naturally, he couldn't accompany them to their destination, be it a stint in purgatory or a more...final situation, but he'd feasted on their wickedness and pain.

She whirled around and said, "First of all, the souls in there? Not up for grabs. Got it?"

He stood straighter and crossed his arms. "No."

"What do you mean 'no'? You follow the rules, mister."

"Precisely," he said. "Do you think the souls trapped within are all innocent? No, the inmates have been joined by some of their former 'care-givers' in a nasty twist of horror. Not that the guardians mind."

She mentally kicked herself. "I'm sorry. I shouldn't have assumed you'd do the wrong thing."

He grinned. "Habit, I'm sure. With your permission," he said, sardonically, "I will take care of the wicked souls, separating the wheat from the chaff for you and your companions. Now, why are we here?"

She jumped, startled, sensing the presence of the entities appearing within the tree line. Darkmore would sense them as well. His reaper senses may have dulled, but he hadn't fully...humanized. His senses seemed to be on par with hers and the other living soul brokers. They were out of time.

"Lazarus, do you trust me?"

His expression changed from amusement to stunned anger. "What have you done?"

"What I had to do to keep us safe and to save the souls. We all have to put aside our differences for the moment and work together."

He growled. The man—corporeal guardian spirit in the form of a man—who stepped out of the tree line wasn't pleased, either, but at least he kept his testosterone-fueled anger under control.

"Ezekiel," the reaper said. "How's the family?"

CHAPTER TWENTY-TWO

"Lazarus, that was ugly and uncalled for!" she hissed.

The reaper was goading Zeke, guardian spirit and her former lover, in a very human jealousy reaction, and it stung. When Vivian let Zeke go, bargaining with Ezra for his soul's freedom, she'd meant for him to cross over into the next life.

Zeke hadn't gone away. Instead, he'd returned to watch over the family he'd left behind from his mortal life, taking much better care of them than when he had actually lived with them. Yes, he'd protected his disabled son from greedy guardian and reaper spirits, but he'd also reunited with his mortal wife, using her new boyfriend as a means of possession. It was all kinds of wrong, but she couldn't help but feel responsible. And jealous. And angry.

But if she could put all of those unsavory emotions aside, the stubborn spirits masquerading as men in her life could, too.

Zeke flashed a wicked grin at the reaper, full of malice and the promise of retaliation. "They're fine. How's life this side of the grave? I could arrange for a return trip for you."

Sparks flashed from her fingertips. She stood between Zeke and the reaper and grabbed both of their wrists, channeling enough light to let them know she meant business.

Neither of the stubborn jackasses blinked or flinched, but they did end the male posturing standoff and turned their attention to her.

"We've got anywhere between five hundred and a thousand damaged souls trapped on these grounds and being held prisoner by guardian spirits. The raid is in progress, and I'm not sure my warning got through to the prisoners. They're..."

"Traumatized," Jeanne said, the young guardian appearing out of the shadows. "We'll keep them out of the line of fire."

She noticed Jeanne wasn't alone. Maggie stormed out of the trees behind Jeanne, a glowing ball of fury. Shit. Would the Grand Dame of Guardian spirits zap them all for this crazy covert ops mission? Or would she just zap Vivian for dragging Jeanne into it?

Jeanne waved a hand at Vivian as if shushing a naughty child. "Vivian, put your hands down. You'll give away our position. My partner, Marguerite, will provide a distraction to keep the sentinels occupied. Who's the traitor?"

A bit chagrinned, Vivian put her sparking hands down and said, "We don't know. Maria Gutierrez, Barry Johnson, and I, we've screened everyone in Briggs' rebel team. They're all devoted to the mission if not Briggs himself."

To her credit, Jeanne didn't express any disappointment or alarm. "I imagine we'll root out the traitor with this operation. Now Zeke, Marguerite, and I will cover you and Darkmore while you take care of the lost souls. Vivian, gather as many of the righteous and damaged souls as you can and hide them. If not protect them."

"Reaper." Marguerite's voice was power held on a tight leash. "You will do what is necessary for the wicked souls of those who once tormented the lost and lonely?"

Darkmore smiled and bowed. "With pleasure, my lady flower."

Marguerite raised her hands to send a blast at Darkmore. Vivian intercepted, taking the blow and, to her surprise, absorbing the energy behind it. Channeling all of the bravado she could muster, Vivian dusted off her shirt, stood tall, and grinned. "Thanks. I needed that. Lazarus?"

She offered her hand to the reaper, ignoring the look of pure murder that almost masked the anguish in Zeke's gaze. When this was over, she had a decision to make. Lots of decisions, but she owed the two men—spirits—in her life answers. Not only the spirits, she owed herself an honest assessment before deciding anything. Between the two, both—ludicrous, but perhaps an option as far as the reaper in his non-mortal form—or neither.

Power at her back, hunger at her side, and determination coursing through her veins, she caught up with her team. B glanced over his shoulder, turned back, and then did a double take. Gutierrez whirled around and cursed under her breath in Spanish. Marguerite frowned in disapproval, but at least she didn't try and blast her teammate this time.

"I brought reinforcements." Vivian nodded. "Barry, Maria, these are the guardians I told you about, the ones on our side. They'll cover us while we wrangle the lost souls and they'll have our backs when we take on the sentinels. Where are the lost souls?"

B scowled. "How we gonna get to them with the cavalry in tow?"

Jeanne beamed at him. "We aren't the cavalry. We're infantry, and Special Forces to boot. Maggie's going to create a diversion. You ready?"

Gutierrez turned her gaze to Marguerite, crossed her arms, and said, "Okay. What's your plan?"

Marguerite smiled, wide and feral. "This."

Her corporeal body disappeared in a cloud of dust less than a second before red lightning streaked through the air. A few of the bolts struck the roofs of outbuildings, starting mini fires. Spirits emerged out of walls and roofs and doorways, some materializing and others taking the time to build corporeal bodies, and moved on high alert. The corporeal entities tackled the small fires with red fire extinguishers while others flew into the air to chase the lightning. They moved as a unit. There was a small fire station and maintenance department in the middle of campus. Humans, probably in league with the guardian spirits since they were always on duty and on campus, fired up the engine of a truck. They'd be heading for the worst of the fires, starting with the emergency generators. Marguerite had chosen her targets well. No lights, so the power had been cut, too. Chaos.

The sentinels wouldn't want mortal first responders or law enforcement to come calling.

Gutierrez wasted no time, grabbing Vivian and Darkmore by the arms and hauling them along into action. They stuck to the shadows, jogging from one patch to another while B and Zeke called out the positions of guardian spirits patrolling the grounds. Most ran off in the direction of one or more fires, but there were enough sentinels remaining to keep the entrance to the Forensics Unit impenetrable without a fight.

She considered blasting her way through, but if they didn't disable all of the sentinels, the rest would come in full force after receiving a distress call. Jeanne appeared in front of them, earning a hiss from Gutierrez. Luckily, the tough as nails soul broker had the presence of mind not to yell.

"Time for another distraction," she said. "Be ready to run in when I've got their attention."

Before Vivian could protest, Jeanne materialized in front of the door and sent a blast from her hands that hit the brick wall hard enough to expose the wood beneath.

"Thought you could hold out on us?" she yelled. Zeke appeared at her side, arms at the ready.

The sentinels surrounded the pair and took aim. They didn't open fire, thank God, but they were poised to strike.

One of the sentinels wearing the form of a young woman, pale and dark-haired, held up a hand, indicating that the rest should hold their fire.

"This area is restricted by order of the Archangel Council. You're trespassing. Go while I'm still inclined to let you."

Jeanne snorted. "This isn't authorized by anyone, guardian, Archangel, reaper, or demon. We know you're stockpiling energy and we know the source."

The lead sentinel scowled. "If that were true, I'd be even less inclined to let you leave."

"Cut the bullshit," Zeke said. "We aren't spies and we aren't rebels. We want in."

Vivian didn't know whether to shout with triumph or run in with spirit light blazing. They were taking a huge risk, bigger than Marguerite's. While powerful, both Jeanne and Zeke were young guardians. They didn't have as much energy or firepower as the older guardian spirits. It worked for their ruse, but if the sentinels decided to strike, they'd be obliterated.

Perhaps sensing her distress, Darkmore took her hand and squeezed it. She wasn't certain, but she thought the temperature dropped a degree or two around her. The sensation should have been uncomfortable. Winter in Mississippi wasn't as chilly as in Tennessee, but it was colder at night, particularly in shadows and in the wake of high winds. The reaper's chill, however, sent waves of calm and comfort, curbing her impulse to attack.

Jeanne's voice broke the spell, and her calm. "You see that?" She pointed to the streams of red lightning flashing across the night sky, striking and creating new fires. "That's Marguerite Bourgeoys, one of the most powerful guardians in this part of the world. As you can see, she enjoys making an entrance."

"That kind of power tends to attract attention," Zeke said. "Another few blasts should bring every powerful guardian within a five-hundred-mile radius to this site. You could take us out, but I doubt you're a match for Marguerite and the legions of spirits that'll materialize in her wake."

Most of the sentinels turned their attention to the sky, jaws gaping or tongues wagging about the apparent legend in their midst. Huh. Vivian had never heard of Marguerite, but she'd never been privy to the history, hierarchy, or inner workings of the guardians. Ezra, or possibly the Archangel Council, had kept her ignorant.

If they lived through this, she'd have to spend more time learning about the world she'd been forced to inhabit.

Jeanne gave the signal and Gutierrez led the way, followed by Darkmore, Vivian, and B. They all tried to remain invisible, one of the powers acquired by living soul brokers, and part and parcel of the reaper's repertoire. She didn't breathe until they cleared the circle of guardians and made it through the open door. Sloppy, leaving it open.

Or perhaps it was a trap.

Once inside, the bright lights left Vivian feeling exposed and disoriented. Fortunately, Darkmore had his bearings and led the group to a utility closet so they could get their bearings and formulate a plan. The scents of dust and mold competed with the harsh tang of cleaners and chemicals and the space forced them shoulder to shoulder, but at least they were hidden. Based on the maps and building layouts Briggs had provided, they should be able to navigate the building as long as they knew where they were going.

They just needed to determine the most likely location of the souls.

Easier said than done. The entire campus was pulsing with spirit light, especially since Marguerite started her little light show. Between the fireworks, energy from pissed off guardian sentinels, and their soul broker teams, the background level of energy was abnormally high.

Unless, of course, she was willing to use her other gift—she'd only used it once before, back when she'd entered the reaper's lair. Gathering the burdens of the damned souls in purgatory, hell, or whatever state the reaper's harvested spirits existed in depending on their crimes in life, she'd liberated them.

Two problems remained. First, she hadn't done it alone. The reaper at full capacity and her guardian mentor Ezra had helped, as had the spirit of her departed sister Mae. Second, it had nearly killed her. Channeling the burdens of tortured souls had proven more taxing than channeling the burdens of the living.

Darkmore met her gaze and, with that uncanny ability of his, said, "I cannot help you here and now as I did then."

"I know," she said. Damn it, she wished she could pace, wished she could think faster, wished she had more time.

Gutierrez looked back and forth between Vivian and the reaper. "Mind cluing us in? Not all of us can read minds."

Vivian almost said that they couldn't, either, but that would be giving away too much regarding the reaper's weakened state.

"I might be able to find the lost souls, but it might take me out of commission." Or worse. God, it always came back to this. Impossible choices, sacrifices, and a heavy price to pay—it was the part of afterlife management that sucked the most.

"What do you mean? And what can we do to help?" B stood straight, determination in his steady gaze. The gaze of a cop, a warrior, and a valuable ally.

Gutierrez rolled her eyes, but to her credit, she nodded and said, "I'm in. Just don't ask me to carry your big ass."

She laughed. "I'll do my best. What I need is cover while I put out feelers for the damaged souls. I can track them by their suffering, but it means I'll have to take some or all of it into me."

"I'll relieve you as much as I am able." The reaper took her hand and said, "And I will be with you all the way."

"Okay." With a deep breath, she squared her shoulders and faced the door. "Let's do this."

———

The bright lights illuminating the hallway were unnerving, a sharp contrast to the darkness she sensed. It called to her, the torment of the long dead, as if their misery and suffering had seeped into the walls and foundation of the building. She opened her senses a bit and followed the dark energy, trying to ignore the flashes of horror that crept into her mind.

A young man strapped to a table, his legs and arms bound by thick leather straps as white-coated men and women wearing masks forced a rubber mouthpiece past his clenched teeth.

His scream, muffled by the mouth guard, echoed in the Vivian's mind, sending chills down her spine.

They hooked electrodes to his temples and threw a switch on the contraption that would send electrical impulses through his brain. The knowledge that the doctors and staff thought they were helping did nothing to ease Vivian's grief, horror, and outrage. Foam leaked from the corners of the man's mouth, tears and snot streaming from his face as the foul stench of emptying bladder and bowels filled the air around them, along with another scent.

Smoke. Burning flesh. Oh, god, the machine had malfunctioned. It was burning the man alive.

"Steady, Vivian." The reaper's cool, soothing voice broke through the terrifying sights, sounds, and smells that assaulted her senses. "It's only a shadow of the past. Nothing more. Mr. Edgar's suffering is over."

"No," she whispered. "Not if he's here."

Arms held her up and propelled her forward. Strong arms, whispered words of assurance, the struggle to remain upright.

Another image appeared. This one more intense. They were getting closer.

A room full of children dressed in everything from old-fashioned homespun to strait jackets to nothing at all filled her senses. There were so many. Bright faces, beautiful and broken, with eyes that didn't track, some with heads too small or distorted features, others with vacant gazes that showed the minds within were elsewhere, all in the small, cramped space.

There were broken toys, puddles of foul-smelling waste, and the stench of unwashed bodies and old feces and blood. A red-haired child in one corner repeatedly bashed her head against the wall, old bruises and blood showing that she'd been self-injuring for a long time. In the center of the room, a young boy with greasy, unkempt hair sat still, his torso covered with old scars. God, they were all so thin. When had they last eaten? Why was no one feeding them, bathing them, giving them even the most basic of human comforts?

"Vivian, breathe."

She inhaled on a sob, suddenly aware of the tears streaming down her face as she walked on shaking legs. So much suffering, it was too much. Her limbs grew heavy and her soul ached, but there were miles to go before she rested. The worst was to come.

"Should we stop?" B's voice shook. Not a good sign. If her current state of being was bad enough to rattle a cop, she was in worse condition that she thought.

"Just a bit more," Darkmore said. "I'll relieve her after we clear the next corridor."

A wave of cool energy caressed her senses, giving her the brief image of snow on the mountaintops surrounding her childhood home, the taste of cool ice cream on a summer's day, the chill of a clean mountain stream. The tremors running through her body eased and she found her footing.

They moved on.

When they turned the corner, all hell broke loose.

CHAPTER TWENTY-THREE

Everything went black as the sounds of hard rains and hacking coughs surrounded her. Lightning flashed, white and blinding. Not Marguerite's. Wherever or whenever Vivian's mind and soul were, they were no longer a part of the battle going on at the asylum.

She'd traveled to another dark time, her essence filled with the collective memories and suffering of souls long dead and lingering, reliving their years of suffering in the mortal world. Lost, lonely, hungry.

They would devour her soul.

Lanterns and candles flickered from what had to be the doorway, the fire illuminating the space with soft light. The clothing and lanterns gave her a few clues about the likely time frame. Victorian era, after the Civil War but not by much—she was standing in the ward for African American inmates, segregated from white patients no doubt housed under better conditions. Separate but equal wasn't even a concept yet, slavery within living memory, and the patients shivering on the threadbare cots were held by the twin chains of illness and insanity. Her visions from other wards might argue that these plagues of humanity were equal opportunity tormentors, but history and the images of agony shared with her by tortured souls made it clear that people of color suffered far greater atrocities in this den of misery.

Off in one corner, an old man rested belly down on his narrow cot, feet sticking out and kicking weakly. He groaned and grunted in pain, the sound louder than the cries of other boys and men sharing what was clearly a sick ward. The stench of vomit, human waste, blood, and sickly sweat permeated the hot, humid air. Bodies slick with perspiration and filth rested cheek by jowl, some practically stacked on top of one another, much as their ancestors had surely suffered during the middle passage.

Nurses dressed in long linen gowns floated around and between available gaps in the stacks of human suffering, their faces weary, vacant.

Haunted.

They'd seen suffering like this before and worse, powerless to do anything for their charges short of offering a murmured prayer or a sip of fetid water.

One nurse coughed, the sound harsh and rasping. She was succumbing to the same illness that would claim her charges. Swaying on her feet, the woman made her way to the old man in the corner. With a gentle hand on his back, she whispered words to him in another language, rich with vowels like liquid rolling from her tongue. He calmed, whispering back to her in the same tongue. How many generations had they kept the memories of their far away homeland and family and traditions alive in the face of oppression?

Vivian's vision narrowed, coming closer. She didn't want to see, didn't want to taste the pain of these poor souls, but it called to her and beckoned her soul to commune with theirs and give them ease. The woman's hand covered a scar on the man's shoulder, but not from accident or injury or even from the lash of a whip, though he bore scars made from one.

This was a brand. He'd been a slave. His masters called him Moses, but he'd had another name, a secret name. His pappy, baba, called him Jagun. He'd seen his wife dishonored and murdered by soldiers in the war, shortly after they'd been declared "free." His children had been sold a decade earlier. Years of searching for them proved fruitless, but he'd soldiered on, scraping by and making a living as a sharecropper.

At least it was on another farm, not the one where he'd been owned, though the two weren't different. Another wife, another chance to sow his seed with the promise of better days for his descendants, at least until she died birthing his son.

Between grief and syphilis, he'd lost his mind and been shipped off to the lunatic asylum where he'd endured more indignities, neglect, and the occasional horror. But he remembered his name. Jagun, his baba's warrior. After all this time, he could whisper his name to the woman of his people who came to carry his spirit to join those of his ancestors.

"What's going on over there?"

Vivian's consciousness spun around at the sound of the angry voice, but not before he saw the nurse flinch, her nails digging hard into Jagun's flesh. Another nurse, this one white, stood in the doorway, two large orderlies looming behind her, their dull gaze full of menace.

The nurse said, "Nothing, ma'am. Just giving this man some water."

"Come here, Beulah!" the woman snapped.

Timid nurse Beulah shuffled over to the angry white nurse, a fresh wave of coughing spasms slowing her progress. Head down, she stood very still in front of Nurse Self-Righteous, so named in Vivian's mind on account of the wooden cross she wore around her neck and the Bible clutched tight in her fingers.

"What were you saying to that man?"

"N-nothing, ma'am—"

Nurse Self-Righteous slapped Beulah across the face, silencing her reply. "You were speaking that vile tongue, devil talk, weren't you? Blasphemous."

"No, ma'am. It's not blasphemy. It's a prayer in the ancestor's speech."

Another slap, another rebuke, and a snap of the finger later and the two orderlies seized Beulah, one placing a hand over her mouth to muffle her screams. Beulah struggled, chest heaving and fighting another coughing fit.

"Let her go!" Vivian screamed in her mind. "She can't breathe."

"Thou shalt not suffer a witch to live. Lock her up. I'll deal with her later."

Nurse Self-Righteous turned on her heel and stormed off, leaving Beulah to the men who would rape and murder her, her screams echoing in Jagun's ears like the long ago screams of his wife.

"No more," Vivian keened. "No more no more nomorenomore."

A jolt of energy hit her in full force as the screams of thousands of souls brought her to her knees.

They'd found the souls.

———

"Vivian!"

Gutierrez's voice brought her out of whatever dark trance that had captured her and back to reality. She blinked, eyes swollen and crusted with dried tears. Vision blurry, she took in the scene. Souls, spirits, specters, they were everywhere. They floated in the air, disappeared and appeared through walls, crawled along the ceiling, or stood still. Many stared into the distance, clearly still lost in their madness. Others couldn't seem to stop moving. There were so many.

A scream from behind her made her sit up and spin around. Fighting a wave of dizziness, she saw the reaper clutching two apparitions. They'd been large in life, big men, but confronted with the reaper, they cowered and keened and would have pissed themselves if they were still capable.

Vivian recognized the spirits.

Mustering her strength, she stood and staggered over to them, rage giving her strength and forcing the burdens she'd harvested and made into potent spirit energy to spill from her fingertips. Without thinking, she shot a blast of red light through both souls, tearing gaping wounds into their essences. She fired again. And again.

Her single-minded purpose was to blast them out of existence.

The reaper's voice stilled her.

"I understand your compulsion, but I have a more fitting fate in mind for these wicked souls."

A vortex opened above them, a familiar portal. He'd called Uphir, the demon, and he intended to give the souls of the orderlies who'd raped and murdered the kind, young nurse, among their other sins. It was fitting. Not by her hand, but vengeance would be served, and justice.

"There's another," Vivian said. "The nurse who gave Beulah to these bastards. Find her."

Darkmore conjured chains of reaper energy around the pair of orderlies and extended his hands, compelling souls of the wicked trapped with the souls of their victims to come to him. One by one they disappeared into the portal, their cries of terror and agony reverberating through the room.

The sounds should have disturbed her more than they did.

At last, the soul of the nurse appeared, spectral gaze wide-eyed and frightened as she chanted. "The Lord is my shepherd, I shall not want…"

Vivian sent a blast of energy toward her, slapping her in the face. Faltering, she continued her chant until Vivian struck her again.

"Good, I have your attention," Vivian said, staring into the wicked soul, all the more wicked since she masked her crimes with the veil of Godliness and righteousness. But she'd known her actions were wrong, were cruel, and she'd reveled in that cruelty.

She'd enjoyed punishing Beulah through the two orderlies.

Vivian sent another blast into the soul of the nurse that sent her into the waiting arms of the reaper.

"Do you remember her?" Vivian asked.

"Remember who?"

Vivian stalked up to her, getting into her incorporeal face. "Beulah, the nurse you condemned to violation and death at the hands of your goons."

"That little Negro nurse? She was a witch. I was saving souls. It was my duty and right as God's chosen instrument and her natural superior."

Vivian was about to open her mouth, but Darkmore's chilly voice silenced her. "Don't waste your breath or your time, my dear. This creature isn't worth it. And I believe in show, not tell."

The reaper spun the nurse around and froze her with his icy gaze. "So full of self-righteousness, even after all this time, this side of the grave, Mistress Lisbeth. Never noticed, never wed, the church and your sense of entitlement were all you had in life, and jealousy, of course. Beulah was beautiful, kind, and compassionate, beloved of her patients and her fellow nurses, so unlike you."

"No," Lisbeth said. "I most certainly was not jealous of such a lowly creature. She was nothing, nobody."

"And yet, she was loved, cherished, and she made the patients she tended feel loved and cherished, unlike you. You wanted them to suffer. You *enjoyed* watching them writhe in pain and misery while you preached salvation in the afterlife. You told them that suffering was the only path to God. But that was only for the people of color on the lower wards. They had to suffer."

"It was God's will," she sputtered.

"You lie," Darkmore said, gripping her essence with his cold hands, digging into it as he might flesh.

"It was their lot. It was the way of things."

"Closer," Darkmore said, moving his face inches from hers. "But still not the truth. You were always jealous of the lovely, dark women on the plantation, the ones you imagined seduced your father, your brother, and your would-be suitors. And then, when they were freed, you grew even more jealous. You saw them free to marry, to bear and raise children they could keep and nurture—children you would never have—and they were beautiful. So unlike you."

"No, they weren't beautiful! They were animals, beneath us. And those damned Yankees marched down here, pillaged our lands, destroyed our way of life, and set them free. And for what? To loiter, steal, be shiftless without the guiding hand of their rightful masters—it was against the natural order."

"The natural order." A broad, malevolent grin spread across the reaper's face, the most beautiful and terrifying sight she'd yet beheld. She'd been wrong. He wasn't human, would not, could not, ever be human.

This was his true nature. He was reaper. He was dark justice, karma, and the avenger of the wronged. This was his purpose.

Fresh tears fell for what she knew she'd lose, for what she'd stolen from the universe.

Not stolen. Borrowed. Saved so she could restore him to his rightful place.

"Let me tell you what's going to happen to you, Lisbeth. I'm going to send you to a realm where the natural order dictates that you are the inferior race, fit only to serve, to toil, to provide pleasure to your masters when not being used as a brood mare. You'll have children, much like the fair Beulah, but they'll be ripped from your bosom and sold as chattel, or worse. You'll toil with them, side by side, watch as they are beaten, raped, dehumanized, and you will be powerless to stop it."

Disbelief followed by dawning realization painted her ghostly features. "That's not possible."

"Oh, but it is," the reaper said, caressing her face. "A lifetime of subjugation awaits you—perhaps several lifetimes. Karma is a fickle mistress."

Lisbeth pulled herself out of the reaper's grasp and flung herself at Vivian. "Please! You're a guardian. You work for God and for what's right. Save me."

Vivian stepped back, recoiling from the vile soul's touch. "I won't save you. I hope you live a thousand lives and suffer a million degradations for the pain you've cause on both sides of the grave you miserable bitch!"

Lisbeth turned to Gutierrez then to B, finding no hope in either of the soul brokers. Both had been ferrying lost and lonely souls to the next realm, righteous souls, souls worthy of peace. Other souls like Beulah and the kind-hearted nurses, doctors, and staff who'd done the best they could for the vulnerable people in their care would join them in peace. Those souls had suffered at the hands of Lisbeth and the other wardens of the asylum. The so-called caregivers who'd tortured and neglected them were now in the hands of the reaper.

"Time's up, Lisbeth. May you find the same mercy you professed to give in your first life."

The reaper channeled his energy and opened a hole in the floor. It was a gateway, smaller than the one she'd first seen him open when she'd first witnessed him at his work. He'd sent a murderer kicking and screaming into his dark realm. With a flick of his wrist, the souls of Lisbeth and the orderlies were sucked into the pit and off to their dismal fate. The reaper grinned, closed the pit, and collapsed in a heap as other damned souls flew into Uphir's realm.

CHAPTER TWENTY-FOUR

Vivian screamed.

"Lazarus!"

While B and Gutierrez saved souls and collected what energy the lost and lonely offered freely during their crossings, Vivian ran to the reaper, crumpled in a heap on the floor. God, it had been too much. He'd used too much energy in his mortal form, and it had cost him.

Had it cost him his life?

She bent over him, turning him on his back and placing her ear on his chest. His heart was racing, his breathing erratic. Energy flowed through her, transforming from violent bursts with killing power to a gentler, healing light. The reaper's broken body drew her light, but she held it in check. The last time she'd healed him, she'd trapped him in his mortal body. Would she make it worse by healing him again?

If he died, it would be much worse.

"Vivian." His voice was soft and ragged. "Feed me. Give me the misery and suffering and anger and pain you gathered and make me whole."

She bent to him, pressed her lips gently against his, and the world melted away. All of the misery, suffering, sadness, anger, guilt, avarice, and every other piece of pain she'd taken in while searching for the lost souls emptied from her into the reaper. Hand on his chest, she felt the steadying of his heart-beat, even breaths, cool skin growing colder as she fueled his reaper nature. She fed him the sorrows, and he gave her peace and restored her in turn.

"You two about finished?"

B's voice broke the spell. The reaper smiled against her mouth and she caught his whispered gratitude. "Better than aged whiskey, fine wine, or ambrosia."

Vivian reluctantly pulled herself away from the reaper, stood, and surveyed the scene. Most of the souls were gone, leaving B and Gutierrez glowing with a surplus of energy, raw power radiating through their beings. The souls who lingered appeared...restored. Sane, powerful, filled with the same energy only a thousand-fold more potent.

Maybe even as potent as Mae.

Vivian recognized the souls she'd met at the crossroads among them. Relief and gratitude washed over her. She'd been so afraid that she'd failed them, but her message had somehow gotten through, thank God. She could help them and, if they were willing, they could help a whole host of other souls.

"Good to see you again. You're free if you want to cross. If you don't, we ask that you join us. Together, we can bring the whole guardian system crashing down and build something new. Something better."

Many of the souls floated silently to Gutierrez and B. By the time the two living soul brokers were finished mediating the crossings, they looked ragged and spent in spite of their energy infusions. Yeah, the energy came with a price. Gutierrez and B would be haunted by the suffering and horror of those lost and lonely souls for the rest of their days. Five souls remained by the end, including the specters of Beulah, Jagun, a small boy with scarred wrists, and a man with a shaved head, emaciated and gaunt. She recognized the boy and man from their meeting at the crossroads and was again filled with gratitude. They'd received her message, and they were willing to help.

The last soul, a short man wearing old-fashioned spectacles, stepped forward. "I'm Doctor Remy LaFleur, or I was." He cocked his head to the side. "I suppose I still am, though perhaps I am a bit outdated."

"Why are you here?" B asked, his voice laced with suspicion. "Figured all y'all who ran this torture warehouse would've been reaper fodder."

Darkmore chuckled, apparently somewhat restored from his former state. "I'm afraid Dr. LaFleur isn't to my taste. Too sweet and...fluffy."

Vivian grinned. "I think what the reaper means is that Doc Remy is one of the good guys. You helped take care of them?"

The doctor bowed, the gesture charming and old fashioned. He might have stepped out of a Charles Dickens novel with his top hat, long coat covering what had probably been a colorful waistcoat when he was alive, and a neck cloth somewhere between a tie and cravat. The striped pants didn't quite match anything else in his attire, but it fit the era, which she assumed was somewhere between the 1880s and turn of the 20th century.

"Then why are you still here?" Gutierrez, ever suspicious, stared at the doctor's ghost, fresh spirit light pulsing beneath her skin. She was itching for a fight. A big one.

But this gentleman wasn't her target.

Before Vivian could speak—or strike—in defense of the doc, he did it himself. "I couldn't leave them." Gesturing to the remaining spirits and to the room formerly occupied by a host of others who'd recently crossed, He continued. "In my time, modern methods of treating patients alienated from their true natures made it possible to understand the damaged mind and it's dissociation with reality. Many of our less severe cases responded. But then..."

Funding cuts, interference from religious zealots like Nurse Lisbeth, or lack of concern by his colleagues came to Vivian's mind as possible explanations. Maybe all three. His answer, therefore, surprised her.

"I was stricken with consumption. My colleagues urged me to travel west and seek relief with the healing springs and fresh air, but I couldn't leave my patients. I had to help them, had to train a new generation of bold residents eager to unravel the mysteries of the damaged mind. These weren't hopeless cases, you see. They could be cured. I knew it."

"You were a man ahead of your time," the reaper said, not without sympathy. "Alas, your untimely death was also the death of your reforms and fresh ideas, at least for a while. Yet, you stayed."

The doctor inclined his head to the reaper. "I couldn't leave my patients, not even in death. Not when so many of them lingered and languished only to be imprisoned by the foul creatures guarding this place." He practically spat the last words.

Vivian knew an ally when she saw one and jumped on the opportunity to take this fight to their allies on the outside who were neck deep in guardian spirits. "Okay, can you communicate with these spirits? I assume they want to help, since they didn't cross."

Dr. LaFleur studied the motley crew of living soul brokers and reaper surrounding them. Naturally, trust wouldn't come easy for this soul or his charges. After having endured more than a century of abuse and neglect at the hands of many of their caregivers, followed by exploitation and abuse by the spirits charged with ferrying them to peace, why would they trust Vivian and her team?

Crap on a cracker, she'd have to show him.

With a deep breath for courage, Vivian let some of her light leave her fingertips and dangle in the air between them, inviting the doctor to accept what she offered, or not, of his own free will. Wouldn't Darkmore be proud of that? No, that wouldn't do. She shoved the snark and anger deep within her psyche and infused her energy with images from her past, from the training with Briggs and the rest of the team, to their purpose.

Doc LaFleur studied the energy with the fascination of a true scientist, walking around it, studying the glow from every angle. He touched it with the tip of his finger and then jumped back, at least as much of a jump as an incorporeal being could make. Under other circumstances, she would have laughed. Luckily, he dusted himself off and touched the light again, a smile of wonder curling his ghostly lips beneath the bushy, old-fashioned beard.

"What is this marvelous substance? It is much like the ether extracted from my patients by our captors, and yet...different. Is red light special? How do you produce it? You are living, are you not?"

Vivian resisted the urge to roll her eyes. Tempering her impatience, she said. "It's a long story and I'll tell you all about it later. For now, take it in and see my story and my truth."

"Make it fast," B said, on edge. They'd all been tracking the flashes of light and sounds of battle outside. "We need to get the rest of the teams and get out."

The doctor placed his hand on the light. It curled around his ghostly form before disappearing into his essence. She'd never seen a spirit pale before, but she feared the doc might pass out or possibly blink out of this plane of existence. After a long moment, he blinked, returning to himself, and stared at Vivian.

"Oh, my dear." He reached out to take her hand. When his ghostly form passed through her flesh, she dipped her hand to maintain the illusion of contact. "You are all like this? Trapped in your own way, between worlds, helping lost souls on their journey?"

"Pretty much. You and your spirits going to help us take on the system and knock it to the ground?" Gutierrez was clearly ready to wrap up negotiations so she could go out and put her sharp shooting skills to good use.

The doctor smiled. "I believe we are."

B had moved to the door and cracked it open. Standing against the doorjamb, he pivoted and pointed his hand straight in front of him and made a slow arc with his body and hands, searching up and down the corridor with slow and deadly precision. Cop instincts worked well with spirit light, apparently. Good thing he was covering them.

Gutierrez moved out the door and down the corridor first, taking the lead. Vivian and the reaper followed the doc, who led the lost and lonely spirits who'd stuck around, their vacant gazes still staring straight ahead and apparently lost in their mental turmoil. Their energy glowed and pulsed around them like a living creature. Were it not for her experience with Mae, she'd worry that they were leading these souls to their former captors like lambs to the slaughter.

Okay, she was worried, but she mustered what faith she had and focused on covering them as B brought up the rear. Father Montgomery, her unlikely ally and even more unlikely friend, would have been proud of her.

The corridor was quiet aside from muffled sounds of fighting or fleeing outside. She hoped the mortal authorities wouldn't show up, wondering how they'd explain a freak lighting storm that may or may not be visible to ordinary humans, let alone a bunch of paramilitary-looking loonies firing invisible spirit light at invisible targets.

The cops would think the inmates were literally running the asylum.

Darkmore moved ahead of her.

"What?" She looked up and down the corridor, trying to spot the danger he saw.

"Your guardian friends are still in parlay with the sentinels who claimed the lost souls. We must proceed with caution."

She hadn't thought it possible with all of the commotion going on outside, not to mention the energy surge they'd produced while ferrying souls to the next realms. Jeanne and Zeke were good. Of course, Zeke was a smooth talker. The thought was like a knife through her heart. She'd fallen under his spell, much as his wife did long ago, before he'd passed. The magic broke shortly after with his wife.

It hadn't ended for Vivian, even after she'd let him go. God, even after he'd come back to her and she found out where he'd been.

No time to deal with it now.

"Maria," Vivian said. "Hold. We've got to get a message to Zeke, Jeanne, and the rest of the teams before we pull out. Exit strategy?"

"Already on it, Red."

B came up beside her, grinning as he tapped his mic. Good. He'd been in touch with the other teams. Briggs was going to go apeshit. Probably try to blast them all into the afterlife for the stunt they'd pulled. Showing up with energy and allies might save their skins and the rebellion.

"Recon?"

It was Maria who brought up the subject they'd been avoiding. They might pull this mission off, but it would be for nothing if they couldn't find the traitor in their midst.

"We got nothing," B said.

If it was Chet, he hadn't yet made his move. None of the other team leaders had behaved out of the ordinary. It was possible he or she was waiting until they got the energy payload back to base. On the one hand, the chaos and confusion of the raid could provide an opportunity to extract the spirit energy and slip away under the guise of taking it back to base. That had been one of the reasons Vivian and her team broke with protocol to safeguard the imprisoned souls and their energy.

On the other hand, the traitor might volunteer for guard duty back at base, taking advantage of post battle euphoria and exhaustion to make off with the cache of spirit energy. It made sense if the traitor was playing the long game, biding time and making sure the mission was a success. Why out yourself on a failed mission and throw away the opportunity for another chance on the next raid?

Shit.

B shrugged. "We can't wait any longer. Let's get our allies and get the hell out of here. The rest can wait."

"Pardon me, young man, but how will you ensure our captors won't follow and recapture us?" The doctor had dematerialized and reappeared beside B. To his credit, the ex-cop didn't flinch, but his veins pulsed hard at his temple and neck, and if he clenched his jaw any tighter, he's likely crack his back molars.

"We're going to use some of the energy y'all gave us to blast them out of this plane of existence."

"You and Gutierrez take the doc, the inmates, and the reaper back to base," Vivian said. "Tell the others to blast as many sentinels as they can. I'm guessing Marguerite took out the strongest, but we don't know how many there are. Be careful."

"And where will you be?"

Darkmore's voice was low, calm, and it made the hairs on the back of her neck stand at attention. God, she'd hoped he'd have enough of his reaper sense left to rise above petty jealousy, but no such luck. She turned to face him, meeting his icy gaze and refusing to look away—no small feat, since he infused as much darkness and otherness as he could muster into that gaze.

Then, for just an instant, she caught a flash of something else, something so heartbreakingly human that it made her drop her gaze and blink back unshed tears.

"I'm going to get Jeanne and Zeke out."

Meeting his gaze again, which had returned to its usual unreadable state, she spoke again. "We have unfinished business, Zeke and I. I have unfinished business with you, too, but this isn't about us. I need you to take care of my team. I need to you look out for the doctor, these damaged souls, and Briggs, and everyone else. Can you do that for me, Lazarus? Please."

After a long moment, he offered her a small, sad smile and nodded. "I can refuse you nothing, Vivian Bedford. I never could. You might ask me for the moon and stars, and I would pluck them out of the sky for you."

Her tears fell freely then, cheeks heating under the scrutiny of her team and the ghosts in their midst. "I'd never ask for the moon and stars."

"No," he agreed. "Too mundane. You ask for things that are far more ordinary. And precious. Go."

Throwing caution to the wind, she threw her arms around him, kissed him hard, and headed down the corridor to the mess waiting for her on the other side.

CHAPTER TWENTY-FIVE

She didn't bother masking her presence with spirit energy. The guardians would see through her concealment, both allies and enemies. Still, she used the shadow of the building and the trees and bushes on the grounds as cover. Sirens sounded in the distance. Not good. The air hung thick with smoke from the rooftop fires Marguerite had ignited, several still burning in spite of efforts by the human firefighters on site.

A blazing hot sentinel in corporeal form stood between two of the firefighters, barking orders. It confirmed that the humans working in the asylum were under the control of sentinels. Guardian spirits unaffiliated with the Archangel Council or the official guardian spirit operation, but just as dangerous as their sanctioned counterparts. The whole corrupt afterlife management system was on the verge of collapse. Good riddance, as far as Vivian was concerned, but without some form of order, operations like this would keep cropping up. The existing high-level guardians would splinter and split power, amassing as many allies and as much spirit energy as they could harvest ethically, steal, or extort from unsuspecting souls.

It would be chaos of the worst kind.

Damn it, she'd signed on to work locally, helping the spirits she could and doing the right thing within the guardian spirit system, operating under the radar. How had she been sucked into a rebellion that was quickly escalating into a war? And how was she expected to rebuild a new system that would better serve the needs of the souls she served?

"No, think about that later."

The whispered thought was as much a plea to herself as a command.

Spotting Zeke and Jeanne, she came as close as she dared, concerned by the way the sentinels surrounding them seemed to be closing in. Should she go in with hands blazing or wait for some signal? Surely Jeanne had an escape plan. Jeanne had been uber organized in life, and she'd proven herself an outstanding, capable, and competent guardian spirit for one so young. Zeke could and would fight dirty, a strategy she approved of since it was her style as well.

In the distance, she spotted Chet's team falling back, melting into shadow and retreating to their planned escape route. Apparently, they'd found some other lost and lonely souls and helped them cross. Vivian detected the spike in energy emanating from the living soul brokers.

And...so had the sentinels.

Time to act.

The lead sentinel held up her hand and shot a blast of energy into the air, two short bursts of light followed by three. Responding to the signal, the sentinels and humans occupied with firefighting and in pursuit of Marguerite abandoned their posts and flocked to the circle of guardians, now splitting into two groups. One pursued the retreating rebel teams and the rest closed in on Jeanne and Zeke.

Vivian took a deep breath, then another, bringing up the horrifying memories she'd collected from the souls imprisoned on these grounds. The energy was dark, thick and viscous, like oil or tar, clinging to her psyche and soul—unclean, profane, a stain that no amount of time or penance could wash away. The cruelty and degradation forged into spirit energy could only be cleansed by fire.

With a cry of grief and rage and madness, she launched herself at the circle of sentinels, unleashing energy darker than any she'd yet channeled, so dark red it appeared black and shiny in the night. Dark as fresh blood in the moonlight, it hit the first sentinel and set his corporeal body on fire. He collapsed into a heap of dust, shaking off the burning remnants of the body he'd constructed, and yet the fire still burned bright enough to light the night sky.

How was such a thing possible? Never had she seen any spirit, guardian, reaper, or lost and lonely soul, burn like that. Non-corporeal manifestations shouldn't be able to burn, but the soul that had strength and energy enough to construct a convincing facsimile of a human body now flickered before her inside unearthly flames, his screams echoing even after he flashed out of existence.

Wasting no time, Zeke and Jeanne turned their own spirit light on two of the other sentinels who'd been distracted by Vivian's deadly show of force. Three others rushed Vivian, hitting her with painful blasts strong enough to knock her body against a brick wall. *Damn it, Bedford, get your head in the game!*

Shaking off pain and brick dust, Vivian sent an enormous blast of energy that split into three distinct streams, one for each sentinel. Again, both corporeal body and spirit within burned out of existence as she stumbled past, back stooped against injuries she'd sustained upon impact.

Stupid. Stupid of her to let her guard down and stupid to get caught up in the spirit light show.

Healing from the injuries she'd sustained was going to be a bitch.

Zeke and Jeanne had disabled their two sentinels and were working together on a third, which left the leader to Vivian. This sentinel looked about fourteen, moved like she was a twenty-something triathlete, and had the burning, fathomless gaze of the reaper. Old. Powerful. Deadly.

And was heading directly toward Vivian in a whirlwind of spirit light and power.

Vivian stood straight and held up her hands, dizzy from excruciating pain shooting through her back. Her breath rushed out as spots danced before her eyes. Unable to draw a breath on account of the pain, she couldn't fire. The powerful sentinel spirit was on her in a flash, fashioning spirit energy into sharp blades that sliced and burned into flesh and spirit.

Her jaw twisted in a silent scream.

She was going to die, here and now, and become the slave of this sentinel, this evil rogue guardian spirit, for eternity, or worse. The price her soul would fetch might make it worth turning her over to the Archangels for a bounty of energy. Either way, she was done.

But the souls were safe, Jeanne and Zeke were safe, and the reaper was safe. The rebellion would live on, and maybe someday they could liberate her soul.

It was a small price to pay.

With her last, gasping breath, she mustered the worst of the memories staining and tainting the unholy ground upon which she'd die. She couldn't fire, but let it seep into her spirit, her body, and her blood. Blood was good. It flowed freely from the slashes and stab wounds and coated the crazed sentinel on top of her. Flames burned her from within as they spilled out of those wounds and wicked up over the sentinel's body, which was gone in a flash. The last thing she saw before darkness overtook her was the explosion of light and fire as she sent the spirit into oblivion with a scream of pure terror.

CHAPTER TWENTY-SIX

She awoke with a start but didn't dare open her eyes. Wherever she'd landed in the afterlife, it couldn't be good, assuming one of the evil sentinels had claimed her soul after she destroyed their leader in a blaze of glory. Maybe Jeanne or Zeke had helped her cross.

Zeke. Something about the scent tickling her nose reminded her of Zeke.

Coffee? Yes, she smelled coffee, and eggs, bacon, and the yeasty aroma of fresh pancakes.

Opening her eyes, she saw an unfamiliar wooden ceiling. Her gaze traveled along the walls of what appeared to be a log cabin, fire roaring in an oversized fireplace, its blaze small and weak compared to the spirit fire she'd unleashed...when? How long had she been out?

She was breathing without pain. Pushing away the thick down comforter that someone had draped over her, she looked down the length of her body. No blood, no aches or pains, and to her surprise and relief, she was able to sit up without pain. Guess she'd been out long enough to heal her jacked up back. Tiny red scars covered her arms, and her torso, as she discovered when she lifted the bottom of a soft tank top.

Someone had cleaned her up, changed her, and taken her away to rest and heal.

But they hadn't taken her back to Briggs' compound.

"Don't get up too fast. You'll get dizzy."

She laughed and it made her dizzy. Talk about déjà vu. Zeke's disembodied voice had been the first thing she heard after waking up from a trip to the reaper's realm long ago. Wait, not so long ago. The past few years seemed like an eternity. Her guardian spirit had saved her then—from her darkness, from the reaper, from herself?

Reaper. Darkness. Briggs.

"What happened?" She tried to yell, but it came out as a hoarse croak. Damn her raw and raspy throat. She must've been screaming. When she rose from the tangle of sheets, she stumbled, tripping over sore limbs and amazed she could even walk. By all rights, her soul should have blinked out of existence after the spirit light blast destroyed her fragile, mortal body.

"Sit down first and eat," Zeke said. He stood in the cabin's kitchen, back to her as he cooked.

Wearing jeans and a button-down shirt with the sleeves rolled up, he looked good. His mortal form was the same as she remembered with heartbreaking clarity. Part of her wanted to fall into his arms and never let go. Another part wanted to rage and scream at him for staying on this plane rather than taking the path to peace she'd opened for him with blood, pain, and pieces of her humanity and soul.

Instead, she sat at the table and filled her plate with bacon, eggs, and fluffy pancakes. Delicious, of course—the man could cook. Surprisingly, not only could she eat, she devoured two helpings, two cups of coffee, and thought about getting another serving.

Zeke picked at his food and watched her eat, a small, sad smile on his face.

"What?" she asked, dreading the answer.

"We need to talk."

They did, but that didn't make it easier to swallow past the lump that suddenly appeared in her throat.

"We do," she said. "But first I need to know what happened back at the asylum. Are the souls safe?"

"Yes, and before you ask, your reaper got out, too. He's on a recon mission right now. I'll tell you the rest after you listen to me."

The note of jealousy in his voice set her off. She stood and started gathering plates, her movements controlled. Breaking someone else's dishes, cathartic as that might be, would be rude. Silverware was fair game, though, and she enjoyed the clank of metal against metal as she tossed them into the sink.

Zeke didn't even flinch, which pissed her off even more.

"So talk." She didn't stop her vicious cleaning. "I'll clean while you do it. It will be better than blasting you across the room."

He sighed deeply and ran a hand through his dark hair, green eyes glittering with barely suppressed rage. She looked away. He had no right to be angrier than she did. Or maybe he did, but she wasn't in the mood to be the bigger person.

"What I did was wrong. With Jen. I haven't done right by her on either side of the grave, but I wanted her to be happy, so I did the only thing I could for her. She deserved to move on with her life."

He didn't say the name of the new man in his wife's life. Not that she blamed him. Beneath the anger boiling to the depths of her soul, she had been jealous and hurt when she found out Zeke had inhabited the body of his mortal wife's new lover. She'd thought it was out of loneliness, something she understood all too well. Or worse, she'd wondered if Zeke had been getting back at her for what he perceived as rejection. But maybe she'd been wrong.

"I had to protect my children. I didn't do it while I was alive, but I could make sure no one from the afterlife went after my son."

Zeb. The beautiful boy with his father's green eyes and dark hair held an abundance of spirit light. Autism robbed him of many things in his early life—speech, engagement with the outside world, and engagement with the people who loved him. Zeke hadn't been a good man in that part of his life, perhaps all of his life. Vivian had never asked about it other than the events leading to his untimely death. Forced to marry Jen when she got pregnant, he'd lost his freedom. And when Zeb had been diagnosed with autism, he'd lost even more. He'd turned back to his old habits, cheating on Jen and neglecting her and his son.

Oh, he'd tried to make amends after a few years, becoming a devoted husband and father. Then Jen got pregnant again, and early signs indicated that the daughter she carried might not be whole and healthy.

He'd been resentful. What was worse, Vivian understood, having experienced the same resentment over Mae. Caregiver fatigue. But Zeke had taken it to extreme. After finding out about the baby, he'd lost it, taking his anger out on Jen before cleaning out their bank account and hitting the road.

He hadn't made it far. Vivian had only seen him once when he was still alive. She'd watched him die after the car crash that was supposed to take her life as well. Zeke had been destined for the reaper's domain. Vivian, for her sins, had been destined to serve the guardian spirits. She hadn't run out on Mae, but she'd contemplated suicide, which apparently constituted the lesser of the evils as far as afterlife management was concerned. So Ezra, the guardian sent to claim her, had taken Zeke instead, robbing the reaper of his prize and getting revenge on Darkmore for a past encounter.

It had left Vivian trapped in the middle with Mae's soul in play. Both sides wanted Mae for her spirit light. But Darkmore had wanted more. He'd wanted Vivian for her own sake.

Okay, that was romanticizing it. The reaper had coveted her power, and she intrigued him. It hadn't been love, at least...not at first? But now, having been cast together as living soul broker and as close to mortal man as the reaper could get, was it love?

She'd been in love with Zeke once. Was she still?

Slumping over the sink, Vivian blinked back tears and resisted the urge to run away. That would be the coward's way out. Strange. Facing the reaper, his dark realm, corrupt Archangels and rogue guardians hadn't scared her as much as facing the men in her life.

"I crossed a line with Jen, another line, and I can't even apologize. I can't talk to her, can't let her know that I'm still around and doing what I didn't do in life, and it isn't fair that I want to. But I do. What I don't want to do is hurt her or the kids anymore, so Jeanne has taken over as their guardian."

Vivian spun around and stared at him in wide-eyed shock. Jeanne? Not that Jeanne wasn't capable, but if anything, the assignment seemed... beneath her wasn't the right word, but in the eyes of the guardian hierarchy, and in the eyes of Marguerite, guarding a single family might be considered too little.

As if guessing her thoughts, Zeke grinned. "You and your band of rebels aren't the only ones looking to buck the system. Marguerite's on board. She'll travel the globe and mediate crossings while Jeanne minds my family."

"That's...good. Jeanne will take good care of them." Treading lightly, she asked, "Will you see them again?"

"No. They're better off if I'm not around. I'll—" He had to pause and clear his throat. "I need to let go, too. It's for the best."

He was right, though her heart ached for him, for his family, and for the whole situation. God, things were just as complicated in the afterlife as they were on this side of the grave. She wasn't sure how else to feel, though she couldn't help feeling for Zeke.

"Why are you telling me this?" She sat back down across from him, her hands moving of their own volition toward his on the other side of the table.

He took her hands into his larger, warmer hands. Guardians could do that, offer warmth and comfort, and comfort rolled off of him in waves. He could probably read her, too. Unlike Darkmore, his powers weren't diminished. And she read him and the truth of his words—the pain of loss and separation from his family, the fervent hope that his sacrifice would make their lives better and end Jen's mourning, lingering regret, longing, and love.

She gasped, tempted to pull her hands away. He still loved her and had never stopped. He'd forgiven her for casting him aside, understanding that she'd been trying to save him.

He held her gaze, his heart in his. "Didn't you know?"

She owed him honest. "No, I wasn't sure. I knew you cared for me, but I thought too much had happened between us."

"Not for me," he said, gently releasing her hands. "The question is, has too much happened between us for you."

God, this was the worst timing. Not that any time would be good for this conversation, but so much remained uncertain—the fate of the rebellion, the guardian and reaper establishment, how living soul brokers would fit in to whatever new order emerged from the ashes.

"I don't even know what's going to happen in the next few hours, days, let alone what's going to happen with us long-term. There may not even be a long-term."

Zeke nodded. "But if there is, I want you. I love you."

She didn't bother blinking back tears. Confusion, fear, anger, and so many other emotions filled her fuller than any burden she'd ever accepted from any soul, living or dead. "I can't make that decision now."

Sadness crept into his green-eyed gaze, but he nodded again. "I know. I'll wait. I'd wait forever for you, Vivian Bedford."

Something tickled the back of her mind, something Mae had said when she'd spoken to Vivian through Mrs. Briggs. "He is with me. Our guardian."

Oh, Zeke.

"You've been with Mae. Looking out for her." It wasn't quite a question, but he smiled at the uncertainty in her voice.

"Well, we've been looking out for each other, really. She's something else, your sister. Something special."

And so are you, guardian.

After all this time, he was still protecting Mae, and protecting her. He'd never stopped. No matter what he'd been or done in life, he was a protector and guardian in the afterlife. He'd become the "man" he'd always wanted to be as a spirit.

"What happened to the rest of the team?" she asked, grateful to change the subject.

Zeke stood and started pacing, a habit he'd carried with him into the afterlife. "The soul brokers made it out. We neutralized or destroyed the sentinels and you took out the last one. Put on quite a light show, too. The souls who stayed behind are safe with the rest of your team. I believe your friends Gutierrez and B are guarding them. Won't even let Chet go near them."

That made sense. They still didn't know who they could trust and wouldn't until they identified their traitor. "What about Briggs?"

He stopped and leveled her with his gaze.

"Briggs is gone. No one has seen him since the battle. Your reaper is looking for him."

CHAPTER TWENTY-SEVEN

Zeke was kind enough to transport her back to base, if travel through the spinning vortex of guardian spirit teleportation could be considered a kindness. Convenient? Yes. Comfortable? Not so much.

Except for being wrapped in Zeke's arms. It wasn't right, enjoying the warmth of his corporeal body and the warmer presence of his guardian powers, but she needed it. With a whispered promise to contact him as soon as she received word about Briggs, she let him go and walked reluctantly to her apartment.

The one she shared with the reaper.

She was glad Zeke sensed and understood. She couldn't deal with both Zeke and the reaper at the same time, not while dealing with the FUBARed mission now missing its leader, possibly at the hands of an unknown traitor who appeared to be operating outside of the rebel teams.

She turned the knob, unsurprised to find it open. The reaper wasn't much for locked doors.

"Lazarus?"

She received no answer, but the gooseflesh on her skin from the chill in the space let her know he was there. Moving from the small living area to the kitchen and then to the bedroom, she found the reaper sitting on their bed, staring at the ceiling. He seemed so human, vulnerable, and beautiful, and she wanted to fall into his arms and let his coolness envelop her.

"Back from your latest rescue?"

His voice was a low, silken purr, and it raised the hairs on the back of neck. He sounded more like the reaper she'd first met, the stuff of nightmares and darkness that you wanted to run from and run toward all at once. He sounded dangerous.

It pissed her off.

"Here's what I need from you, reaper. I need you to focus on this mission. I need you to put aside whatever jealousy your human side is conjuring so we can find Briggs, give the big, bad loa what he wants, and restore you to your former state. You with me?"

He pushed his body up from the bed slowly, gracefully, with the controlled movements of a stalking predator. Blue-eyed gaze, icy and fathomless, locked on hers. Her hackles rose, but she held her fear and anger in check. If she was angry, he was, too, and rightly so, she supposed. Zeke had once rescued her from the reaper's clutches, and she'd once loved her guardian. She might love him still, but her emotions were too tangled for her to be sure of anything.

The reaper had saved her more than once, including when he took a blast of spirit light that would have been lethal to her. He'd sacrificed his immortality, his ability to move between spirit realms as an incorporeal reaper and the material world—her world—as a corporeal spirit. He'd stayed with her, aided her, and even fought alongside Zeke for her.

Vivian wasn't prepared to let him intimidate her, but she would allow him to speak his mind. She owed him that.

"Am I with you?" The question was rhetorical, so she didn't bother answering. "I've been with you since the beginning, little soul broker, and you've challenged me every step of the way. You resisted, you offered to *save* me from my realm, you asked me to be your insurance policy against the guardians you served, and you asked me to accompany you on this fool's errand to join a rebellion so you could restore me."

God, but he could make her squirm. Fighting the urge to drop her gaze, she said, "All of that is true. You saved me and lost your immortality. Whatever humanity you've found can't be worth the price you'll pay when you die!"

Tears flowed down her cheeks unchecked, and she let them. She was tired of crying, tired of grieving and mourning, tired of guilty, of being pulled between two worlds, two men, and a destiny she couldn't understand and never wanted. But she would not allow the reaper to suffer an eternity of torment for her sake.

"Free will, Vivian. Would you deny me mine?"

"I already have!" she yelled, fists curled at her sides, holding the energy sparking from her fingertips. "I stole your free will when I healed you and made you mortal. You didn't have a choice, and I have to make it right!"

The reaper smiled, his face transforming from menacing and otherworldly to something so very human. He took two steps to reach her, took her face in his palms, and wiped her tears away with his thumbs.

"I have a choice now, and so do you. You may take me as human or as reaper if you insist on letting the loa restore me to my previous state. I would take you in any form."

Oh, God, how could she choose? Zeke was first, but Lazarus Darkmore meant as much to her as Zeke did. Zeke had spoken of love, but the reaper had never betrayed her. Zeke hadn't exactly betrayed her, but his actions had crossed many lines and damaged their relationship. Could it heal? Could she live without the reaper? Could she live without Zeke?

With a heavy sigh, Darkmore let her go and put space between them. "You don't have to decide right away, but soon. For now, I suggest you secure Briggs' grandmother."

"Is she in danger?"

"Your leader is missing, presumably taken by someone who wants what he has. What is his most valuable resource?"

God, she was stupid. The traitor would want what any soul broker, guardian, or reaper covets—energy. Briggs' grandmother was his repository. Forget quashing the rebellion. If the guardians got their hands on the mambo, they could use the vast quantities of energy to defeat those who resisted the status quo and as the means to channel a host of dangerous and powerful spirits, demigods, demons, and God only knew what else to do their bidding.

"Who else knows about Bijoux Briggs?"

Darkmore said, "No one in the rebellion, and none of the other cells are missing members. Your friends checked."

It was her turn to pace. "But that makes no sense. Maeve's vision, the loa's bargain, they all point to a traitor, someone who'd cross Briggs to stop the rebellion."

"Assuming it's about the rebellion." Darkmore seemed lost in thought, which was still odd to her. She was used to the confident, almost omniscient reaper. He was the man who had all the answers, even if he didn't share or gave her pieces of the puzzle wrapped up with bows of cryptic obfuscation.

Now he seemed as lost as she was. She could really use the other guy right now.

Think, think, think.

Okay, so if it wasn't about the rebellion, what else could it be? Did Briggs have enemies this side of life? Probably, but would they know about his afterlife management business? Not likely. Closer to home?

She froze. "Lazarus, what kind of read did you get from Aunt Olive?"

The reaper cocked his head to the side and thought. "She's a true believer in the Christian faith, uncomfortable with the traditions of her charge. Protective, loyal, zealous—she wants to save souls."

"How badly does she want to save souls? Bad enough to pair up with the establishment?"

The reaper grinned. "Possibly. Probably. We should pay her a visit."

"Not without backup," Vivian said. "We'll go alone, but I want the others to know what kind of hunch we're playing. Tell Gutierrez, B, and Chet. I need to let Jeanne and Zeke know in case our firepower isn't enough to stop her."

To his credit, Darkmore didn't balk at her mention of Zeke. He simply nodded and left to inform their allies on site while she summoned Zeke. Zeke didn't like her going with just the reaper—not out of jealousy, thank God, but because the reaper couldn't protect her in his current state. She countered that no one could protect her from the Archangels if they'd gotten to Bijoux Briggs.

No one except Mae.

And the only way to Mae was through the mambo.

What she had to do was get to the mambo, get her to safety, find Briggs, and fulfill her end of the bargain to the loa. The reaper could help, and he'd be on hand for the loa to restore.

"I don't know how to do this?" she said.

Zeke grinned. "You've always been a fly-by-the-seat-of-your-pants gal. What's different now?"

"The stakes." If the Archangels got the upper hand, they would crush all of the living soul brokers, the guardians who aided them, and would continue to hold innocent souls for ransom to increase their power. "It's not about Mae anymore, or me, or you, or even the reaper. It's about everyone."

Zeke took her hands and kissed her on the forehead. "I have faith in you, and I'll be there, just outside with Jeanne and the souls you liberated. Your reaper will be with you. You won't be alone."

———

It was dusk when she arrived at the home Briggs' grandmother shared with his aunt, her caregiver and protector. It was something Vivian had in common with the woman. Hopefully common ground would help her negotiate with someone who she suspected was doing the right thing for the wrong reason.

She and the reaper had left their reinforcements behind, approaching the house on foot from several blocks away. It probably wouldn't matter if the Archangels had infiltrated Briggs' inner circle, but if Olive was operating alone, as they suspected, she would be more likely to let Vivian and Darkmore in than a host of strangers. They hadn't risked any of the incorporeal spirits by sending them on a recon mission. Too risky if other spirits were involved, or if the loa Mrs. Briggs channeled were disinclined to trust unfamiliar spirits.

Approaching the front steps, Vivian rang the doorbell, tense and wary as shadows moved inside, behind sheer curtains. A well-manicured hand pulled the curtains aside, revealing Olive Briggs in her matronly glory. Vivian was struck again by how well the woman was put together, albeit like a throwback from a bygone era. She smiled warmly at Vivian and unlocked the door. The smell of fresh coffee and some mouthwatering baked good wafted from the kitchen.

She'd been expecting company, then.

"I thought you and your friend might stop by," she said, turning her megawatt smile to Darkmore. It was so strange, the attraction she had to the reaper. Most living souls who were on the right side of good and evil tread lightly around the reaper, leaving the bad souls to fall under his spell.

She didn't want to think too hard about her own attraction to him. Whatever it meant, the rapport Olive had with Darkmore would get them in the door and maybe get them some much-needed information. Olive stepped aside and allowed them to enter. The den appeared much as it had on their first visit, only darker, seeming to close in with claustrophobia-inducing tightness.

And the air was thick with spirit energy and power.

Olive invited them to have a seat while she disappeared into the kitchen. She came back with a lovely serving tray filled with cookies and small cakes, a pot of coffee, and three mugs, helping herself to the treats when Vivian and Darkmore politely declined.

After a delicate bite of cake and a sip of coffee, she asked, "I assume you're looking for my nephew?"

"Yes. Do you know where he is?" Vivian had a million questions for creepy aunt Olive, but she decided to keep it direct and simple, following creepy aunt's lead.

"Of course I do. I know everything, including how he sold his soul to that desert demon when he was in service. He's not been the same since, meddling in things better left to God. I mean to put a stop to it."

She drew in another breath to speak, but Darkmore's hand on her thigh stopped her. "Of course he hasn't been the same, my dear. No mortal would remain unchanged by an encounter with Ereshkigal, let alone being claimed by her."

Olive narrowed her gaze at the reaper, speaking after a second sip of coffee. "You speaking from personal experience."

"I am. She claimed me when I was little more than a babe. It was a mercy, really. Nothing for me on this side of life."

Vivian wanted to kick Darkmore. When a religious zealot complains to you about her nephew's deal with the devil, you don't go and tell her you get it because you made one, too. Then again, could he have actually made a deal with the reaper at such a young age? Free will in humans has a minimum age of consent, and if he couldn't consent to turning his soul over to the reaper, who had?

Someone must have worked a bit of dark magic or traded the innocent child Darkmore had once been to get out of his or her own sentence. Darkmore's mother sought healing for her child, something a wicked person wouldn't necessarily do. She could have smothered him in his cradle. No one would have suspected murder in his condition. Or, if she didn't have the stomach for murder or mercy killing, she might have abandoned him to the desert with a shaman's blessing.

"Who traded your soul to the reaper?" Vivian asked.

Laughing too loud, eyes a little too bright, Olive leaned closer, gaze burning with interest. "I'd like to know that myself. I should have known about you. The devil was said to be the most beautiful angel in the heavens, at least before he fell. You fit the bill."

Darkmore smiled that sensual, come-hither smile he used when trying to seduce a soul. Its charm almost masked the predator within him. "I'm not the devil, dear lady. Ask my companion. She thought I might be when I called on her, but she soon learned there were much darker entities lurking just beyond our perception."

Olive appeared to consider. "Be that as it may, she's corrupted my nephew and she's using his mother to undo God's order in this life and the next. I can't abide that."

Against her better judgment, Vivian spoke up. "Know what I can't abide? The guardian spirit who used me to disrupt what you call God's order so he could settle a personal grudge, and he did it with the blessing of the Archangels. They aren't who or what you think they are."

Olive's gaze went wide. "You know them? Are you sure, dear? The serpent is subtle, you know. He tells pretty lies to lure lost souls like you. You fell in with this evil creature," she said, gesturing to Darkmore, who didn't seem particularly offended. "And you fell in with my wayward nephew."

"He's not wayward. He's trying to make things better, fairer. I've met souls the so-called angels left behind, souls that became prey for those who were supposed to help them find peace. If you knew their suffering, you would want to wreck the whole corrupt system, too."

Olive smiled, a pitying smile disguised as benevolence. "This reaper of souls has his purpose, and so do the angels, all except those who turned the living into their instruments of chaos. You and my nephew and the others like you are abominations. Not your fault, of course, but you'll find justice in the next life. You'll help the angels track down the traitors who made you what you are."

Vivian stood, rage threatening to spill over as uncontrolled jolts of spirit light.

"I am not an abomination. I have purpose, just like your nephew, and we're going to bring this whole corrupt system down."

A familiar voice almost knocked her on her ass. "Not without energy you ain't, little gal."

Her head whipped around. Standing in the doorway to Olive Briggs kitchen was Ezra, her former mentor, the guardian spirit who'd made her what she was to settle a grudge, or for the greater good, possibly both. And behind him, the diminutive form of the Archangel Uriel stood and smiled.

They'd been found. Worse, they'd fallen into a trap that would doom the rebellion.

CHAPTER TWENTY-EIGHT

Ezra bound her in a cage of spirit light and led her to Bijoux Briggs' garden in the back yard, cast in the menacing shadows of night and a chill that neither guardian spirit nor angel bothered to chase away. The reaper followed. No cage for him. Perhaps Ezra and Uriel underestimated him in his current mortal state. Or maybe, as Olive said, he was accepted as a part of the establishment, not an abomination.

Not like her.

As usual, Darkmore kept his cool. The bastard was unflappable, and even seemed to find something funny if the slight curl to his lips was any indication. She hoped he had a plan.

She certainly didn't.

Briggs sat crouched at the feet of his grandmother, bound by ropes of energy that cut into his wrists and ankles. The stench of burning flesh assaulted her senses. God, they'd burned him. Not only that, they'd tortured him. The light of his bonds revealed angry, blackened streaks on his face, disappearing beneath his shirt. They'd tortured him.

But why? They had him, and now they had her and the reaper. Presumably they could find the rest of the rebels and the remaining lost souls who'd escaped the true enemy. They had the mambo and her energy.

Or did they?

Bijoux Briggs' elegant face appeared twisted and malevolent in the half-light of her grandson's bonds. One of the loa had taken control of her body, mind, and soul, and it was angry. It turned the mambo's gaze on Vivian, the reaper, and their captors, splitting Mrs. Briggs' face into a wicked grin.

"You brought me a sacrifice? How thoughtful."

Uriel bowed. The Archangel wore a tailored suit in charcoal grey. It added a touch of class to his mortal form, but the lack of height muted the effect. He was a less hairy Hobbit in the garb of a mobster. It was fitting.

"You weren't inclined to bargain for your descendant's soul. Will this creature sweeten the deal?"

The loa met Vivian's gaze. "You're late."

She stood straight, ignoring the smoke and flash of pain as parts of her body made contact with her cage. "I got a little dinged up on a rescue mission. Am I too late?"

It was a gamble. Having no idea if the loa had a plan to salvage the situation or if it would honor their agreement if and when it did, the question had more than a few layers. The loa wanted a minion on this plane of existence, a powerful essence trapped in a corporeal form it could control and use to exert its power in the world of the living.

It could serve as another vessel for the loa to inhabit. That was it. Bijoux Briggs wasn't long for this world, and when she passed, the loa would have a tough time finding another vessel. Waylon Briggs didn't have the gift, and as far as she knew, he was the last of the mambo's direct line.

Was that it? Did the loa think she could pull off encasing a guardian or an angel in a mortal form?

The loa's gaze sparkled. "Oh, no, child. You're just in time."

Crap. She couldn't pull it off. What she'd done to Darkmore had been an accident. It was an act of desperation meant to save the reaper. She had no desire to save Ezra or Uriel, and in spite of all they'd done to wrong her, she wasn't inclined to turn such powerful beings into playthings for the loa, an entity that might be more wicked and dangerous than the guardian or angel.

The loa's smile widened. "Life's full of tough choices, isn't it?"

Ezra looked between Vivian and the loa, his gaze full of speculation.

Damn it, beneath the overalls, beard, and country bumpkin persona lurked a fiendish and calculating mind. Not good. Of course, he might be planning to double cross the Archangel. Ezra played both sides and switched allegiances like most folks switched clothing. Perhaps he planned to save Vivian and Briggs. He owed Vivian, since he'd gotten her tangled up in afterlife management in the first place.

Then again, she'd double-crossed him by forming an alliance with the reaper. But considering that he'd cheated the system and left her in limbo before claiming her as one of his soul brokers, she preferred to think of it as self-preservation. At any rate, it made Ezra a wildcard in this scenario, much as she was from the others' point of view.

Wonderful.

Reaching through the bars of the cage, Darkmore's hand landed on hers, cooling the heat from her burning wounds and soothing her soul. Nice, but unless he had any bright ideas, she was going to have to make some tough choices or face a more horrifying fate than she'd ever experienced or imagined.

And she'd experienced and imagined plenty.

When the reaper pulled away, she turned her attention to Briggs. "You okay?"

He was glowing and not just from his bonds. They'd captured him before he had a chance to make an energy deposit into Gran. That might help. She needed all the help she could get.

"I've had better days, Red. You get to those souls you told me about?"

She smiled, vision blurring from unshed tears. "Sure did. You did a good thing. Better than you know. No matter what else happens, remember that."

He chuckled, grimacing when the movement stretched and twisted his burned flesh. He made it worse by arching a brow and cocking his head to one side. It was such a brave, defiant gesture in the face of death and eternal torment. She had to laugh through the tears. She reached through the bars of her cage, burning clothing into flesh, and took his hand, taking in his pain, suffering, and burdens as an act of camaraderie and good will.

"Thanks," he said, voice raspy and wry, "but I'm dead anyway. So are you."

She leaned in and whispered, "I brought someone back once before. I think I'm supposed to do it again tonight. Twice. Be ready."

"For what?" His grip on her hand tightened and his gaze met hers, wary.

"I don't know. Not yet. But I'll think of something."

The cage tightened around her, forcing her to let go of Briggs' hand. Uriel forced her to kneel before the mambo inhabited by the loa. She took perverse satisfaction that she was still almost eye level with the little shit of an Archangel. Ezra looked away, the coward. Maybe she could get in a good blast to that no-good, double-crossing, traitorous good old boy spirit who'd convinced her not once, but twice, that he was on her side.

"Shall I dispatch these two for you?" Uriel asked. "In what manner will their shed blood and deaths best serve you?"

The loa grinned through the mambo's face, showing small, white teeth. "Your kind hasn't gotten your hands dirty for centuries, not like you used to. Blood magic and sacrifice haven't been a part of your rituals since the slaughter of your one true lamb. Think you're up for this?"

Uriel looked down his nose, comical for such a short corporeal form. "You've been out of the loop, to borrow a phrase from this era. The holy wars of this age are just as bloody as those of the past, and death is more efficient."

"More energy for your little pyramid scheme and more souls to conscript into guardian service. Real efficient." Briggs earned another lash for his words, proving they were accurate. It was sick, insidious.

"Greed is good, huh? I get it. Never our style. We were too busy helping our descendants navigate life in chains. Your kind didn't help with your bad PR and forced conversions."

For an instant, Uriel's confidence faltered. The Archangel had apparently made some powerful enemies during the millennia of his reign. Christianity didn't like competition, and Voudon had been a favorite target, as had its practitioners. How many pagan gods, loa, and ancient spirits like Maeve had the Archangels pissed off by stealing or killing their followers? Robber barons and the sharks on Wall Street had nothing on cutthroat angels.

Recovering, Uriel spread his arms wide. "That was rather short sighted of us. Perhaps tonight can be the beginning of a new era of cooperation between us, established spiritual intercessors? These," he spat, looking at her and Briggs huddled on the ground, "are the true enemy, our mutual enemies. They serve no one but themselves, hoarding energy and wasting it by fighting us."

"We're all fading," the loa said, waving the mambo's thin wrist in dismissal. "Some of us are just moving along a little faster."

"But it doesn't have to be that way. With just a tenth of the energy these foolish mortals have harvested and stored in your vessel, we could crush the rebellion and get back to the business of mediating the crossing of righteous souls. Naturally, we will offer your side a percentage of the souls for harvest."

"How generous. What percentage?"

Uriel considered for a moment. "I was prepared to offer ten percent, but as a gesture of good will, I will agree to twenty-five percent. Think about it. Twenty five percent of our followers would double your get."

"All of that for the energy these rebels have collected? That's no way to run a business, and you are the ultimate businessman. What's so special about these mortals? Why do you need their energy in particular?"

If she hadn't been so tightly caged, Vivian might have pumped her fists in the air. This loa was good. Bet the ugly Archangel hadn't counted on working with such a shrewd negotiator. Hope bloomed inside her soul, intoxicating and dangerous. She couldn't count on the loa to do the hard work for her. And even if it spared her and Briggs, she'd still have to bring someone back from the dead or trap a soul in a corporeal form in order to restore Darkmore and get another chance to commune with Mae.

Mae.

If anyone could get them out of this, her sister could. The power she'd first experienced from her sister's soul hadn't faded, not even after a trip to Darkmore's realm and the liberation of countless souls. That was it. She just had to get the loa to release Mae.

Uriel's words brought her back to the present and sent ice through her veins. "These two have been a thorn in my side and I want them gone, painfully, with the promise of eternal torment."

"It's personal, then. No wonder you're making such shitty deals."

"The reasons don't concern you," Uriel snipped. "All you have to decide is if you want these two tasty souls and the promise of legions more in exchange for the energy they collected."

"You could give them to the reaper...if he were still here."

Vivian craned her neck along with the other entities in the yard. Darkmore was gone. Briggs swore under his breath. Vivian didn't know whether to laugh or cry. While she fervently hoped the reaper had gone to warn the others and/or fetch help, part of her could see how he might cut and run in his current state. If Ezra wanted another shot at revenge, now would be the time, with Darkmore at his most vulnerable.

Yeah, maybe it was better that Darkmore had quietly vacated the area. Then again, she needed him here in order to restore him to his former state. Was that why he'd left? He'd asked her to come away with him into hiding. It would give him the chance, for the first time, to experience a true mortal life. And it would give her what? A friend, a lover, a loyal companion, and love?

He hadn't said he loved her, but he'd shown her in a thousand different ways that she mattered to him. Wasn't that enough? Zeke had professed his love, and he'd seen her through some tough times, saved her life and her soul, but would he stick around? As a former playboy and self-centered narcissist of a mortal man, he might well fall back into his old habits. After all, eternity was a mighty long time, and there were plenty of guardians, reapers, demons, and angels who'd love to spend time with the handsome and charismatic guardian spirit.

Would she be enough for him, or Darkmore for that matter?

"Bedford! Get your head back in the game." Briggs growled through the pain, nudging her cage of spirit light so it burned her back to reality.

Right. No time to wallow about her love life. Love afterlife? What had she missed?

"Forget the reaper," Ezra said. "He's no threat to us now that this little gal turned him human. I'll catch up with him later, I expect. As far as what to do with these two so-called rebels, I don't recommend killin' 'em. They'll become martyrs and we'll be chasing their followers for hundreds of years."

"You son of a bitch, Ezra," she whispered.

"I ain't gonna miss your sass, Miss Vivian, and I surely ain't gonna miss your foul mouth."

Uriel quirked a brow. "If not their destruction or eternal damnation, what did you have in mind?"

Ezra grinned, his damned beard twitching. "You got yourself a powerful mambo with an even more powerful loa in the driver's seat, so to speak." Turning to the loa, Ezra said, "How about you wrangle some of your kin and see if they'd like to take possession of these two fine, hale human beings. We can send 'em back to their rebellion and wreck it from the inside."

Briggs struggled to stand and lunged at Ezra, tripping over his bound feet and cursing. Vivian glared at him, anger rising like the tide at the moon's call. She wanted to blast him into kingdom come, strangle him, rail and rage at him. Ezra of all people knew the horror of being trapped in a body that no longer obeys the mind, and possession on the level he was talking about would leave her essence, and Briggs', buried far into the subconscious, nothing more than a powerless observer, or completely unaware.

It would be akin to eternal damnation.

Uriel's triumphant smile sent chills down her spine.

The loa said, "I can do that, but not with any old spirit. The loa prefer to ride those of their own line, and it requires an invitation from the ridden. A forced riding, or possession in your parlance, requires the blackest of magic made by a bokor. You ain't got one of those."

"Well, then," Ezra said. "Guess we're going to have to convince our two ornery little soul brokers here to issue an invitation."

He walked over to Briggs and kicked him in the kidney. Vivian screamed, "Ezra, no!"

Turning to face her, he yanked Briggs by the collar and held him up so Vivian could get a good look at his grimace of pain, the burn scars over his face, and his defiant gaze.

Ezra kicked him again. Hard. "I say ladies first. Miss Vivian doesn't like to see anything suffer, as I recall, but she might have a stronger constitution after whoring around with the reaper. Should we test that?"

Slamming Briggs into the ground, he turned to the loa. "She can heal him when the new occupant takes ownership of her." Then he turned back to her and said, "But it'll be harder if he's dead. What'll it be, little gal?"

She turned to face the loa wearing the face of the mambo. Then it dawned on her. The key was in the words of the loa, in permission to be ridden by someone of her line. With a leap of faith and a silent prayer to whatever goddess or god might be listening, she nodded at the mambo. Opening her senses, her heart, and her soul, she summoned her spirit light and let it course through her veins.

After one last look at Briggs, the mambo, the Archangel, and Ezra, Vivian closed her eyes and said, "Come on in."

CHAPTER TWENTY-NINE

She came to herself disoriented, confused, and panicked. Cold on her skin, pain throbbing through parts of her body like...like nothing she'd ever felt before. Not...bruises. That was the right word. Bruises. She'd had bruises, most of them from flailing limbs that seemed to have a mind of their own, rarely going where she asked them. This was like pain from fever, only stronger, and only concentrated in some parts of her body.

Was she back in her body? She hoped not. Nothing in her experience had prepared her for the joy, peace, and freedom when she left her body in a rush of power and...light.

Terrified, she told her fingers to move, and they did! Arms, legs, and body did what she asked...sort of. Her only other experience with a body was the body of Sister. It was strange and wonderful, being with Sister, in Sister, finally able to speak to her. Sister had red hair and a crooked smile. Her laughter was like ice cream. She'd loved ice cream when Mother and Sister fed it to her. Sister touched her skin and brushed her hair and cried for her. Why did she cry?

She knew now. It made her chest tight and her stomach feel sour. She didn't like that feeling. She didn't like it when Sister cried, when Sister was sad.

A gentle hand shook her by the shoulder. She was in a body, but it wasn't her own.

"Anyone home, little gal?"

That voice. She'd heard it before, long ago, or maybe not. Time never meant much to her when she was in her body, and the Others told her time was different in the place of afterlife. But she'd heard that voice in the place of darkness with the man in white—and with Sister.

She opened her eyes and saw the man who was not a man. Spirit. Yes, he was a spirit like her, but he could make a body. The Others told her she could make a body, too, but it would take time for her to learn how to make a body that was right. Her body wasn't right, not like other bodies. Her body was...different, not in her control. This body was under her control. She lifted her hands to his face and felt the wiry hairs of his beard. Her lips curled into a smile. His beard tickled, like the hair over Father's lip had tickled. She liked the sensation.

"I know you," she said. The words still felt funny in her mouth—the mouth that came with this body. Strange and wonderful, it was good to speak. So many thoughts had flooded her mind after she first left her body.

The Others had taken her in, pleased that she brought so many spirits from the place of darkness with the man in white. She'd seen glimpses of him from the place of the Others. He helped Sister.

Sister...

Sister was here, in her mind, urging her to do...something. What? How could she help Sister? Sister had never been in her mind before, no one had, except the Others.

The man smiled. Sister, somewhere in the back of her mind, growled. Sister didn't trust this man—spirit. That's right. This spirit wanted to steal her from Sister, wanted to make Sister do his bidding and had...betrayed sister? But this spirit had come to the place of darkness with her to free the spirits there.

The spirit leaned closer, whispering in her ear. "Tell her I'm sorry for making her doubt me," he whispered. "And that I knew you'd come. You're going to have to save us again, little doll. You're going to be doing a lot of saving from now on."

Saving...she liked that. She would save the spirit and Sister from the one who meant them harm.

The Archangel, the small spirit, is the one who means us harm. Save Briggs, the beaten, burned, and bloodied man, and the old woman who let you speak before.

Sister didn't ask her to save the bearded man—Ezra. His name was Ezra. But that was okay. Sister got mad a lot, but Sister was good and kind and always took care of everyone. Sister was good, even if Sister didn't always believe it.

Ezra helped her to her feet. She stood on wobbly legs and smiled in wonder. Sister's legs worked, her mouth worked, and she could see so far, so many things. She looked at the beauty all around her, things she'd only seen in glimpses before with the eyes in her own body. Green things were everywhere, visible as far as the dim light of night, and bursts of color from flowers that also smelled sweet and lovely. Cool air chilled skin and blew through hair.

How marvelous. She stumbled toward a flower with Ezra's support, wanting to touch, to smell deeply, to experience. Living things sang in the night, their songs so much richer heard through Sister's ears.

Sister sobbed in the back of my mind. Sister was sad. Why?

Because you were cheated in life. You never got to see, hear, smell, and experience all of this. People like me take it for granted, but not you. You see the beauty and the wonder. You should have been like the rest of us, taking it for granted because you were too busy living a full life.

"No, Sister. You and the rest of the living should be like me of now, me of then. Taking in everything. It is a gift."

Ezra chuckled. "It surely is. Now then, I need you to play along with me. Don't go striking out right away, no matter what your ornery sister says, and don't get your feelings hurt. It's all pretend."

A sound came out of her throat, her sister's throat. *It's called a snort and it's totally appropriate.* Sister was right.

"I am not stupid." The words were louder, angry. Some people said she was stupid, retarded, not worth being alive—those people made Mother and Father angry. They made Sister angry, too, even when Sister wondered if they were right. She was glad to show Sister that those people were not right.

I'm glad, too.

"Of course you're not stupid, darlin'. You're a good girl, and you're going to help us make some people who've been stupid do the right thing."

Ezra patted her hand. He wasn't speaking to her now. He was speaking to the small man with power, the Archangel. Uriel was his name. She was confused. Angels were good.

No, the Others told her that some angels were corrupt, like the angels from long gone times, those who defied the Good. She was supposed to defend the Good, like the Others. Sister asked her to save them from the Archangel. Sister didn't lie.

The Archangel came closer. Ezra helped her stand on her feet, steady. She set her legs wide as he did. It was easier to stand. The Archangel looked strange, but she wasn't used to looking down at people. He smiled at her, but it was a wrong smile, the kind of smile people used to give her when she was in her own body. They talked to her like she was stupid.

He thought she was stupid.

Let him think that, Mae. If he thinks you're feeble and weak, he'll let his guard down. When he does, you hit him with all the light you've got.

"When Ezra says?"

"When Ezra says what, my lamb?"

She had spoken out loud instead of in her mind. That was stupid. She would not be stupid again. She would be clever and sneaky, like the reaper. Like Sister when she was tricking the angels and guardian spirits so she could help the Good.

"When Ezra says, I can smell more flowers? I can eat good food and see pretty things?"

The Archangel laughed and it was wrong. He was not happy. He did not think she was funny. He thought she was stupid. Good. She would show him. Later.

"Of course, lamb. And when you are comfortable, you will work with us, yes?"

She curled her lips into a smile. "Yes, I will work for the Good."

"Most excellent. Your energy will help so many, dear Mae."

She froze. The Archangel knew her name, knew who she was. But he was not afraid? He had not been there in the place of darkness where she unleashed her energy to bring the many souls home. He thought she was stupid. He thought she was a tool for him to use. She was not his weapon.

Ezra's grip on her arms tightened. That was good. She must not show anger. She must pretend that she was stupid, foolish, and willing to do what the Archangel wanted.

"Now then, what shall we do with your wayward descendant?" Uriel said, turning his attention to the small woman seated in an outdoor chair. She was old, older than Mother, and she was filled with the soul of another. That soul, that loa, was the one who'd called her forth to speak with Sister and had brought her into Sister's body.

The broken and bloodied man on the ground was hurt badly. His spirit would leave his body soon if not healed. Sister could heal him.

Yes, I can. I will. But first we have to destroy the Archangel.

Destroy. The Others did not destroy. The Others worked for the Good. Confusion filled her. She had never destroyed before.

Oh, Mae, I'm so, so, sorry. I don't know what the consequences will be with your...Others, but if the Archangel gets away, he'll destroy innocent souls and the ones who protect them.

A funny feeling filled her. It was cold, unpleasant, a roiling sensation in her stomach worse than hunger, worse than sickness. She'd experienced it when Mother took her to the doctor, when she had trouble breathing in her own body, and when Sister became angry, the night Sister went away to the place of darkness the first time.

I'm sorry.

She'd forgiven Sister long ago. Sister came back and cared for her, made her well, kept her safe, brought another spirit who filled her with warm light and happiness.

Zeke.

Zeke was a good guardian. Sister loved Zeke. Zeke and the man in white, the Reaper, were both in Sister's heart, but she could not hold them both.

Don't worry about that for now. Worry about the Archangel. If you can't destroy him...disable him so one of us can.

She didn't want to destroy, didn't want Sister or other spirits to destroy. The voice from the old woman, the mambo, came. The loa spoke. He was a trickster, like the man in white, like Ezra. He did not like the Archangel, did not like what Uriel had done to the bruised and bloodied man who was his kin.

The loa inside the mambo laughed. "His Daddy won't do. Never was good for much this side of life, let alone the next. There's an old friend that might do."

Uriel smiled. "You've done well with the woman. I trust your judgment with this man."

She smiled. That would be the angel's second mistake. His first was putting her into Sister's body.

"Careful what you wish for."

CHAPTER THIRTY

Before the Archangel's wicked smirk fell, Briggs rose. The black marks on his face shrank into nothingness, leaving smooth skin behind as broken bones popped and snapped into place. Vivian saw through a haze, looking out through her own eyes, but through the lens of Mae. Her sister's soul surrounded her, full of love and hope and so much power.

Vivian hoped she could shield Mae from what needed to be done. Mae's soul was pure, innocent, beautiful, and using her power to kill—if that was the right word for the destruction of an Archangel gone bad—would destroy that. That first taste of darkness in the reaper's realm, and in her own soul, had changed Vivian forever, and she'd been far from innocent.

Concentrating on her body, she flexed her fingers experimentally.

What are you doing, Sister?

"Don't worry," she said in her mind. "I might need to sit in the driver's seat if things get as bad as I think they will."

Driver's seat? We are not in a car.

She fought back a chuckle. This was no time to laugh, but being able to talk to Mae, listen to her, share her knowledge in a big sister kind of way, was a wonder and a miracle.

"What I mean is, let me have control of this body when the fighting starts. I'll keep us safe." And she would keep Mae safe from killing.

Mae's presence...faded. Her sister was still there, seeing, listening, feeling, but she'd given Vivian control. Vivian stood straight and jerked out of Ezra's grip, turning to shoot a look of pure murder at her former mentor.

Ezra's gaze narrowed, but he let go, nodding. He didn't want Mae harmed or forced to harm, either.

Clearly nervous, Uriel took a step back and clenched his fists, power surging beneath his skin. Briggs, or rather, whoever had hopped into Briggs' body, turned his neck back and forth with popping sounds, rubbed his hands together, and smiled at Uriel.

"Uriel, Light with the Fiery Sword, it has been long since our paths crossed. When last I saw you, you guarded the only gate to the afterlife and denied the first souls entrance. I see you have not changed."

Uriel frowned, his gaze narrowed in thought or calculation. "With whom am I speaking?"

The thing inside of Briggs laughed. "You don't remember me? You once bowed before me as Queen of the Underworld."

Waves of shock rippled across the angel's face, his true form showing beneath the veneer of the corporeal form he'd chosen. Light and power surged beneath his skin, melting it away to reveal his true form. No white wings or gentle, benevolent protector, this angel was a warrior, his hair flaming as red as his fiery sword and crimson wings. He was tall, terrifyingly beautiful, and the most frightening creature she'd ever seen. His glowing gaze fell on the creature wearing Briggs, that of the reaper who'd claimed Briggs on a faraway battlefield and the same reaper who'd once claimed Darkmore.

That creature smiled through Briggs' eyes, red light glowing as bright as the flames from the Archangel. A flaming sword emerged in Briggs' palm, shorter than Uriel's, but long and gleaming in the low light, edge sharp, as runes in a language she'd never seen glowed and sparked. Magic, soul energy, spirit light—whatever it was matched the Archangel's power, making the creature within Briggs a formidable warrior.

Vivian took a step forward, but Ezra held her back, as did Mae's presence within her. "Easy now, Miss Vivian. It ain't the right time and this ain't your battle. You'll know when to strike. You and Mae."

The pair of powerful entities circled one another, swords whooshing and swinging, showing deadly skill and the reach of weapons as they sized one another up. At last, they stopped, feet apart, while still moving to find weight and balance, and the fighting began. The angel moved his sword from a straight, shoulder level to, in a quick slash, forward, moving to meet the thing occupying Briggs and crossing blades. Fire spilled from the point of contact as a shrill, unearthly clang echoed.

Uriel pushed, sliding his sword across the Queen's in an attempt to stab her—Briggs—in the neck. The Queen bent Briggs' body at an unnatural angle to avoid the strike. Twisting the body she inhabited, she swept at the angel's legs, then kicked Uriel between his legs. The Queen fought dirty.

So did Uriel. The angel brought the sword down on Briggs' head with a skull-splitting crack. Vivian screamed, but Ezra held her to the spot. Blood gushed from the head wound, but the Queen still managed to push her sword up and through the angel's torso. Uriel cried in pain as he stumbled back.

Angels bleed red, too, Vivian thought with horror.

The battle continued, brutal, ugly, and faster than her human eyes could track. Somewhere in the process, the pair began casting spirit light at one another. Shots that didn't find their targets hit shrub and tree foliage, flowers, and the elegant lawn furniture in Bijoux Briggs' backyard paradise. Small fires burned in patches of grass, sending up billows of acrid smoke.

Olive, to her credit, ran out and covered Bijoux's body with hers, and Ezra put himself between Vivian and the stray blasts of light. Minutes passed like hours with no signs of the battle stopping. Blood splattered as the combatants moved, struck, dodged, and charged.

How long could they keep going before one or both expired. And where would they go? God, what if they simply rebuilt corporeal bodies and fought for eternity? No, they couldn't—the Queen couldn't. Not unless she discarded Briggs' body.

The angel was bigger, much bigger, than the Queen of the Underworld in Briggs' body. This was bad. She'd survive the damage to the vessel she occupied, but that could and likely would leave Briggs mortally wounded or dead.

"What's her name?" Vivian asked, trying to pull her body out of Ezra's grasp. He pulled harder, using his supernatural strength to immobilize her.

Mae stilled within her, reading her thoughts and knowing what she meant to do.

"Damn it, Ezra, I'm not going to strike! I need the Queen of the Underworld, dark angel, demon, goddess, or whatever the hell she is to leave Briggs' body before he gets hurt!"

Ezra swore, which was a shock to the system. She'd never heard the old coot swear. He'd always admonished her against swearing, blasphemy, and other unbecoming words. Good. He realized the stakes now.

"She has a whole slew of names—Ereshkigal, Irkalla, Hecate, Hel, Isis, Kali—"

"Pick one!"

The reaper's voice called out, flooding her heart and soul with hope—at least until she remembered how vulnerable he was. God, was he still on good terms with his former mentor, or captor?

"Eloah. Hear me, your first child, your loyal one, the one who serves you." Darkmore appeared, flanked by Jeanne, Zeke, and the souls from the asylum.

Crap, why had he brought them? They were supposed to stay out of this battle and flee if and when it went to hell, which it had. Ezra smiled, the crazy old coot, clearly pleased by this turn of events.

"Hold!" The loa's voice boomed from Mrs. Briggs. "Let the reaper speak."

The angel and the queen lowered their weapons with inhuman grace and faced the reaper. Darkmore removed his hat, a sure sign of reverence and respect, and bowed low to the Queen of Darkness. "I see time has not diminished your power and warrior's grace."

"Flatterer. But you always were, my Damu. You were once a god. What name have you in this time and place?"

"Lazarus Darkmore," he said with a small smile.

The feminine laughter was so odd and disturbing, coming as it did from Brigg's mouth. It was even weirder to see Briggs saunter over to Darkmore with a sensual, feminine gate. If she kissed Darkmore with Briggs' lips, it would be too much. Not that she had a problem with two guys, but how did one reconcile consent when an entity takes over the body of another?

Briggs deserved a say in whether or not he was okay with his body being used in a deadly battle.

"It suits you," she said. "Resurrected, yet still reaper. Her doing?"

The thing inside Briggs gestured to Vivian, turning a fiery gaze upon her. Damn it, was this creature—Eloah—curious, jealous, or simply irritated? Vivian held no more significance to the ancient and powerful reaper than a speck of dust, no matter her soul broker powers. Darkmore had been intrigued by her, but this creature? No, she had nothing to offer and no way to defend herself from this potential threat, or to prevent the creature from claiming her.

"Yes," Darkmore said. "It is a rare and wonderful gift for one such as I."

"I gifted you more. You ruled the underworld as my consort for untold ages, and I shared my kingdom with you, a god to my goddess." The creature's gaze returned to the reaper, cool and...sad? Crap. She was jealous. No good could come from earning the jealousy of a goddess.

"That you did. I do not believe I ever thanked you for it. Delights of the flesh and spirit, darkness and light, all that I was and all that I am were your gifts to me."

"Were..." She paused to wipe the blood from her face—Briggs' face. The slash was no longer gushing, but it had not fully healed.

Darkmore sighed. "I've come into my own, as all acolytes do. My regard for you, and my love, has not wavered. It has changed, to be sure, as have I, but I am here now to fight at your side. And so are they." He gestured to the guardians and freed souls.

"What about you?" she asked Vivian. "Will you fight at my side and defy your master? Think carefully. One who betrays one's master will surely turn on a new one...eventually."

Biting back ugly words that would do her no good, Vivian took a deep breath and spoke. "I do not serve Uriel. His...organization no longer serves its purpose and souls in need. Once I learned that, I worked for change from within. I have stood beside guardians," she said, nodding at Ezra, Jeanne, and Zeke. "And your reaper. I will fight for a system that is fair and just for all souls, one that does not exploit the most vulnerable among the living to fuel the power of those in charge of their crossing. If that is what you stand for, then I'm with you. I ask only two things."

The creature wearing Briggs disappeared and reappeared in front of Vivian, flaming sword at her throat. Ezra's power flowed through her body along with Mae's. A shield. The Queen of the Underworld stopped. Whether by her own control or by the protection of Ezra and her sister, Vivian didn't know. Or care.

"You dare make demands of me, human?"

When Vivian remembered to breathe, she said in a voice that shook only a little, "Not demands. Requests, on behalf of humanity and for the sake of peace as we, for lack of a better word, restructure afterlife management. You have the power to choose how we move forward, how the souls in limbo move through their penances or to their own personal paradises and from there to...wherever they go."

She'd never asked what was next. If her slice of enchanted woods where flowers bloomed eternal near a cool, bubbling stream would be her final resting place or a stop along the way. Once upon a time she'd visited it, her place as Ezra called it, and she'd asked Zeke to look out for it while she was busy on earth or trapped in the Darkmore's realm. It was her paradise but not yet where she belonged. She hoped she saw it again. Someday.

The Archangel slashed his sword through the air in what appeared very much like a fit of temper. Vivian shifted her gaze as best she could, not daring to move her neck. Damn it, why did he have to speak up now? This was not how negotiation was supposed to work. Flaming swords of eternal damnation had never been a part of her agreement with Ezra.

If she survived, it was definitely time for contract renegotiations.

"You would bargain with this creature, you impudent wretch. You are nothing. You have no idea what's at stake if this malevolent so-called goddess overthrows the council. Archangels have ferried souls since your kind first stood on two legs, bowing before the sun, and you think to change it?"

Taking a risk, Vivian snorted. The Archangel already thought she was impudent. Might as well live up to the image, and perhaps a bit of bravado would buy her more time with the Queen. "Yes, I'll bargain with her. You and your angel buddies had your run and got greedy in the process. I'd like to see what new management can do."

"So would I."

The voice gave her more hope than she'd had all night. Marguerite appeared, taking her place next to Jeanne. Maeve appeared beside her, and shortly after, Uphir. That was a powerhouse of light and dark energy on their side. The Queen took the sword away from Vivian's neck.

The Archangel hissed. Maeve's hand rose and she pointed at Uriel with an index finger. Uphir smiled, her teeth no longer human. Marguerite made a gesture unfamiliar to Vivian, but she could guess the meaning. More figures materialized. They shouldn't have fit in Bijoux's back yard, but the walls between this life and the afterlife had grown thin.

All of the energy concentrated in the small area must have helped. Vivian hoped it wouldn't cause a permanent rip. Not the solution she was seeking.

Uphir stepped forward. "We will all bargain with you, Eloah. Before your scion's pet speaks on our behalf," she said, giving Vivian a sly smile. "It would be fitting for Uriel to call on his brethren so that they might also judge him for his crimes, or answer for theirs."

"But please, your...highness..." Vivian hoped that was the right word. "Will you release your, um, scion Waylon Briggs and allow me to heal him? I owe that debt to the loa."

The Queen narrowed her gaze at Vivian. Before Vivian could blink, a blast of light exploded in front of her, knocking her back from the impact.

CHAPTER THIRTY-ONE

When she came to, Ezra stood over her with such a strange mixture of pride and fury and exasperation painted across his face that she had to laugh. Zeke and Darkmore flanked Ezra. Great. The unholy triumvirate of the dead men in her life all stood above her newly conscious body.

"At least I know I'm not dead, or at least I'm not in hell."

"I'm here," Darkmore said helpfully.

"So am I." Zeke wasn't quite so chipper.

Ezra swore—again. Twice in one night. That had to be a record. He yanked her off the ground, hard. "You'd better go take care of your leader before she changes her mind."

Vivian groaned, fighting the urge to stand upright as her head spun and her legs wobbled. "Why are you so testy? You didn't get shot by the Queen of the Underworld."

Ezra's grip gentled. "You gotta take care of our little doll. Miss Mae's still with you. We need her."

Didn't that just spark a million questions? She settled on, "Why?"

Ezra grinned. "You'll just have to trust me on that."

Vivian grinned, pulled back, and punched the old guardian square in the jaw. Zeke tried to stay stern, but his eyes danced with mirth. Darkmore smiled.

"I've been waiting a long time to do that."

Before Ezra could reply, she spun on her heel, saved herself from falling by bracing her arm on one of the fallen lawn chairs, and spotted Briggs, his body a limp pile of flesh and blood on the lawn. Panic surged, but the slow rise and fall of his chest eased it. He was still breathing.

Trying to remember the feel of the energy as it surged through her body and soul the night she revived the reaper, Vivian stumbled to the ground next to his body and placed trembling fingers on Briggs' battered body. She thought about healing, visualizing blood flowing through intact vessels after being pumped through a strong, healthy heart. In her mind, smooth skin free of cuts, bruises, gaping wounds, and burns appeared, bones set at natural angles, tethered to solid muscles by tendons, organs working in harmony to maintain the healthy, strong man who had become a worth ally, if not a friend.

Nothing happened.

Crap. How could she replicate what had happened with the reaper? She didn't care for Briggs the same way she cared for Darkmore. Briggs might be dying, but it wasn't the same. When she'd raised the reaper, she'd been panicked, adrenaline coursing through her veins after battle—a battle in which she'd participated. Darkmore had saved her by taking the fatal energy light blow.

Replicating those conditions didn't seem like a good idea, but what else could she do?

Let me help.

Mae's voice inside her was calming, a steadying presence in her mind and heart. She wasn't alone. Not everyone in this crowd of gods and monsters loved her, but Mae did. So did Zeke, and Darkmore, and maybe even Ezra. It would have to be enough.

"Okay," she said.

Trust me. This may feel...too much.

Before she could ask what that meant, energy flowed through her body like an electric current, more intense, and strange, and wonderful than anything she'd ever experienced. God, she'd only had a taste of Mae's light before, back in Darkmore's realm. This was a thousand, thousand times more brilliant. Pleasure, wonder, hope, sat on the precipice of pain and oblivion. Or eternity. How could one being encompass so much...

Too much.

Vivian's eyes flashed open and her hands clutched Briggs. Rather than the burst of energy she'd expected, healing light trickled out like a gentle stream, dropping like rain and flowing over Briggs' body. His breathing deepened, muscles tensed and relaxed, tensed and relaxed, and the low groan that escaped his throat turned into a growl.

"Get off me, Red." Briggs' voice was a rumble.

"Welcome back. Think you can sit?"

He accepted her help as she first pulled on his broad shoulders and then pushed when she managed to lift him off the ground. He examined his hands and feet, ran a hand over his skull, and then cast his gaze all around. When it landed on the figure she hadn't noticed before, his lips curled into a wry smile.

"Long time no see, Ala. Did we win?"

The woman, goddess, Queen of the Underworld, stood before them, a tall figure with dark, glowing skin, gossamer wings, dressed in a flowing tunic of purple and gold, brandishing her sword. This was the figure Vivian had seen in her vision from Darkmore. Reaper, warrior, justice bringer, powerful and deadly—what more, she couldn't say.

But Briggs clearly could.

"We await the outcome. I believe this woman who healed you has another request before we proceed."

"Of course she does," Briggs said, smiling. "It's good to see you again."

Vivian stood, steady on her feet, thank goodness, and feeling more like herself. The healing mojo hadn't only cured Briggs. She let Mae come forward in her consciousness. They looked out over the gathered beings, including a host of six glowing, winged creatures who stood near but apart from Uriel. Someone had apparently called his colleagues while she was out. Raphael and Gabriel appeared the same as they had when Vivian had been summoned before the Archangel Council. She hadn't met the others. Darkmore told her that only Uriel, Raphael, and Gabriel had been involved in a war with Watchers, Watchers being guardians who mated with human women.

Had their offspring become demigods, the first living soul brokers, or possibly both?

The fact that the other four Archangels hadn't been involved seemed important.

Vivian and Mae took a deep breath and spoke as one. "We do not wish to destroy anyone in this place, not even Uriel."

Some of the parties present gasped. Others spoke loudly in a cacophony of languages, most in opposition to the plan. She didn't understand everything, but the gist of the main argument was about justice, punishment, penance, or vengeance. Vivian gently nudged Mae to the background.

"I got this, sis."

She hoped she was right.

"I don't mean that he should go unpunished. As far as I'm concerned, all of the establishment should spend a few millennia in whatever passes as a prison for your kind—especially those who went after the Watchers and their wives. But if we are to build a fair and just new system for ferrying souls, we can't do it with blood."

The Archangels split, leaving Raphael and Gabriel standing apart, not quite beside Uriel, but away from the others.

"What do you know of the Watchers?" Uriel spat. "They broke divine law and created abominations—"

"Lies!" Eloah said. "You and your kind craved power and control, and you demonized those among your legions who disagreed, who shared knowledge with humanity. They and their offspring became the best of humanity. They honored all divine beings who cared for them."

"Until you became greedy," said a female figure radiating power. A goddess from the Hindu tradition, Vivian thought.

"Y'all have quite the monopoly going," the loa said.

One of the four Archangels, one Vivian didn't know, stepped forward. "I am Michael, Angel of Death. On behalf of my brethren, I wish to negotiate a truce. I did not sanction Uriel's activities, and I do not believe my brothers Raphael and Gabriel knew the full extent of his treachery."

It wasn't quite a question, but Raphael and Gabriel nodded solemnly, stepping back into the fold and leaving Uriel to stand alone in his defiance.

Looked like even angels threw one another under the bus to survive. They were closer to humanity than their mythos led people to believe, apparently —much more like gods from the so-called pagan traditions.

Whatever. As long as Michael was at the table, they could salvage the situation.

Something tickled the back of her brain, a sense of dread and the urge to act. That made no sense. They'd stopped the battle between a goddess and a rogue angel. Briggs was safe. The Archangels minus Uriel had come to the table. They were poised to negotiate instead of halting all of afterlife management. And after that, she could restore Darkmore and...well, they'd work that out later.

So why was she on edge.

You'll know when to strike. You and Mae.

Ezra's words flashed through her mind a second before she lunged, blocking Uriel's flaming sword strike with a blast of energy. Mae's energy flowed through her hands, blended with her own, and struck the angel.

Uriel fell to the ground. Vivian screamed. What had she done? What had she made Mae do?

"Waylon? What's happening?"

Vivian turned to Bijoux Briggs, mambo asagwe, and the old woman was...herself. No longer inhabited by the loa, Mrs. Briggs focused on her grandson and Olive. Auntie Olive, who seemed to have had an epiphany, stepped back, gaze on the ground, and made room for Briggs to fall into his Gran's embrace.

"It's all right," he said. "I'll take you back inside. It's time for your stories and then we'll get you in bed."

A beautiful smile lit the old woman's face. Energy still swirled around her, and in a moment of clarity, she reached up and touched Briggs' face. "I couldn't be prouder of you, grandson. You make sure these beings do right by souls."

Choking on his reply, Briggs said, "Yes, ma'am."

He carried his Gran into the house, Olive on his heels. Vivian turned her attention back to the angel, but he was gone. Had she killed him?

No, Sister. No destruction. It will be fine now. There will be peace.

Vivian was about to ask what Mae meant by that, but the angel stirred and then rose. He wore the corporeal form of a small man in a tailored business suit, which seemed odd. The other Archangels kept their imposing and beautiful angelic forms, so why had he changed?

Uriel opened his mouth to speak. Vivian expected a protest, but instead was greeted by the voice of the loa.

"Well done," he said, smiling at Vivian. "You kept your end of the bargain. Two lives, many souls."

"So this is your zombie?" A loa using Uriel's corporeal form to control the angel was bad. Very bad. Destruction might have been kinder.

"No, he'll be all right and I'll let him go...eventually. Right now, he's leverage."

Okaaaaay.

Which left two questions. What was the cost of her...service and where was the rest of the payment?

The loa laughed. "The cost and the price are the same, child. Your sister is yours, but she's with you."

Wait, Mae would possess her forever?

"Until you make your choice, she's yours."

CHAPTER THIRTY-TWO

Vivian stood inside the apartment she'd shared with the reaper at Briggs' compound, empty of their belongings. After several days and nights of tense negotiations, the Archangels, members of Briggs' living soul broker rebellion along with rebel guardians and reapers, and the many and varied divine beings with a stake in the business of ferrying souls had reached an agreement. It would take decades, maybe centuries, to fully implement. Faith traditions were slow to change.

Immortal beings were even slower.

In the meantime, living soul brokers would work with guardians and reapers to mediate soul crossings. Extra energy, including the huge cache the Archangel Guardian Council had stolen and squirreled away, would be turned over to powerful souls, the Others as Mae called them, for safe-keeping and distribution. The souls from the asylum who'd chosen to remain, Jagun, Beulah, the boy, and the emaciated man, and Dr. LaFleur had joined them. The Blues Legend dropped by to check in, since he'd be ferrying souls for the reaper's side.

The reaper...

He'd kept his distance since the night of negotiations. So had Zeke. They were waiting for her to decide.

"You outta here, Red?"

She grinned. Briggs, taking time out of training the remaining recruits, had come to see her off. He looked good. It would take time to recover from the trauma he'd suffered at the hands of Uriel, but he'd conquered past demons. He'd manage.

Eloah would help.

"I guess so," Vivian said. "You good?"

He laughed. "Good as I'll get. Lot of work to do."

It was a jibe, but she'd take it. Briggs wasn't the sentimental sort. It was as close to an "I'll miss you" as she'd get.

"Jeanne and Marguerite are worth a hundred of me," Vivian said. "I'll be serving elsewhere. Besides, you and I couldn't work together. One of us would kill the other, and I sure would miss you."

He laughed, offering his hand. She accepted, holding his with both of hers and taking in his burdens. Breathing easier, he released her hand and said, "You take care of yourself. Keep in touch."

"Yeah, you'd better." Maria Gutierrez and B came around the corner.

After exchanging hugs, Vivian asked, "So, you never told me how to part ways with a reaper."

Maria smiled. "You made up your mind, then?"

"Yes, no...oh, hell, I don't know."

"Well, if you do, it's pretty straightforward. You find someone else to give him."

"Or her," Briggs said. "Eloah let Darkmore go for good. She's got me now."

Vivian nodded. Good to know, on all fronts.

Never one to prolong goodbyes, she hopped in her car and drove away, knowing somehow, they would all meet again. Like Briggs said, there was a lot of work yet to do. She still had miles to go before she could sleep.

Leaving behind the grey of Mississippi for the springtime splendor of Tennessee, the ache in her heart eased as soon as she took the exit to the parkway that would take her home. Of course, things would never be the same, but she had friends and loved ones waiting for her. Ezra assured her that they would remember her now. It would be as if she'd simply gone on vacation and then come back.

Her house was the same as the night she'd left, with no trace of the renters who'd kept it for her. Cozy, comfortable, and full of loitering spirits. Since she didn't have any food in the house, she asked Junior, a rascal of a spirit she'd rescued—the first lost and lonely spirit she'd liberated, actually —to clear them out. He promised to keep them away for a week or two until she got settled.

For the first time in a long, long time, Vivian Bedford was well and truly alone.

Except for Mae, a quiet, peaceful presence content to see and experience the world through Vivian's eyes. For now.

Her friend Kay Clemmens had stopped by after she settled, helping Vivian clean several months' worth of dust off her furniture and freshening up the place to keep her mind occupied. That was good. There were too many questions running through it. When would the loa free Darkmore from his mortal state? What would happen when it did? What would happen to Mae if and when she left Vivian's body? Would she see her sister again? What was Mae's purpose in this new world they were building?

Before she left Mississippi, Ezra told her to stop fretting. The answers to all of her questions would be revealed in time. She hated to admit it, but the old coot was usually right.

Taking a glass of wine with her, she stepped out onto her back deck and took a moment to savor the spring evening with its cool breeze carrying the sweet scents of blooming flowers, freshly mown grass, and a cloudless sky filled with stars. Her strange journey into the world of spirits had begun on a night like this one.

Are you sorry, Sister?

"No, Mae Belle," she said, an odd sense of peace falling over her. "I'm not."

Suddenly, she knew what to do—the choice wouldn't be easy, but it was the right choice for everyone. For her, for the reaper, Zeke, the lost souls of the world and, most importantly, for Mae.

With a deep breath for courage, she whispered his name on the wind and summoned the reaper.

Darkmore appeared in his white suit, white hat, and wearing a smile so beautiful it broke her heart. Vivian took two steps and pulled him into a fierce embrace. She'd missed him.

He pulled away first, perhaps sensing her intent. Before he could stop her and before she could change her mind, Vivian placed her lips on his and infused the last of her healing power, the last of her light. The reaper struggled, but then, as his spirit separated from a now temporary mortal coil, he relaxed as she set him free.

She only had a few more moments.

"What have you done?" he whispered.

"What I had to do. I can't walk through life with you as a mortal. The loa told me I would never be free of my ties to the guardian spirit world. But Mae can. Will you walk with her and keep her safe? Show her the world and all of its wonders, love her and accept her love in return? She has so much to give and, together, the two of you will change the world."

Sister, what is happening? You cannot leave me!

"I love you, Mae," Vivian said, feeling the pull of the afterlife. "And I love Lazarus. I give you both this gift. Take care of one another. I will see you again on the other side of eternity."

Vivian wiped away a single tear from the reaper's cheek, kissed him softly with her last breath, and left him in Mae's keeping.

And Mae in his.

EPILOGUE

Time was different on the other side. Her crossing had been surprisingly uneventful, but pleasant. This time, she didn't arrive naked. Her old friend the Padre, known in life as Father Lloyd Montgomery, led her soul to the next place. He'd stayed with her for a few hours.

Or was it a few days? Months?

Her place was as she had left it, a little patch of paradise set in the middle of the woods in a warm eternal summer. A worn footpath wound its way through a tree-covered path, past the delightful old springhouse, half concealed by thick vines, and down to the bubbling, lazy little creek that flowed left of the trail. She'd spent her first nights there, camped near the spring without a care for time or such trivial things as hunger, thirst, or discomfort. Her hammock stretched between two trees and served as the perfect place for a nap.

Of course, the soft grass worked for naps, too.

The water of her creek teemed with small fish, frogs, salamanders, and turtles. She'd spotted a pair of otters...yesterday morning? She didn't remember them from last time. Birds sang while butterflies, bees, and a host of other insects flitted and buzzed about. No stinging or biting insects lived here, but rabbits, deer, and a few predatory creatures that never gave chase, oddly enough, came to visit—coyotes, bobcats, and even a few friendly domestic cats.

After a few weeks, or maybe months…she didn't want to think too much about time, she made her way to the log bridge and crossed the meadow to find the most beautiful part of her paradise.

It was still there.

As far as her eyes could see, the rolling hills were bursting at the seams with black-eyed Susans. Their yellow petals waved to Vivian as if welcoming her home.

Wait, something had changed.

In the distance, on top of one flower covered hill, sat a two-story log cabin. Outside, on the front porch swing, sat a man. He had dark hair, and even though she couldn't see them at this distance, she knew his green eyes were sparkling in the noonday sun. She smiled, her heart in her throat, and she took off running.

He was faster.

He caught her in his arms, lifting her and spinning around as he laughed through tears. She understood. Her vision had gone blurry with her own tears of joy. She slid down into his arms and kissed him deeply. Then, looking back at the cabin, she said, "I like what you've done with the place."

Zeke grinned, placing his forehead against her. "It wasn't home until you came back."

"How did you know?" she asked.

"I didn't. But I hoped. You gave that to me the night we met. You gave me hope."

"And you've given me so much more."

Zeke's joy gave way to a wariness that she hated to see in his beautiful face. "You didn't come to say goodbye, did you?"

"No," she said. "I said two goodbyes that broke my heart into pieces. Think you can mend it? I mean, we'll have to go back…someday. We'll be needed. But for now—"

"For now, and forever, this place is yours."

"Ours," she said.

Then together, hand in hand, they walked to their respite.

THE END

Thank you for reading! Did you enjoy?

Please Add Your Review! And don't miss more urban fantasy novels with HOUSE OF ASH & BRIMSTONE. Turn the page for a sneak peek!

SNEAK PEEK OF HOUSE OF ASH & BRIMSTONE

Gisele Walker landed in the fighting pit face-first, and her mouth flooded with mud. Bruised, she scrambled onto palms and knees, spitting out the warm red clay.

Her stomach churned as she struggled to her feet, wiping her chin with the back of one arm. Mud sucked at the hem of her jeans, had plastered her tank top to her chest.

This wasn't how she'd planned to spend her Friday night.

Overhead, a rich green-and-gold circus tent arched, burnished with ropes of amber globe lights. Empty stands surrounded a checkered stage that extended out from the pit. After hours, the place was quiet, deserted aside from the show's performers.

The ringmaster, a bald, jaundice-skinned demon in a crimson jacket and gray plaid kilt, leaned over the lip of the ring—at least fifteen feet high —to leer down at her. A cobra tattoo wound up his neck to swallow the top of his head, two fangs dripping venom into his greenish-yellow eyes.

"Thought you could s-steal from us-ss?" he stutter-hissed.

Well, yeah. Actually, she had.

At a quarter past two that morning, she'd crept through a country field littered with smashed popcorn and gummy worms, sneaking up to the tightly circled caravan of circus boxcars. She'd broken into the one with

"Curios and Oddities" hand-painted on its side, and from a dusty display case, she'd filched the Mardoll—a shrunken head on a straw doll body. It was the magical curio her client had hired her to find, and for the last fifty years, it'd been on exhibit with the traveling entertainers, demons known as the Curators of the Cursed.

Breaking in had been *easy*. Sneaking back out? Not so much.

One of the Curators, a sword swallower she'd seen perform as she'd cased the circus earlier that evening, reached his entire arm down his throat. With a hacking cough, he extracted a heavy, dinged-up cleaver sword. "This the one you wanted for her, Canaan?"

Mother-of-pearl ornamented the two-handed hilt. It gleamed beautifully in the amber light. But the wide blade appeared dull and scratched—tarnished with age.

Wide-mouthed, the ringmaster grinned, and Gisele saw that his teeth had been filed into points. "Give it to her. Ss-so we can place betss."

Canaan turned, signaling to someone she couldn't see with a flourish of his hand. The entire stage rattled beneath the approaching clomp-scrape of heavy hoof steps.

Oh, no. It had to be the cow-headed beast from the 'taming' exhibition mid-show. Her heart had panged while he'd charged around the stage, bull-whipped and slavering. She'd watched as they'd spun plates on his shoulders and horns.

Then, he'd just snorted and clacked his teeth in protest. Now he brayed, piercing her eardrums—the sound like boulders cracking together.

They'd brought out the minotaur.

The sword swallower tossed the cleaver into the mud, and Gisele dove for it as the monstrous demon barreled into the pit. She rolled, then crawled, elbows digging into the ground as she dragged the heavy sword to her side.

Stomping one hoof, the minotaur regarded her with unnerving, side-slitted eyes. He stood upright like a man but on backward bent legs, at least seven-and-a-half-feet tall, and crushed her hundred-and-twenty-five pounds by a good five hundred more. Stocky, with wide sloped shoulders, his body was a solid mass of muscle. Mud-splattered, dark brown fur covered him from top to hoof-tip, and a dirty, black mane lay matted to his head and neck. Two large, curved horns, one of which had been cut in half, curved out from his temples.

He wore only what appeared to be a rawhide loincloth, and she did not want to know what was underneath the flap.

"Um, this is a little awkward," Gisele said, belly-down in the mud.

With a snort, the beast charged for her, faster than she would've thought possible. His meaty three-fingered hand tangled in her dirty-blond hair, lifting her onto her knees.

Heart kicking like a rabbit on the run, she swiped for his legs. Blood flowed, and he bellowed, flinging her across the pit. She landed with a flailing splash, and a round of jeers exploded from the rim of the ring. Popcorn fluttered down like buttery snow as the Curators leaned over, hurling both insults and food.

"Don't let him kill you before he breaks your leg," a strongman shouted. "Be a doll and win me an extra two-fifty!"

Groaning, Gisele tried her best to tune them out.

She crawled to her feet, trembling, scraping the tip of the sword through the mud as she backed away. As a half-demon, she was stronger than a human, but the weapon felt unwieldy in her grip.

Again, the minotaur stomped a hoof, preparing to advance.

"Easy, fella," Gisele said, one hand outstretched to placate the beast. "I didn't come here tonight to hurt you."

Intent mattered, right?

His nose was black and wet, nostrils flaring wide as he sucked in breath. He hesitated, and she took her chance.

"Right now," she blurted, "they're taking bets on us. Thinking you're going to kill me. But you don't like doing what they want, do you? And they *don't* know everything about me. Like how fast I heal. You can gore me, trample me. Choke me. I'll get back up again." Eventually. "So instead of chasing me around this ring 'til we're both tired and hurting, why don't we turn the tables on these creeps and get the hell out of here?"

"S-stalling won't sssa-ave you," the ringmaster warned.

Sword up, Gisele sidestepped, walking a slow sweep of the ring that the minotaur mirrored. When he stepped forward, she jabbed with the cleaver and he retreated.

Live and learn. Hopefully.

She licked her lips, tasted clay mixed with blood. "All I'm saying is, I could really go for a stiff drink and a hot bath after this, if you'd care to join me."

The minotaur leveled her with guarded, teal-blue eyes, contemplating. Then he flicked an ear in agitation. Violently, he stomped a hoof into the ground.

His left hoof. He'd been doing it off and on all fight. What was it about...?

And then she saw it. He was wearing a metal cuff around his ankle, so coated in mud that she hadn't noticed it before. The cuff had been in place for so long, it'd rubbed the fur around his ankle raw. It was a collar, a cage.

Palms suddenly sweaty, Gisele swallowed against what felt like cotton candy lodged in her throat clogging her airway.

With a terrifying bellow, the minotaur charged. She twisted and ducked, lashing at him with her cleaver. He knocked the blade aside, opening a bone-deep slash in his arm, and got her in the gut with his fist.

The air exploded from her lungs, and she doubled over, in a world of pain. The Curators roared and stomped their feet, clamoring for a bloody, drawn-out finish.

If she couldn't get the cuff off of him, one of them was going to have to kill the other. And despite what she'd said...she wasn't sure she'd be the one to walk away.

Gisele retched, then sucked in heaving gulps of air. She rolled away before he could grab her again, and as he lumbered after her, she dropped, sliding in the mud. His cuffed hoof stomped near her head, and she got a good look at the magical device. It was remotely powered, pulsing as it fed from an external source. The metal was tarnished silver and etched with symbols she didn't recognize.

Whatever spell it cast was powerful, but the cuff itself didn't look too difficult to break. Wielding the sword like a bat, Gisele swung the flat side of the blade against the ankle cuff hard enough that her entire arm went numb on impact.

The cuff looked undamaged. Frustrated, she grabbed it with a bare hand and felt electricity arc through her body. She screamed and wrenched away, palm scorched.

Leaping leviathans from Linger! The damned thing was a shock collar.

How the hell did the minotaur withstand it? And more importantly, how the hell was she going to get it off him?

Before she could come up with another plan, the minotaur reached down and clamped a thick-fingered fist around her neck. He lifted her by her throat, and she choked, sneakers dangling off the ground. His breath blew hot in her face, gusted her bangs off her forehead, and coated her own tiny horns with sweat.

Her pulse shot into a wild, adrenaline-fueled race.

He was going to kill her.

Stupid godforsaken minotaur. He hadn't given her enough time.

Her vision swam red, and her head pounded. Her nails bit into the palm of her hand around the grip of the sword, sharp as claws.

She bared her teeth at the minotaur. They cut into her lower lip, drawing blood as if she'd suddenly sprouted fangs, but if he noticed, he didn't react. He was too busy, turning—winding up with all his strength to toss her into oblivion—and then she was flying, sailing high overhead. She crashed hard into a boxy metal unit, hurting and disoriented.

Her side screamed, ribs bruised or cracked.

Moaning, it took her several moments to realize that she was actually above ground.

He'd tossed her onto the stage, near the best seats in the house—front and center. *He'd thrown her right out of the pit!*

Curators scattered like loose marbles. Twin acrobats and a bird-masked harlequin scrambled to flee while a fire breather in a brass dragon-scale corset rushed for her. Planning to roast her on the spot? She was welcome to try.

Others—including an improbably milky-eyed fortune-teller—screamed at the minotaur, furious and panicking.

Oh, yes. Gisele was going to make them pay, every last one. She was going to rend them from neck to navel.

She just needed to get up first.

Her head throbbed, her normally tiny, knobby branching horns feeling thick and heavy where they jutted from her skull. She blinked back the headache from Hell, focusing in order to take in her surroundings.

The equipment she'd landed on hummed low with power, and Gisele's excitement soared as she realized what it was: a transmitter. The Curators must need to keep it within range of the cuff. And the minotaur had hurled her right into it.

That beautiful, brilliant beast.

Miraculously, she'd kept a grip on the cleaver through the crash landing. Struggling up onto her knees, she jabbed the full length of the blade into the front of the power box and was blasted backwards from the resulting electric surge. Heat sliced up her skin. The unit sparked and fizzled, leaving the acrid taste of charred magic in the air. It was dead, and the binding spell with it.

There was nothing controlling the minotaur now.

A soul-shattering bellow erupted from the pit, so intense that the ground shook. The minotaur clambered out of the pit and charged the ring-master with unnerving speed, horns angled down, ready to gore.

She didn't want to watch, but couldn't tear her eyes away.

Canaan recoiled and fell. Blood sprayed from him in a thick mist that sifted through the air. His jacket was torn, red strips gaping like an open wound over his muscled abdomen.

It happened so fast that she wasn't sure how exactly the minotaur had hurt him. But maybe he hadn't. The viperous demon was laughing full-bodied, shaking, hissing. The minotaur's efforts to kill him... *They amused him.*

And then he sobered, fury burning in the depths of his eyes. "Well, you sssu-ure do know how to put on a s-sshow," he said, arms swept out wide as he gestured to the chaos Gisele had caused.

"Happy to oblige," she scoffed, and surely would've crammed her foot further into her mouth if the fire breather hadn't chosen that moment to spew a mushroom cloud of death at her face. With a yelp, Gisele dove back toward the center of the stage, ribs throbbing, heart thumping as she stood on shaky feet.

Considering she was up against thirty-some Curators, the others could have rushed her. Instead, they retreated warily, giving her a wide berth.

Good. Let them cower. Let them see what they were up against—a girl with a banged-up sword who had held her own against a monstrous minotaur.

It was almost laughable. Except that she could feel her own violence like a dark aura, swelling within her.

The minotaur bellowed again, but in pain rather than anger. His thick fingers tore at his pelted chest, now misted with blood. Gisele cringed, hating that he was hurting because of her, that he might soon be recaptured by the Curators working to surround him. Mardoll or not, now was the time when she should probably run like Hell. But she needed the payoff from this contract job if she was ever going to strike out on her own. And she was just battered and ticked off enough to want some revenge—for the both of them. Oh yeah, she was going to make these dill-weeds regret ever tangling with her.

"You have what I came for." Gisele raised her sword at the ringmaster. "I want it back."

"Hate to sssa-ay, little s-sstealer. But the head don't belong to you." Canaan spat at their feet, and the dirt began to sizzle and melt as his saliva ate a shallow hole into the ground. He patted the left breast pocket of his tattered jacket. "I'll keep it ss-safe right here."

Okay, so his spit was corrosive. That wasn't great. But he still had the curio on him. And *that* was.

"I'm not going to ask again." She closed the distance between them as the minotaur lunged for the ringmaster from behind.

Canaan sidestepped the beast easily, fluid as a dancer. Gisele kicked hard at his crotch, but he saw it coming and twisted, taking the blow in his thigh. He spat at her, and she screamed as his saliva seared through her once-white T-shirt and into her left shoulder. Then he grabbed her by the throat, and she reacted on autopilot from years of self-defense training, swinging her elbow into his jaw with as much force as she could muster. The impact knocked him backward, and she was free.

The minotaur used the opportunity to grab Canaan around the shoulders, a meaty arm encircling his neck as he dragged the ringmaster around to face Gisele again. Canaan struggled and cursed, but the minotaur held him firm, an expectant look on his dark, cow-like features. His eyes flicked to the sword in her hand.

The beast flexed his arm, squeezing Canaan's neck until the man's sallow face turned bright red.

Gisele had never killed anyone before and wasn't keen to start now, though if anyone deserved it, it might be the ringmaster. She had, however, beaten a bloody life lesson into more than one street punk in her line of work and had no qualms about dishing out some punishment in order to get the curio. The minotaur would just have to settle on some broken bones for his revenge.

Surging adrenaline drowned out the pain in her body. She inhaled deeply as her cracked ribs began to mend, hurting worse than the initial injury. With a grimace, she threw her whole body into a kick to Canaan's knee that cracked the joint with a sickening pop. His ensuing wail was music to her ears.

"That's for tossing me in a fighting pit," she said. "And this is for the minotaur."

She snapped the heel of her hand up into Canaan's crooked nose.

Hot blood gushed onto her palm, scorching the skin. She wiped her blistered palm on the leg of her jeans, cursing. Even his blood was venomous to the touch. No wonder he looked like his skin was flooded with bile.

"Holy Hell-balls," she breathed, but neither Canaan nor the minotaur seemed to hear her. One of them was laughing again, and the other braying, cradling his arm where it had been sprayed by the ringmaster's blood.

A gust of fire blasted past her shoulder, narrowly missing the edge of her hair. The strongman closed in, grabbing for the minotaur's half-cut horn.

Her plan was rapidly unraveling...for the second time in one night. She needed to wrap this up and get the hell out of Dodge with the curio safely under her arm.

Or at least, that was the idea. She found herself having second thoughts when Canaan speared up and then up again, much taller than he'd been before. He swung side to side, arms dangling, the movement hypnotic. And then he rose even higher, straightening to look down on her with spittle-flecked lips split in a sneer.

"Sss-surely that iss-sn't all you'ves-s got," he taunted, eyes flashing murder.

The words slurred out slower around two new bone-white fangs. As thick and long as her forefingers, they curved over his jaw, downright wicked looking. The demon had begun to shed his human appearance in favor of his true, more lethal form.

He snickered, darting a fat, forked tongue to lap the drying blood from his upper lip. "S-shall I introdussshe you to my widowmakers-ss?"

————

Don't stop now. Keep reading with your copy of HOUSE OF ASH & BRIMSTONE available now. And sign up for the City Owl Press newsletter to receive notice of all book releases!

Want even more urban fantasy? Try HOUSE OF ASH & BRIMSTONE by City Owl Author, Megan Starks. And find more from D. B. Sieders at www.dbsieders.com

———

Hell has come to collect, but Gisele Walker has no plans to pay the debt.

Being a paranormal bounty hunter is flirting with death, even for a half-demon like Gisele Walker. An orphan with no memories of her childhood, she's spent the last decade working for the foster father who saved her from the city's streets. But when she's partnered with Shade, an infuriatingly handsome demon who's keeping secrets, her jobs spin sideways.

Determined to ditch Shade, Gisele takes a contract to steal a mysterious curio and accidentally opens a portal to Hell. As a nightmarish ghoul hunts her down, and parts of Baltimore burn to the ground, she finds joining forces with Shade may be the only way to undo her unleashed mess.

A white-hot attraction ignites between them, until Shade's secret is exposed. The contract bringing them to Hell is nothing more than a ploy to lure Gisele to Hell's royal court, where her devilish brother and aunt lie in wait. It's a family reunion that has her wishing she'd remained an amnesiac orphan.

To save herself and Shade, Gisele must face her past and venture into the twisted heart of the demon court where she was nearly murdered a lifetime ago.

———

Please sign up for the City Owl Press newsletter for chances to win special subscriber-only contests and giveaways as well as receiving information on upcoming releases and special excerpts.

All reviews are **welcome** and **appreciated**. Please consider leaving one on your favorite social media and book buying sites.

For books in the world of romance and speculative fiction that embody Innovation, Creativity, and Affordability, check out City Owl Press at www.cityowlpress.com.

ACKNOWLEDGMENTS

I thank my amazing community of writer friends, colleagues, and publishing partners. This book took a long time to finish, mostly due to a breast cancer diagnosis in April of 2018. I put my life and writing on hold to focus on treatment decisions, planning, surgery, radiation, and recovery. I came back to writing in order to escape into a fantasy world of my own design that, while dark, would always be safe. This fictional world is one where I have control. The reaper lives only in my head, the ghosts fleeting images flashing through my mind, Vivian's tragedies and triumphs exist as bits of data stored on my computer and on various external drives. But knowing they were still there, waiting for me, was a gift and a comfort. Coming back to this world allowed me to heal a little more. Healing is a long-term process, a lifelong process, as I've learned that cancer is forever.

That doesn't mean that cancer wins. It means that I've had to find my new normal as a cancer survivor. Along the way, I've come to know and love a wonderful, beautiful community of survivors. They are strong, smart, happy, funny as hell, and have taught me that life can and does go on and it is still amazing and full of possibilities.

Thanks to Victoria Raschke for beta reading and giving me wonderful, constructive feedback.

I am grateful to my editor, Tee Tate, for her work on this book. She came to me after the first two books in the series with an open mind, boundless enthusiasm, and a wealth of ideas on how to make the project better, richer, giving each character an authentic voice and agency. Thank you to City Owl Press for being an amazing publisher. Tina Moss and Yelena Casale were supportive in spite of the delay, and stood with me, offering encouragement, support, and love. Thanks also to Mibl Art for the gorgeous cover art. This one is my favorite!

And, as always, thank you to my family for giving me the freedom to be a writer, and to my furballs for keeping my lap warm. I have the best job and support system to sustain it!

ABOUT THE AUTHOR

Award-winning author D.B. Sieders was born and raised in East Tennessee and spent her childhood hiking in the Great Smoky Mountains and chasing salamanders, fish, and frogs. She loved to tell stories while sitting around the campfire.

She is a working scientist by day, but never lost her love of telling stories. Now, she's a purveyor of unconventional fantasy romance featuring strong heroines and the heroes who strive to match them. Her heroes and heroines face a healthy dose of angst as they strive for redemption and a happily ever after, which everyone deserves.

www.dbsieders.com

facebook.com/DBSieders

twitter.com/DBSieders

goodreads.com/dbsieders

amazon.com/D.B.-Sieders/B00D18ZPOY

ABOUT THE PUBLISHER

City Owl Press is a cutting edge indie publishing company, bringing the world of romance and speculative fiction to discerning readers.

www.cityowlpress.com